WITHER

J. G. PASSARELLA

a novel

POCKET BOOKS
New York London Toronto Sydney Tokyo Singapore

POCKET BOOKS, a division of Simon & Schuster Inc.
1230 Avenue of the Americas, New York, NY 10020

ISBN: 0-671-02480-9

Designed by Laura Lindgren

Printed in U.S.A.

For
Andrea, for her faith, love, and understanding
and
Dave Hodgson, longtime friend and fellow Fangorean

ACKNOWLEDGMENTS

In Los Angeles: Janet Yang, Lisa Henson, Naomi Despres, and Mark Levine, of Manifest Films; Amy Pascal and Michael Costigan, of Columbia Pictures; David Colden and Joel McKuin; and everyone at United Talent Agency.

In New York: Emily Bestler, Jason Kaufman, and Naomi Nista at Pocket Books; and Gail Hochman, of Brandt & Brandt.

Thanks also to Carol Gangemi, Mike Werkheiser, Greg Schauer, and Andrea Passarella for reading a (very) early draft of the novel. And for helping *Wither* graduate from high school, a special thanks to Steven Katz.

As long as children continue to believe in witches ... they need to be told stories in which children, being ingenious, rid themselves of these persecuting figures of their imagination.

—Bruno Bettelheim, *The Uses of Enchantment*

It is commonly said that sleep is disturbed by dreams; strangely enough, we are led to a contrary view and must regard dreams as the guardians of sleep.

—Sigmund Freud, *On Dreams*

BOOK ONE

"AWAKENINGS"

September

From *DesPres Guide to*
U.S. *Colleges,* 1999 edition:

Danfield College
Windale, Massachusetts

Number of Students: 3,128   Tuition: $10,645
Admissions: Selective   R&B, fees: $5,120

Situated in a quiet community forty minutes outside of Boston, Danfield College offers students an affordable alternative to Beantown's pricier institutions of higher learning. The surrounding village of Windale was once a thriving textile center for the region, and many of its dilapidated old mills still stand as testament to an industry that long ago abandoned the frigid New England weather for sunnier climes. But if you're partial to thermal underwear, and you've got a taste for living history, Danfield may be the perfect place for you. The town prides itself on being one of the oldest in the country (the community was established by Puritans in 1684) and, like neighboring Salem, has built a small but thriving tourist trade around one of its darker chapters of history: the witch hysteria that swept New England in the late seventeenth century. Today, Windale celebrates its brief "witch fever" of three centuries ago with everything from street names ("Witch Hill," "Familiar Way") to the emblems on police patrol cars (a shield with a broomstick-riding witch in profile). This modern-day "witch fever" culminates each October, when the town holds a "King Frost" festival and parade on Halloween night.

CHAPTER ONE

The house was growing. Eight-year-old Abby MacNeil heard it at night—the low groan of the walls, the floorboards creaking, the radiator pipes letting out long and shuddering sighs. Abby would lie still in the dark and listen as the old house complained about its aching wooden bones. It was their first house—she and her father had lived in apartments ever since her mother left, and before that, a trailer—and so she accepted its growing pains as something old houses did in the night.

When they'd first moved to this house a month ago, in the dead of summer, her father had argued that this third-floor room would be too hot for a bedroom. And, in fact, it was stifling up here, where the heat seemed to thicken the airless shadow beneath the slanted ceilings. But Abby still loved it. The room was round like a fairy-tale tower, with a pointed cap roof of green shingles. From its high windows Abby could see the backyard and the weedy fields beyond, and farther still, the woods, cool and green and inviting. At night sometimes, with the window open, they seemed to whisper to her, as if there were children there at play just out of sight behind the trees. Calling to her, an invitation to come and play....

She'd listen to them, and the sound of the house's long sighs as it settled in for the night, and then she'd fall asleep . . .

. . . And wake in darkness. Tonight. Around her, the house had grown still, and was silent. Her eyes searched the surrounding black, and she felt a tickle of panic. She was alone, and awake. In the dark.

She reached out to turn on the bedside lamp, gave its tiny chain a tug. Click-click. Nothing. She felt for the lightbulb and was surprised when her fingers felt something soft instead: small, feathered, dead. Like a stuffed bird stuck in the fixture. She pulled her hand away with a tiny gasp. Smelled her fingers. Moldy, like decaying leaves.

Now her eyes were beginning to adapt to the deep darkness. What she saw made her frown with its unfamiliarity. The room was bigger than she remembered from just hours ago, when her father had switched off the light.

In the textured darkness, she saw the walls as supple, like skin. Curious now, wanting to touch it, Abby swung her legs out from under the covers. Stood, feeling the natty weave of the rug beneath her bare feet. Began venturing out into the dark, groping ahead of her. Touched the wall—and recoiled.

The wall had flinched. She jerked her hand away, as if stung. But more curious now than afraid, she approached again, lay her palm against the wallpaper, more gently now, as if it were a nervous animal. Moved her hand slowly over the wall, soothing it.

She felt its pulse. Deep, slow . . . confused it with her own. She was almost certain now the house was breathing . . .

. . . and that she was dreaming. She understood that dreaming was sometimes just as vivid as the things she did in daylight. But she had yet to develop the adult reflex to pull away from a dream, to deny what was happening so sharply that she woke herself up. So Abby accepted the dream, and decided to explore it.

She groped along the floor, venturing farther from the bed. Some of the things she found in the dark were familiar, her grandmother's rocker, the glass doorknob on the closet (it looked like a big diamond), her rolltop desk. But there were other things here as well, things long since lost. A doll with a hard plastic head, a favorite toy when she was three. (She could feel its bristly eyelashes on its open eyes.) A wooden duck that paddled after her when she tugged its leash. She hadn't seen that since she was a toddler.

She left these curiosities and continued to explore the growing dimensions of her room. She followed the round walls with trailing fingers, discovered the variations in its texture, sometimes smooth and sometimes furred, sometimes rough like bark. She found a chair that wasn't there in the daylight, its cottony insides bursting through a rip in the fabric. She found a bookcase, and pulled down one of its heavy volumes. She opened the book and tried to feel the words with her fingertips, like a blind person. She explored farther, realizing now with a glimmer of uneasiness that she had ventured very far from the safety of her bed.

Then she found the staircase.

It waited, disappearing below in the darkness. Not the stairs that were outside her room in daylight. These stairs were formed from smooth stones, the grit of dirt between them, cold against her bare feet.

She sat down on the top step and deliberated exploring farther. Already this dream had lingered much longer than the others. Already she'd ventured too far from the bed she knew. Could she find her way back now if she descended these stairs?

She would try. She stood, and took one exploratory step down. That wasn't so bad. She took three more, feeling braver now. She descended each step carefully, pausing before the next. She could feel the cool, open space waiting below for her. Cool like a basement. It smelled like a basement, too, cool and dank, though there were none of the chemical smells—of paint cans and rusting tools—found in her own basement.

How many steps had she gone down? She'd lost count. Finally she put her foot out for the next step and found there were no more. She'd arrived at the bottom. The floor here was earthen, gritty and hard beneath her bare feet. The darkness seemed deeper here, too. She couldn't see the room ahead, but she could smell its vivid contents, a dizzying potpourri of scents ... dried flowers, raisins, dead leaves, and stagnant water. Then beyond these scents, others: candle wax, animal fur, ashes. She was disoriented, and with the disorientation came fear. She retreated a step toward the security of the stairs but couldn't find them now behind her. Like a stage set that was moved while the audience was distracted.

She fumbled, groping for the missing stairs. Couldn't find them. And became even more disoriented.

Her fingers fluttered in the open air, trying to find something firm, an edge or corner. Some reliable surface to lead her back home ...

Nothing. More open space.

And then suddenly, something: her fingers found cloth, worn cotton or lace, folded and creased. Was it a curtain? A fringe of table-cloth. She clung to it, not quite solid but still reassuring against this absolute dark. There was so much fabric, and beneath it something more solid, stuffing or soft wood. She explored its shape with her hands, recognizing carved wooden feet and arms. A chair. She felt a little better. She could curl up in this chair and wait for morning. Wait for her father to find her. She tried to climb up into the seat ...

She reached up to feel the back of the chair and was surprised when her hands felt something rough, not the smooth cushion she'd expected. Rough and weathered, like leather ... A face.

Someone was sitting in the chair.

Before Abby could snatch her hand away from that face the mouth opened suddenly and her fingers were sucked in.

Abby sat bolt upright in her bed, screaming. She shivered, gasping for breath.

The door to her bedroom opened, and with it came light from the hallway. Her father was there, profiled in the hallway light. Groggy and mad. "What's going on in here?"

He came in, sat on the edge of her bed. Yawning, taking her into his arms. "All right now, you're okay," her father said. "Musta had a bad dream. I told you not to eat chips before bed."

Abby clutched him tighter. Already now the dream was fading, her room was small and round again. She stared beyond him, trying to wipe the sticky saliva from her devoured fingers on his undershirt.

Hours later, she was too deeply asleep to hear the *thump* overhead as something heavy came down from the sky and landed hard on her little pointed roof. She was too deep into blissfully dreamless sleep to hear the chittering across the green shingles overhead as the thing that had invaded her dreams paid a midnight visit. The roof beams creaked beneath its weight, then were silent as her visitor leaned over the edge of its new perch, claws curled over the rusting gutter, and looked in.

⛤

The shrill buzzing of the alarm clock sounded like a fly exploring Wendy's ear. She swatted at it, missed the snooze but managed to sweep most of the contents of the bedside table onto the floor. She flopped over, yawning. Gave her senses time to wake at their own pace. Sight first: white ceiling, obnoxiously chipper sunlight. Then smell: this morning's coffee, yesterday's incense.

With a long sigh, she struggled out of bed and surveyed the chaos that had been her room for the last three years. Her mother had left it alone for once. Everything scattered where she'd left it: clothes, charm bottles, crystals, books, jewelry. Wait—not everything. Her pentagram. Must've flipped itself upside down during the night. Now it hung on the wall with two points up, the symbol of the goat. Bad mojo. She spun it on its nail, transforming Goat into Man. The symbol of white magic.

Her parents accused her of being disorganized, but Wendy (who was taking an intro. psychology course this semester) countered that she was simply a right-brain organizer. That argument didn't discourage her mother from her midnight Clean and Organize missions. Yet another problem with living at home instead of in a dorm. But paying for room and board at a dorm a quarter mile away from home was even tougher to justify to her parents than her sloppiness. Especially when your dad was president of the college, and you lived in the president's mansion. The college waived her tuition, but not dorm housing costs, and her father made it plain that if she wanted a dorm room, she would be footing the bill.

She dragged herself onto her exercise bike and began pedaling mechanically. Gotta establish the rhythm: eyes closed, upper body swaying. Exercising was brutal this morning, especially after another restless night of weird dreams. The odometer stood at 1,249 miles. She'd thumbtacked a U.S. map to her wall, marked how far she'd managed to pedal—in spirit at least—away from here, this quaint little freckle on the backside of Massachusetts. Today's aerobic session should bring her to the outskirts of Jacksonville, Florida. She closed her eyes and tried to imagine herself there. Gators. Sunshine. Anywhere but here ...

A half hour later and a few hundred calories lighter, she made the long trek to the shower. She reemerged ten minutes later, swaddled in a Big Thirsty towel. She hopscotched her way across the book-littered floor, being careful not to stub her toe on the Western canon. School stuff—a psych text ($68.50), a weather-beaten English lit reader (a compulsory course for freshman). Then the scattered syllabus of her own independent course of study: classics of numerology, pyramid power, astrology. Titles like: *Witchcraft through the Ages. Wicca. Gaia's Grace. Trance Channeling Understood.* The most recent purchased with an employee discount at the New Age shop downtown where she worked. She spent most of her paycheck before she'd even walked out the door.

She kicked these few titles out of the way, searching for today's wardrobe. Color coordination wasn't an issue: practically everything she owned was some shade of black. She found a relatively unwrinkled blouse, her I-feel-frumpy-today jeans, black sandals. She dressed quickly, lingering only when it came to accessories.

She settled on old favorites: a crystal pendant, silver bangles, a black onyx ring. She deliberated when it came to earrings. Lately she'd even been considering letting the holes in her earlobes close. She'd taken out her nose ring for good her junior year of high school, when she realized even the class valedictorian had one. The navel ring had been a complete waste of time and pain since she was way too embarrassed to ever flaunt a bare abdomen in public. That left her pierced ears as the only remaining bit of sentimental body mutilation left…wouldn't it be a radical move to let them heal! But she was waffling and decided to let the issue go another day. In went the dangly silver crescent moons. At least piercings could close up if you got sick of them. The tattoo of a quarter moon and three five-pointed stars above her right ankle was something she'd need a goggled technician and a laser to get rid of someday.

She threw her books into her backpack and sprinted out. Downstairs, the folks were finishing breakfast. She gave her dad a quick peck on the bald top of his head.

Wendy reached around to straighten his tie. "Why the three-button blazer today, *pater*? Bankers?"

As president of Danfield College, her father's days were spent raising funds for the school's endowment. Either locally, or in Boston, Cambridge, and the technology-heavy Route 128 corridor.

"Biotechnology. Someplace in Cambridge."

Wendy stole a sip of his coffee, a bite of his toast (black; dry). She said, "Nice, Dad. Soliciting funds from bioterrorists."

Her mother appeared with a glass of OJ for her. "Actually, dear, they make skin."

"Skin?"

Her father lowered his newspaper. "Synthetic skin. For grafts, burn victims, that sort of thing."

"Didn't realize there was big money to be made in skin," Wendy said. But there must be, if her father was traveling all the way to Cambridge to meet with the skin-mongers.

As she dashed toward the door, her mother caught her sleeve. "What about breakfast?"

"Late for class."

"Eat something anyway." Of course her mom had already been up since dawn, assembling the impeccable ensemble she now wore: silk blouse, cream-colored skirt, a single strand of freshwater pearls. Accented by an hour's worth of cosmetics. Classy. Would you buy a house from this woman? Her mother certainly hoped so.

Wendy scooped a handful of Raisin Gravel into her mouth, chased it with a gulp of juice and turned to go. Her mother followed her out to the foyer.

"Honey, I need to talk to you for a second." Using her Quiet Voice. Something urgent, to be kept secret from her father.

"What's up?"

Her mother hesitated, unsure how to begin. "I know classes are casual, sweetheart, but couldn't you find something a little less... wrinkled?"

Wendy rolled her eyes. "C'mon, Carol, I don't have time for this."

"Wendy." Sharper now. Not just nagging. "I know you want to just pretend that you're...the same as every other freshman. But you're not. You're the president's daughter. Believe it or not, that makes a difference."

Wendy's jaw set in an angry line. "Actually, Mom, I couldn't care less about being 'the same' as every other freshman. Conformity isn't exactly a high priority in my life."

"Maybe it should be." Her mother said quickly. Rewind. "That's not what I meant. I only meant to say...people notice. What the president's daughter does. How she dresses...." Her mother's face softened. She touched Wendy's hair. "I always liked your long hair. Won't you consider letting it grow out again?"

"I gotta go." She rolled her eyes and ducked out before her mother could try to hug her.

Outside, the day was hazy and hot, Indian summer coming to a reluctant end. Wendy jogged across the rolling lawn, which was wet from the sprinkler system the college's landscapers ran around the clock, drought-be-damned. Her car was waiting in the long gravel drive, a battered Gremlin she'd chosen over the more sensible Accords and Civics her father had offered when she turned sixteen.

As she was unlocking the hatchback, her father appeared on the front doorstep with his briefcase. "Try to keep it on the road today," he called. "It runs better without shrubbery in the grill."

"Okay, so I thought it was in 'Park,' " Wendy called back.

Her father crossed the lawn toward her. His own car, a silver BMW, waited a few car lengths—and several rungs up the automotive evolutionary ladder—away. He slipped an arm around her waist and looked at the Gremlin's glossy black chassy. He secretly admired the battered piece of shit. Probably reminded him of some psilocybin-inspired road trip during his own college days, maybe a girl with armpit hair and a Navajo blanket in the backseat . . .

"How's the paint holding up?"

"Starting to chip a little."

He grunted, looking where she pointed. When they'd bought the Gremlin it had been a sickening bioluminescent green, the color you want to imagine for nuclear waste. Together, they'd spent the better part of a weekend and $69.99 repainting the car to its current glossy black. Where the paint sported nicks, however, its former florescence glowed through.

Wendy looked up at her father suddenly. "Would you like me better with more hair, Daddy?"

He considered a moment, smart enough to know his answer mattered. "Not if it means you'll start spending as much time in the bathroom as your mother." A nonanswer. He gave her a kiss and headed off for Cambridge.

She opened the Gremlin's hatchback carefully. Beeswax candles, overdue library books, and empty Diet Coke cans spilled out at her feet. The car was a four-cylinder Dumpster. She tossed her backpack onto the heap and checked her watch. Five minutes to class.

The president's mansion was on the college's west side, which meant a dash across campus to student parking, out in the hinterlands with Maintenance and the tennis courts. A five-minute drive on a good day, which this wasn't. Twice she almost hit frat boys on bikes darting out from parked cars. (One flipped her off.) Then when she yielded to pedestrians at the lone traffic light on campus the Gremlin conked out. By the time she got it started again she had an audience, including two hecklers beside her in a converted jeep/date-rape mobile. "Dyke!" one called as they sped off, leaving her in a cloud of blue exhaust.

"Thanks," she said. "You have a good one too." Pretending it didn't sting. She slipped the Gremlin back into gear, and it lurched ahead.

With only three thousand students and a dozen academic departments, Danfield's campus remained self-contained. Most of the classrooms were clustered around Parris Beach, which had been nicknamed for the central lawn with its narrow reflecting pool. In good weather, sunbathers populated the lawn. The whole place was surrounded by a low brick wall. All interconnected with cobblestone bike paths and little grassy quads. *Très picturesque.* But a nightmare for commuters. Scoring a campus parking permit required a Byzantine journey through the administrative netherworld, and being the president's daughter apparently didn't count. ("Honey, I'd help you," her father said early in the term, "but you can bet there are a dozen little would-be Woodwards and Bernsteins on the student paper just dying to uncover evidence of presidential favoritism.")

When she finally arrived at her freshman comparative lit class, the seats were already nearly full. Three hundred fellow frosh, gulping down breakfast lattes and Cokes from the student center, grumbling at the early hour. Wendy stood at the base of the stairs looking up the tiered ranks, scanning for an open seat. Very aware that the class bell had rung five minutes ago.

Professor Karen Glazer appeared at Wendy's elbow, pointing up to the back of the hall. "There are a few seats left in the nosebleeds." She gave Wendy a disapproving look. "I'm still signing drop/add slips if you're having trouble making it to my class on time, Wendy."

"Sorry," she mumbled, then hurried up the stairs, receiving plenty of amused stares from her classmates.

As fate and the chaos theory of student seating would have it, she had to pass right by Jack Carter, Danfield's blond, toothy quarterback, whose mission it was to stamp out individuality wherever he saw it.

"Look, it's the black hole of Windale," he whispered to his mini-entourage of Jensen Hoyt and Cyndy Sellers, both of whom giggled obligingly. Wendy discreetly blew him a kiss with her middle finger.

She caught a lone smile among the sea of hostile faces: Frankie Lenard, the pudgy little blond women's studies major from Los Angeles who had befriended Wendy at orientation. Frankie gave her a sympathetic quirk of the lips as Wendy climbed the stairs past her and slumped in the first open seat she found.

"Here, you missed this." A voice spoke quietly beside Wendy. She turned and found the second sympathetic smile of the day, this one unexpected. Lanky guy, nice eyes—was that a scar over his right eyelid—something reluctant about his smile, like he expected to get in trouble for it. He was dressed in khakis and a loud Hawaiian shirt. Fashion throwback or ... nonconformist? She liked that in a guy. Scuffed-up pair of Ray Bans on his stack of texts. Maybe he thought he was at the University of Honolulu. Boy, did he have a surprise coming in about four months.

He showed her a photocopied page. "She handed these out before you got here. You can look off mine if you want."

"Thanks." Wendy glanced at the page, which described the parameters for an upcoming class term paper, eight to ten pages, three cited references, yadda-yadda-yadda.

"I'm Alex," the Good Samaritan said, and actually offered a hand to shake. She laughed, and gave his hand a squeeze. "Beat you here by about thirty seconds."

"Wendy," she said, introducing herself.

"Guess you wouldn't be late if you didn't have to park all the way over in East Lot," Alex said, then, at her confused look: "Black Gremlin, right?"

"How...?"

"You almost ran me over the other day." Matter-of-factly. "It's okay, really. My fault. I was jaywalking, headphones on ..."

Wendy shook her head, smiling. "Sometimes I think that car's possessed. It's always—"

"Wendy!" Professor Glazer interrupted, her voice sounding nearby in the acoustically sensitive lecture hall. Wendy snapped away from Alex, saw her prof glaring. She was a ferocious little woman, Professor Glazer. Even six months pregnant.

"Yes, ma'am?"

"Since you're so chatty today, why don't you help us get started with Hawthorne . . ."

⊕

Karen Glazer looked up at her student at the back of the lecture hall and waited. Wendy Ward, daughter of the college president, looked embarrassed to be caught flirting with the handsome guy next to her. Mortified now to be on the spot.

"Hawthorne, professor?" The poor kid's voice came out a squeak. Karen took pity.

"Give us your impressions of Hawthorne's *House of the Seven Gables*. Go ahead, throw out anything. Help get us started on a Monday morning."

An uncomfortable silence. Then, suddenly, the girl actually came through with a response. "Well . . . Hawthorne comes right out and says the moral of his book in the preface. Which was kind of surprising. I mean, usually writers disguise their morals in symbolism and whatnot."

Whatnot? Karen let it slide. "And what is Hawthorne's moral?"

The girl was thumbing through her copy of the novel. She found the passage and read aloud: " 'That the wrong-doing of one generation lives into the successive ones.' "

"Exactly!" *Bless you, child,* was what Karen really wanted to say. *Bless you for actually reading my assignment.* She did a quick mental shuffle, reclassifying Larry Ward's kid from the overcrowded Space Cadet classification to the more rarified category Promising Student. An endangered species.

"And what are the 'wrongdoings' that haunt the generations in *Gables*?" Karen prompted, building momentum now, opening the question up to the entire class.

Silence. "C'mon, guys, this is an easy one."

Finally, an anonymous reply: "Witchcraft?"

"The *accusation* of witchcraft," Karen corrected. "Colonel Pyncheon falsely accuses his enemy Matthew Maule of witchcraft—and Maule is hanged! What do you think of that? Kinda appropriate this time of year, don't you think?" She looked out at the gallery of blank faces, searching for some glimmer. *Nada.* If anything, they seemed embarrassed for her and her enthusiasm for this 150-year-old book. Karen felt herself deflate a little before their critical gaze. An unpleasant feeling. She was losing them.

She felt a sudden sharp kick from the baby, and put a hand to her belly. *Thanks, kid.* Her own daughter joining the chorus of disapproval. She felt the gap between generations yawning suddenly wider before her. Felt a vertiginous lurch, toes at the precipice. Looking across the chasm at those blank, dispassionate faces on the other side of youth. Her students. Somebody's children. Each year she felt the distance from them growing. Was it simply a matter of age? At thirty-eight, Karen didn't feel old, exactly, at least not physically. In fact she felt for the first time her right age: she'd been thirty-eight for the last two decades. Back in college in Boston, then grad school, she'd always been a little out of sync with her classmates. Even from her friends, whose companionship felt more like a coincidence of common sensibilities, interdepartmental alliances, than true kinship. Would her daughter's love be similarly coincidental? A matter of convenience, of cohabitation? Would they grow apart, like roommates who drift out of touch because they were never really friends? Would her own daughter someday give her the same glazed-over look of incomprehension as this gallery of strangers?

"Professor?" A girl's voice. Karen snapped back into focus. Saw a raised hand—Wendy again.

"Yes?"

"Did you assign this book to hint that we shouldn't celebrate witch killing?"

Karen smiled. "Not exactly the best reason to have a parade, is it? But no, I don't have a secret political agenda in assigning Hawthorne. That's later in the term, when we read *The Scarlet Let-*

ter." She perched herself on the edge of her desk and looked up at Wendy, grateful to the girl for helping get her back on track.

"I picked *Gables* as our first novel because it's fun—if you bother to read it—and because it takes place in a New England town similar to our own beloved Windale. And because it's a big ripe American novel by a guy who wasn't afraid of literary special effects."—a few smiles now among the crowd, when she picked out individual faces—"So there's plenty for us to chew on together." Karen opened her edition to the first passage she planned to talk about. "Shall we?"

Forty minutes later, Karen popped a cough drop into her mouth and watched her students filing out. She'd left them the assignment of reading the next three chapters of *Gables*; a few had looked at her like she'd asked them to transcribe the text into ancient Greek.

Eva Hartman slipped into the lecture hall from her own classroom next door, where her contemporary German lit (conducted entirely in the original tongue) was just letting out. "You want to catch lunch later?" she asked Karen.

"Rain check. I've got my monthly with the obstetrician."

"How are you feeling?" Eva was a vet when it came to pregnancies, with two startlingly blond, bilingual children in the Friends Select school favored by faculty parents.

"Not bad," Karen said. "She kicks a little more vigorously than I expected."

"Keeping you awake at night?" Eva asked, then explained her concern: "You've been looking tired."

"Bad dreams, actually." She flashed a smile to show she wasn't crazy. "Last night was this incredibly vivid tour of colonial Windale. Quite spooky."

"Too much Hawthorne before bed," Eva said, nodding with a smile toward the copy of *Gables* in Karen's arms. "You better take care of yourself, Karen. The last trimester can really suck the life out of you. Don't think you'll catch up on missed sleep after the baby's born."

"Don't worry," Karen said with a little laugh, "I'm not that naive."

✶

Wendy casually gathered her books and notebooks into a manageable pile as Frankie came up the steps toward her. Most of the other students had rushed by—including Jack "Quarterback" Carter, who shook his head and gave her a thumb's down followed by a finger up—how original—when she realized Alex was hesitating over his own pile of academia. Waiting for her?

"Alex, thanks again. . . ."

"No problem," he said, propping his sunglasses in his hair.

You can do better than that, Wendy. She smiled, "So, what's your short and sweet here at Danfield?"

"My 'short and sweet'?"

"You know, your bio, personal sound bite, facts and figs," she said. "Look, I'll go first. Wendy Ward, freshman, biology major, dabbler in the arcane and, sadly, a townie." She left off the 'college president's daughter' section of her résumé. "Favorite color? Much too obvious."

Alex laughed. "Let's see...Alex Dunkirk, freshman, finance major, dabbler in the track and field here at Danfield, Minneapolis born and raised. Favorite color? Paisley."

Now Wendy laughed. "Paisley? Really?"

"Just kidding."

Frankie had sidled up next to Wendy, all smiles and ears.

"Athletic scholarship, right?" Wendy asked Alex.

"Walk-on, actually."

Something unrelated clicked for her. "You know, I think you're in my astronomy class."

"That would probably be me."

Frankie had been looking back and forth between them. "Fine, if you guys are gonna ignore me anyway, I'll go chat with the prof."

Wendy snagged her sleeve.

"That's okay," Alex said, scooping up his books and backing away. "I'm about to be late for macroeconomics anyway. Nice meeting you, Wendy," he said, again offering his hand. She shook it, couldn't help grinning like a...like a schoolgirl. "And you...?" Alex said, looking at Frankie.

"Frankie," she said with a cursory smile.

"Nice meeting you too, Alex," Wendy called after him, with a halfhearted wave after he'd already turned his back to her. She looked at Frankie and headed off the avalanche of questions by saying, "If you want to talk to Professor Glazer, you'd better hurry. Think she's about to leave."

✪

"Professor Glazer?" Karen looked at the girl before her and struggled for a name to match the round little face, the tight blond curls. Blank. But she was with Wendy, so Karen gave her points for keeping good company.

"I just wanted to say, professor, that I really think it's great, what you're doing." Behind her (Frankie! That was it!) Wendy looked embarrassed for her friend.

"What exactly am I'm doing?"

"Having a child. On your own, I mean. As a single parent," Frankie said, putting a hand on Karen's arm. "I think it's a really strong thing for a woman to do. We talked about it for, like, an hour the other day in class."

"You talked about my pregnancy in a *class*?!"

"Freshman seminar, actually. Contemporary women's issues. Professor Bennett."

Ah, Jessica Bennett. Danfield's own home-grown Camille Paglia. Very vocal in her support of Karen's pregnancy...though Karen secretly suspected Bennett was Patient Zero in the epidemic of interdepartmental speculation about the identity of the father of Karen's child. Karen was tempted simply to quash the gossip by announcing that she'd gone to a sperm bank. Tempted, in other words, to lie.

"Tell Professor Bennett I'm honored to make her syllabus," Karen said to Frankie. Wendy tugged her friend away by the arm before she could bury her Birkenstock any farther in her mouth. She flashed Karen an apologetic look. Karen was liking her more and more.

⊛

"What?" Frankie said as she walked double-time to keep up with Wendy, her sandals slap-slapping in the hallway.

"I can*not* believe you just said that!" Wendy rolled her eyes heavenward.

"Why? I think it's very strong of her. I wanted her to know I support her decision."

"I'm sure she's grateful, Frankie."

As they exited Pearson and began to power walk back in the direction of student parking, Frankie asked, "So who's the guy you were flirting with?"

"That wasn't flirting. It was fraternizing."

"With the enemy."

"What, you don't like guys now that you're a women's studies major?"

"I'm physically attracted to them, yes. But that's just biology. I have no control over that." Getting out of breath now.

"Let me guess, that love charm I gave you didn't work."

"Great big round zero," Frankie said. "Besides, intellectually, I disapprove of everything men stand for."

"Which would be?"

"Aggression. Warfare. Organized sports."

"Then you definitely wouldn't like Alex. He's on the track team." She flashed a wicked little smile. "Track guys have great legs."

"And just where exactly is this going?"

"Nowhere," Wendy said, suddenly darkening. "It was probably a random blip. The blind squirrel finding an occasional acorn. Next class, he'll probably sit on the other side of Pearson. Chat up some other coed. End of story."

Wendy and Frankie reached the Gremlin and battled traffic all the way to the campus radio station, WDAN. By the time they arrived, Frankie had prattled on for twenty minutes and Wendy didn't mind seeing her leave. Frankie leaned in through the Gremlin's open passenger window for a final piece of advice: "Ask him out. But don't expect any sympathy from me when it all goes sour."

"Good-bye, Frankie."

Her friend turned to go. "And don't forget to listen to my show!" she said, pointing to the call letters stenciled on the radio station's door.

Wendy turned on the Gremlin's old dashboard stereo. A man's voice announced, "Stay tuned for 'Sisters in Song,' which will be on just as soon as your host, Frankie Lenard, decides to show up . . ."

⬟

Art clicked off the studio mike and cued a PSA cart. Over the speakers, the public service announcement (Art's own prerecorded voice) warned whoever was listening at ten in the morning that "Swimmer's ear is more than a summertime nuisance . . . untreated, it can lead to painful swelling, infection, even hearing loss!"

He pushed away from the console and tipped his head back, closing his eyes and for the moment, letting everything fall away except for a heightened awareness of his breathing. The breathing meditation was supposed to help Art center himself, empty out a cluttered head, but usually all he achieved was a heightened awareness of how shitty this job was anymore. His eyes snapped open suddenly: overhead he saw crumbling acoustic tiles, badly water damaged. With an annual budget in the low five figures, no advertising, and a staff of unreliable volunteers, WDAN was a leaking ship awaiting decommission. And Art was the only guy holding a bucket. He looked at his watch: ten-fifteen. No Frankie Lenard yet, no "Sisters in Song." He cued a second PSA to stall. ("Do you have an eating disorder, or know someone who does?") The student DJs who signed up for airtime did it for fun, or (in the unlikely event they were communications majors) for a half credit of Independent Study. Could he really blame them for being late? These kids were out busy discovering life, reading Walt Whitman, figuring out all the various interesting combinations for genitalia. Art envied them. He'd been envying them for the last fourteen years.

Some of the student DJs Art had managed back then were now MDs, JDs, PhDs. Christ, some were on the *faculty* now. And Art? Fourteen years later, he was still behind the console, filling in for another tardy kid. Recording PSAs for Big Brothers/Big Sisters and the National Association of Podiatrists. And still chasing down that last little bit of research for his own dissertation.

Actually, he was going to have to start thinking of the dissertation in the past tense. No longer a work in progress. He'd submitted it two weeks earlier, and its absence on his desk still haunted him like a phantom limb. Which opened up a whole other avenue of dread ...

What would happen when he was awarded his degree? It had been two weeks now since he submitted his long-awaited dissertation, which examined the social impacts of the textile industry's rise and decline in Essex County (in general) and Windale (in particular). Suddenly he'd no longer be a PhD *candidate*, he'd be ... well, an *alumn*. A doctor. What next, then—professorhood? That's exactly what he'd been avoiding these past fourteen years, choosing to offset his tuition in the graduate program by managing the campus radio station, instead of becoming a TA, or pinch-hitting for profs on sabbatical. Those jobs required exponentially more contact with students and faculty than Art wanted. Just the concept of facing a lecture hall of students sent him scuttling back to his breathing meditation, on the brink of hyperventilating. Tenure, academic infighting, publish or perish ...

He realized he was tugging on his ponytail, a nervous habit. No getting around it. It was due time he figured out what was next in life, the way most grown-ups already had by the time they were forty. The old cocktail party line he'd used for years ("I'm in public radio") no longer came as quickly to his lips. (Of course, invitations to cocktail parties weren't coming as quickly either, so that problem took care of itself.)

The door of the studio opened and Frankie peeked inside. "Sorry sorry sorry...," she said, ducking beneath Art's disapproving gaze and taking the swivel chair he vacated for her.

"I pulled some CDs to get you started," Art said, handing her the tall stack of jewel cases. "I used your last playlist."

"You're the greatest!" Frankie said, donning headphones and giving Art a wave that was both mea culpa and dismissal. He left, shooting her one more warning stare through the Plexiglas studio window, and went to fetch the mail.

An FCC bulletin, last issue of *Stereophile*, a couple of photocopied take-out menus for the overnight DJs from local pizza joints and sandwich shops...Art shuffled through the mail on his way back through the dingy cinder block halls of WDAN. He found an official-looking white envelope at the bottom of the pile, addressed to him. From the history department's graduate program. He felt his stomach drop.

Art took a breath, closed his office door behind him, cleared a space on his desk, pushing aside the bonsai tree he was busy killing, the Magic 8-Ball, promotional copies of new albums. He tore open the letter. Started to read, just as Frankie's "radio" voice piped through the little radio Art kept on the windowsill. She really enjoyed getting into her sultry voice for the airwaves. Compared to her normal squeaky Frankie voice, it almost seemed like a superhero's secret identity. "Good morning, sisters in song! We've got new tunes today from Tori Amos ..."

The sound dropped away behind Art. The world dropped away. He looked at the letter in his trembling hand.

His dissertation had been rejected. Not a qualified rejection, not a "we'd like to discuss certain aspects of your research" sort of rejection. Rejected absolutely and definitively. Everything but the rubber stamp.

"It is the opinion of this Board that the subject of your dissertation does not meet current requirements necessary for the degree of Doctor of History," Art read aloud with disbelief, then continued reading in stunned silence.

Typically, doctoral candidates receive guidance from an assigned faculty advisor, so that situations such as this unfortunate one are avoided before candidates invest time and resources on research. As you know, dissertation topics must be preapproved by both the assigned faculty advisor, as well as this Board. Your situation is unique in that all of the members of the original Board who approved your dissertation topic have since retired from Danfield College, while the original faculty advisor assigned to you—Professor Emeritus Karl Lundt—has passed away. Typically, when the Board rejects a dissertation, it accepts a measure of responsibility for inadequate academic guidance throughout the development process. However, given the protracted amount of time you have taken to complete your research and dissertation, the Board feels it cannot accept such responsibility. What we can offer is our deep regrets, and warm wishes for your future academic pursuits.

The letter was signed (respectfully) S. Leigh Himes, Chair, Board of Graduate Studies.

Art picked up his Magic 8-Ball and hurled it across the room. It smashed against the opposite wall in a spray of blue-tinted water. He felt immediately remorseful, like he'd kicked a dog.

He scooped up the telephone and punched in his brother's cell number.

Paul answered on the second ring. "Leeson Contracting."

"They fucking rejected my dissertation."

A beat while his brother processed. "They can do that? After fourteen years?"

"Of course they can! They're Nazis." He was about to rant on some more when he heard something on his brother's end of the line, like the buffeting of a strong headwind. "Where the hell are you?"

"On the roof of a beautiful Queen Anne that's seen better days. Out on Old Winthrop Road."

"Well climb the hell down and come take me out for a sympathy beer," Art said.

"I'm sorry, bud," Paul said. "The homeowner wants an estimate this afternoon—the ceiling's been leaking on his little girl. " Art heard his brother shift the cell phone to his other hand. "You should see this roof. Looks like someone dropped a tree on it."

"I feel like someone dropped a load of shit on me today, too," Art said glumly.

"I bet," Paul said, genuinely sympathetic. "Listen, I'm booked up today, but what do you say I buy you lunch tomorrow at that vegan place you like—the one where the waitresses don't shave their legs?"

"That's okay. I know you're busy." He knew his brother usually wolfed down a sandwich driving between jobs. A two-hour pity lunch would be cutting into the man's livelihood. "I gotta be here for an FCC inspection."

"Then come over for supper, sometime. How about this weekend?"

"Sure," Art said unenthusiastically. That introduced a whole other circle to Art's hell, as he got to sit across from Paul and his girlfriend—whom Art had loved since high school. "That sounds . . . nice."

Paul must have heard the defeat in Art's voice. "Take it easy on yourself, bud. You'll figure this one out," his brother said, concerned. "You're the brains in the family."

They hung up. Art stood wearily and crossed the room, stooped down and began picking up plastic shards of ruined Magic 8-Ball from the carpet. He found the little twenty-sided oracle die tangled in the sopping shag. (It was an icosahedron. What a useful fucking thing to know.) He picked it up and gave a humorless laugh when he saw its forecast: OUTLOOK NOT SO GOOD.

※

Anticipating another restless night of bad dreams, Wendy stopped by the health food store on her way home from work for the ingredients to a homeopathic hot toddy. While the herbs were steeping on the stove, she took a hot shower. When she came down a few minutes later to fetch her concoction, she found her father standing over the saucepan, a spoon in his hand.

"What the hell is this?" he asked, making a sour face.

"Shouldn't you ask that before you taste? What if I told you it was a powerful herbal laxative?"

"I've learned my lesson. What are all the floaties?"

"Licorice. Lemongrass. Peppermint. Valerian root. Skullcap," she said, counting them off on her fingers. Missing anything? "Oh! And good old chamomile tea."

"Think I'll stick to bourbon," he said, searching the cupboards for one of the everyday highball glasses (as opposed to the presidential Waterford.) He was enjoying a rare night alone—Carol Ward was at a seminar on new Essex County zoning policy—which meant he could indulge a little. He found a highball glass and opened the freezer for ice.

"Trouble sleeping, kiddo?"

"The usual. Bad dreams."

He closed the fridge, dropping ice into his glass with a satisfying clink. "Garden variety, or something we need to talk to psych services about?"

Wendy considered a moment before answering. "Somewhere in between, I guess." Something in her voice caught him, and he looked up at her with concern.

"What kind of dreams?"

"Just—weird. I don't know, I can't really describe them." Or want to. "Very vivid. Like I'm being watched by someone I can't see."

She could tell she was spooking him. "This doesn't have any sort of connection to the real world, does it, honey?" he asked. "You're not being stalked . . . ?"

"No, daddy. It's okay." She flashed a smile to signal he could drop back to DefCon One. "Really. I mean, being followed around by guys is definitely not a problem I'm having. I should be so lucky . . ."

He was relieved and gave her a kiss on the temple that made her slosh her herbal tea all over her bare toes. "I thought you've looked a little tired lately," he said. "Your mother and I noticed."

"I figured. Mom left me a tube of Revitalizing Eye Gel on my nightstand. That's her idea of getting to the root of the problem."

He laughed, and she gave him a quick peck good night. Minutes later she lay burrowed under her down comforter, sipping the citrusy tea and reading Hawthorne. Already her eyelids were feeling heavy. She put the book aside and gave herself to sleepy thoughts. Free association . . . Frankie, and Professor Glazer, and the Gremlin, and . . . Alex. With the uncertain smile. Her thoughts kept circling back around to him like a recurring melody in a piece of jazz.

And on that smile, she fell asleep.

✪

Midnight. Throughout town a dry wind blew, quick and mischievous, animating bits of trash and overturning garbage cans with a clatter before retreating to the restless treetops. At the Grocery King on Main, the breeze set a shopping cart rolling across the empty parking lot; while out on Old Winthrop Road, at the all-night Stop-N-Go, it blew insistently enough to trigger the automatic doors, startling the night clerk with a gust of sudden litter.

Across town, in the tiny business office of Holy Redeemer Church, Father Joe Murray heard something clatter on the roof slates overhead and looked up from his faded paperback. At first he mistook the sound as laughter, but before his ears could identify its source the sound was masked by the steeple bells chiming midnight. Father Murray scowled. He hated the digital chimes, which had replaced Holy Redeemer's original bells two years ago. Just the latest sad concession to technology. Before that, the parish had been forced by the insurance companies to replace the ranks of votive candles with vulgar electronic ones to remove the risk of fire. It wouldn't be long, Father Murray sometimes grumbled, before the parish would decide to replace *him*—he imagined by a laptop computer on the altar.

Thump. This time the sound was so loud Father Murray left the business office and walked into the dark chapel. Had a tree branch fallen? The night was certainly windy enough, and he'd been meaning to call the O'Neill boy to have a look at the diseased elms that overhung the church.

The digital chimes were just beginning the second verse of their tinny hymn when the church shuddered violently, and Father Murray heard a terrific crash. The digital chimes slurred, leaden, then were silent.

Father Murray bolted through the dark chapel and out through the church doors. He turned and looked, craning his neck to see what had happened. He could just make out the steeple, still standing in profile against the night sky. Its side was gaping, the wood splintered. What the hell had done that? A wrecking ball?

The breeze shifted, carrying a dark smell to him. He felt his hackles rise in response to the musky, fetid smell—the stink of spoiled meat, left to rot. He shivered, suddenly afraid. On the roof of Holy Redeemer he saw a fleeting motion, a shadow darting across the scrim of stars—

CRASH! Another phenomenal concussion, and now the steeple was falling in slow motion toward him. The crucifix it had held aloft for three decades came tipping forward and broke in two on the roof shingles ... the ruined steeple slid down the slanted roof and landed in a splintered heap on the lawn at Father Joe Murray's feet.

⊛

Wendy slept, if not exactly fitfully, then at least without interruption throughout the long night. There was a storm front moving through, and it tossed the branches of the old maple outside her bedroom hard enough that it clacked repeatedly against her window. But still Wendy slept, deep into the night, and dreamed. Behind closed lids her eyes scanned rapidly left to right, left to right, and her breathing was quick and troubled. But she did not wake—or couldn't.

Not even at the sound of the heavy thud overhead as something stronger than the agitating currents of the storm front landed on the roof above Wendy's bed, waiting.

CHAPTER
TWO

Eight-year-old Abby MacNeil fell sick in late September and missed an entire week of third grade at the newly opened Thorburn Public Elementary School. Whether the illness was viral in origin or the result of sustained exhaustion was never diagnosed, because her father maintained a basic mistrust of doctors (a hostile orthopedist had once testified against him in a workman's comp claim) and an even baser discomfort with clinics. (The only people who went to clinics, he often said, were poor blacks looking for free birth control and Portuguese factory workers with gonorrhea.) And so Abby lay in bed that first Monday morning following another weekend of feverish nightmares, beneath the critical eye of her father, until he rendered his diagnosis: "You're sick—you should stay home. But if you're screwin' around with me, girl, you're gonna get a beating."

With those words he left her alone for the morning while he went downtown to get his unemployment check. He returned at lunchtime with a bottle of NyQuil and a thermometer he'd purchased at the CVS. The little girl was running a temperature of 102 by then and had become dehydrated. After she'd choked down the viscous adult flu medicine and some tepid tap water, she dropped off into a feverish delirium. Sunlight climbed the faded wallpaper before reddening, dying, and succumbing to the time-lapse shadows. Around seven that evening, on his way out to the Tap Room, her father paused in her doorway, frowning at the sight of his daughter in the grip of sickness: fetal, sheets kicked off her flushed young body, her breathing quick and hot. Something bothered him about the sight of her, beyond the fever itself, and kept him on the threshold of the sickroom. Something wrong with the way the shadows seemed to cling to her sweat-sheened limbs. Something wrong about the limbs themselves. She looked . . . longer. Was it a trick of the dying light, or could he see the teenager she would become already showing herself lightly beneath this child's skin? And yet she was sucking on the two long middle fingers of her right hand, an infantile reflex. He'd never seen her do that before, not even when she *was* an infant. He left hastily.

By the next day the fever had broken, though Abby's horrible body aches kept her home from school yet again. Out her bedroom window she could hear her school bus rumbling by, and she was sure she could even distinguish the individual voices of her friends. Her hearing was getting sharper. She could hear mice in the basement. She could hear voices in the current of the wall sockets.

Later that morning, the man her father had hired came to begin work on the ceiling over Abby's bedroom, so she moved her convalescence to the sofa downstairs in front of the TV. The repairman—he introduced himself to Abby simply as "Paul"—seemed surprised to learn her father had left her alone in the house. (She'd let him in to use the bathroom when he appeared at the back screen door.)

"Do you need anything? Some water or something?" he asked when he came back from the bathroom. She shook her head.

"D'you have a little girl?" Abby asked him suddenly.

"A little—?" Her eyes seemed strangely older than her years, heavy with sad understanding. "No, not . . . yet. Soon."

Abby nodded gravely, and returned her attention to the television. He felt with certainty that he'd been dismissed. And yet he lingered a moment before returning to work. He searched for a business card in his shirt pocket and handed it to Abby. "Do you know how to use a telephone?" he asked her.

Abby turned those too-wise eyes to him with a pitying look. "Are you kidding?" she asked.

"Right. Dumb question," Paul said. "Well, if you need anything while you're dad's out and I'm up on the roof, you just call this number. I carry my cell phone with me." He slapped his hip, where the cell phone was clipped beside a tape measure, a pocketknife, and a pager. Then he left the little girl staring blankly at the flickering television.

By noon Abby had grown bored with Nickelodeon reruns: *Gilligan's Island*, *Brady Bunch*, *McHale's Navy*, *Partridge Family*. After *Bewitched* she pulled on her best school clothes and quietly ventured outside for the first time since falling ill. She was shaky, unstable on her aching legs, but she couldn't bear to remain cooped up in the house a moment longer.

Outside on the porch, Abby sat on the steps and tried looking up at the blue sky, streaked with the cottony contrails of long-gone airplanes; but it was too penetratingly blue for her tender eyes, and she had to look away. She felt hot, flush in the face, as if the fever might be returning.

Her eyes found the inviting shade of the woods beyond, at the edge of the weedy lot behind their yard. The woods looked cool and peaceful, back where the details of individual trees melted into a deep and leafy blur. Abby stood and decided, on impulse, to seek refuge in its shade. She slipped her bare feet into the dusty pink jellies she left beside the screen door—her summer play shoes—and strode off purposefully across the yard, stepping without hesitation beyond its mowed border and into the waiting field of tall weeds and witchgrass.

Without a backward glance she disappeared into the shade of the woods.

A child left alone outdoors long enough will always find her way to water. Minutes after she'd entered the canopy of shady woods, Abby discovered a creek, a tributary from some unseen spring. It babbled gently over mossy rocks that were green above the water-line, cool and slimy below. She followed the water to a kind of tide-pool and watched a water bug skating across the placid surface, its legs barely dimpling the water. She found a school of minnows hovering in the shallows by a muddy bank. She investigated a shoal of fragile foam beside decomposing leaves.

The creek fascinated her for an hour and led her deeper within the woods. When she finally looked up from her investigations, she found herself in an unfamiliar clearing. She was alone and, she supposed, lost. She wasn't afraid yet, though. Shafts of sunlight angled down through breaks in the high canopy above. She found a fallen tree that crumbled beneath her weight when she tried to climb up onto it. Inside it was dry and rotten, roiling with ter-mites.

She ventured farther into the clearing. The trees here seemed different from the others in the woods. They were thicker, which meant (recalling a life sciences project in the second grade) they were older; if you cut one in half it would have many rings, one for each year. These trees must be very old, and like old people they were twisted and bent, barnacled with strange misshapen growths and burled, tumorous swellings. Their bark was mottled, scarred, split in places to reveal raw sodden wood beneath. One trunk bore great fatty lobes of fungus. Another wept a treacly black sap. All rose up from visible roots that clutched the moist humus of the for-est floor like arthritic hands.

Abby realized the clearing had fallen strangely silent, like a church. Gone were the bird calls, the ever-present susurrus of insects. No more breeze in tree branches overhead, or the distant rumble of airplanes.

But Abby still wasn't afraid, she was curious. And when she found the gravestones, she ceased to be simply a visitor to this place—she knew she'd found a home.

They lay in a tumbled heap, three stones so old they almost seemed natural rock. Abby kneeled down to peer at the first name carved into the green face of the first stone. She read the letters eroded by three hundred seasons of wind, rain, and snow.

SARAH HUTCHINS
CONDEMNED WITCH
HANGED THIS DAY 1699.

She had to read the words slowly, sounding them out. She traced a fingertip through the shallow grooves, feeling each letter. Quietly, with reverence.

The woods watched. The trees held their breath, as if afraid to startle away the timid visitor to this secret place. But Abby felt no impulse to flee this quiet place. Just the opposite, in fact. She'd found a new secret place of her own.

⊗

Wendy was late for work. She turned onto Theurgy Avenue, which was part of the sleepy business district located within three miles of the main Danfield campus. The Crystal Path was nestled within a block of nine quaint shops, painted in different pastel flavors, each one sporting a gingerbread trim of awning and an old-world charm that made you want to tack "Ye Olde" to the front of every store's name.

The store tenants had unilaterally agreed that street parking be reserved for customers, so Wendy was spared the embarrassment of parallel parking the Gremlin, which she found to be a nightmare even when the little car cooperated by not conking out on her. The long narrow lot behind the row of stores handled the spillover customers and employees. Just her dumb luck to get stuck in the spot next to the big, smelly Dumpster.

Wendy opened the door to the tinkling sound of hanging silver chimes in the shape of quarter moon and stars—Alissa hated buzzers—and the pleasant aroma of a vanilla candle. As always, just walking through the door of the place seemed to soothe Wendy. "I'm sorry, Alissa!" Wendy called instinctively. Her boss was often in the back of the store practicing her yoga breathing or postures, even when she was technically in charge of the register. In other words, when she was alone in the store. Her regulars usually browsed for a while before requiring any sort of sales assistance. Newcomers were often at a loss as to what to make of the shop anyway and needed time alone to acclimate.

"Wendy? Is that you?"

"Reporting for duty!" Wendy called to the back of the store.

While she was alone, she took a moment to look at the store anew, as she imagined a first-time visitor would see it. Arranged around the front of the store were jars and baskets of daisies, lavender, jasmine, and roses, some fresh and some dried. Various handmade jewelry items—mostly crystal or silver—were on display in the glass cases that formed the cash register's U. At each corner of the island stood an oversize palmistry model hand, with all the lines and whorls of the palm reader's art plainly illustrated and labeled. Each hand was suction-cupped to the smooth glass countertop.

On the walls on either side of the register were shelves featuring crystal balls and polished stones, including amethyst, blue-laced agate, sapphire, tiger eye, and rutilated quartz. Farther back on the left side were the many jars of dried herbs—thyme, rosemary, sage, and hawthorn among them. Opposite this display were drawers of muslin bags, candles of numerous sizes and shapes, empty bottles and jars and decorative baskets, shelves with simple and elaborate candleholders, wooden mortars and pestles, and even an assortment of tarot decks.

Wendy stepped inside the cash register U and high-fived the nearest palmistry hand, smiling as it wobbled back and forth like one of those inflatable punch clowns that always came back for more. She tossed her backpack on a low shelf under the register. Alissa didn't mind if she caught up on her class assignments if business was slow, as long as the store was properly presented: swept, watered, dusted, folded, and alphabetized.

"Traffic bad?"

Wendy spun around to face Alissa Raines, who had a disconcerting habit of gliding wraithlike throughout the shop, making about as much noise as a passing thought.

"Traffic bad. Gremlin worse."

Alissa had an ethereal presence and an inner tranquility about her. A youthful face with hauntingly pale blue eyes framed by long white hair, usually bound in a loose ponytail. Since she'd taken up yoga, she more often than not wore flowery scarves and wraparound skirts over her exercise leotard. She kept an exercise mat in the back room, along with her own personal mandala, so she liked to be able to strip down quickly to her leotard for a twenty- or thirty-minute yoga session.

"Gwendolyn, I do believe that car is the only thing blocking you from true inner peace." Whether consciously or unconsciously, Alissa always seemed to use Wendy's formal name when she was in mentor mode.

"I know," Wendy said, chagrined. "More trouble than it's usually worth."

"Why not get a bike? A good ten-speed could get you around campus and back and forth to work easily enough."

"I need a place for all my stuff," Wendy said sheepishly. *Besides,* Wendy thought, I *already have a bike. It's up on blocks, in my bedroom.*

"Most of your stuff is trash you forgot to throw away. You know, we do have recycling bins in back."

Wendy nodded. She planned to get organized . . . just as soon as she got some free time. "So . . . how's business today?" Wendy asked.

"Change of topic. Okay, I can take a hint. Business? Well, you know what I always say, we only get two types of customers . . ."

"Tourists and true believers."

"Well, the tourists are scarce today, and the true believers must be all stocked up," Alissa said with a wry smile.

"What do you want me to do?"

"Got in a shipment of books." Alissa tapped a large brown box with the toe of a slipper. "Shelve those, give the place the once-over with the magic duster, and you're free to crack open the books for the rest of the evening."

"Oh, joy!" Wendy said with a wry smile.

"If you need me I'll be in back, for a little pranayama." Breathing exercises. Wendy was starting to remember all the "anas" and "amas" of yoga.

She took the box cutter out of the drawer and sliced the top of the book carton open. She made three trips to the back of the store, stacking the books in a loose pile on the floor. All the books were shelved by topic, not by author, so when she got to the book on water dousing, she had to decide whether to file it in the W section for water or in the D for dousing. She settled on D, since that was more specific. Sitting on the carpeted floor with no customers to help, no sounds but her own humming to intrude, she felt a creeping lethargy seep into her bones, as if she were being pulled down into sleep by a strong hand. She yawned so wide her jaw cracked. After she shelved these books, she had a whole pile of her own textbooks to absorb. Another yawn. "Oh, boy," she mumbled through the hand pressed to her mouth, "it's gonna be a long evening."

After a full afternoon of classes and one graduate seminar ("Proust, Joyce, Faulkner: Architects of Memory"), Karen was exhausted. Driving home in her red Volvo, she wanted nothing more than a cool drink, a magazine, and a few uninterrupted hours on the porch glider before sunset.

Alas, her evening wind-down wasn't to be. As she turned off Main onto Lore Avenue, she saw Paul Leeson's blue pickup parked outside her house, and the man himself taking measurements on the wraparound porch. Karen sighed and told herself she should be glad to see him. Like many a successful contractor, he juggled her renovation along with half a dozen others, assigning priority to the homeowners who shouted loudest when he went MIA for more than a day. Too often, Karen found herself low on that priority list.

Paul looked up at the sound of the Volvo's tires on the gravel driveway and raised a hand in a kind of minimalist wave. He was a plain-featured man, always just shy of a sunburn, and handsome if you caught him in the right kind of light—this kind, in fact: a six-thirty sun. He wore a contractor's standard-issue jeans (he kept a pair of pressed khakis for delivering an estimate) but somewhat uncharacteristically favored old golf shirts in wash-faded pastels, monogrammed with little alligators or polo players. Sometimes Karen thought he looked more like a golf pro—up there on his A-frame ladder—than a general contractor.

"Need help?" he called as she lifted a stack of blue exam books from the passenger seat of the Volvo. She shook him off, but he came anyway, closing the Volvo's door for her, taking her shoulder bag from her.

"Did I catch you actually planning to do some work?" she asked, tempering the jab with a smile.

"You feeling neglected?" he asked.

"Just cranky," she said. "Been a long day. My feet hurt. My back hurts. The baby's been doing jumping jacks all afternoon." They climbed the porch steps, Karen throwing a forlorn glance at her antique glider. Paul had laden it with tools.

"We've got to talk about the bills, Professor Glazer," he said as he held open the screen door for her. She was singling out her house key, trying not to lose the slumping stack of exam books.

"Oh yeah?"

"I'm afraid I can't do any more work until you settle some outstanding receipts. How would you like to pay?"

"Inside," she said, pushing the heavy door open. He followed her into the cool foyer, the place smelling comfortingly old, like carpets and deep closets. Part of the reason Karen had fallen in love with it. She turned within the sudden circle of his arms and kissed him. She felt his five o'clock shadow, like fine grit sandpaper, though with his fair hair the stubble wouldn't be visible for hours.

She fumbled behind her to close the door on their little display. He broke the kiss and gave her an amused look. "Don't want the neighbors to know you're carrying on with the handyman?"

"Just chilly."

"Bullshit," he said, not unpleasantly. She slipped away from him and into the living room. Long streaks of honeyed sunlight lay across the oriental carpet, the only time of day the sun was low enough to breach the ramparts of the deep porch. Karen dropped the exam books on the piano bench, tossed her keys into the basket atop the old spinet. Paul slipped a hand across her belly as she flipped through the day's mail.

She asked him, without looking up, "Do I really owe you money?"

He grunted and said, "Fifteen hundred," his touch turning into a caress.

"That much?"

"It's the cedar siding. Expensive stuff, particularly for the quality you want." She'd returned her attention to the mail, using her finger like a letter opener. He took advantage of the moment's distraction to slip beneath her radar. "You know, there's a simple way we could economize . . ."

She was only half-listening. He felt like a shrink planting a posthypnotic suggestion: "I could put my place up for sale, move in here, we turn my mortgage payments into your renovations." He nuzzled her throat, slipping his arms around from behind.

She sighed. "Paul."

"Don't worry, professor—it's not a marriage proposal."

She turned to face him. "But it's not a good idea, either." She tried to say it gently, but he darkened nonetheless.

"Why?"

She headed into the kitchen. He followed on her heels.

"I'm just beginning to get used to this being *my* place," she said. Her parents had deeded it to her when they moved to Panama City.

Paul trapped her in the corner where the kitchen counters met. "Okay, so it's your place"—he touched her belly—"but this is *our* daughter."

She looked away. She hadn't yet gotten used to thinking of the baby as theirs together. In unguarded moments she still found herself thinking of the unborn child as somehow a solo act of creation. Ridiculous, she knew, and usually checked herself for thinking it; but even quashed, the thought left an aftertaste of possessiveness. And Paul sensed it.

"She is going to be *our* daughter, isn't she?" he asked. "Or am I overstaying my welcome?"

"Of course not." She flashed an irritated look, forced him to let her out of the corner. Went to the fridge and began rooting around inside, improvising supper. "Honestly, Paul, I think sometimes you wait to spring this shit on me when I'm at peak exhaustion. It's like you know my resistance is weak."

"Trouble sleeping again?" It was more observation than question.

"Bad dreams."

"No kidding," he said, and she saw the worry etched around his eyes. Good, kind Paul Leeson. Nothing duplicitous about this man. Nothing hesitant or uncertain about his feelings for her. He deserved no less in return, and once more Karen felt ashamed she couldn't return his love without qualification.

"You were talking in your sleep again last night," he said, taking a beer for himself from the door of the fridge and twisting off the cap with a calloused palm.

"Anything memorable?"

"You called me a 'son of a whore' at one point," he said, and took a meditative swallow of beer. He wiped his frothy lips and belched quietly. "Oh yeah! And a 'pig fucker.' I sorta liked that one."

She looked troubled. "I'm sure I wasn't talking to you . . ."

"Who then? Department chair?"

She looked up at him, concerned. "I don't remember," she said finally, finding it easier to lie. For in fact she *did* remember, if not the name then certainly the face. The particulars had evaporated in daylight, but the man's hard, flinty face remained, seared like a phosphor-flash afterimage on her retinas . . .

Her accuser.

✦

"Let me guess, " Art speculated later that evening, as he and Karen and his brother Paul lingered over coffee on the front porch of 131 Lore. "You're teaching *Seven Gables* again. Couple that with 'new parent anxiety.' What you have is a recipe for a nightmare in the shape of seventeenth-century Windale." The sun had just slipped beyond the western rim of the world, setting ablaze the century-old textile mills that loomed there in stark relief against the smoldering sky. Night was coming on from the east, bringing with its first scatter of stars an early rumor of winter. If Halloween had a smell—and it did, to those inclined to remember it—then tonight smelled prematurely of that holiday, still a long month away.

"I hope that's all it is," Karen murmured absently.

Paul lit a cigarette and aimed his smoke out at the night, away from the porch. "So what are you gonna do now that they rejected your dissertation?" he asked Art.

"I don't know. I'm appealing the board's decision, but it's probably a lost cause."

Paul nodded once. "You could always come work with me?"

A beat of surprise, and Art gave an involuntary laugh. "Working *for* you, you mean—"

"Hear me out, I've been giving this some thought," Paul said, raising a hand. "With you on board, we could go after some of the choice historic renovation projects in Essex County. You've been researching this town's history for the past fourteen years, Art. Right now I'm just Paul Leeson, General Contractor. We team up, suddenly we're Leeson Brothers, Preservationists."

Art smiled, touched. Even as a kid Paul had always tried to remedy any and all family disharmony. "We'd be more convincing if I had my PhD," Art said, which was the only way that occurred to him at the moment to sidestep his brother's offer without hurting his feelings.

Karen said, "Why don't you come up with a new dissertation topic? One that salvages as much of your existing research as possible, but gives it a sexier spin?"

"Sexier how?"

She gave Art a pitying look. "You're really clueless about academia, aren't you?" He flashed her a helpless look, and she gave him a crash course: "Okay. Who chairs the history department? Leigh Himes. She's pretty well known in her field, actually—Danfield's lucky to have gotten her. She's published pioneering social histories of women during the Industrial Revolution and the Second World War. Now take a look at the faculty who've been granted tenure since she took over as chair," Karen said and began ticking them off on her fingers: "Weber, Getty, Olsen. What do they have in common?"

"They're all women . . . ," Art said.

"Wait a minute," Paul said, looking surprised. "Is that legal?"

Karen shot him an amused look and said simply, "We've come a long way, baby." She turned back to Art. "Don't get me wrong, I'm not suggesting Leigh Himes has been denying any male faculty advancement solely on the basis of gender. After all, she hired two new adjunct professors this year, and approved tenure for a third—all men. But it's naive to ignore the fact that Danfield's history department has become a feminist enclave. If you think that's unfair, you can go apply to another program with a bias more to your liking. Or, you can put a spin on your research that will appeal to the current Powers That Be."

"You mean like, 'Women of the Textile Mills of Essex County'?"

Karen stood, began gathering their empty coffee mugs and dessert dishes. "I would think you could recycle whole chapters of your old dissertation."

Art was getting excited now. "Christ, it's all there already! I'd have to do a little more research, of course, and probably a year's worth of writing, but . . ."

"You're welcome," Karen said, opening the screen door with her elbow and carrying the ceramic mugs inside.

"Let me help you with those," Art said, following Karen through the screen door. He gestured for his brother to stay. "Finish your cigarette. I'll help with the dishes."

Inside, Art joined Karen at the kitchen sink, drying the dishes she handed him. He talked excitedly for the next ten minutes about how he could recast his dissertation. He realized she was only half-listening. She'd slipped away again into her own dark thoughts and was washing each dish mechanically, scrubbing it long past clean. Lost in the rush of the tap, the slosh of water.

Art watched her furtively, taking advantage of her inattention. She was wearing a light wool cardigan, and each time her sweatered shoulder brushed against his he experienced an almost static electric charge. Their soapy hands touched as they exchanged a plate. He knew Karen was aware of his "crush" on her, which had first bloomed in high school, and he was pretty sure she was flattered. That's what had kept it innocent all these years, and somehow permissible. It was a secret they maintained together, like a balloon kept sweetly aloft on the thermals of mutual affection. Only in Art's blackest periods, and in close quarters moments like this, did it become nearly unbearable.

"Do you want to talk about these dreams you're having?" Art said now, paying special care not to drop the porcelain creamer he was attempting to dry.

"It's okay, Art," she said. "I'm fine."

"I'm sure it's nothing to worry about. You know, just random neurons firing. Or some side effect of all the hormones you've got sloshing through your—"

He noticed then that she was crying, silently. He stood helpless, drying his hands so he could put an arm around her shaking shoulder. The tears stopped coming, but he still felt a tremor shiver through her as she pressed herself against the edge of the sink.

"I'm afraid, Art," she said, her voice blurry with tears. She was trying to be quiet, so Paul wouldn't hear. "Something's wrong... with the baby... I don't know what exactly..."

"Have you talked to your doctor? What does Paul say?"

"They think I'm paranoid. That I'm just stressing because I'm having a baby at thirty-eight."

"Are you?" he asked gently.

"No. Not any more than any pushing-forty mother-to-be would. And all the early tests show the baby is normal." She nodded in the direction of the ultrasound stuck by a magnet to the refrigerator door. She snatched a paper towel from the dispenser over the sink, blotted her eyes. "I just have this terrible feeling, like a sixth sense." She wadded the paper towel into a ball, angry at herself for crying.

Art's arm was still around her. He felt a momentary twinge of guilt that he was here with his arm around Karen while Paul was outside, but that was quickly replaced by a deeper satisfaction that he could somehow provide a comfort his brother could not.

Karen was looking at the windows above the sink, which had darkened to the point that they'd become mirrors of the kitchen. They reflected back at her the haunted image of her own face, missing its eyes.

"Something's wrong," Karen said, as much to herself as Art. "Something's wrong with my baby, and my dreams are trying to tell me."

✪

Night. The woods rustled quietly, the trees whispering to one another as if afraid to wake the child sleeping in their midst. Sleeping sweetly upon a bed of moss and composted leaves, with a gravestone for her headboard.

Abby dreamed . . .

She is Sarah Hutchins and stands across a long table from her husband.

Roland Hutchins is much older, but powerfully built through his shoulder and arms. He is eating meat off a wooden trencher with his hands. He struggles to get comfortable in his banister-back chair, but it creaks beneath him with each movement. He curses, stands, and kicks the chair across the room. "Useless!" he shouts, then glares at her, and it is apparent he's not commenting on just the chair.

Sarah says nothing. Instead she looks down to avoid his angry eyes.

He sits at the long bench, moving his meal and tankard of beer with him. He chews his last piece of meat lustily, then wipes his hands on a linen napkin. "More meat," he says, breaking off a hunk of bread from a loaf in the middle of the table. "Too hard," he mutters with a disgusted shake of his head. He washes down the bread with a mouthful of beer. "You are a failure as a wife. Where's my meat, woman?"

She hurries to the stew pot in the center of the table, attempts to ladle more meat onto the trencher, but her hand is trembling. His eyes glare into her, and she shudders, splashing hot gravy on his hand. His face goes white in an instant. Her hand recoils from her mistake . . . and the back of her hand spills the tankard of beer across the table.

She gasps, hands pressed to her face, fingers splayed across her mouth. "I beg . . . I beg forgiveness, husband."

"Can you do NOTHING right!"

He is rising from the bench, shaking hot gravy from his large hand. She stands on the other side of the table, unable to move. "I pray forgiveness . . ."

He comes slowly around the table, his face a leering mask. As he flashes a wicked smile, she drops the ladle at her feet. He enjoys her fear as much as his power over her. "I am done forgiving," he says. "Fourteen years old and never learn the simplest of lessons."

She wants to run, to hide, to huddle in a corner. Her legs tremble, but her feet seem glued to the floor. She cannot move.

He is now on her side of the table, towering over her, the stink of his sweat an overpowering odor. He shows her the gravy on his hand. "See that?" he asks her. She gulps, nods quickly, acknowledging her mistake, but it will do no good. There will be no clemency. His arm is a blur as he backhands her across the face with his soiled hand. She crumples to the floor, her hand clamping over her cheek, now smeared with his gravy and the blood from her split lip.

He reaches down, clamps his hand around her upper arm and lifts her to her feet. Too unsteady to stand on her own, she merely *sags against him, silent tears trickling down her face. If she sobs it will be worse, much worse.*

(Asleep on the grave, Abby whimpers softly, pulling her arm from an invisible grip.)

He shakes his head again, looking at her coldly. "Perhaps a good beating will remind you of your duties!" he bellows.

Just then, a knock. Three quick raps on the keeping room door.

"Who comes at this hour?" Roland asks, his voice uncertain. He stands and faces the door and the dark he knows waits beyond. Behind him, Sarah scrambles to her feet, brushing at her petticoat.

The flames in the wall sconces gutter. An unseen hand moves the door latch and the door swings inward. She stands there, cloaked in shadows, but her face is pale and her eyes reflect the candlelight and blaze toward him.

"I would speak with your kind wife."

Roland stands slack-jawed before her, the fire of his rage snuffed out. Sarah notices his hands twitch slightly as he says, "G-good evening, Widow Wither."

Wither says. . .

✪

". . . Good evening," Wendy said, snapping awake from her sitting position on the floor. Disoriented. She looked around, realized she had been leaning against the wall of New Age wisdom, the concentric swirls of the mandalas above looking like a hypnotist's tools. The Crystal Path, of course. She had been, ahem, working.

"Who are you talking to?" Alissa asked, standing over her with a curious smile.

"I think I zoned out there for a minute." Wendy rubbed her face, sighed heavily. She stood, listened to her joints creaking and cracking in protest.

"Zoned out?" Alissa asked with a knowing smile.

"All right, busted," Wendy said with a sheepish grin. "I dozed off for a minute or two. Honestly, I don't know why you even bother to pay me at the end of the week."

Alissa massaged her shoulders. "You're still adjusting to your new schedule: college life, employment, and piles of homework. Give yourself time to adjust. But you must get your sleep, Gwendolyn. Sleep is essential."

"I do sleep," Wendy said. She looked down. Somehow she had managed to shelve all the new books before nodding off. "But when I sleep I dream and ..." She shuddered. "I have these nightmares." She walked toward the front of the store, subconsciously walking away from her problems perhaps, or at least the discussion of them.

Alissa followed, relentless as usual. "What sort of dreams? Showing up in class naked? Taking a test you forgot to study for? Being chased, but you're legs won't move fast enough?"

"It's a little more involved than that," Wendy said.

"Those are anxiety dreams. Consciously you're worrying about something while, behind the scenes, your mind is trying to work it out."

"I'm always worried about something," Wendy said with a quirk of her lips. "These dreams aren't even about me, they're about some other person, like I'm looking through her eyes ..."

The door chimes tinkled and a curly blond strolled into the store, taking in the inventory with one wide sweeping gaze.

"Frankie, what are you doing here?" Wendy asked.

"I never forget a promise," Frankie said. "And I promised to look this place up some night so that I could torment you at your place of employment."

"I think our dear Gwendolyn has quite enough tormenting her," Alissa said, looking at Wendy. She missed Frankie mouthing "Gwendolyn?" with her eyebrows arched impressively high. "I'm Alissa," Wendy's boss said.

"Pleasure to meet you—cool store!" Frankie replied.

"Thank you," Alissa said, then turned back to Wendy. "So let's hear about these dreams."

"Um, it's always about the late seventeenth century, I think," Wendy said. "Puritans."

Frankie looked knowingly at Alissa, "You see, it figures. Talk about male-dominated oppression of women. You go back a few centuries and forget about it! We're talking about that now in my Founding Mothers class."

Ignoring Frankie's commentary for the most part, Wendy sat down on the stool behind the cash register. "It feels like I'm dreaming about events that really happened back then," Wendy said. "In Windale."

"This town certainly has a long history," Alissa said. "Maybe your college studies are filtering into your subconscious and giving you historical nightmares. What's happening in the dreams?"

Wendy frowned at her and said, "Sometimes I'm flying over Windale, how it must have looked back then, houses made of squared timbers, a commons where livestock graze, a meeting house and church."

"Flying dreams?" Frankie said, "You're talking sexual repression there, sister." Alissa frowned at her and Frankie closed her mouth abruptly, making a key and lock gesture in front of her mouth.

"And . . . there's this feeling of darkness and . . . fear in the town. I feel like I'm watching over it, but I'm not afraid. I'm just watching and there's this sense of . . . purpose, of manipulation, like I might be the cause of the fear. I don't know. Does that make any sense?"

Frankie and Alissa were staring at her, but she just shook her head, unwilling to say more. Alissa spoke first. "I still think these are anxiety dreams, Wendy. In Windale, an interest in witchcraft, in white magic, isn't all that unusual, considering our town's heritage. But now that you are in college, you may be feeling the pressure of being different a little more strongly now."

"Maybe," Wendy conceded.

"One bit of advice," Alissa added. "No meditation. When you're dealing with negativity and self-image problems, avoid meditation. It has a way of concentrating the bad stuff. What you need is action, a way to work out those feelings without dwelling upon them. Or, you might consider aromatherapy. I can give you the card of a good aromatherapist. She's a sweet little lady, and a good aromatherapy massage might be just the thing."

"Thanks," Wendy said. "I'll think about it." But already Wendy was thinking along other lines.

"Anyway, I'll go in back and leave you two alone," Alissa said, padding softly toward the back of the store, her skirt the merest whisper of fabric.

Wendy grabbed the duster and came out from behind the cash register. "Follow me," Wendy said. "Nothing looks sadder than dusty crystal balls."

Frankie looked around conspiratorially. "So, Wendy, are you still planning on doing your . . . ceremony thing, out in the woods."

"Why not?" Wendy asked defensively.

"I don't know," Frankie said. "I'd be creeped out, after having those dreams, that's all. I mean, sitting bare-ass naked out in the woods, alone at night." She shivered.

"That's a very small part of it, actually," Wendy said.

"Just how did you get into this . . . wicca stuff, anyway?"

"Being born and raised in Windale can do strange things to an impressionable young girl. But what really hooked me was this time in high school . . ."

A field trip. It was a science experiment where you made a ring out of a wire clothes hanger and tossed it like a Frisbee. You walked to where it landed and sketched whatever fell inside the boundaries of the ring. The idea was to identify whatever you happened to find by chance. But Wendy was getting bored with the plain old grass and rocks she kept finding within her ring. So she ventured far from the main group, deep into the surrounding woods, and found a small clearing that had an air of mystery about it. Wendy's hanger ricocheted off an ash tree, landing within a clump of red and white toadstools.

She noted the tree and made her sketches. Later, her teacher identified the toadstools she'd drawn as fly agaric and told her that witches were said to use the hallucinogenic toadstools as an ingredient in the body grease that enabled them to fly. The hallucinogenic property might explain a lot of the myths. From her later reading, Wendy discovered that these witches made their broom-sticks from the wood of ash trees.

"And that led me to Alissa and this store, where I've since spent entirely too much money. I became an employee for the discounts, otherwise I'd be penniless."

Frankie whispered, "You're telling me Alissa sells these magic mushrooms? Too cool! I know a couple frat houses I'd like to buzz over."

"Nothing hallucinogenic here, sorry," Wendy said, grinning.

"But you don't really rub your body with these flying mush-rooms, do you?" Frankie asked, wide-eyed.

"Personally? No, I do not."

A sudden image of flying filled Wendy's mind. She was looking down on log homes and the commons of colonial Windale, on the sheep that darted and ran from the distorted moon shadow she cast upon the ground. Their primal fear filled her with a sense of power.

Frankie was shaking her. Wendy shuddered.

"Are you okay?" Frankie asked, her easy manner replaced with concern now.

"I'm . . . okay."

"Could have fooled me," Frankie said. "You're white as a ghost."

Wendy hid the trembling of her hands with quick passes of the duster. She forced a smile and a light tone as she said, "Maybe somebody walked on my grave."

CHAPTER THREE

On the last day of September, and with the provisional blessing of the Board of Graduate Studies in hand, Art embarked on his new career as a feminist.

Not quite a card-carrying feminist, Art harbored no particular political agenda, and he was smart enough to recognize that he knew next to nothing about contemporary feminist debate or the intellectual tradition on which it was founded. What he *did* know, however, was the history of the textile industry in Essex County, which had employed a large number of lower- and working-class women throughout the nineteenth century. He knew statistics about salary inequalities; employee racial and ethnic demographics; attitudes of management toward its female workforce. (Much of this information lay unused in Art's overstuffed filing cabinets, or had been relegated to footnote status in his dissertation.) If this specialized knowledge made him a feminist... well then, Art supposed he was a feminist. And, surprisingly, he was beginning to warm to the idea.

What had started as a mercenary undertaking had soon sparked an excitement Art hadn't felt since the early days of grad school. He spent a week poring through his old notes and files in preparation for today, when he'd begin his fieldwork. He bought 400-speed 35mm film for his camera, a fresh stack of the three-by-five note cards he preferred (wide ruled, a medium card stock), and—for spiritual guidance—a new Magic 8-Ball.

The first stop on his itinerary was Windale's tiny one-room historical society, which shared office space and a single underpaid secretary with the Clerk of town records. Her name was Mrs. Florence Reader, age seventy-one, and she was as much living witness to the region's history as its curator. As Art entered the small offices, Florence called out to him.

She kept her focus on centering an ancient folio within a glass table-case. Florence recovered from her fright and beckoned Art to join her at the display case. "Oh, Arthur! Come see our latest acquisition! It's a journal, dating back to the early eighteenth century. A local farmer's wife."

"Have you read it?"

She looked horrified. "My stars, no! It's too fragile." She closed the glass lid of the display case and locked it, suddenly suspicious Art might try to touch it.

Art peered in at the folio, which wasn't a bound volume but simply a collection of brittle pages held together between two loose covers, secured with leather cords. "She must've been a *wealthy* farmer's wife, if she could afford paper in the early eighteenth century."

"Yes! I was just about to type up a note saying as much, for the display. This paper probably came from one of the few commercial paper mills. My guess is the Rittenhouse Mill in Germantown, Philadelphia."

Art straightened, surveying the historical society's digs. It was almost wholly dedicated to a single chapter in the town's long history: an October day almost exactly three hundred years ago, when, on a grassy spot now occupied by an old Howitzer-turned-war-memorial, three of Windale's daughters were hung by the neck until dead. Despite the simple brutality of the act, it didn't seem like much of a story, in Art's opinion. Not even in the same league as Salem's witch persecutions. Salem's trials had been a bona fide hysteria, a series of lurid courtroom confrontations presided over by a colorful fire-and-brimstone preacher, Reverend Parris, that ended in the executions of many innocent women—for the most part condemned on the basis of "spectral" evidence. The mere fact that the accusers said they saw the "specters" of the accused women tormenting them was admitted into a damning form of evidence. Talk about "insubstantial" cases. By the time Windale's blip on the historic radar occurred seven years later, the new Commonwealth of Massachusetts had outlawed spectral evidence in witch trials. Though Windale's three witches were blamed for a long list of wordly and otherworldly woes (unexplained fires, stillborn children, sudden illnesses, inconvenient weather), what ultimately brought them to trial were a series of very real crimes, all with the same outcome: murder.

And so, as far as Art was concerned, Windale's witchy past was actually a criminal—not a hysterical—one.

Of course, try explaining that to Mayor Dell'Olio or the town board of trustees, all of whom salivated over the potential tourist revenue generated by Windale's past. (*Isn't it interesting—the cynic in Art thought—that Windale's interest in its own history began right after its flagship industry collapsed?*)

Hence the original street signs (Chestnut, Oak, Maple) rechristened (Witch Hill, Familiar Way, Black Cat Crossing). Hence the new emblem on Sheriff Bill Nottingham's patrol car—a witch in silhouette, complete with broomstick. Hence the annual King Frost Halloween Parade, with its witch float and brigade of sexy witch-majorettes . . .

And hence the Witch Museum, the entrance to which Art could just see now, annexed off the historical society's one-room headquarters. It was more of a wax museum really, and a pretty pathetic one at that. (Art had once visited a more impressive museum in Vermont dedicated to the history of maple syrup.) Oh, they had a few spooky dioramas, with a half dozen old department store manikins tricked out in colonial garb (no one seemed to mind that these Puritan women wore eye shadow and lipstick). And Florence had tried to lend a little class to the displays by hanging wall placards that outlined the scanty details of the event. But don't fool yourself—Windale's witch museum had no loftier ambitions than the average carny Chamber O' Horrors.

Florence caught Art's disapproving look in the direction of the Witch Museum entrance, and said gently, "I always enjoy your visits, Arthur. It's nice to talk to someone who is interested in real history."

"I hope you can help me, sweetheart. I'm trying to find a list of the thirty-eight women who died in the mill fire of 1899."

"You want names?" Florence said with a discouraging look.

"That's the idea."

She sighed at the task and led Art into a back room heavy with the smell of moldering newsprint, and together they searched the archives. Art noticed Florence's hands trembling as she brought forth old newspaper clippings; the skin of her liver-spotted hands was nearly the same papery texture as the fragile clippings themselves. He thought he caught a whiff of something medicinal on her breath, and decided finally that it was scotch.

"No names in the Boston papers," Florence announced after several moments of close reading. "Just a record of the tragedy itself. 'Thirty-eight Souls Perish in Inferno.' My, but that's rather biblical."

"I'm not having any luck with the local daily, either," Art said. Then his eye snagged on something curious in the yellowing text. He read aloud, " 'Though arson is suspected by police officials, local opinion, particularly among the elder citizenry, attributes the blaze to a centennial curse laid upon the town's founding fathers.' " Art looked up from the news clipping. "Know anything about a curse, Flos?"

She flashed him a proud look. "I wouldn't know, that's *long* before my time."

Art put an arm around her and gave her a squeeze. "Of course it is, sweetheart. I only meant, when you were a little girl, do you remember any of the old-timers talking about a town curse?"

"In fact, I do remember some talk. Campfire stories. My Uncle Reginald would scare us with stories about Windale's curse. I'm afraid I'm a little fuzzy on the details," she said and made her own spooky-story face. "But there was talk of a restless evil in the woods . . ."

She took the newspaper clippings from Art and began refiling them according to her own eccentric system. "Speaking of woods, if you really want to find the names of your thirty-eight mill workers, you might try visiting their graveyard out in Milton Woods."

"Graveyard?"

"Yes. The mill owners donated a little parcel of land on the outskirts of town to the families of the dead. That's how businesses settled out of court in those days. The women who died were all poor immigrants anyway and couldn't afford grave plots in the Catholic cemetery." Her eyes twinkled. "Not many people know about that graveyard!"

Art gave her a kiss. Her cheek was downy, soft as tissue. "That's why I came here first!" he said and slung his camera strap over his shoulder.

Twenty-five minutes later he was hiking along old deer paths (or, perhaps, mountain bike trails) in the dense woods that encircled the Milton textile mills. He'd had to park on a gravel shoulder off Old Winthrop Road to gain access to the woods, because if he'd parked any closer to the condemned mills he would've quickly drawn the attention of the local police. The great rusting mills stood like shrines to a forgotten faith, and like all condemned places they drew a steady traffic of pilgrims looking for the illicit. Which for Windale meant fraternity pleebs, vandals, amateur photographers, and the more adventurous teen lovers. Trespassers braved not only the general spookiness of the place, but also tetanus, sprained ankles, and the wrath of the local police department. Nonetheless, the textile mills still held a nostalgic fascination, and Art wasn't the first townie who sacrificed his virginity on the iron altar of these rusting cathedrals.

Within moments of entering the woods, Art was lost, though he wouldn't admit this to himself for another quarter of an hour. He wasn't particularly concerned, since his instinctive directional sense had been honed during a childhood spent tramping through woodlands. He knew with innate confidence that these woods were bounded on one side by Old Winthrop Road to the south and Miller Creek to the east, that if he wandered too far to the north he'd emerge in the manicured backyards of the new single-family developments of Darley Springs. But he'd expected to find the graveyard Florence had told him about in closer proximity to the mills, and after three quarters of an hour now of persistent searching he'd seen no sign of it.

That was when he stumbled upon an entirely different graveyard.

He almost tripped over the little girl. He let out a startled yelp at the sight of her, lying still on a sunny patch of grass among tumbled gravestones. For a split second he was certain she was dead; something about the play of shade-dappled sunlight made her look broken. He took two panicked steps backward and fell, tripping on tree roots and landing hard on his tailbone. His teeth clacked together and he winced, tasting blood. His heart trip-hammered behind his ribs as he spun out the implications of what he'd found ... a dead girl ... a serial killer's dumping grounds—

Then she whimpered. Art felt his fear shift palpably within him, just as the little girl shifted in her sleep, and become something less focused: curiosity, surprise, confusion. He steadied himself against the tree that had tripped him and waited, the way you wait a few moments before trying again to start a flooded car. The girl was sucking on the two middle fingers of her right hand.

Art climbed to his feet and moved a little closer. *What in the world is this little girl doing alone in the woods?* From the sight of crayons, storybooks, and stuffed animals nearby it seemed this was her secret place. He followed that thought up to the gray screen of trees beyond, and wondered in which direction her home lay. How far could a child this young travel? She couldn't be older than seven or eight.

He moved closer now, and examined the gravestones that had undoubtedly attracted the little girl to this place.

SARAH HUTCHINS
CONDEMNED WITCH
HANGED THIS DAY 1699.

Before he could even question why he was doing it, Art had snapped the lens cap off his camera and captured four shots of the gravestone. Near it lay two others, with similar epitaphs, differing only in name: REBECCA COLE, ELIZABETH WITHER.

The Windale witches. It had never occurred to Art that they might actually have graves. Finding them here somehow diminished them in his mind, and Art couldn't help feeling a twinge of disappointment. We want our historic figures to keep their mystery, to inhabit that hallowed place in our collective consciousness we keep for the vaguely unreal, like movie stars and saints. Finding these graves only reminded him now that they were *real* women, who had suffered real lives of savage brevity.

Why had they murdered? The question of motive—the first question of any self-respecting homicide detective—had gone unasked for the forty years of Art's life in Windale. He couldn't remember, and had a nagging suspicion he'd never really known. Did anyone remember? Was motive such a twentieth-century concern that it had escaped the historic record? Young women in the colonies, particularly religiously fanatic ones, didn't routinely murder their husbands and neighbors. What, then, had pushed these three to those types of crime? Art felt a tremor of excitement as that single, simple question began to branch and bifurcate into a more intricate pattern of inquiry, blooming in his mind's eye like a fractal flower. Suddenly his dissertation seemed ugly by comparison.

Click-click-click-click. Art spent the rest of the 35mm exposures capturing the gravestones from different angles. He had to step over the sleeping little girl and felt guilty doing it. But she seemed to be sleeping peacefully enough, and anyway it was just for a moment . . .

He rewound the roll of film, slipped it into a canister, recapped the camera. Now to the little girl. Should he leave her? Wouldn't she be even more frightened to be woken by a stranger?

He crouched down beside her and touched her arm. Immediately, his decision was made: she was hot, burning with fever. He knew with primal certainty that what he felt was danger, another animal in distress. And now, closer to her, he could see the strange bruising beneath the skin of her face and neck.

She whimpered a little as he slipped his hands beneath her. When he went to move her he saw that she seemed entangled in the weeds on which she lay. Almost as if the ground itself was sending runners to hold her down, like Gulliver among the Lilliputians. The sun suddenly disappeared behind a cloud and the day took on a chill. Art stood and staggered a step beneath her unexpected deadweight. It was going to be a real trial carrying her back through the woods. He set off, his feet crunching through the underbrush.

Behind them, the trees rustled in agitation.

⬠

Wendy sighed deeply as the class finally ended. She gathered her books and notebooks into a pile, wondering if she'd ever be able to make sense out of all those arrows she'd drawn. Notes taken in class had a curious way of becoming as indecipherable as hieroglyphics in about a week's time.

"Don't forget, people!" Professor Gorgas called out over the general hubbub. "Your list of lab assignments and due dates are down here. Pick them up before you go. I won't listen to excuses later. You have plenty of time. And be sure to *show* your work!"

"Shall we?" Wendy asked, indicating the stack of assignment sheets.

"Ladies first," Alex said, with a sweeping gesture.

"This is *real* late in the late twentieth century, you know," she said.

"Then I won't offer to carry your books or toss my coat on mud puddles."

Wendy laughed. "I don't know, that mud puddle thing might come in handy."

She stuffed an assignment sheet in her notebook without looking at it, handed another to Alex, who made the mistake of looking at his paper before filing it. He frowned, "Who knew stargazing could be so much work?"

Wendy stepped out the main doors of Locke Science Center. Professor Gorgas's astronomy class was not shaping up as she'd expected. Wendy had selected astronomy as an elective, imagining nightly field trips to the Crown Observatory. Definitely *not* imagining long formulas that tried to cram as many Greek letters in them as an Athens telephone directory.

"You parked in East Lot, again?" asked a familiar voice behind her. She turned and saw it was Alex.

She nodded. "Why do you ask?"

"It so happens I'm headed that way." Alex winced and quickly put his sunglasses on. Wendy stood beside him, watching Alex grin, then replied. "I may be . . . but you've got to be fast!"

She laughed and quick-stepped down the tree-lined walkway to East Lot, for the moment not caring who might see her acting goofy. When they reached the Gremlin, she was out of breath, more from laughing all the way than from the actual distance they'd covered.

Wendy had the feeling he was about to say something. Something about her? "So, where exactly are you headed anyway?" she asked.

"Run some laps," he said.

"SPEC's the other way across campus," Wendy said. SPEC was the new, sprawling Schwartz Physical Education Center. "You just wanted to spend a little quality time with me, right?" *Oh, my God! I can't believe I just said that. Maybe Alissa is right. Maybe I am cracking under the pressure of non-Windalers.*

Alex just smiled. "That's probably a better reason than the real one," he said. "I'm going over to Marshall Field."

A *better reason?* Hmm... "Marshall Field? That place is a dump. Why go way over there?"

"Solitude," he said. "I like to run several miles a day without a lot of distractions. Helps me focus. Coach doesn't mind if I practice at Marshall on my own time."

"Well, that's a long walk," she said. "Why don't I drive you over?"

"Don't you have a class or something?"

"Free period," she said. "I was going to spend it in the library with my psych text, but I can spare a few minutes. Just give me half a minute to clear some space for you." She opened the passenger door and quickly shoveled the clutter from the front passenger seat and floor onto the clutter already piled in back. Checked quickly for spilled soda, grease, old gum. All clear. "Have a seat," she said.

Alex was quiet on the drive over to Marshall Field, which was really at the ass end of the campus. Out of the corner of her eye, she caught Alex looking at her legs. She smiled briefly, then turned a little red when she realized he'd been checking out the moon and stars tattoo above her right ankle. Her legs were in good shape from all the excer-cycling she did, but they were pale, even for a New Englander. Alex hardly seemed to notice. After a few moments, the silence weighed too heavily upon her. "So what's the real reason for the sunglasses?" she asked. "Anything to do with that scar over your eye?"

"What if I told you I was in the witness protection program story?"

"Sorry, Charlie."

"It's much more interesting. Really."

"I demand the truth, Mr. Dunkirk."

"Ice skate," he said.

"Skating?"

"Ice hockey, actually," he said. "As a Minnesotan, I'm embarrassed to admit it, but I really suck at hockey." She laughed good-naturedly. "I went down, spun out of control, and got an ice skate lodged right about there." He poked his scar.

"Ouch!"

"Blood on the ice, that day," he said. "I can see fine, but ever since, I'm really sensitive to bright light, even fluorescent lighting. Sadly, the glasses are much more than a shallow affectation. This is where I get off." She pulled up the gravel driveway to the fence around Marshall Field. It was an unmaintained track surrounding Danfield's old football field, used mainly for scrimmages now. The bleachers had fallen into a severe state of disrepair—condemned, actually—and the field was now generally deserted.

Wendy got out of the car and walked with him to the gate. "Thanks for the lift," he said.

"No problem...," she said, wondering why she was lingering around. "Guess I better get going."

"Right," he said, "the library."

She nodded. Still standing there. *Say something, stupid!* Wendy thought, then realized she wasn't sure if that thought was directed to Alex or to herself. "You know, you're gonna need a ride back."

"Don't worry about it," he said. "That'll be my cool down."

"I don't mind," she said. "It's quiet here...actually, it's quieter than the library. I'll just sit and read my psych book. I have no fear of condemned bleachers."

"Okay," he said, "Thanks. I appreciate it."

As Alex made his first lap around the track, Wendy settled in and heard a slight creak beneath her. Maybe a healthy fear of condemned bleachers was called for, after all. The rusting steel framework was the last obstacle preventing the long wooden bench seats from becoming several tons of mulch.

Alex rounded the far turn of the track, streaking by the visiting team bleachers. In a few moments, he would come around the near turn, and she didn't want him to catch her staring at him like a lovesick little fool. Maybe offering to stick around had been a little over the top. She could have offered instead to stop by after the library.

Alex passed in front of her, and she waved but was suddenly struck by a sharp pain surging down her fingers to her fingernails. They ached, as if someone were squeezing them with pliers. She examined them and saw the lavender crescent at the base of each fingernail had darkened and spread. Now the entire surface of each nail was tinted a deep shade of purple, reminiscent of winter days so cold her hands ached and her rings slid easily around her fingers like tiny bracelets.

Alex was heading for the far turn. Wendy stared down at her purple fingernails. "He'll think I'm weird," she whispered, "God, why *am* I so weird." She stared down at her purple fingernails.

And what the hell is happening to me?

✸

By the time Art staggered out of the woods carrying the little girl, his back was screaming at him in four different languages. He dropped her without ceremony on the gravel shoulder of Old Winthrop Road (but she didn't seem to notice) and leaned against his parked Volkswagen bug, leaning forward with hands on his knees and waiting for the searing pain to subside.

When he'd recovered, he managed to wrestle the sleeping child into the passenger seat without doing himself any further injury. He'd been drinking a Big Gulp on the drive here, and now he soaked an old T-shirt from the backseat with the remaining ice chips for a cold compress. She recoiled at the touch of the damp cloth, her lip curling back from her teeth in a soundless snarl.

Hospital or police? He didn't know the protocol for lost children, though the high fever was tipping the scales toward hospital. Weren't fevers particularly dangerous in children? (He vaguely recalled a medical acronym, FIB—Fever in Baby.) He started the Volkswagen and peeled out from the roadside with a spray of gravel.

As he navigated the winding road back into town he kept glancing over at the little girl. He hadn't managed to get the seat belt on her, and now he wished he'd taken the extra time to secure her. Thanks to the jostling ride, her fingers had slipped free of her mouth, and now her lips worked feebly, recalling a newborn's sucking reflex. Art leaned over to lift her dangling hand back up to her mouth, noting now that her middle fingers were elongated, calloused, dark beneath the nails. *Christ, what's wrong with this kid?* Art thought, then saw he'd allowed the Volkswagen to wander into the oncoming traffic lane. He swerved back into his lane. The violent motion shifted the little girl against the door, and she groaned.

"It's okay, honey," Art said, hoping she could hear him. Hoping he sounded more convincing than he felt. "I won't do that again."

She responded with a low growl. His blood ran cold. He glanced over—

And saw her eyes. The lids were open now, though the eyes were rolled so far back in their sockets he saw only pupil-less whites. And then she sat bolt upright.

Art swerved, reacting as she flew at him. He tried to pull away, but she came at him across the brief space separating them, shrieking like a feral thing. He tried to throw up his hands in defense against her snapping teeth, and the Volkswagen went out of control. He felt them hurtle into a spin. . . . Felt a sudden stabbing pain as her diseased fingers found his right eye. . . . Saw the sickly crescents of her own eyes, a yellow-white beneath fluttering lids as . . .

Wham! The Volkswagen glanced off something on the roadside, and they were weightless for one suspended instant before the impact—

and the little girl was jerked away from him as if by a cable. With his one remaining eye Art had this time-slowed image of her sailing backward through a curtain of glass.

He lost consciousness almost instantly, and so he didn't hear the broken sounds of the next few minutes: the hiss of the ruined engine's radiator, the tinkle of bits of metal falling free of the wreck, the whimpers of the frightened little girl somewhere out of view. Only the approaching sirens managed to penetrate the deep receding blackness into which he plunged, like a stone dropped down a well, and by the time they arrived even they weren't loud enough to find him where he'd gone.

✶

She dreams she's flying. Not like a bird, tethered to earth, beating its wings to stay aloft on the currents. No, she is different. Weightless. Drawn to a different gravity—the gray and silent moon, looming above like a watchful parent. She swoops above the patchwork landscape, taunting the earth. Below sprawls her hunting grounds. Fields. A farmhouse. A town. Huts of wattle and daub, homes of timber. Each golden with window light. They hide indoors tonight, her prey. She tastes their hearth smoke on the wind.

A giddy rush of vertiginous flight, and the town rushes up to meet her. Gliding past she sees the town hall, church spire, homes huddled like children. She swoops above the rooftops . . .

. . . and descends effortlessly to the grassy commons, where livestock stand in stupid clusters. Gliding silently down among them now she sees the cows roll the whites of their eyes. Sheep scatter, bleating in fear.

Suddenly, she realizes she is not alone on the common. She sees a man. Staggering, a drunk, coming across the common. He stops at the sight of her. His clothing is wrong, ragged and crude. His eyes go wide and she smells his piss as it soaks his pant leg. He retreats a step, turning to run, and she comes shrieking at him—

Pointing at her accusingly, he screams, "Witch!"

Wendy woke with a start, banging her head against the bathtub soap shelf. Lavender flowers clung to her body wherever it emerged from the water.

All the *images* of the recurring nightmares were as familiar to her as her own backyard, but each time she awoke the fear was fresh and the *details* dissipated like smoke rings, eluding her grasp. It would be comforting to chalk up the colonial dreams to her comp lit course's study of *Gables*, but the dreams had come before she'd started reading the book. Of course, the parallel was hardly helping matters. And she certainly wasn't looking forward to *The Scarlet Letter*. Obviously she was identifying with the people of colonial times. Sometimes it seemed they were being persecuted; other times preyed upon. But was she observer or participant? Wendy was feeling more like an outsider than she ever had in high school. Could it all be just anxiety dreams? It didn't matter really. She had decided to go through with the ceremony.

Her knees rose from the bathwater like the coils of some sleek sea serpent. The Loch Knees Monster, she thought. She flipped the drain switch with her toe, stood and used the showerhead to rinse clinging lavender petals from her body. The cleansing power of the flowers and her meditation in the bath were both designed to prepare her for her ritual that night. Sleep hadn't been part of the plan but was clear evidence she was now centered, relaxed.

She walked to her bedroom wrapped in a towel, hoping she hadn't slept too long. That morning she'd decided her out-of-body exercise bike tour would take a turn west to New Orleans, her next colorful stop, rather than continuing down to Key West and back up the Florida peninsula.

Second thoughts began to trouble her, but she pushed them back. It's not as if she were going to be sitting in the middle of the quad. She would be utterly discreet, completely secluded. Nothing to worry about.

She dressed in a cotton blouse and baggy slacks. From the cedar chest at the foot of her bed she removed a white linen robe belted with a soft rope and a smaller wooden chest she would take with her to the forest glade.

She crept quietly down the stairs, praying they wouldn't squeak. It was seven-thirty, and she could hear the television, her parents talking softly. All clear. She carried the chest and robe down to the basement.

Regrettably, she shared the basement with her father. His end looked like the set of a cable-access show: a paneled room with a missing fourth wall. His mounted game trophies—bucks with massive antlers and glass eyes—hung from two walls. Against the back wall was a desk with a leather chair. Two hunting rifles and a twelve-gauge shotgun rested on wall racks. She called his side of the basement The Hunting Horror.

Between her father's room and Wendy's end of the basement was the old wooden frame pyramid Wendy's father had built for her two years ago, after a lot of coaxing. She'd finally convinced him the pyramid would help her geometry grade. Back then she could often be found meditating on a folding chair within the confines of the pyramid, absorbing its ancient mystical energies. Or so she had hoped.

Wendy's side of the basement was separated from The Hunting Horror by a linen curtain ... and a state of mind. When she pulled the curtain along its ceiling track, the basement became her herb cellar.

On tiered wooden shelves mounted above an old desk, her herbs, seeds, flowers, and stones were separated and labeled, each variety in a separate airtight jar. For simplicity and portability, the herbs and flowers were labeled in linen bags in their jars, the stones protected in muslin pouches. She selected bags of sage leaves and chamomile flowers, ground monkshood rootstock and leaves, then a small sachet of anise flowers. Next, she took a flat gray moonstone, rose quartz, and a jagged tektite stone. On a last-minute whim, she grabbed her red jasper.

From the center desk drawer, she took several sheets of parchment and a charcoal stick. Finally, from the bottom shelf, she removed a full mandrake rootstock, her prize possession. The root of *mandragora* resembled a human figure and had been considered magical since primitive times. Anyone found to possess the root during the Middle Ages had been summarily accused of witchcraft.

Wendy placed each of these items, along with a mortar and pestle, in a large duffel bag she kept beside the desk. She gathered up her robe and wooden chest and went back up the steps, pausing to listen for anyone in the kitchen. Satisfied, she snatched her car keys from a hook on the wall and slipped quietly out the back door. She circled around to the front of the mansion, hoping the sprinkler system wouldn't pick that moment to douse her. She hurried down the horseshoe driveway, slipped into the Gremlin, placing her bundle of items on the seat beside her. Remarkably, the car started on the first try.

The sky had darkened already, but the night air was dry and not too cool. She had worried that it might be too cold at night to follow through with her plans. But so far, so good.

As she pulled out of her driveway and cut over to College Avenue, she saw the first of the roving packs of Friday night revelers. Six girls working the Gap's fall fashion line. Standard-issue accessories—the hoop earrings, the chunky black shoes, the boyfriend's baseball cap.

On College Avenue the pedestrian traffic was heaviest: whiskered Phish in tie-dye and dreadlocks, Birkenstocked Liliths with their goateed lampreys. There went a trio of predatory lacrossers, all teeth and testosterone, cruising these waters for sorority frye. And there went whole schools of identical frosh, carried along on the whims of the tide.

She turned onto Gable Road, its blacktop beginning to crumble around the edges. She passed the Windale Motel and Restaurant and glanced at her odometer. The clearing—her clearing—was less than two miles ahead. She had centered herself, she was ready to perform the ritual, the ceremony. She smiled, then bit down on her lower lip at the sudden thrill that filled her, an exquisite anticipation of the unknown.

✷

Jack Carter made a habit of driving over the speed limit. Speed limits were designed for people with normal reflexes. As a well-conditioned athlete, he should be able to operate a motor vehicle at higher speeds than your average, slack-jawed Joe Beer-belly could. And frankly, the quicker he got through depressing little Windale, the better. Oh, yeah, freshman orientation had been a real hoot. The town was so fucking proud of itself and its "heritage of witchcraft." They slapped a stinking historical monument plaque on every other building. Must be the odd numbered ones got the special treatment.

None of that mattered at the moment, of course. He'd finally asked Jensen Hoyt out instead of Cyndy Sellers. He'd better not tell

Jen he'd made the final decision with the flip of a coin. It had been a literal toss-up between the two. They both acted like they'd enjoy some quality time with him, but neither seemed incline to share. Cyndy had the better rack, but Jen was slender, with a nice little ass. And he really liked Jen's generous smile. Jen's smile seemed legit. Whenever Cyndy smiled, he had the uneasy feeling she was smirking . . . at him, maybe?

Jen was an art history major and always carried that damn sketch pad with her. Even tonight, she'd tossed it on the backseat. He'd left the top off of his roll-bar Jeep, because he liked the rush of air as it whipped around the windshield. After the next major pothole, he expected the sketchpad to fly out the back. Whatever. Maybe sometime he'd pose for her, if she wanted.

He looked over at her and could tell she was just as excited by the rush of air whipping back her long, straight black hair. She was wearing a white, sleeveless sweater with a plunging neckline to show off what little merchandise she had up top and a short, peach-colored skirt that was blowing back up her thighs. If she hadn't kept her hand pressed to the material, the *What color are your panties?* question would be answered in short order. Maybe she went *au naturel* down there. Jack smiled at the thought.

Jen noticed Jack's smile and responded with one of her own high-wattage, come-hither looks. "Where are we eating?" she asked.

"Best place in this weak little burg," Jack said. "Moody Inn. Got a bud works there won't give my fake ID a second look."

When they arrived at the Moody Inn and Tavern (established 1660, according to the obligatory plaque), Jack parked the Jeep himself. He never let the valet dipshits touch his wheels. Thanks, but no thanks, Bro. Jen waited for him to open her door—well la-dee-da—so he walked around and held it open for her, getting an eyeful of her legs as she stepped down, one hand on his shoulder for balance. She was about four inches shorter than his six two. Tall for a girl, but a good fit. He hated slow dancing with short girls. Their asses were completely out of reach unless he hunched over like a fucking troll.

Jen finger-combed her long hair back behind her ears, then patted down her skirt before they went through the iron-bound oak doors. Just as long as she didn't feel the need to reapply the minimal amount of makeup she wore, Jack was cool.

Jack ignored the maître d' and signaled for his frat brother, Rich, as if he were hailing a cab. After Rich had a brief, whispered exchange with the maître d', Jack and Jen were seated at one of Rich's tables. The maître d' left two menus on the table with a curt nod. After he left, Rich stepped forward and said, "Man's got a major stick up his ass. Can I get you something to drink?"

"Just roll a keg of Coors up to the table, my man," Jack said. Jen ordered a strawberry daiquiri.

"Okay. Make like you're showing me some ID . . ."

Jack reached into his wallet and whipped out his student ID. Rich nodded, then looked to Jen, who fished a credit card out of her clutch purse. Rich nodded, hurried off, and returned a few minutes later with a draft beer and a daiquiri.

Jack looked to Jen, who nodded. Jack ordered the rib eye, rare; Jen—who frowned slightly at Jack's choice of entrée—asked for the vegetarian platter. After Rich took their menus away, Jen leaned forward and asked Jack about the football team.

"Can't complain," he said. "I made starting QB by the first game of the season. We're two and one. Would be undefeated if our special teams didn't suck ass."

"Do you ever dream about making it to the pros?"

"Let's be honest, okay? I'm not exactly playing in the Big Ten," Jack said, swigging his beer. "Blew out my ACL my junior year in high school—in a scrimmage, for Christ's sake! Can you imagine that? Don't get me wrong, I've got the arm strength, but I'm about as mobile in the pocket as a three-wheeled wagon. Turns out Danfield's football program has been a joke five years running. They offered me a full scholarship knowing I was damaged goods. Who knows? Maybe it will even be worth their while."

"Well, you're certainly off to a good start," she said.

Jack smiled, nodded. That's what he thought. Always look on the bright side.

"What about you? How long you been doodling on sketchpads?"

"Probably since I could pick up a crayon," she said. "Not that that's my choice of artistic medium anymore."

Jen seemed to think she'd made some sort of joke that Jack wasn't getting, but he smiled anyway to humor her. She was thinking that Jack was the kind of guy who got ahead in the world. A natural leader. You had to be a leader to be a quarterback, right? To lead your team to victory? That's the kind of thing businesses looked for. . . . Jen surely didn't want to get stuck with some introspective, navel-gazing loser. Guys who weren't "take charge" material were always on the sidelines, watching the other guys grab the glory. So what if he was a little self-absorbed, she preferred to think of it as natural-born confidence, a healthy ego. She could be the introspective, artistic one in a relationship—Christ, a relationship? This was a first date, no more.

Throughout their meal, Jen made sure to keep the small talk going, trying to keep Jack comfortable, and trying most of all not to ask Jack why he had to eat his meat so bloody?

⊛

The Gremlin sputtered in complaint as Wendy slowed through gravel and litter on the shoulder of Gable Road. When she saw a battered hubcap, she slowed to a stop. She had found the spot.

Under the driver's seat, she found the old T-shirt she used whenever she checked her oil. She tied the shirt to her door handle so any passersby would assume she had abandoned the car and had walked to the nearby gas station for assistance. That should delay any embarrassing investigations, at least for the few hours she would need to perform her ritual.

She gathered her belongings from the passenger seat, locked the car, and took her keys with her. After a minute or two she located the winding trail, probably used by deer as a runway before launching themselves between automobiles. She ducked and dodged often to avoid the tangle of branches above, stepping carefully to avoid the deadwood below. She was surprised to find herself remembering her childhood fear of the dark, a primal tremor. Her brief journey was made more difficult by the burden in her arms, but soon she saw the bright disk of the full moon high overhead, its light shining through the silvery leaves of the ash tree on the far side of her chosen glade. The clearing was roughly fifteen feet long and eight feet across.

This was the clearing she had discovered over a year ago on her field trip with the wire hanger, the place where she had found the ash tree and the fly agaric toadstools, Frankie's "magic mushrooms." If she continued through the woods, on a line away from Gable Road, she'd eventually come out into Bonsall Park, where that long-ago field trip had begun.

Now she stood in the center of the clearing, her grove. She placed her bag on the ground, laid her robe on top of it, then opened the wooden chest and removed her meditation mat. Next she brought out a jar of flour and a pointed peg, which she used to dig a groove in the dirt. When she was finished, she filled the rut with flour poured through a paper funnel to form a white circle on the ground. She put away the jar and peg, then used a compass to mark east, south, west, and north. She placed four white candles, each in an antique brass holder, at each point of the compass. She then set a bowl of rice beside the north candle to represent earth, to the west a silver cup filled with wine to represent water, to the south a brass burner filled with kindling to represent fire, and lastly, to the east, her latest antique store find, a brass incense holder with holes for three sticks, representing air.

She unfolded her meditation mat in the center of the circle, lit the candles and the incense, then laid out her pouches with the mandrake root on top of the wooden chest. Careful not to break the white line, she stepped outside the circle with her folded linen robe and duffel bag. The robe had sleeves, but she wrapped it around her body like a cape, keeping her arms free within it. She tied the robe at her neck but left the waist unbelted.

She looked around nervously then, the light cast by the five fires dancing with the shadows. For a moment, she thought she saw an animal moving back in the brush, a deer or something smaller. But she was confident the fire would keep it away, whatever it was.

She took a deep breath and thought, *Now or never.* Whenever she felt self-doubt, she would issue a challenge, a dare to herself. Her arms moved within the loose confines of the robe, her fingers unbuttoning her blouse from top to bottom. She slid if off her shoulders, then tugged each sleeve down separately. After she folded the blouse and placed it in her duffel bag, she kicked off her shoes, unfastened her slacks and stepped out of them. Finally, she removed her bra and panties and carefully placed them in the bag as well. Then, wearing just the robe, she stepped back into the circle.

She stood on her mat for a moment, her senses prickling: she could taste the blended, acrid tang of candle smoke and incense, and behind these scents the rich, earthy musk of the forest. Beneath the soft robe, her entire body felt electrified; it was a feeling of exhilaration that made her wonder if she might be a closet exhibitionist. Somehow, she had never dared take her magic this far. She listened for the sounds of the night.

But the forest was silent, and she felt a powerful isolation in the dark, the moon shining down on her alone. Even within the circle of fire, the night was chilly. *Why am I hesitating? I'm all alone. I have no reason to be afraid. Right? What's the worst that could happen? Okay, the worst would be an arrest for indecent exposure. No, that wouldn't be the worst. The worst would be if everyone at Danfield knew I'd been arrested for indecent exposure.* And her father's position as college president . . . ? *Oh, God!* She spent several seconds trying to control her breathing, the nervous trembling of her body, trying to ignore the heightened sense of the soft cloth of the robe rubbing her bare flesh. *Stop that! I'm just being silly. I'm all alone. You can't make a fool of yourself by yourself. Okay? Okay, then go ahead . . . , I dare you.*

She reached for the collar string knot, tugged it loose.

Alex Dunkirk felt like a grade A creep, a real bottom feeder. At least he was above classifying his activities as surveillance. That was way too noble a word for what he was doing. Spying? No, still too self-important. Stalking? Bingo! Give the man a Kewpie doll. Stalking and . . . peeping? Now you're hitting a little too close to home.

Sure, he'd been curious about Wendy's hobby, if you could call it that. He'd heard a whispered rumor here and there about witchcraft or white magic in reference to Wendy. Frankie Lenard called it wicca, and she seemed close enough to Wendy to know something of the truth of it. Until then Alex had assumed all the whispers were sheer rumor. It was expected in a town that celebrated a history steeped in witchcraft. And Wendy was a local, who invariably dressed in black, wore handmade silver jewelry and crystal pendants. At first he'd merely thought she was a bit more interesting than your average coed. She defied categorization in any of the standard cliques that served to categorize most of the three thousand students attending Danfield. She was attractive without seeming preoccupied with her appearance. She almost dared you to find the beautiful girl beneath all the witchcraft trappings, an impressionist painting that could only be appreciated from a discreet distance.

So why the compulsion to follow her, on this night of all nights? Did he really expect to witness some black mass, a human sacrifice, a bubbling cauldron? He supposed he could blame Frankie. After all, she'd been the one who planted the seed in their calc class, told him about this ritual Wendy was going to perform. Frankie had not only confirmed the "wicca" rumors he had been hearing about Wendy, but had also actually mentioned what night she would perform this mysterious ceremony. Alex had been hooked. He had to see for himself.

And so now he watched with utter fascination, hidden behind the trunk of an old maple, as she unfastened the neck ties of the robe and let it drop down, around her ankles.

A lambent moment hung in the balance as he stared at her nakedness—golden and pure in the candlelight—with a mixture of pride and chagrin. She truly was unique and wonderful and a lovely girl besides. A splendor of nature before him, communing with the earth. In that moment she was a vision of all he could ever want, secretly revealed to him, a grandeur so simple and extraordinary that it brought a hard lump to his throat. He was completely unworthy of her. The magical moment burst like a child's soap bubble, and he felt as if a slimy coating had descended over him, tainting him in his own eyes, if not yet in hers, his physical arousal only making it worse. The moment passed as she sat down within the circle of her fallen robe. Strangely, it felt like a dismissal. He was an outsider here, uninvited and unwelcome. Just as she had turned her back to him, nature chose to exclude him at this moment. This was not how he wanted to see her and it certainly wasn't how he wanted to see himself.

Slowly, he backed away from her . . . her clearing, her moment alone in the night. Backed away so that he would know if she turned and saw him. Frankie should have kept her damn mouth shut. Despite her own warped agenda about male-female relationships and occasional feminist diatribes, he'd assumed she was playing the role of matchmaker, not saboteur. Enough of that, he told himself as he jogged back to Jesse Oswald's station wagon. It took several tries to turn over the engine, but once he was back on Gable Road, he made it a point not to look back.

✪

Jensen Hoyt's plan had misfired. She had boosted Jack's ego so much that he'd lost all restraint, thinking there was no way he could lose with her. He might as well have had a keg sitting beside him, for all the beer he'd gone through. Talked so much, he'd left most of his bloody, soggy meat sitting on his plate all night for her to stare at and be repulsed by.

Out in the parking lot, he was walking with a swagger that had become more stagger than anything else, his arm looped heavily over her shoulders as he sneaked glances down her sweater. She wasn't wearing a bra, but her white camisole was probably giving him fits. Not that she minded the visual attention, but he smelled like a brewery, and she doubted he'd be able to drive his Jeep in his present condition.

"Maybe we should call a cab," she suggested.

"Fuck we need a cab for?" he said. "Got my Jeep, soon as I can remember where I parked it. Ah! There she blows."

"It's a little chilly, Jack," she said.

"So I noticed," he said with a big smirk and wink and a tug at her sweater.

"I meant it might be more cozy in the back of a cab."

"Don't worry. I expect things to get heated up soon enough."

"Are you sure you're okay to drive?" she asked, finally taking the risk of coming across as judgmental.

"I'm fine," he said, standing up straight. "What? You want to give me a field sobriety test?"

"I guess not," she said and let him help her into the Jeep. She watched closely as he pulled out of the lot. They drove for what seemed like miles. "Look at that shit?" Jack said, suddenly jabbing his finger at the windshield.

At first Jen thought he was literally complaining about a blob of bird shit on his windshield, or maybe a splattered bug, then she saw he was pointing to the old factory ahead. "It's a mill, I think," she said. "An abandoned textile mill."

He turned the Jeep into the back road that paralleled the mill. Through a stand of trees, she could see the old brick building with holes for windows. She shuddered, thinking it looked like a swell home for ghosts. And Jack was having trouble staying on this narrow lane that circled up toward a covered trestle bridge. She saw a sign indicating they were about to drive over Miller Creek. Jen wondered if they'd be driving *through* Miller Creek.

"Jack, I've never driven a Jeep," Jen said, groping for enough tact to get her out of this situation in one piece. "It must be really exciting. Can I drive for a little while, back here where it's safe." She was hoping once she was behind the wheel he'd nod off. For a moment, she thought her ploy had worked. He swung the Jeep roughly to the side of the road.

"Nobody drives the Jeep but me," he said. "Don't think I don't know what you're trying to do."

"I just wanted to see what it felt like," Jen said, feigning innocence. Just how shit-faced was he, anyway? "It's gotta be exciting," she said, squeezing his thigh for emphasis. Maybe if he thought it would get him laid, he'd turn the keys over. Otherwise she was in for a long walk down to the main strip to hitch a ride back to the dorm. The bastard.

"What? You tryin' to make it worth my while, huh?" he said with a lewd wink.

"Maybe," she said, really struggling to prop up her smile. Her face felt glassy.

He reached into his jacket pocket and pulled out a joint, which he lit with a disposable lighter. He pulled on it with a ludicrous intensity. "Want some?" he asked.

She couldn't help it, she rolled her eyes at him. Why not put out a fire with some lighter fluid, you dipshit? Got some PCP in the other pocket? She was starting to reach the conclusion that Jack was a self-destructive asshole. And that was definitely not in her plans.

"You know, my father played for the Lions," Jack said. "The Detroit Lions. Caught a pass in one of those fucking Thanksgiving Day games, if you can believe that shit. Tight end. Wasn't even the starter." Jack shook his head with a bitter laugh. "I think he was cut before the end of the year. Three fucking months of pro ball and you know what? He never forgot it, never lets me forget it."

"What happened?" Jen asked.

"I don't know," Jack said, making short work of the joint. "He doesn't talk about that part too much. I think he just wasn't good enough. Anyway, what difference does it make? He was there and I never will be. That just about sums it the fuck up, doesn't it."

"It's not a big deal, Jack," Jen said, taking his arm. "You can make your mark in other ways."

"Right," he said with another bitter laugh. "Maybe I'll win the Nobel fucking Prize."

"Give me that," Jen said with her best leering smile.

Jack held up the joint. "This? No shit?"

He handed it to her, what little was left of it. She tossed it out of the Jeep.

"Aw, what the fuck you do that for?"

"Because," she said, grabbing his square jaw in her hand, turning his face toward hers and kissing him wetly on the mouth.

"Well, in that case..." He returned her kiss, adding a little tongue.

She took his hand and slid it up under her sweater, letting him get a good feel. She pressed her lips to his ear and whispered, "Why don't you let me drive us back to my dorm?"

But she'd miscalculated. Jack jerked away from her with a curse. "Forget it! Just forget it, okay! You're not driving the fucking Jeep. You can keep your cozy little tits to yourself."

"Fine," Jen said, "I'll walk back to campus."

"Be my guest," Jack said. He took the keys out of the ignition and climbed out of the Jeep.

"Now what are you doing?"

"Making my little contribution to the historical society of Windale," Jack said. He rummaged around in the back of the Jeep and found a can of black spray paint he'd obviously used before. He shook the can vigorously, the little mixing pebble rattling around as he walked to the covered bridge spanning Miller Creek. "My own little commemorative witch plaque." Jen sat in the Jeep, arms crossed, biting down on her lips. At least he wasn't trying to drive anymore. Maybe he'd pass out from his little excursion, though she'd have a devil of a time dragging him back to the Jeep.

She watched impassively as Jack spray painted a lopsided pentagram on the side of the bridge, leaning precariously out over the creek with one hand. A chill wind had suddenly kicked up, swaying the tree branches. Clots of dark clouds scudded across the sky. Dry leaves, autumn's early fallout, skittered across the blacktop.

"You're going to break your neck, Jack!" Such an asshole, she thought.

"You know what," he said, "this little thing lacks the ... artistic statement I'm going for. How about a big old fucking pentagraph they can see from planes passing overhead. Now that's a fucking canvas even Jensen Hoyt could be proud of. Am I right?"

He somehow managed to grab hold of a tree branch and swing himself up on the peaked roof of the covered trestle bridge without dropping his can of spray paint or pitching headfirst into the creek. He made a wobbly ascent to the peak. Would marvels never cease? "Nice view," Jack said. "You should bring up that sketch pad. Really." He laughed.

"Jack just get down, okay?"

"You know what? Screw the pentagram," he said. "Maybe I'll just write 'Jen Hoyt's a Big Cock Tease' instead. Bet they'd see that up in first class!" He laughed, bent over, and began spray painting the sloped roof of the covered bridge.

"You're a royal asshole, Jack Carter," Jen said, not caring anymore. She'd walk back to the dorm and let him break his neck up there. Serve him right.

She was climbing out of the Jeep when Jack exclaimed, "What the fuck?"

She looked up at him and saw he was looking up into the sky.

"Did you see that?" he asked.

There was a sound among the topmost branches, clacking violently together, as if a body had been tossed through them. Leaves rained down like confetti. Jen rubbed herself to get rid of the sudden chill she felt, something unnatural, an icy breath down her spine.

"Jack get down!"

Jack had lost interest in his graffiti. He was turning in a slow awkward circle as he straddled the peak of the covered bridge. He was looking up, not at his footing. "Biggest damn thing I ever...," he said, still searching the sky.

A long shadow rippled across the road, up the side of the bridge, fluttered across Jack as he stood skylined on the bridge. The backwash brought a sour smell to Jen's nostrils, part sewage, part rotting flesh, part maggot-ridden garbage. Her hand clamped over her mouth as she fought back the gag reflex.

"Jesus!" Jack said hoarsely. Jen had the feeling all the alcohol and marijuana had been miraculously flushed from his system. Clean and sober, he looked at her. "Did you see that fucking th—"

It streaked up from behind him, out of the sky, darker than the shadows it had cast, a gleam of long teeth and baleful eyes as its clawed hands snatched him off the roof of the bridge as a hawk snatches a rabbit. Its eyes met Jen's and she thought it let out a predator's shriek, but she couldn't be sure. Jack's scream drowned out any sound the flying creature had made as he writhed in its grasp, completely overwhelmed by the size of the thing. In a moment, it was gone, lost to the night with its prey.

Jen staggered against the Jeep, her legs all but completely numb. She wondered at how she could still hear Jack screaming. A long time passed before she realized the raw, primal sound was coming from her own throat.

✪

Wendy sat naked and alone in the moonlight, cross-legged in the circle of cloth formed by her fallen robe. A wave of goose bumps flowed down her arms and legs.

I hope I remember everything. What happens—will anything happen—if I get it wrong, screw up somehow?

She faced east, the direction of sunrise and new days, hope and opportunity. Before she could commune with each element, she must find her center, her core, her own essence, everything that was Gwendolyn Alice Ward. Long minutes passed, her eyes closed, her breathing deep and regular, before she felt completely at peace, all tension and distracting emotions dissolved like ice in a glass on a hot summer day.

She opened her eyes, her gaze to the east. With a woodstove match, she lit the sandalwood incense sticks in the antique holder. She watched the smoke rise, forming ribbons lighter than air, imagined herself being carried up into the sky in the embrace of those tendrils. "Welcome my mind to your essence, Air," she said. Did the incense smoke drift nearer her? She turned to the south; the burner greedily consumed the kindling. She imagined herself as flame, as fire, hot and passionate, demanding and bright. "Welcome my heart to your essence, Fire," she said. She faced west, the silver cup of wine shining in the candlelight. She pictured herself as liquid, water flowing, caressing all of life, supporting it, but first producing it, the ancient home. "Welcome my life to your essence, Water." She sipped the wine, tasted the sweetness and tang of life as it rushed through her, warmed her, claimed her. She turned to the north, facing the bowl of rice—uncooked, because she planned no Earth magic tonight. Still, she must recognize the element. She gave her thoughts to the embrace of the ground. Earth Mother gave life and received death, just payment. "Welcome my body to your essence, Earth," she said. Finally, she faced east again to close the circle.

Now I begin, she thought, trying to quiet her nerves.

She had purified her stones in a freshwater stream, but she had bought the herbs in a store—even though The Crystal Path was where she worked, it was not as pure as growing or finding your own herbs in the wild—and she needed to consecrate them before she made her magic. She offered each to the essence of the four elements.

She ground the chamomile flowers with the mortar and pestle, mixed them with her jar of springwater in a ceramic cup and drank the infusion. Then she tied the sachet of anise flowers to her crystal pendant. These flowers would awaken in her body the powers she needed for magic. *Ready for the first spell.*

As she had with the chamomile, she ground the sage leaves into a coarse powder. But this time, she poured the powder into the palm of her hand and faced east. This would be an Air spell for the health and beauty of Professor Glazer's unborn baby, a girl. She should probably even give her prof a charm, and would have already if she knew it would be accepted in the spirit it was given. She visualized her holding a healthy baby girl.

"Air, please carry now the good of this sage on your swift and mighty winds." She inhaled a slow, deep breath, then blew forcefully, as if facing a birthday cake with a hundred candles. The powder scattered, a momentary mist that rose and vanished in the branches far above her. "I thank you, Air."

The next spell was for her. She was tired of the verbal abuse so many of her classmates directed at her.

While the code of white magic would not allow her to curse anyone, she felt justified in taking preemptive measures. She wrote quickly with a charcoal stick on a piece of parchment. In her left hand, she held the tektite stone; in her right she held a corner of the parchment paper. She repeated the words scrawled in charcoal three times. "Let others not attack by word or deed, and by the Fire will Gwendolyn be freed." She touched the corner of the parchment to the flame and let the ashes fall into the burner to complete the banishing.

Next, she'd perform a healing spell to rid her of the pain and discoloration in her fingernails, and the psychological pain of the nightmares. She dropped the poisonous monkshood rootstock and leaves into her burner, then took out her rose quartz. In a few moments she retrieved the ashes and held them up in her hand where the light breeze would blow them from her. In her other hand, she clutched the rose quartz to her chest, where she could feel her slow, steady heartbeat. "Oh wind, please take away these things which ail me, I know great wind you will not fail me...." The ashes fluttered from her palm.

Before she began the next spell, she almost changed her mind. Oh, well, it's no big deal. Mother Nature would certainly understand. In a moment she had written another message on parchment paper, but not to burn. She held the red jasper, the stone she'd taken with her from home on a last-minute whim before the flame, felt the heat on her fingertips, saw the fire sparkle through the stone, investing it with the element's power. She read the message aloud, three times as well: "Bring to me a new romance, may Fire consort with Fate and Chance." Then she carefully folded the paper in half three times and, together with the red jasper, placed it in a small box, which she would keep sealed for a full cycle of the moon. She hoped she still had a chance with Alex, that she hadn't scared him off completely by hanging around at Marshall Field.

Now she knew she should quit, but sitting on the ground, naked to the world and alone with the elements of nature, she felt unfettered and empowered, absorbing strength from her inner circle, while the outer circle maintained her power, kept it concentrated like white heat. Yet somewhere in the back of her mind was a seed of doubt, not doubt in her confidence, but doubt that she would ever come back to this clearing this way again. A feeling that what she was experiencing now was like dream strength, dream courage, and that when she awoke she would be amazed at the words she had said and things she had done while asleep.

Just one more spell, she told herself. *Like nothing I've ever tried before.* And the pure confidence was exhilarating.

Wendy had missed the weather forecast, but the night sky was cloudless and starry. This could be the quickest proof of her power. Witches had been known to create storms, some to destroy crops, others to sink ships. But Wendy only wanted a small sign that the elements' power flowed to her this night. To confirm that what she felt was real and not imagined.

She began her meditation anew. She had read how to control the weather in one of her books, how to bring rain and storms. She crossed her arms below her throat, covering her crystal, concentrating on water: the feel of it as it dripped from her hair to her cheeks and shoulders, snaking down her back; the smell as it dampened her clothes, moistened the ground; the sound of it tapping the leaves, plunking in puddles, gathering and rushing in streams; the sight of it, falling in countless drops, a procession of infinity.

First she imagined and her imagination was clear, completely focused on the rain that would come, must come. Then she visualized with a clarity that was breathtaking. In her mind, behind her closed eyes, the clouds gathered from afar and came as she beckoned. The winds marshaled to her command, gusting with a sense of primitive duty. The branches seemed to sway above her, the leaves rustled with an urgency that she alone could hear, the rush of air swept down and caressed her naked body, thrilling her every pore. The hair on the back of her neck bristled and she shuddered with a chill that whipped down her spine with the speed and power of thought.

She brought the clouds, mother of rains and father of thunder, soft and harsh, bright and dark, alive with lightning. So real were the sights and sounds and smell of the rain she had created in her mind that Wendy was surprised to discover that her hair was actually wet, that drops of water were falling from her eyebrows, to her cheeks, to the valley between her breasts, rolling softly over her abdomen.

Her eyes opened wide. Beads of water clung to her eyelashes. She smiled, then laughed. She hugged herself, almost giddy with the thrill of it. "I did it!" she cried. "It really worked." She clutched her pendant and looked up into the sky. A dark shape or shadow— her storm cloud?—streaked across the sky, unnaturally fast, with tendrils that flowed oddly like gesturing arms. And as quickly, it was gone. *Of course, it's magic!* Lightning flashed without an accompanying crack of thunder. Slowly, though water still dripped from the leaves, she realized that the rain had stopped. *Her* rain had stopped. All she had wanted was a sign that what she had felt was real, and now there could be no doubt.

The ground was not completely wet, but all the candles had been extinguished with protesting hisses. The burner flame flickered, sputtered, then regained strength. She noticed that her protective circle of flour had been broken in several places, no longer a complete ring.

You enjoyed the power, said an inner voice. Wendy shuddered, from the cold, she thought. She reached for a woodstove match to relight the candles, but a sudden cramp caused her to stop short. She reached again, and again winced in discomfort. Her fingernails ached, as if she had held them in flame for a long time. *Not again!* She looked down, half expecting to see her nails cracked and blistered. They had lost their recent purplish hue and were now completely black.

You enjoyed the power.

She stood up, lifting the robe with her, but dropping it as another cramp doubled her over. The cramp was accompanied by downward pressure, below the stomach, pushing, pushing. She almost cried out, gasped instead, stumbled forward. Another cramp, worse still. And then the blood came.

The thick, clotted flow streaked her inner thigh. She fell to her knees and wondered why it was a week early, why it was so painful this time. *Why now?*

All her confidence was gone, extinguished as quickly as her candles had been. Her rapport with nature had been whisked away. The trees seemed menacing, concealing unimaginable horrors lurking in the dark. Nature had become a trap for the unwary. She wanted to be home in her bed more than anything.

She was confused, but she knew several things. She knew that she must thank and dismiss the elements. She knew that she would dress quickly, in just the robe if necessary, filling her duffel bag and wooden chest with all her belongings. Then she would stumble to the car and drive home, arriving well before her parents' rented film festival ended, sneaking into bed before them but not falling asleep until well after. She would suspect with dread certainty that that one spell had consumed a week of her life in the blink of an eye. And she would wonder, before she dreamed the dreams again, if she just might be losing her mind.

Jack Carter was flying. In those dizzying first moments he thought he was dying, thought the exhilarating rush of sight and sound was that last roller-coaster moment before you plunge into the vortex. He saw stars, a blur of treetops, heard the screaming of the wind and saw a scatter of distant house lights below him . . .

Then he was dropped into darkness . . .

And woke in darkness. But it was at least a lighter darkness than the oblivion of unconsciousness. He shifted, disoriented, and suddenly felt a lancing pain so fierce it made its own temporary flash of light—like a fountain of sparks behind his eyelids.

He winced, testing his limbs. Trying to pin the pain down, localize it. There—the overextended bones of his shoulders and arms. He couldn't move his right arm at all. Shit, his throwing arm.

As his eyes began to adapt to the dark, he could make out a little more clearly where he was. Inside. At first he thought he might be in a cave of some kind, but some sixth sense told him this place was man-made. Wooden. And yet, confounding him, he saw high above a patch of night sky. Wherever he was had a patchy roof that let the starlight in.

A barn. His nose discovered his location before his eyes. Beneath him was a thick layer of hay clumped with dirt and manure. Beyond those immediate smells were odors of old wood, chaff dust, the sweet stink of dead rodents. And something else. The instant he tasted that smell his balls seized inside him, so powerfully had the odor become associated with terror. It was an animal stink, hot and ripe, like some sour mix of shit and burning hair and unwashed bodies. And yet he recognized it as human. It was a primal recognition of his own kind. But so much worse . . .

He had to get out of here. Out of this reeking darkness.

Now that he knew he was in a barn, his eyes were able to unravel some of the puzzling geometries they saw. The place was old, like no barn he'd ever seen before. The support posts seemed hewn from whole trees and still bore the marks of amputated branches. He came up into a crouch and stood, wincing when his dislocated shoulder shifted outside its socket. He held the dead arm close to his side, and took a shuffling step in the dark. Both his knees felt weak, unreliable. Even after the most brutal sack, you never let them see just how much you hurt. He took another step, regaining hope, strength with each inch of yardage. In the darkness, distances seemed to stretch. Another step.

And then he fell—

He let out a single yell as he dropped. The cry turned into an airless gasp as he landed hard, the wind driven out of him. He blacked out for a split second, a blink of unconsciousness. Then he was awake again, listening to the dusty rain of hay from the loft above. He sat very still, listening, hearing noises . . .

He wasn't alone in the barn. Far above, huge black shapes unfolded themselves from their places among the rafters.

Go! Get the fuck out! Jack scrambled up, surprised he still had any strength in his arms and legs to stand and coordinate into a run. Pure adrenaline rush. He ran full tilt into a wall, then hit it again as he tried a second time to run through it, until he told his panicking mind to try another way out. He slid along the wall, hearing the dry leathery sound of movement high above in the rafters. He wanted to push himself into the grain of the wood, to hide in the knotholes.

Then he found it—the door. It was warped, crude and tall, wide enough for livestock. Through a crack between door and wall he smelled the clean breath of cool night air, bright as ice water.

Behind him the rafters boomed with the weight of the huge things leaping from one beam to the next.

The door would not budge. Jack pressed himself through the crack, ignoring the pain in his sides, the narrow gap constricting his chest. Something gave and the door swung outward. He stumbled out into the cool night. He took several deep agonizing breaths and cut right, an evasive maneuver, crashing headlong through tall grass and weed. He didn't look back.

He fell, came up in a crouch and kept going. Ahead were trees, pale trunks luminescent in the moonlight. If he could make it into the trees maybe the things in the barn rafters wouldn't be able to find him. They were so goddamned big, maybe they'd have trouble maneuvering through the dense woods. These were the thoughts he whispered to himself in cold comfort.

Just before he reached the trees, a foul blast of wind hit him. Jack gagged, stumbling against a tree as he puked up his dinner, the beers he'd drunk a hundred years ago coming up again as acid. He ran, leaves clotting around his ankles. He tripped again and again, snagged by tendrils of vine and thornbushes. Tangling him like barbed wire.

Then, ahead, he saw window light. A house, just beyond the stand of trees. He veered in its direction, crashing through the underbrush and lunging out into the weed-choked backyard. The house was old, its roof buckling as the place sagged on its foundation. An ancient pickup truck stood in the driveway, the hulks of older cars decomposing around it.

The screen door of the house clacked open and shut, an old man emerging onto the ramshackle porch. He met the crazed teen halfway across the yard. The old man held a shotgun. Jack nearly impaled himself on it as he staggered forward gratefully. Given what he'd been through tonight, a shotgun was nothing.

"Something's after me—please—you gotta HELP ME!"

"Get back." The old man's eyes were black and glittering. And there was something wrong with his face.

"Please! They're coming!" Jack said. "We have to get inside—"

The old man grunted. "Ayuh, they'll be along soon," he told Jack; his voice was cracked and gravelly with disuse. "I'm sorry, son."

"What!?" Jack seized the old man by the shirt and tried to shake him. But despite his thin build the old man was solid, like something carved of wood. His face was hard, weathered as old board, and fixed in an expression of infinite sadness. Like the weary acceptance of a cenotaph martyr, guarding the dead.

Jack released his grip on the old man and took a step back. The old man's glittering eyes looked beyond Jack to the banshee wailing coming from the woods. Jack smelled the hot stench he'd smelled before but didn't turn this time to look.

The old man said simply, "They're here for you, son."

The ground thundered behind him. Finally, not really wanting to, he turned slowly and saw the death that had come for him... the three crooked shapes looming over him, as big around as trees, almost nine feet tall, seething with hunger. *Vultures*, he thought with dread fascination until he saw the clawed hands that reached for him. Only then did he understand...

They tore him to pieces, and fought amongst themselves for the scraps.

BOOK TWO

"THE CHOSEN"

October

From the *Essex County Examiner*, October 7

WINDALE. The search continued throughout Saturday for eigh-teen-year-old Jack Carter, who disappeared a week ago under suspi-cious circumstances in the vicinity of a condemned industrial site.

According to a female friend who was with the Danfield College freshman at the time of his disappearance, the youth was allegedly under the influence of both alcohol and marijuana when he attempted to scale the old trestle bridge, which fords Miller Creek. Though the witness maintains Carter was abducted, town sheriff William Nottingham feels a more likely explanation is acci-dental death, and speculates that the intoxicated youth probably fell from the bridge and drowned in the rapids of the creek below.

To date, efforts to locate the boy's body in the creek or the neighboring Hadleyville reservoir into which it flows have proven futile.

The underage witness had a blood alcohol level below the legal limit for the State of Massachusetts, and tested negative for mari-juana and other hallucinogens. Her bizarre testimony is being attributed to the acute psychological distress of Carter's disappear-ance. Danfield officials have not yet decided whether any punitive action will be taken against the young woman for violating that school's policy regarding underage drinking.

CHAPTER
FOUR

The old man in the rocking chair set aside the newspaper and took up his tin cup of chicory tea, swallowing the bitter liquid in a futile attempt to wash away the thirst that had haunted him for more than a hundred years.

Today Matthias had added hard spirits to his morning draught, as he'd done every other morning of this goddamned week, in an equally futile effort to forget the boy he'd seen devoured in his own backyard. But hard spirits had long since ceased to affect his wits. Like water on stone, they only darkened the color of his mood. (And that was how he imagined himself now, as a stone, a fossilized thing.) He remembered once what it was to be drunk, the dizzy thrill of it, but it was a sensation remembered at a great distance, like the memory of happiness. Memories were brittle now, so fragile they fell to dust at the slightest recollection. Only fear remained as bright as the first time he'd tasted it . . .

That first time had been over a century and a half in his past. And it was his father who'd introduced him to it, an even harder man than Matthias. *We're caretakers, our kind*, his father had said as he led him through the forbidden woodland path to the old barn. Even as a boy, Matthias had understood that he was to inherit whatever secret waited in that barn, just as his father had inherited it from the father before. Matthias recalled that he had felt a childish pride on that long walk through the woods, perhaps the last human emotion he would ever feel. Moments later, pride was replaced forever by fear—as his father pushed him alone through the barn door, locking him in darkness where something darker crouched. It was Matthias's initiation.

Matthias coughed on his chicory tea now, choking on the memory. Yes, the fear was still fresh, though he'd made many trips in the years since to the barn, and no longer was surprised by what slept there.

He was due there this morning, and he was dreading it, which was why he lingered over his newspapers. (Once, he'd been an educated man, and he'd kept the habit of following the turnings of the world—though he was no longer a part of it.) He rocked a moment longer on the porch, the chair's old runners creaking torturously beneath him. The morning smelled of dampness and impending light, the hard autumn sky softening toward dawn. *Just a little longer*, he thought, willing daylight to overtake the world. The things in the barn were weakest in the strong light of noonday. But god help the man who met them in the night . . .

Or the boy. The unwanted sight of the week before came again to Matthias—the three of them tearing the boy in two, fighting over the scraps. Matthias had turned away as soon as it began, but no matter how quickly he walked he couldn't escape the wet sounds of them feeding . . . the cooing noises the one made . . . the other's mad cackling. . . .

He wished they would finish the boy quickly, or at least take their meal back to the barn. It wasn't the boy's cries that bothered Matthias so much—those were over quickly enough—but rather the sound of the feeding itself. It conjured an unwelcome memory from the dust motes in Matthias's brain of the time he'd served them up his own wife. But he'd had no other choice. They were most dangerous when they were hungry. Fortunately their hunger came less frequently than a man's, and they were content to lie dormant for whole decades, like the seventeen-year locusts that had returned this summer. When Matthias sensed they needed feeding he would buy a few head of dairy cattle and shoo them through the barn doors. The three would be so sluggish with their long sleep he'd have to slaughter the cattle himself and leave the steaming carcasses in the dark.

For decades they were content with this fresh kill. But then they would begin to emerge from their slumber, reawakening with an appetite for a more savory meat. If Matthias did not satisfy this hunger they would begin to venture forth in the evenings to hunt—a risky time, when Matthias felt most vulnerable to discovery. (He'd learned to take precautions to eliminate all traces of their slaughter, and had taken pains to burn the most recent boy's shredded clothing in a pyre out behind the springhouse.) The last time they'd awoken—a century past—Matthias had done what he could to feed them. And so he had led Mary through the woods to the barn, as his father had led him once, though for a different purpose. His wife had thought it a game when he pushed her through the open door into the dark. He'd stood with his back to the plank door, trapping her within, and he remembered how she'd laughed, never knowing that behind her the crouching shadows were stirring...

Such was the price a man paid for longevity.

Matthias carried his shovel to the barn.

⊛

For a change, Wendy arrived early for comp lit in Pearson Hall. Even though the Gremlin had stalled twice on the way to the East Lot, she still arrived at Lecture Room 100 five minutes before class. It was easy to be on time in the morning when you couldn't sleep at night. She had been awake and showered well before her bedside alarm clock let out its first shrilling buzz. Not that she was feeling particularly chipper that morning. The last couple of weeks had granted her fitful sleep only grudgingly. The dreams were so viscerally disturbing she felt more relaxed in the wicker chair by her window at night, sitting a silent vigil for the sun.

She was walking down the hall, navigating on autopilot, when Frankie Lenard spotted her and plotted an intercept course. From the opposite direction, Alex peeled off from a group of guys with whom he'd been joking, and hurried toward her. Wendy thought, amused, that if she stopped short, the two of them would probably collide with each other.

"Wendy," Frankie said in a forceful whisper, "I can't take it anymore. It's driving me crazy!"

"Wendy," Alex said, arriving a split second later on her left, "I want to ask you something."

She looked blankly at both of them, twice. I *need more coffee*, she thought. A *gallon or so should do it.*

Frankie placed an arm possessively on Wendy's shoulder. "Ladies, first and foremost." Alex nodded, didn't budge. "A little privacy, please," Frankie said. "This is women talk."

"Wouldn't want to hear any of that," Alex said. "Must be some sort of gender rules violation."

"Yes," Frankie said, grinning wickedly, "punishable by castration or frontal lobotomy. I guess, for a guy, it's about the same either way."

"Such a die-hard romantic, Frankie," Alex said. "Wendy, I'll save you a seat, okay?"

She nodded. The moment he stepped through the lecture hall doors, Frankie steered a yielding Wendy back toward the wall. "I'm dying to know how it went out there, alone . . . naked in the woods. You and Mother Earth doing your thing. You did do it, didn't you?" Wendy sighed heavily, said nothing. "You chickened out! Jeez, I knew you'd never go through with it. Well, that explains it. You've just been too embarrassed to tell me you wimped out."

Wendy squeezed by her, but not before she said, "For your information, I didn't wimp out."

Frankie's jaw dropped a couple of notches as she caught up to Wendy. "You really did it! Tell me."

"Not much to tell," Wendy said, feigning disinterest. "Made a circle, lit a few candles, cast a few fire and air spells. Rather uneventful, actually."

"You're joking, right?"

Wendy started up the lecture hall stairs, Frankie about as close as a pilot fish on a shark. "Well, it was a . . . brisk evening."

"Oh, I'll bet it was, Lady Godiva," Frankie said, soft enough for Wendy's ears alone.

Wendy noticed Jensen Hoyt sitting in the back of the crowded class, completely alone with her thoughts. She looked as if she hadn't been sleeping well either. Cyndy Sellers had moved to another little clique. And, of course, Jack Carter was gone, missing and presumed dead. The police thought drugs were involved, but apparently Jen's story included some details that had been too farfetched for the official police record. Between the reported details and the truth of Jack's disappearance was a twilight zone of inner turmoil for Wendy. Somehow she couldn't shake the feeling that she had been involved in Jack's disappearance and probable death. Hadn't she clutched the tektite stone and performed her banishing spell? Even though she had only wanted him to get off her case, was it possible the spell could have been much more powerful than she intended. She *had* made it rain, hadn't she? That couldn't have been her imagination, though the days since then had been a confusing mental game involving internal smoke and mirrors and self-deception. Half the time she convinced herself the rain had just been a coincidence; the other half she was filled with doubt and guilt that not only had she altered the weather pattern over Windale but also had somehow killed Jack in the process.

As Wendy reached the desk across from Alex, Frankie clutched her shoulder and whispered in her ear, "I'm not letting you off this easy, Wendy."

It could have been her own conscience speaking to her.

Alex smiled at Wendy after Frankie continued back a couple of rows to a free desk. She settled into her desk and already the pull of lethargy was strong. She glanced at her watch: 9:02.

"Prof's late," Alex said. "On exam day, no less."

"Is that what you wanted to tell me," Wendy said, smiling to take the sarcasm out of her words. She couldn't figure out what to do with her hands. Her fingernails were still pitch black, a shade she had often painted them in the past. She had debated covering the "natural" black with a more "girlish" shade like hot pink or rouge red, but in the end she thought that might draw more attention to her fingernails than the black they had become. And it wasn't even the black color that bothered her as much as the thickening of the nails, which made trimming them with clippers almost impossible.

"What I wanted to ask you," Alex said, "is if you'd like to be my partner."

"Your partner?" she was confused, still lost in her own thoughts.

"Well," he said, "I couldn't help noticing that moon and stars tattooed on your leg."

Oh, Christ! she thought, embarrassed. *I'm balling my fists to hide these fingernails and he's staring at the stupid tattoo on my leg.* She crossed her legs at the ankle so quickly that he laughed.

"No," he said, "I think it's kind of cool, actually."

"So did I," she said wryly. "About a year ago."

"It's just that it got me thinking, you know, about these astronomy lab assignments coming up."

"Ah, yes, those pesky lab assignments."

"I figured you must have the inside scoop on the moon and stars and stuff," he said. "And I thought these labs would be a little more interesting if we tackled them together."

"You did."

"Sure," he said, a little more comfortably into his pitch now. "We have that sunrise-and-sunset calculation one coming up next week. We could get together this weekend and figure it out..."

"Well, true, I've got the moon and stars covered," she said, "but the sun is a whole different tattoo. You'll never guess where Bruno said he'd have to draw that one."

He grinned. "Well, if you'd rather do it alone..."

"No, no, I think we should team up," Wendy said. "I'm not really a morning person, so you could do the sunrise calculations and I'll take the sunset. Fair?"

"It's a date," he said, offering his hand of course, which Wendy dutifully shook.

A *date*, she thought. *I like the sound of that.*

⬟

For the first time in her teaching career, Karen was late to class. She arrived ten minutes after the class bell, flush and flustered from her breakneck drive to campus. She'd overslept, exhausted after a late night with Paul, worrying about his brother. And of all the days to arrive late to class, it had to be this one—she'd scheduled an essay test on *House of the Seven Gables*.

She dropped the shrink-wrapped bundles of blue exam books on her desk and heard an audible groan go through the lecture hall.

As she began distributing the books, one girl in the front row voiced the collective disbelief of the class: "You're not actually still thinking of giving us this test, are you?"

"I don't want us to fall behind schedule so early in the term."

"But, professor, you were late!" the girl said with an angry pout.

"I know, and I apologize," Karen said. "But don't panic—the exam shouldn't take you more than twenty minutes." She fanned out the sheets of exam questions (they could choose any one of five) and sent them up the rows.

With that accomplished, Karen slumped behind her desk, already exhausted by a day that hadn't even begun. She knew she looked like hell, dark circles beneath her eyes, her hair a lusterless tangle. She crossed her legs on her desk and leaned back in her chair, her notes for her afternoon seminar lecture on Faulkner's *The Sound and the Fury* propped on her belly. The baby, who seemed to be somersaulting all morning, grew uncharacteristically still, and Karen found herself suddenly alert to the silence, the way you do when a background noise suddenly stops. When this happened she had an almost eerie sense that the baby was listening to Karen, in a kind of silent standoff between mother and child.

Her eyes unfocused as she turned her senses inward, attuned for movement. *When did it first happen?* Karen thought. *When did her unborn daughter suddenly cease to be an extension of herself and become a stranger?* And implicit in that thought was a more taboo one Karen hadn't yet allowed herself to speak aloud: *When did she first begin to fear the baby?*

Around Karen, three hundred pens scribbled in a kind of cumulative whisper. She felt her eyelids growing heavy. Just for a moment, she told herself, but of course that wasn't a decision for her to make . . .

He is watching, he will come: the dread inevitability of nightmares. His face is lined with deep creases, as if it has been carved up then sown back together with a coarse black thread. He wears a waistcoat and linen shirt, knee-length breeches, hose, and black shoes. She knows he is watching with his black, narrowed eyes.

The pleasant aroma of bayberry wax on her hands and clothing is a cruel background for the nightmare. But she is a chandler, trading her candles for food, sometimes clothing. And since she has not remarried since her husband's death, the trades are becoming more difficult.

She passes the town hall with its row of pillories and stocks. Goodman Osgood stood haplessly in one pillory, marked for the drunkard again, the letter D dangling from his neck.

Across the commons, opposite the town hall, is the lofty church. It always pains her to see it. She still attends services on Sundays, but the memory of her husband's death in the church's construction is, at times, too much for her to endure. It is all too easy to imagine that the church scorns her, has abandoned her.

She feels the touch of a black breeze that smells like the magistrate. The steady thumping of an unseen samp mortar, pounding corn into a coarse grain, keeps time with her steps as she forces herself to continue on: THUMP . . . THUMP . . . THUMP . . .

Across the commons, beyond the grazing cows, Goody Gable maneuvers her well sweep. Young Timothy Brown rushes by Rebecca, cradling a fire scoop as if it were the queen's jewels. The

Browns always have such terrible luck keeping their chimney fire lit. She wrinkles her nose at the foul smell of wood ash lye and burning grease as she passes the Goreys making soap over a bubbling, smoking kettle.

THUMP ... THUMP ... THUMP ...

The Moody Inn is to her right now. She can never avoid it in the dream. And, as her gaze falls on the iron ring handles, the doors burst open.

He is laughing as he steps out.

He inclines his head, clasping hands behind his back and smiles with a rotting charm. She fights the urge to run. "Good morning, Widow Cole," he says, bowing neatly from the waist.

"Good day, Magistrate Cooke," she answers quickly. She attempts to continue past, but civility is never enough to escape him.

He steps in front of her again. "Please, do call me Jonah," he insists. "Surely you are not too busy to exchange greetings with a gentleman of the most honorable intentions?"

"Please forgive me," she says, attempting unsuccessfully to sidestep him yet again. Honorable was the last word she would attach to his intentions.

He rubs his jaw, displeased with her. "There are rumors, ... new accusations in this very town."

"It has been years since Salem. I had hoped Windale would be spared."

"Some say a witch caused the burning of Goodman Jones's house."

THUMP. The samp mortar sets the dull, heavy rhythm for her heart.

"They say it was witch fire that done it." He pauses for effect. "You sold candles to Goody Jones, did you not, Rebecca?"

"Only candles, nothing more," she says, holding her basket of candles close.

THUMP.

"I have heard it said that these ... fits of yours, these fits of the mind have brought great ill to Goody Hale's hens."

"Goodman Howell says that my fits are merely an ... epilepsy. There is nothing of witchcraft in them."

"Goodman Howell is an excellent physician, but guileless in the matters of witches and witchcraft. I know better, Rebecca. Some say that the very moment the devil slips into your body to cause these fits, foul things happen. That your fits let the Old Boy do his work. Do you not smell the stench of brimstone?"

"Sometimes ... a foul odor, but there is nothing of the devil in my epilepsies."

"The stench of hell, I say. The devil come calling and you his willing servant. Do you not see apparitions of the damned?"

"I know nothing of the devil. They are merely visions—"

"They are the devil at work and yourself a witch," Cooke says. "Nothing says the devil's chosen shall always have the face of the hag. I could believe a woman as pretty as yourself might be a witch." THUMP. "What really caused the Jones's fire, Rebecca, your candles or your fits? Are you ready to confess it?"

THUMP. "I never ..." Her breathing has become shallow, the laces of her bodice constricting her chest. She is suffocating. Almost wishes it for the foul odor that suddenly surrounds her.

"As you know, it is quite within my influence as a magistrate to ... shall we say, dispel certain of these accusations. There are inter-rogatories, certain tests and examinations." She nods nervously, all words lost to her lips. Her mouth has begun to twitch slightly, her eyelids to flutter. "Perhaps you might visit me this evening, to ease these concerns?" A thick eyebrow arches expectantly.

The pounding of the samp mortar comes from within her now, her heartbeat, quicker and deafening. His hand reaches out and touches her face with icy fingers. She pulls away and stumbles. The basket slips from her nerveless fingers and the candles scatter on the ground around her feet. Light flashes around Jonah's face. Black demons articulated from smoke seem to caper above his head, taunting her. Voices whisper urgent nonsense into her ears.

Jonah's hands reach out to her, but instead of helping her, he seems to be pushing her. Pushing her down. She falls with a gasp. Fear clenches her stomach. The seizure pulls her down into a helpless darkness and she is hardly aware as ... people begin to gather *around her, where she lies in the dirt, twitching and trembling. They look to one another, darting glances, looking for something fearful they expect to happen. Rebecca Cole is in a seizure. Is it not then that strange, foul deeds happen?*

Wither pushes through the crowd, toward the prone woman. Jonah Cooke, the troublesome magistrate, stands over the spectacle, a look of disgust on his face, not the slightest inclination to help. She does not doubt his unwanted attentions are somehow at the root of Rebecca's fit.

"Move! All of you!" Wither kneels at Rebecca Cole's side and sneers up at them, finally settling on Jonah Cooke. "You would stand here and do nothing for her?"

Cooke clears his throat. "I had planned to find Doctor Howell."

"A plan long in its execution, then," Wither says disdainfully. Her hands move swiftly over Rebecca's body, seeking.... Finally, her hands settle around the thrashing woman's face, grip it tightly. "She burns brightly, this one," Wither says softly. "Her mind burns, like to burn itself out." Suddenly the convulsions stop.

"The devil's own work!" Cooke says, his voice thick with fear. "You took the spell away. The very same spell you must have placed yourself. You are a witch—"

"Nonsense," Wither says, but smiles at his discomfort.

Rebecca's strained muscles relax and her face becomes peaceful.

Her eyes flutter open and slowly focus. She stares first at the sky, then at the strange woman who cradles her head in her lap.

The samp mortar is suddenly still.

And Rebecca says with a touch of awe, "Widow—"

Karen's eyes snapped open. She saw distant lozenges of institutional light, and realized she was looking directly up at the fluorescent lighting of the lecture hall. A face was nearby, just outside her frame of vision. Speaking: "Professor? Can you hear me?" The voice was distorted, as if traveling through water.

Wendy. Recognition came after a disorienting delay. Wendy was crouched down on the floor beside her, holding Karen's hand.

In a circle at a safe distance away stood more students, looking wary, as if what Karen had might be catching.

Karen tried to rise. Wendy put a firm hand to her shoulder. "Maybe you should lie still for a second. We've called for campus security—they're sending an ambulance."

Karen sat up anyway, her head throbbing. Through her hair she felt an angry knot at the base of her skull. She tasted the coppery tang of blood.

"What happened?" she asked Wendy.

"I think you had a seizure. You made a noise, like a groan, and flipped out of your chair onto the floor." She took a clean tissue from her purse and touched it gently to Karen's lip: it came back bloody. "I think you might've bitten your tongue."

"How long was I unconscious?"

"Maybe thirty seconds," Wendy said, speaking quietly.

"That's all?" Karen said.

"Seemed plenty long enough," Wendy said, and Karen could see the girl was concerned.

Karen looked into her student's eyes and had the strangest feeling of déjà vu. The present as flashbulb afterimage on a dream . . . or a past memory?

Art woke to antiseptic light and an out-of-kilter world. The right side of his face felt sore and lopsided, and when he lifted a hand instinctively to the bandages he saw intravenous lines trailing from the back of his hand.

"My eye . . . ," he said, feeling a dread sinking in his chest.

A voice told him: "Don't worry—you still have them both."

Art turned in the direction of the man who'd spoken. He was standing in Art's temporary blind spot, in the doorway of the private hospital suite.

Sheriff Bill Nottingham was Art's age and twice his size, big across the chest and shoulders, with the hangdog expression of a man with teenaged daughters. They'd gone to Harrison High School together, though of course they'd run in different crowds—Bill captaining the swim team while Art engineered the perfect bong.

"What do you remember?" the sheriff asked, taking Art's return to consciousness as an invitation to enter.

"Being prepped for surgery," Art said.

"Before that."

There was a plastic cup of water on the bedside table, and Art sipped it. "You mean the accident ..." He frowned, tried to bring it back into focus. "Isn't much there. Just fragments ... Hitting my head on the steering ... And the paramedics ..." He shook his head and instantly regretted it. He looked at the sheriff, now standing at the foot of his bed. Tried a smile. "Christ, Bill, I don't think we've spoken since high school."

"This isn't a reunion," the sheriff said flatly. "I've got questions to ask. I'd like to get the answers to them now, but I'll come back if you're not ready."

Art chilled at his tone. "My god, the little girl. . . . Is she dead?"

The sheriff's expression tightened, controlling any show of emotion beyond the professional. "Her neck is broken. She'll never walk again."

Quadriplegic. Art felt the room swoon sickeningly around him. He clutched the cold steel bed rails to steady himself. *Worse than dead . . .*

The sheriff watched Art's reaction through clinically cool eyes. When Art began to speak again, they narrowed to slits.

"I remember she ... had some kind of fit. She attacked me—"

The sheriff held up a hand. "I want to hear this. All of it. But I have to tell you before you say any more that you have the right to remain silent..." Art looked at him in surprise while he delivered his Miranda monologue.

"I'm under *arrest*!? What do you—?"

"Do you understand your rights as I've described them to you?" He glared at Art.

Art's mouth was dry, so he only nodded.

"When did your relationship with Abby MacNeil begin?" He gave the word *relationship* special emphasis.

"But I'd just found her . . . in the woods. . . . She was unconscious—"

"When?"

"A half hour before the accident. I never saw her before that." He was confused, put on the defensive by the cop's accusation tone. "The car wreck was an accident, Bill. I lost control when she attacked me. You see what she did to my eye."

The sheriff's jaw tightened again. He crossed his arms and his jacket opened, revealing his service Glock and handcuffs. When he spoke again, it was in a deadly whisper. "You keep pissing in my face like this, we're gonna have a serious problem. Now, I'll give you one more chance to tell me how long you've been doing this to the little girl."

"Doing?!" Art felt tears of frustration well up in his one good eye. "I told you—I just found her a half hour before the accident."

"Bullshit!" The cop was trembling with restrained fury. "Listen to me, Leeson. All we've got you on now is reckless endangerment of a minor—it isn't much, but it's enough to hold you until we can make the more serious charges stick. And I will make them stick."

"Serious charges. But what am I suspected of?"

"Kidnapping. Attempted rape."

The words hit Art like a slap. "My God, no." They thought he was some kind of—child predator.

"That's right, Art," the sheriff said. "While you're lying there healing, you just think about what you've done to her."

Art was too numb to protest. He couldn't shake the memory of the little girl asleep on the witches' graves. He said weakly, "Does she remember anything?"

"She won't speak. She's in post-traumatic shock. No one can help her now." He'd spent all his rage, and was left now only with a weary sadness. He hesitated at the door to Art's hospital room. "Only you. You can do one thing right by this little girl: accept responsibility for what you've done to her."

⬟

On his way down from the perp's fifth-floor hospital room, Sheriff Bill Nottingham stopped off at the Pediatric Intensive Care Unit to check on the little girl. He found the child's father at the nurses' station, flirting with one of the RNs. Randy MacNeil, twenty-nine, had problems with Massachusetts open-container laws. Nottingham had personally administered field sobriety tests on two occasions to the younger man, the second resulting in a DUI conviction. It was to this prior confrontation that the sheriff attributed MacNeil's discomfort now whenever they were alone together.

The sheriff tipped his head in silent greeting to MacNeil, who looked stricken at the sight of the police officer approaching from the elevators.

"How you holding up?" the sheriff asked, and put a hand on MacNeil's shoulder. The young father startled at the sheriff's touch.

"You know." He gave an equally vague shrug, like a kid called on the carpet by his guidance counselor. He hadn't shaved, and his red whiskers were coming in patchy, like a rash.

"You mind if I look in on her?"

Randy MacNeil looked relieved. "Yeah sure, go 'head. I think she's awake." He waved his hand vaguely in the direction of his daughter's room.

The sheriff nodded and continued past the nurses' station, steeling himself for the sight of the little girl. A father himself, he dreaded these moments when the random ugliness of the world chose a child for its victim. He put a hand on the Plexiglas partition that separated Abby's area from the rest of the ICU pod, and looked in.

She was lying on her back on a special hospital bed designed to prevent bedsores in paralyzed patients. The heart monitor chirped quietly from its mechanical stand behind her. There'd been some concern at first that her spinal chord had been severed so high up that she would lose all autonomic function and require a respirator for the rest of her life to do her breathing for her. Thank god for small miracles, Sheriff Nottingham thought now, as he noticed that she'd been taken off the ventilator since his last visit.

Randy MacNeil had been wrong about his daughter: she wasn't awake. In fact the little girl was deep into REM sleep, her eyes scanning left-to-right rapidly behind her closed lids.

She was dreaming . . .

Sarah Hutchins slides the warming pan under the linen sheets of the single-posted jack bed. The embers in the copper pan warm the bed while the ale her husband drinks from his tankard warms his stomach. The ale, however, will produce a fatal heat from which he will not escape. He will take that secret to his grave.

Her arms ache with each movement of the warming pan. The bruises along her arm and ribs have faded to yellow. Three days have passed since the last beating. Enough time to give her the courage to administer the poison Elizabeth has given her.

Even though she has been waiting for the sound, it still startles her. The wooden tankard falling over, ale spilling out, spreading over the long table with a wet, gurgling rush. A moment later, his head strikes the table.

She places the warming pan carefully on the floor. "Roland," she calls, afraid to turn, afraid that he has found her out and is playing along to reveal her treachery. "Roland?"

Sarah turns slowly, conscious that she was holding her breath. Now her fate is truly cast with Elizabeth and Rebecca. She whispers to herself, "There is no one else now."

Moonlight shines through the triangular-shaped windowpanes of leaded glass, lighting the floor of the keeping room in a pattern like arrowheads on her husband's back. The flames in the fireplace and lantern seem stirred to urgency, impatient for her to finish her task, as if they are emissaries of the devil come to oversee her sin. "The worst is over," she says. "But all is not yet done."

He wears his looped jerkin, deer-hide breeches tied at the knee, and knitted wool stockings. He has been still and silent since his head fell to the table. Not snoring, as the poison has taken him to a deeper place than sleep, where the blackness of his mind matches the blackness of his heart.

She wraps her hands under his arms, grips the cloth of his vest, and pulls him back from the bench. He is a big man, and she struggles with the weight. "Take your time," she whispers, "You have all of the night to make it complete."

Her knees buckle under his weight, and she falls back, banging her head against the hard wood floor. She squirms out from beneath him. "Even in death you have the power to abuse me."

She looks at the window, expecting half the town to be staring back at her. Bent into a crouch, she pulls him across the floor, her fingernails biting into the cloth of his jerkin. "Did you think I would ever give a child to you? Each day you made such beautiful furniture, yet each night your hands had only ugliness for me. I would never give a child to your ugliness. Elizabeth saw to that outcome with her bitter potions, which I gladly drank." It is only passing strange to her that his death has freed her tongue to speak the endless grievances against him. All the things she could never say to him while he yet lived.

She struggles with his weight, down the narrow staircase to the basement. If she is not careful, she could fall and break a limb or split her head open. Carelessness now will produce the same result as if she had shared the deadly draught with her husband. She grunts with effort, realizing with each step that she leaves traces of dust and wood splinters on his clothing, signs that he has been dragged. She will have to clean his jerkin and breeches. "How many times has Elizabeth performed such dark chores?" she asks herself, sweat beading her brow.

Her heart pounds. Sunrise is still hours away, yet the thought of daylight's revelations fill her with sick fear. She has begun to appreciate the night, the concealing darkness. Here in the basement, the darkness is almost complete. She imagines Roland looking up at her, waiting for a careless moment to clutch her throat, to squeeze the life out of her as easily as water from a rag. One last beating.

She runs upstairs for a candlestick. The fireplace hisses and spits its disapproval. Taking the long candlestick from the windowsill, she hurries to the betty lamp, pulls its wick out with the chain pick, and lights her candle from the bear fat flame. A chill races up her spine and a lump of dread makes its home in the pit of her stomach. What has she seen out of the corner of her eye? What movement?

She looks over her shoulder, her mind filling with excuses never to be uttered. If she is caught now, she will not fight the accusations. The night knows all about her now. It knows the exact moment she stopped being the girl with the quick laughter and the moment when months of fear blossomed into a willingness to commit murder. Yes, the night knows Sarah Hutchins well.

So be it. She turns around swiftly, prepared to meet her accuser. Shadows move across the banister-back chair. Someone rising...? It is just her shadow, cast by the now higher flame of the betty lamp. But she has faced down her own accusations. Or so she thinks.

Roland is waiting for her in the basement, lying beside the stone well, flat on his back, head hanging awkwardly to one side, one hand bent over his waist. Such large hands, she thinks. She had seen strength in them once. Now she knows them only as instruments of his brutality. She sets the portable candlestick beside her as she brushes the dust and wood splinters from his clothes. "When you go down the well, know my fate will not follow you," she whispers.

In a few moments she is ready. She lowers the bucket first, hears water splash against the wood. Daylight will reveal that he fell trying to retrieve the bucket. She lifts him, first to a sitting position, then turning him over, pushing up, her arms under his legs. His arms and shoulders now hang over the pit.

She will throw him in with enough force to crush his skull or break his neck against the side of the well. Otherwise, she must hope that it will appear he simply drowned in an unconscious stupor.

She sucks in her breath, feels her arms and legs trembling with exhaustion and a residue of fear. With a grunt of effort, she heaves him over the edge, her fingernails clawing at his breeches. His body, free from her grasp, spins wildly, his foot nearly kicking her lip, narrowly missing her nose, as he falls. His head strikes the stone with a heavy thud, then she hears him crush the bucket as he lands on it. Water splashes up from the mouth of the well.

The candle flame hisses, then dies. The darkness swallows her whole. She fights the urge to run upstairs, and the equally strong urge to empty her stomach. Instead, she crawls on hands and knees, searching for the candlestick. She feels about blindly, her fingers sweeping across the cold floor, splinters of wood.

His foot! Standing before her . . .

She screams . . . but it is only one of his shoes. She flings it into the well after him, then picks up the candleholder and hurries upstairs.

"Now am I truly free, Elizabeth, free to join you and Rebecca." Her voice is a tremulous whisper of self-reassurance. She knows she can not turn back. Trembling, she curls up in the short jack bed, waiting for the sun to rise, clutching the linen sheets to her chest. "I am finally free . . ."

Then she is plunged into darkness again.

⊛

While Abby dreamed in the PICU, Karen sat shivering four floors below in a paper hospital gown, in a forgotten corner of the ER where she'd spent most of the afternoon suffering the various scans and pricks and indignities of modern medical science. As if the humiliation of convulsing before an entire freshman class wasn't enough, Karen's day had included puking on the bumpy ambulance ride over, receiving a pelvic exam from a former student doing his obstetrics rotation in the ER, suffering the claustrophobic treat of MRI and CT scans, the painful impalement of an amniocentesis, and, now, wincing her way through the sixth blood test of the afternoon's latest trial: a glucose tolerance test.

"Ouch," she said without much conviction as the kid drawing blood—a third-year med student with shaky hands—missed her vein for the second time. "Sorry," he explained sheepishly, "this is my first day." He hit the vein on the third try, capped the vial, and scurried away.

Thirty minutes later, Maria Labajo, Karen's OB/GYN, appeared with the results of the final blood test in hand. "Well, your pancreas is functioning perfectly. I just want to perform a quick ultrasound as a final precaution, and then I'll send you home to get something to eat." She rolled the portable ultrasound and monitor cart through the curtains that had been drawn around Karen's bed for privacy. Maria was a tiny woman, Filipino by birth, and yet she manhandled the cart with force.

Five minutes later, Maria began expertly maneuvering the transducer across Karen's jelly-slick abdomen. As always, the image that appeared on the monitor was murky and throbbing, an animate Rorschach test welcoming interpretation. It was possible to lose yourself in the rhythm of that heart-thrumming land-scape, to peer so intently at the echoing contours of your own insides that you became mesmerized. So enrapt was Karen in deciphering what she saw that she began to hear the accompanying soundtrack, hallucinating the agitated thrush-thrumping percussion of the baby's amplified heart. And now she could see the child, her daughter, a grotesque thing suspended in the pixilated gloom...a goblin crouched within her, mouth open in a ravenous yawn—

With a cry, she knocked the transducer free of Maria's hand. The ultrasound monitor went dark. "Karen! It's okay—"

"There's something wrong! Something's wrong with the baby!"

Maria put her hands on Karen's shoulders and held her until the panic had abated. Paul returned then from the cafeteria to find them like this, Karen crying, Maria hushing Karen with calming words in Tagalog, the language of her childhood.

"What's wrong?" he said, his eyes going stony, preparing himself for the worst.

"She had a fright," Maria said. "Everything's okay now."

Karen clung to Maria's hand as the obstetrician began to pull away. "What's wrong with the baby? Tell me."

"Nothing. The baby's heartbeat is strong. She's large for twenty-four weeks. She's going to be big, like her father." Maria looked up at Paul, tall and awkward within the little tent of curtains, like a befuddled magician at a child's party.

"I don't believe you," Karen said. Paul kissed her and stroked the hair away from her forehead. She bristled, brushing him away. She didn't want to be touched. Didn't want to be consoled like some crazy woman.

Maria said, "You'll believe me when the results of the amniocentesis come back in a few days."

"What caused her seizure this morning, doctor?" Paul asked.

"That's going to remain one of the great unsolved mysteries," Maria said. "At this point, my money is on old-fashioned exhaustion."

"She hasn't been sleeping," Paul said.

"Bad dreams," Karen said. It was becoming her mantra.

"Pregnancy demands a lot of a woman's body," Maria explained. "You've got a lot of hormones surging through you right now. Mix with exhaustion, and you've got a pretty potent cocktail." She looked at them both, asked them as a couple: "Have you been under a great deal of stress?"

Karen exchanged a look with Paul. "Paul's brother was in a serious car accident earlier in the week. They think he's lost part of the vision in his right eye . . ."

Maria's face darkened. "He is in this hospital?" Paul nodded. Karen tried to intercept the rumor before it found another convert. "What they're saying about Art and that little girl . . . It isn't true."

Paul said, "The police interviewed me all afternoon yesterday, I tried to tell them . . ."

Maria nodded and said unconvincingly, "Of course." Karen could already see her reevaluating them because of their association with Art. She said, "The little girl's condition is very serious."

"We're all praying for her," Paul said, and Karen frowned. It was such an unlikely thing for him to say that she felt a hot rush of anger at the world, at this community, for forcing him to say it.

Maria nodded, and gestured toward Karen. "She's had a long day. I'm afraid we've worn her out in our efforts to prove she's suffering exhaustion. You should take her home." Karen sensed a coolness in Maria's voice, and resigned herself to it.

She expected to hear a lot of it in the coming days.

Even though it had already been an impossibly long day, Karen and Paul decided to extend it a bit longer and visit Art. Paul had already looked in on his older brother earlier in the day, updating him on Karen's seizure and learning of the sheriff's visit. Now, after convincing Art that Karen was all right following the seizure scare, they returned again to the topic of Art's arrest on suspicion of attempted rape.

"They think I kidnapped that little girl," Art said, his voice trembling. "They think that I—"

He began to break down, and Karen went to him, kissing his temple and calming him as she herself had been calmed only a little while earlier.

"I've found a lawyer," Paul said. "Neil Katz. I filled him in on the situation, and he's agreed to represent you."

"Why do I need a lawyer?" Art said miserably.

"Because the little girl was found in your car. Because you've admitted to being alone with her in a secluded place in the woods. Because you've got scratches on your face made by a terrified child fighting for her life. Because she's paralyzed."

"But I didn't do anything!"

"You're not listening to me. What do the police see when they look at you?—A forty-year-old recluse with a ponytail, no wife and kids, not much of a job, that dope arrest still on your records from college. It isn't that big a leap for them to start seeing you as a sexual predator." At that, Art recoiled with a horrified look. Paul didn't relent. "I'm sorry. But until that little girl starts talking, that's how they're going to keep seeing you. We can't be naive and assume they'll give you the benefit of the doubt just because you're a hometown boy. We've got to start protecting you, and that means no more talking to police without Neil Katz present."

"But if I stop talking, it's like admitting I'm guilty." He turned from Paul's unrelenting gaze and searched out Karen. She gave his hand a squeeze.

"Paul's right, sweetheart. They'll help you make your own noose if you let them."

"I've got to get out of here," Art said, giving his head a violent shake. "Shit!" He put a hand to his bandages as he felt a searing white bolt of pain lance through his injured eye.

"Do you want me to get a nurse?" Karen said. "Do you need more pain medication?"

"I'm okay. It does this sometimes," Art said.

"Antibiotics," Art said, already beginning to absorb some of the jargon. "Pharmaceutical equivalent of an A-bomb. So far this infection is resistant to everything they throw at it."

"A staff infection?"

Art shook his bandaged head. "They don't know what it is. But it came from under the little girl's fingernails." He cast a sidelong glance toward the nurses' station, and dropped his voice to a whisper. "I've been bribing an orderly to sneak me information on her status. He said the little girl's infected with it, too. It's all through her." He tried a weak smile to cover how frightened he was. "Who knows where that kid's hands have been."

Karen felt Paul tugging on her sleeve, trying to draw her away from Art's bedside.

"Hon, maybe you shouldn't sit so close . . . the baby . . ."

Art said, "Don't worry. Apparently, you can only contract it through direct blood contact."

He fell silent. Paul paced to the window. "What happened out there, Art? Do you have any idea?"

"She was running away," Art said quietly. "The graveyard she found was her hiding place, she felt safe there. That might sound creepy to you or me, but she's just a kid, she hasn't learned to be afraid of death yet. Hell, she probably saw the word *witch* on those headstones and the first thing that came to mind was Tabitha, not Margaret Hamilton—"

"What do you mean, 'witch'?" Karen said, feeling discomfort at the mention of the word.

Art looked surprised. "Didn't Paul tell you?" He turned to the bedside table, where a photo lab envelope rested among magazines. He shuffled through the five-by-seven glossies, singling out several for Karen. "The police let me keep them after they saw there were no kiddie porn shots in the roll. Of course, they kept the negatives."

As Karen flipped through the close-ups of the gravestones, Art explained, "I always assumed they were buried in an unmarked grave somewhere. But here they are—the infamous Windale Three. Elizabeth Wither, Sarah Hutchins, and—"

Rebecca Cole, Karen's thought blotted out Art's words, the name resonating in her mind as she held the gravestone bearing that name in trembling fingers. Her eyes grew distant, and for a moment she seemed to drop sideways out of the flow of time. Her expression—blank, unseeing—was enough to alarm Paul, but by the time he reached for her she was back, the world's unspooling ribbon of film finding its sprocket again with a sharp snap into sync. She shivered, fighting a wave of nausea.

"I'm sorry, I—"

"Are you okay?" Paul said. "Are you going to be sick?"

"No, no, I'm fine now," Karen said, lying for his sake. "Just light-headed for a moment."

Art was watching her curiously. Something in her reaction puzzled him, and he wondered if it had anything to do with her colonial dreams. "Karen?"

"Saying their names just makes them seem so real." Karen said. The room seemed to have gotten darker, and airless.

Later that night, as the night float nursing staff began hanging paper Halloween decorations all along the pediatric wards, and the ER's on-call residents dealt with a violent addict convinced he'd seen monsters in the moonlit skies above Windale, Art's doctors met over their sleeping patient's bed to discuss his prognosis.

The infection in his right eye was proving stubbornly resilient to the broad-spectrum antibiotics they'd ordered; the fear among the surgeons was that the microbe would begin to spread from the eye to surrounding structures and even the brain.

It was the opinion of the chief surgeon, Dr. Phelan, that if the spread of the infection could not be checked within the next forty-eight hours, the patient should again undergo surgery to have the damaged eye and infected tissues entirely excised. The gathering of serious men disbanded, satisfied that an appropriate course of action had been determined. The patient would lose his right eye but would keep his life. And for that, frankly, he should be grateful, as it was the unspoken opinion of Dr. Phelan and his colleagues that this particular patient deserved no better.

In this they were unanimous; but then, all four doctors were the fathers of young daughters.

CHAPTER
FIVE

Paul woke suddenly in the predawn darkness. He'd always been an early riser, and by five was usually wading in from the deep, fathomless waters of dream to the shallows that broke on the shores of morning. Now he came awake with a start and lay still on his back, wondering what had woken him.

He listened and heard nothing out of the ordinary, only the smotheringly heavy quiet of the early morning in a rural town. He heard Karen breathing from the cocoon of blankets beside him, heard the slow mechanical turn of gears as the backlit numerals on the old bedside clock tumbled one moment forward in time.

His heart was skipping along rapidly, an adrenalized flutter, his senses becoming oversensitized to the expectant silence. He listened, motionless, and was finally rewarded . . .

There. A sound, tiny and warbling, from within the bedroom itself. He froze, and heard it again, coming from Karen. From *within* Karen.

From the baby.

He knew now that he must be dreaming. He rolled onto his side facing Karen, studying the outline of her face in the dark. He put his face close to hers and smelled each sour exhalation. He shimmied lower in the bed, in the blood-warm dark beneath the down comforter, to the place where Karen's belly swelled beneath her nightshirt. As gently as he could he brought his ear to her stomach. He heard the liquid sounds of her insides, the muffled thump of her heartbeat (or maybe it was his own heartbeat, smothered in his ear), and beneath them the distant creaking sounds that lived in the mattress.

And then he heard it again, that warbling coo. It was a faraway sound, a growl, distinct from the peristalsis of her digestion, as much a feeling sensed on the taught surface of the skin—a tremor—as it was a sound.

Certain that he was dreaming, he spoke a single clumsy greeting. "Hello?"

Instantly the warbling stopped. As if the child within Karen had heard him and stopped its feral cooing. And was now listening to *him* ...

Overhead, the pitched ceiling of the third-floor bedroom creaked as something heavy shifted. Paul looked up, tracking the scrabble of claws across the ceiling. The scrabbling ceased and he heard a thud, the house shuddering slightly, as it did in winter when the old boiler kicked in.

He looked at the clock: 5:35. He swung his legs free of the comforter and stood in his socks, stretching. Outside the blowing curtains of the bedroom windows, he saw the first light, a blush of morning. He went downstairs to make coffee, fetch the paper, and have a breakfast cigarette. In another hour he'd swing by the YMCA to pick up the hitchhiker he'd hired as cheap temporary labor. (He paid $7.50 an hour, all under the table, for cleaning up work sites, hauling lumber scraps to the Dumpster, light demolition, etc.).

Downstairs, Paul stood barefoot on the cold kitchen linoleum listening to the coffeemaker burbling away cheerfully, and found his thoughts drifting to the tension that had thickened the air of late between him and Karen. Was this simply first-time mother-hood jitters, or something more serious, tremors from a deeper fault line in their relationship? When he was feeling surly and irri-table, he allowed the thought to surface that she was ashamed of him, ashamed of the fact that he'd never gone to college and made his living as a contractor. When he was in this mood he took her suggestions—a book he should read, a movie he might like—as con-descending recommendations for self-improvement, as if she wanted to play Henry Higgins to his Eliza Doolittle. Once, she'd recommended A *Farewell to Arms* to him, thinking he would respond to the stark sentences and romantic fatalism; but when he'd preferred *Light in August* she seemed surprised, as if she'd thought Faulkner beyond him.

He poured himself a mug of coffee and slurped a scalding mouthful. He opened the front door and walked out onto the front porch. The smooth boards underfoot were damp with dew. The kid who delivered Karen's *Windale Gazette* had horrendous aim, and Paul was just fishing the newspaper out of the forsythia bushes when he suddenly froze midstretch . . .

Froze, as his eye traveled out to Lore Avenue . . .

And saw his pickup truck overturned by the curb, resting on its crushed cab.

As was every other car along the Lore, overturned in their driveways.

It was October 20.

Wither is watching the magistrate, Jonah Cooke, as he smokes a clay pipe, but the man is unaware of her presence. It is as if she is a ghost in his house. In a very real sense, she is an apparition.

Thunder rumbles as dark clouds roll across the face of the moon, casting the keeping room in deeper darkness. The candle-light from a single wall sconce is unable to push back the redou-

bled gloom. Heavy rain begins to sheet outside. In a moment he hears the light rapping on the door. Wither has been expecting the caller, while Cooke seems mildly surprised.

He places his pipe carefully on a metal charger then rises and opens the door. A figure in a red, hooded riding cloak stands before him. "So, you have come, after all?"

Hands reach up to reveal the long red hair and fair face of Rebecca Cole. Rain pelts her mercilessly as she stands patiently before them. "If you will stand for me at trial, I am agreeable to your proposition."

"The only sensible course," he says. "Come in out of the rain."

He motions her inside, and she keeps her back to him as she walks to the middle of his keeping room. "My fits have left me but my accusers remain. They say I am cured for pleasing the devil and continue to practice witchcraft. Only you, magistrate, can put an end to these hateful rumors. And save me from the hangman's noose." She is shivering. "I fear I have caught a chill." She wraps her arms tightly around her cloak.

He lights a stick of pitch pine at the wall sconce then takes it to the fireplace where he gets a steady fire going. Lightning flashes, but with her back turned to him, he can not see the wild look in Rebecca's eyes. There is something of the feral animal in that look. "Allow me to take your cloak. Warm yourself by the fire."

She clutches the cloak tightly. "Then you will ... search me, for the devil's mark...the witch's teat. So you will know I am not his willing servant."

"So I shall." The lecherous gleam waxes in his face. "A most thorough examination, Rebecca. Anything less, and the devil's mark might go unnoticed in my haste. If you are free of his mark, I will use my influence with the other magistrates ..."

"I take you at your word, Magistrate Cooke." Rebecca opens her cloak and is satisfied with his startled look. She wears nothing but a nighttime shift underneath the red cloak. "I would not falter in haste. Please forgive my inappropriate dress."

"Forgiven," he says, his gaze lingering overly long on the slender lines of her body. "Ah...but let me hang your cloak to dry." As he walks to a peg board on the wall beside the door, Rebecca smiles and runs her hands down the sides of her body, taking a deep breath. She whispers, "A fish firmly set on my hook."

He turns back to her, his harsh face set in shadows like lumps in his countenance. A thoroughly unappealing face, she thinks, even more so with that hideous smile. "The devil may place the mark anywhere on the body of his servant, a nipple of inhuman, unfeeling flesh so that he or his familiar may come to suck the blood of the witch, and a measure of her soul along with it. It is a cold bit of flesh, unfeeling to the prick of the needle. Or to the stroke of a hand …" His hands lift hers and he makes a show of searching between her fingers, her palms, wrists, the undersides of her arms. His fingers are dry and scaly as they sweep over her shoulders and back down to her elbows. He lifts her long red hair and looks behind her ears, down the nape of her neck. "Obviously, if you wear his mark, the Old Boy has hidden it well."

"Search where you will to convince yourself I am free of it." She is still playing her part, the frightened accused, allowing him to think he is in control of the situation. They both know his search is a pretense. Nor is she foolish enough to believe that Jonah Cooke will be true to his word. He will never stand by her if she is accused and goes to trial. His hollow promise is but part of his lecherous game.

"Your feet are splattered with mud," he comments. She has come in bare feet, delighting in the sensuous feel of the earth beneath her feet on this night. "Yet I doubt the Old Boy would stoop himself to suckle at your feet." Jonah likely does not wish to get his hands dirty in the details of a thorough search. He kneels behind her, content to check her calves and the back of her knees. "I have checked all that I can see. You must remove your shift."

"Of course," she says, smiling wickedly. She pulls the loops free under her neck, and the shift becomes loose enough for her to pull over her head. She tosses it aside and stands naked before him, no longer the demure girl.

He gasps at her brazenness, but he is not about to object to her unseemly display. In a moment he begins fondling her buttocks, the pretense of conducting a search for the devil's mark immediately forgotten. She smirks in satisfaction. He clears his throat. "I see...nothing here that offends." His hands stroke up and down the back of her thighs, his fingers trembling. Good.

He comes around before her. His lecherous stare is captivated by her full breasts, his hands tentatively reaching out toward her. Briefly his eyes meet hers, and they are wide with excitement. He gulps and croaks out something she can not understand, yet she knows what he wants. "Be assured," she says, taking his hand and pressing it to her breast. She guides his hand across her nipples, feels them rise with her excitement, an excitement that has more to do with her power over him.

"I see a mark," he says softly, "here and here."

"Merely freckles," she says. "Surely not cold."

"No, never cold." His hands wander again to her breasts, her nipples, sliding down her abdomen and even venturing lower. "I . . . I must have . . . you understand . . . ?"

She nods, her hungry smile wide as she unfastens the loops on his jerkin. "You will find no part of me cold to your touch," she promises. She has the clothes off his scrawny, knobby-kneed body even as his pawing continues unabated. "Do what you must," she says, "take me to your bed."

His mouth falls to her right breast, his tongue to her nipple. Odd that he, who searched for the witch's teat on her, now suckles of her himself. "Ha!" Rebecca shouts as a peal of thunder shakes the house. Lightning flashes brightly enough to fill the room... and reveal Elizabeth Wither—or rather, her apparition—standing in the corner of the keeping room. She nods to Rebecca, whose eyes are locked with her spectral gaze in that split instant.

"The taste of you," Jonah Cooke says, ". . . seems strange to me."

"Ointments and potions on my body," she says, "to excite you all the more." Rebecca steers him toward the bed, keeping his eyes away from the corner that hides Wither's specter. Simple, since he can not avert his eyes from her nakedness even for a moment. The fire inside him grows higher and she has stoked it well.

She pushes him back on the bed and climbs astride him.

"You are a wanton!" he gasps, his breath ragged. "Surely, a succubus!"

But he is beyond the point of rational thought. As she mounts him, she chuckles, "You have no idea!"

At the critical moment he grips her waist and attempts to hold her firm, but she rides through his pitiful climax, throws back her head and laughs wildly. He can not control her, ever again. His moan becomes a strangled cry. Thunder shakes the house. His hands fall away from her sides, limp as the rest of him has surely become. The sinews in his neck relax, but his wide, frightened eyes continue to stare at the ceiling, already collecting dust.

"So much better than you deserved, wouldn't you say, you disgusting old goat?" She says, leaving his bed with a satisfied chuckle.

"Attend the fire," Wither's specter whispers.

Rebecca nods. She has already killed him and now she will destroy his corpse. She lights a stick of pitch pine in the fireplace and walks toward the bed . . .

Wendy sat up in bed, covered with the damp, clingy sweat peculiar to bad dreams. The light of the waning moon shone down on her bed, where the sheets were rumpled and . . .

She snapped on a bedside lamp and looked down at her bed. The sheets were torn, long gashes as if an animal had smelled raw meat beneath them. She held them up to examine the parallel, ragged tears and discovered the extent of the damage beneath. Furrows had been gouged through the fabric of the mattress, the stuffing exposed in long tufts.

For a moment she could only stare. When she had fallen asleep, everything had been normal . . . Except that she had taken an infusion, made from the rootstock of valerian. The cup was still on her night table, sediment at the bottom. She wore her moonstone and amethyst in a linen pouch pendant.

She had decided to use dream magic to combat the strange dreams, to free herself from the endless repetition of seventeenth-century Main Street. But she had been successful only in moving to another dream. A predatory dream, a murder. Who were these women she kept dreaming about? Persecuted women or accused witches? The Windale witches? Wendy had never given much credence to Windale's witch persecution era. She chalked up that time in history to hysteria. Besides, white magic wasn't what those times or witch trials had been about. People used to believe the world was flat, but that was no reason for her to take up the cause. White magic was a natural cooperation with and acknowledgment of Mother Earth. No pacts with the devil, no summoning or demons or dolls stuck with pins. Like it or not, she must be identifying with them, imagining their lives as persecuted outcasts. But, in her mind at least, they weren't just victims anymore.

She sat by her window as the sun climbed over the trees, but it did not warm her. Her sheets were curled into a ball in her trash can. She had flipped the mattress over to hide the gashes, laid fresh linens over it, but had not slept upon them. She had outlasted the night, her secrets safely hidden. In that at least, she and those distant women were alike.

With the arrival of morning, she felt the need for normal routines and rituals. She climbed slowly out of the folding chair by the window, her muscles creaking, joints cracking with an achy stiffness. She might have slept on concrete by the way her body protested.

With a weary sigh, she straddled her exercise bike, checked the odometer: 1299.1. According to her wall atlas, she was about fifteen miles east of Tallahassee, traveling west on Interstate 10. The Florida panhandle seemed ungodly long, with her next big goal, New Orleans, still hundreds of miles away.

Closing her eyes, she thought only of Tallahassee. She doubted she'd pull off fifteen miles in her present condition, but reminded herself every long journey starts with the single turn of the wheel. She pedaled swiftly, the sound a rachety whisper, a cleansing through exercise. Sweat out the impurities, work out the creak in the joints. Her fingers curled around the padded handlebar grips as she gritted her teeth. Today she was not content with her normal leisurely pace. She pushed herself to the edge, seeking physical exhaustion, a relief to the tension that had been building in her since her ceremony in the woods. Her legs pumped, faster and faster, her feet straining against nylon pedal guards. She was vaguely aware of her forearms cramping, sweat streaming down her face and neck, soaking her gray Danfield T-shirt, the frantic hiss of the belt on the bicycle wheel.

Why am I seeing these things in my dreams? These Puritan women and their crimes? I never cared that much about their criminal chapter in history. Never obsessed about Windale's minor bout of witchcraft hysteria. So why am I obsessing over it in my dreams...?

Knocking.

Startled her. She shook her head, her thoughts numbed, waking from her trance, and stopped pedaling. Someone was knocking on her door, loudly. "Who—is it?" she croaked, her throat painfully sore. Her tongue was swollen and dry. "Come in," she managed to say.

Her father poked his head through the doorway, uncharacteristically angry. "Just how long are you planning on keeping up this racket."

"What?"

"It's Saturday morning, Gwendolyn," he said. "Your mother and I would like to eat breakfast in peace and quiet. Give it a rest. Come down and eat something." He closed the door.

She stepped down from the bike, and whimpered in pain. Her thighs ached, and now that she was supporting her full weight, her legs trembled. She almost fell but caught herself on the handlebars.

"I feel like an invalid," she said, glancing at the odometer. "And I've only ridden"—she did the subtraction—"thirty-seven miles." She looked again at the black and white numbers of the odometer. "Thirty-seven miles!" She checked her alarm clock. "In . . . an hour." She had pedaled the bike almost forty miles per hour. All in a trance. "*Jesus!*" She touched the metal tire and yelped as it burnt her fingers.

✺

Karen was napping in her book-cluttered office when the call came. Her office hours were Tuesdays and Thursdays in the afternoons, at which times students were welcome to seek help on term paper topics, or discuss ways to resuscitate a struggling GPA. This early in the term Karen typically had few visitors, and lately she'd taken advantage of the downtime to catnap, curled up in the comfortably upholstered armchair that had accompanied her through three colleges and a half-dozen apartments.

When the phone rang she'd just been drifting off, lulled by the sound of a brisk October breeze stirring the loose windows in their panes. She came awake with a start at the sound of the old-fashioned telephone clanging in the cloistered silence of the cinder block office. (The English Department needed to update its office equipment, but when it came to the distribution of infrastructure funds, Danfield gave preferential treatment to its big grant-winners, like Biophysics and Women's Studies.)

She unfolded her legs from under her and crossed to her desk.

"Ms. Glazer?" the voice on the phone asked. "This is Renee from Dr. Labajo's office. Doctor Labajo would like to schedule a time for you to come in and discuss the results from your amniocentesis."

Karen felt a sudden knot of dread. "What were the results?"

"I'm not allowed to give out test results on the phone. Doctor Labajo would like to schedule—"

"But they're my fucking results!" Karen said. She heard the girl on the other end of the line suck in her breath in surprise. "I'm sorry, I didn't mean to—"

A cold silence. "Ma'am, don't yell at me. I'm not allowed to give out test results."

Especially when there's a problem . . .

"I'm sorry, you're right." She put out a hand to steady herself against the desk. The room felt suddenly too small. "When? Can I come in, I mean."

"Doctor Labajo has cleared her schedule for you after three-thirty this afternoon."

Cleared her schedule. Normally, Karen had to make appointments weeks in advance to get an audience with the obstetrician.

Karen closed her eyes and said into the phone, "I'll be there."

⬦

"This is quite a place you live in," Alex said as Wendy led him to the spacious kitchen of the president's mansion. He was lugging his astronomy text, a couple notebooks, and a scientific calculator. Wendy had already set her stuff out on the long table.

"Four spare bedrooms upstairs," Wendy said. "Huge foyer and entranceway, a den, and a library. Everything about this place is huge. Sometimes, when I'm alone, I yell and I can hear an echo."

"You yell when you're alone?" he asked, smiling.

"Primal yelling," she said, grinning. "Scream therapy. Never heard of it?"

"No," he said, setting his books down catty-corner to hers.

"You should try it sometime," she said. "And of course, I only yodel when no one else is in the house."

"Now you're joking," he said, catching on.

"Yes, but not about the screaming part," she said. "This house is like a big, empty cave half the time."

"A cave with central air and heating," he said.

"Well, a nicely appointed cave," she said.

A few minutes later, they were each drinking Diet Coke from a glass and looking over their astronomy lab instructions in the kitchen. Alex flipped through several pages of his textbook and said, "So we're supposed to find the exact time of sunrise and sunset for the day we graduate, which is the second Saturday in May, three years and seven months from now. Can't we look this up in a farmer's almanac or something?"

"We could, but remember Gorgas said to show our work."

"Well, I would list the page number in the almanac."

"It won't be so bad," Wendy said. "I think it only has to be accurate to within one minute."

"Oh, so it's no biggie, then."

She smiled. "We can be wrong by sixty whole seconds and still pass with flying colors."

"Color me relieved," Alex said, shaking his head. Then he read the lab assignment again. "I think we need to calculate the coordinates of the sun for the midnight before and the midnight after."

"No, she's given us those figures, right ascension and declination. That's the alphas and deltas. Oh, and we're to use Boston, level horizon at sea level. And she gave us the latitude and longitude."

"Well, that Professor Gorgas is just taking all the fun out of it."

Wendy ignored the comment, except for the quirk of a smile. "We calculate the local sidereal times, then"—she flipped back a few pages in her text—"convert those to Greenwich sidereal times. Well, those conversions don't look so bad . . . comparatively speaking."

"Mind if I take those," Alex said. "I'm a finance major, and we're not supposed to get much fancier than accelerated depreciation calculations."

She laughed. "Fine. I'll work on the local sidereal times."

He watched as she flipped through the text, made quick notes in her notebook, plugged numbers into her scientific calculator, and jotted down her results. "I just love to watch you do that."

"Oh, really?"

"Nothing sexier than a woman whipping out sidereal calculations."

She stuck out her tongue at him.

"On second thought, that tongue thing definitely works for me."

She laughed. "You know we're never going to get through this at this rate."

"You mean with me interrupting every five minutes?" He held up his hands. "I'll be quiet." Wendy nodded and went back to work, scribbling down some more figures.

Alex kept his head down for the next twenty minutes and methodically worked through his calculations. Despite his pretense at mathematical incompetence, he seemed to have no trouble doing the conversions. Wendy would have a hard time coming up with a less romantic study date topic than a laborious series of calculations. But she guessed you had to play the hand you were dealt....

"All done," Alex said, looking up and around for her. "At least I think they're all right. Wanna check?"

"You know what," she said. "I think we need a break. Wait here a minute." She ran off before he could ask a question. Down the hallway, up the ridiculously grand staircase, down the long upstairs hall to a linen closet. She rummaged around, finally found the bundle she was looking for, and returned to the kitchen.

"That's a blanket," Alex said. "You want to take a nap?"

"No, silly," she said. "It's an astronomy class. Let's forget about all the numbers and foreign letters for a little while and look at some stars."

"Now why didn't I think of that?"

"You were too busy trying to be charming," she said.

He stepped beside her as they walked by the door to the pantry. "Was I?"

"Occasionally."

She flipped a switch by the back door. "What's that?" he asked. "Sprinkler system," she replied. She flipped a couple more switches. "Those?" he asked. "All the lights in back. It's much darker back here than in front. Moon's just a sliver, so we should be able to see some constellations."

They walked out onto the spacious backyard where Wendy had already seen tents go up several times for various functions on the president's lawn. She wouldn't be surprised to wake up one day and find the Ringling Brothers Circus tents being pitched. Tonight the lawn was uncluttered and relaxing. They walked far enough out from under the long second-story balcony to get a clear view of the sky, the black velvet darkness and the twinkling of stars a wondrous canopy. She spread the blanket out with a snapping motion reminiscent of a magician about to make a costumed assistant disappear. "Welcome to the Gwendolyn A. Ward Observatory," she said, indicating the blanket. "Please be seated. Our show is about to begin."

⬠

When she returned home later in her Volvo, she saw with relief that Paul wasn't there yet and she had the house to herself. The overturned cars that had greeted them this morning—the most ambitious act thus far of a particularly creative band of vandals—had all been towed away, and the street and sidewalks and driveways along Lore Avenue were sprinkled with chips of safety glass sparkling in the late afternoon sun. Karen piloted the Volvo carefully into the garage, which had spared it from the vandals, and entered the house through the laundry room.

She made herself a cup of tea and sat in the living room among the lengthening shadows. She turned the television on to the local news and lowered the volume to a whisper. Her eyes unfocused before the newscast, where a local reporter stood in a pasture describing the prior night's livestock mutilations in a neighboring town.

The local news went to commercial, and the screen filled with the image of a baby sitting inside an all-weather radial tire. Karen looked away.

Some uncertain amount of time later, she heard the thump of a car door closing in the driveway. Paul entered in his work boots and flannel shirt. She listened to him, disappointed to have the silence she'd cultivated interrupted by this loud presence: the front door closed too brusquely, his humming, the jingle of keys and pocket change.

"Hey! I didn't see you sitting there," he said. "How was your day?"

Fine.

"You should've seen it out there this morning. It took every tow truck in Essex County to clear the street. Did you see anything about it on the news?"

No.

"I got a rental. It's a pretty sweet ride, I'm thinking about talking to Dick Hollins about leasing one just like it. You wanna see it?"

Maybe later.

He watched her as she stared into her tea, which sat untouched between her cold hands. Suddenly he reached across the kitchen table for her hand. At his touch a tiny static electric spark leapt between them, and she startled. It was the first such shock of the season, and it reminded her that winter was coming on.

"Karen, I want to talk to you about something," he began, giving her hand a squeeze until she lifted her eyes to his.

Please. Not now. (But she didn't say the words.)

He showed her a gentle smile, and she tried to harden her heart against the look of open love and concern he gave her. "I've been really stupid lately," he said.

Please, don't.

"Just really dumb, like a teenager, like these stupid fucking kids I hire for seven bucks an hour. Thinking I can just stroll along and take life as it comes to me. Make decisions about my life, about us, as if they're no different from decisions about what grade of lumber I need for a job, or what kind of truck to buy." He frowned as he struggled to put the words together, as if what he rehearsed wasn't jibing with what was coming out of his mouth. She saw him back up mentally and come at it again from a different direction. "I guess what I'm saying is I've taken a lot for granted, important things. You. Our daughter. I've been sitting back and letting these—wonderful things—just happen to me. I realized that today, how lucky I am, and how little I'd done to deserve it."

Now Karen spoke. "Paul, don't talk like this. You've been perfect."

"No. I've been complacent. Look at us. I pretend because we're both almost forty I can leapfrog right over marriage, we should just move in together, it's not about romance, just two grown-ups talking things through." He smiled again, guilty and repentant. "But that's not what I want. To back up into love."

He began rooting in his shirt pocket. He held the engagement ring out to her with nicotine-stained fingers, and she looked at it blankly, as if it was an alien object.

"I'm asking, Will you marry me? And, Will you forgive me for not asking when I should've?"

When she began crying, at first he took her reaction for tears of joy, and grinned in relief. But then she looked up at him with such sadness in her reddened eyes that he felt something harden inside his chest, as if part of him had turned to clay.

"What? Karen, tell me—"

"The baby," she said, and it became a wail. "Oh Paul, our baby . . ." She began to sob.

When she calmed enough to tell him, he sat and listened expressionlessly, the life draining by degrees from his face. She told him about the amniocentesis, about the mysterious and profound birth defects detected within her womb; she told him between bouts of sobbing of the insidious growth of their gestating child, a growth unchecked by nature, speeded up like time-lapse photography by some fecund gene that lay coiled within their tainted chromosomes. And as she reached the end of her confession, she concluded with the same prophecy Maria Labajo had given her: "It will probably end in a spontaneous abortion, sometime before the end of term."

She looked at Paul and saw him sitting like a statue. His eyes were fixed on the engagement ring resting on the table between them. He looked up to her, and she saw emotion building behind his eyes, though he was a man and the tears wouldn't come easily, even now. He came to her, shuffling forward awkwardly from his kitchen chair, wanting to hold her. She made it difficult for him by not rising, and he was forced to kneel on the cold linoleum before her. She kept her hands folded across her stomach as he took her in his arms. She felt a stab of guilty anger as he began to sob too, angry that he felt some claim on this sadness. She wanted to be alone, didn't want to share her misery.

"I need to be alone," she said, recognizing even as she said it that it was the most unreasonable thing she could possibly request. He pulled away from her, stunned and hurt, and searched her face for some sign of regret. But she had accepted herself as a villain, accepted her selfishness in her grief, and she did not blink.

"Karen, my god, you can't be alone. Not now," he said.

"I'm tired Paul. I need to be by myself. I need to think."

"But I don't understand . . ."

"I'm sorry," she said flatly. He scowled, and she saw his own grief suddenly flare brighter.

"She's my daughter too," he said fiercely, the first hot tears coming now, freed by his anger. "I'm losing something, too."

When she met this with more silence, he suddenly turned from her and swept the contents of the table across the kitchen floor—bills, a calculator, place mats, magazines. Somewhere in the debris that went flying was the engagement ring, antique, once his grandmother's.

He stormed out then, slamming the front door hard enough that it shook the frame. She sat in the echoing aftermath of his rage and stared at her hands long into the night, while the house grew cold around her.

"Okay," Alex said, lying beside Wendy on the blanket in the backyard of the college president's mansion. "I was never good at finding constellations. But there's no mistaking that one. It's the Big Dipper right above us. Am I right?"

"Sorry," Wendy said. "That's the Great Square of Pegasus."

"Come on," he said. "That has to be the Big Dipper. See the handle, coming right off it."

"That's part of Andromeda, the chained lady," Wendy said, pointing straight up into the sky. "Go two stars up the handle then turn right. That little fuzzy blob is the Andromeda Galaxy."

"Not all that impressive for a galaxy," Alex commented.

"It's over two million light years away," Wendy said, with a wistful air. "It's actually bigger than the Milky Way."

"So, if that's the Great Square and Andromeda," Alex said, "where's the Big Dipper?"

"It's too close to the northern horizon now for us to see," Wendy said. "Out at sea, we might be able to see it."

"No thanks," Alex said, "I'm kind of comfortable right here."

Wendy smiled. "Look over to the northwest from the Great Square. . . . That's the Northern Cross." She lowered her arm and her hand brushed Alex's. She moved her arm away slightly, but he reached over and covered her hand with his.

"Tell me a fatal flaw," she said quickly.

"Excuse me," he said.

"Fatal flaw," she said. "Something you don't want anybody to know. A closely guarded secret about a personal shortcoming."

"Well, that depends . . ."

"On what?"

"Is this to be used in a blackmail context?"

She laughed. "Secrets under the stars are never told."

"Did you just make that up?" he asked, sitting beside her.

"Yes," she readily admitted. "But I promise not to tell."

"Because this is a big thing you're asking," he said.

She sat up beside him. "Do you have something dark in your past, a felony perhaps? *Oh, my God!* Alex isn't your real name. *You* really *are* in the witness protection program!"

"My true past as Vito Cortizone is exposed . . ." He shook his head, laughing. "A fatal flaw, huh?"

"I am sworn to secrecy," she said. "Your secret dies with me."

"Okay," he said, then cleared his throat. "Here goes . . . I have webbed feet."

"What?"

"A little webbing between the toes." She burst out laughing. "Hey, it's not like I'm the Man from Atlantis."

Wendy wiped a tear from her eye. "Have you . . . have you tried out for the swim team?" She was still laughing.

"No," he said. "I don't swim."

"Wait a minute," she said, "isn't Minnesota the state of a thousand lakes or something? How can you not know how to swim?"

"They wouldn't let me wear my shoes in the wading pool," he said, causing her to burst into another fit of giggles. He smiled and shook his head. "I thought the other kids would think I was different."

"And you think wearing shoes in a swimming pool would make you look normal?"

Now he was laughing, too. "I didn't think it through that far."

"Let me see your feet," she said, reaching for his shoelaces. He spun away from her, swinging his sneakers out of reach. In a moment she had her arms around him.

"No peeking until you tell me *your* fatal flaw," he said.

She gave him a peck on the cheek then sat back on her heels. "I guess that's only fair." She sighed deeply. "Here goes. My fatal flaw is ... I'm a wallflower."

"A wallflower?" he said, incredulous. "*That's* your fatal flaw."

"Uh-huh."

"Musical arrhythmia?" he said. "I'd hardly call that a fatal flaw."

"That's because you've never seen me dance," she said. "I look like somebody lit my socks on fire."

He laughed then. "I'll let you see my feet when you let me see you dance."

"Argh!" she said. "Stalemate. Okay, then you have to answer a personal question," she said.

"Am I missing a list of rules or something?"

"My yard, my rules," she said, grinning. "Just answer the question." He nodded. "What's with the Hawaiian shirts?"

"Mind over matter," he said.

"Come again?"

"Brutal winters break your spirit," he said. "I wear Hawaiian shirts to change my state of mind. It can be ten below zip in January, but in my mind it's always balmy."

She stared at him for a moment, impressed. "And that keeps you warm?"

"No, I freeze my ass off," he said. "But I have to keep trying. . . . It's all about self-improvement." She gave him a good-natured shove. "Had you going, didn't I."

"*Yes*," she said. "Mind over matter! I believe that shit."

"Hey, so do I," he said but couldn't help laughing.

"Another personal question," she said.

"When do I get to ask the questions?"

"In due time," she said, her tone becoming serious. "Why did you come over here tonight?"

"Because those sunrise calculations looked like a real pain in the ass."

She jabbed him in the arm with her fist. "I'm serious."

"Well, that is part of the reason," he said. "The other part is, I like spending time with you."

"You don't think I'm odd?"

"Well, you're different . . ."

"Different." She was sitting straighter.

"Unique," he said. "And that comes from a web-footed, fashion-impaired Minnesotan, so I wouldn't put too much weight in it one way or the other."

"I see," she said.

"I think you're, I don't know, exotic," he said. "I find that intriguing."

Exotic, she thought. *I can work with exotic.*

"So, is it my turn?"

"Go ahead," she said, leaning back on her palms. She smiled. "It's about the tattoo isn't it? You want to know where Bruno wanted to put that sun tattoo?"

He smiled, shook his head. "No, I was wondering about the . . . stuff you do."

"Stuff?"

"You know, the white magic, the wicca stuff," he said.

"What do you want to know about it?" she asked. "Go ahead, ask. My skin's gotten thick over the years." She clenched her fists, conscious of her black, hardened nails.

"Well . . . I, um, have a confession to make first. . . ."

She sat forward, no longer leaning backward on her palms. That position seemed too vulnerable suddenly. "You don't really have webbed feet?"

He smiled wryly. "It's not that." He looked her in the eye for a moment, then looked away, over her shoulder. "I'm not real proud of this. I don't know what got into me actually."

"What? You wrote my phone number in the men's room? Tell me?" Her smile was forced.

"I followed you," he said. "That Friday night ... when you went into the woods."

"Were you alone?" she asked, her jaw clenched so tightly it ached. She imagined Jack Carter, Jensen Hoyt, and Cyndy Sellers traipsing through the woods to watch the naked girl commune with nature and laugh about it later.

"Of course, I was alone," he said. "What are you thinking?"

"I don't know," she said coldly. "What were *you* thinking? You were the one stalking me."

"I wasn't stalking you," he said. "It's just that Frankie told me about your ceremony and—"

"Frankie told you where I was!?"

"She said that if I was curious about the magic stuff I should follow you and see for myself—"

"If you were curious, you could have asked me! I can't believe her!"

"Look," he said. "I know it was way out of line. I really didn't know what to expect, so when you took off your robe ..."

Oh, Jesus, she thought, feeling her face start to crumble. She pressed her hand to her mouth and fought back tears. "I can't believe you," she said, "I trusted you. I thought you were different."

"I'd give anything to take back those few moments ..." He reached out for her arm, but she jerked away.

Then a troubling thought crept up on her. Just how much had he seen, how much had he witnessed. "So ... I suppose you waited around to get a good eyeful."

"Wendy, it's not like that," he said. "I just wanted to see what the white magic stuff was all about. I didn't expect you to ... I mean, the second I saw you take off the robe I left."

"So, the sight of me in my birthday suit scared you off," she said, with a bitter little laugh.

"No! Wendy, you are a really beautiful person, a beautiful woman ..." He shook his head, trying to sort out his own emotions. "I felt like I was violating you and—"

"Good! Because that's exactly what you did." At least he hadn't seen the rain spell and ... what came afterward. "And even if I had left all my clothes on, you would have still been violating me, my privacy."

His chin was all the way down on his chest, where only minutes ago he had been contemplating the stars. "I know it," he said. "I'm sorry."

Wendy stood up abruptly. "Get out."

He looked up. "What?"

"Just get out," she said. "I can't talk to you now, I can't look at you."

He stood slowly, stunned. "Please, Wendy, I'll do anything to make it up to you . . ."

"Good," she said, "then get out. That's what you can do for me."

She strode back toward the house. Alex stood on the blanket, hands widespread. "Can't we talk about this?"

"No!" she shouted.

He walked slowly toward the house, then stopped when she slammed the back door shut. Moments later she opened the door and tossed out his textbook, notebooks, and calculator, which broke open on the patio. "Wendy . . ."

She poked her head out the door. "Sorry if I got you all hot and bothered out there in the woods. This should cool you off." He saw her reach for a wall switch, then dropped his head as the sprinkler heads popped up and soaked him.

When he gathered his books—the scientific calculator was ruined—he could no longer see her through the back windows. Sopping head to toe, he trudged slowly around the house. "Well, that could have gone better," he said.

Wendy ran upstairs to the guest bathroom closest to her bedroom, shut the door, and sat down on the toilet seat lid. She put her face in her hands and cried silently. "I'm such a freak," she said. "Real sideshow material. All the boys come poke their sticks at my cage." She shuddered. *Why did I ever think he might be different?*

Soft knock. "Wendy? Are you okay?"

Wendy sat up straight, wiped her nose. "Fine, Mom."

"Has Alex gone?"

"He had to leave," Wendy said. "Track meet in the morning."

"Sorry I missed him," her mother said.

"I'm sorry too, Mom," Wendy said.

She sat for several long minutes, regaining her composure. She wiped her eyes and decided to check the damage in the mirror. *Not too bad,* she thought, *little blotchy. Can barely tell I had my dignity stomped on.* She looked at her fingernails, and in the fluorescent lighting, they appeared to have lightened to the dark purple shade that had preceded the black. *Almost as if they approve of me dumping Alex,* she thought. "What's that all about?" She looked back in the mirror. And she screamed.

For a moment her face had been replaced by a hideous visage, an oversize, black leathery head, with wisps of hair and incredibly long teeth. But it had been the yellow, wolflike eyes that had scared her the most. They had been feral yet cunning, and they had looked right through her, right into the depths of her soul, and they had seemed to know her, to claim her. Those eyes seemed like the last thing she would ever see.

Her mother didn't bother to knock this time. She just opened the door, pure maternal fear clouding her face. "Wendy, my God, what's wrong?"

"Nothing, Mom," Wendy said. "It was nothing."

"I know nothing when I hear it," her mother said. "And that was definitely something."

"Just a spider," Wendy said. "A jumbo, piston-legged beast in the sink."

"A spider?"

Wendy nodded. "I was washing my face and there it was..." Her mother looked skeptically at the spotless sink. "I, uh, I washed it down the drain."

"You're sure you're okay, dear?"

She hugged her mother. "I'm really okay, Mom. I just need some sleep." *Long, dreamless sleep...*

CHAPTER
SIX

Alexander Ian Dunkirk decided he needed to think outside the box, and he did his best thinking on the run, which meant jogging. He usually jogged the night before an exam, right before he began a cramming session, but now he had a different dilemma to resolve. Wendy. And after a restless night, he decided to hit the streets of Windale, leaving the familiar campus far behind.

Once he had jogged beyond the campus buildings into the heart of the town, he began to see its age. Windale was a town over three hundred years old, and it showed its age in more ways than the number of historical monument plaques. The town had died a little death with the collapse of the textile industry. It had revived the town's history of witchcraft in hopes of generating tourist dollars, but the truth was that Windale's potential as a tourist stop was severely overestimated by the chamber of commerce, despite the proliferation of quaint street names.

His weak economic prognosis for the town was getting him nowhere. And, he suspected, was merely a way of helping him avoid the issue.

Alex had screwed up with Wendy. And maybe there wasn't anything he could do to make things right again. Sometimes mistakes are unintentional, only obvious with the benefit of twenty-twenty hindsight. His mistakes had been obvious every step of the way. He should have known better from the start. Wendy had smashed his attempted "clean slate" across her knees and sent him packing. So what next?

The main problem wasn't even her sense of modesty. At first he thought that embarrassment might be the source of her anger but soon realized it was more than that. She had opened up to him, brought him into her emotional circle, so to speak. And by spying on her, he had shown himself unworthy of her trust. It didn't really matter what she had done in private or how she had been dressed or undressed while doing it. The sticking point was that it had been a private thing. *You can't unring a bell*, he thought. Maybe time was the only thing that would help her get past his betrayal, if she ever did. If not, Wendy Ward would likely be one of the great regrets in his life. And that was something that really made his insides ache. *I can't give up on this*, he decided. *She's not ditching me that easily.*

He slipped on something slick in the road. For an instant he hung poised on the treacherous line between maintaining his balance and the fall. Then he pitched backward, arms swinging in slapstick circles. He knew before he hit that he was going to be hurt. When the pain came it seemed to be registered by a different sense, a texture and a thudding pressure, a rusty color, a sound like a mallet striking a faraway drum. Then it *hurt*.

He landed on his ass in the sticky slick mess that had caused him to slip, his head whipping back a split second later, smacking the blacktop. After a dazed moment, he rolled up onto his hands and knees, the dark mess squeezing between his fingers. As he tried to push himself up, his palms shot out in front of him, and he fell face first, his nostrils filled with the nauseating stench.

An explosion of gore, covering the entire width of the road. It smeared his clothing, had soaked through his sweatpants, plastering a clammy swatch against his thighs. He felt it drying on his face. He wanted to scream, but the running and the sudden fall had startled any sound out of him. A dozen feet away the carnage seemed heaviest, a dark heap. He saw bits of spotted hide, shreds the size of washrags, a jagged fence of splintered ribs. A long skull trailed vertebrae and ruptured muscles, the snout crushed in bluntly. A lolling tongue—

A cow, Alex thought, part of his mind still screaming irrationally that he'd wandered into the human wreckage of an automobile accident. But no, a cow...it was just a cow. He wiped the gory mess from his hands on the cement road, leaving long crimson smears. Bad luck and some ridiculous need for self-flagellation had caused him to stumble right into this...granddaddy of all roadkill.

The cow must have wandered free of its pasture, been hit by ...what? Nothing short of a Mack truck could have done this much damage to an animal, and a large truck seemed unlikely on this small road. Maybe another prank by some of the more inventive frat members. Tired of simply tipping or spray painting the cows, they had decided to use them as four-legged tenpins. But where was the car? Where was the fucking wreck? They would have totaled the car after striking a heifer that violently. The cow had literally exploded. Alex wondered, belatedly, if some explosive device had been concocted in Danfield's chemistry lab. But that, too, seemed far-fetched. What the hell had happened to this cow?

It wasn't until twenty minutes later—the sleepy police on the scene and Alex's bloody clothes stinking in the early morning sunlight—that Alex thought of another possibility. He climbed a short distance up a hillside and looked down at what seemed like an evenly distributed blast radius... He tipped his head back and watched a carrion bird wheeling slow figure eights high above. The cow hadn't been struck, it had been dropped.

✸

Over breakfast in the physicians' cafeteria, Dr. Jim Phelan called up to the eighth floor on his cell phone, and spoke to the posting clerk:

"I'd like to schedule an add-on surgery for today. Patient is named Leeson, Arthur A.," Phelan said, "Born 12/14/59, room 712. I need to get him on a table this morning."

"So he's Class Two?" the clerk asked, and when Phelan confirmed the priority status, said, "What's the procedure?"

Phelan dictated slowly. He knew the clerk was writing it down. "Excision of necrotic right eye, with exploration and debridement of rectus and oblique muscles, optic nerve, retinal artery, and vein. Got that?" The clerk grunted. Phelan added, "Oh, and Dr. Gangemi will be assisting."

The clerk said, "We'll page you when we've scheduled an OR."

Phelan closed the cell phone just as three of his colleagues entered the doctors' cafeteria deep in solemn consultation. Howard Sanders and Richard Green were well-respected oncologists; Keya Khayatian was the hospital's chief pediatric resident. Phelan picked up his Styrofoam cup of coffee and approached the men. He knew Khayatian was attending on Abby MacNeil.

"How's your girl?" he asked.

Khayatian was postcall, and his bloodshot eyes showed it. "Not good. She tried to crump on us last night, spiked a high fever around midnight, and followed it with a nice febrile seizure."

"Christ."

"Tell me about it. We finally got her defervesced by one, but it was scary there for a while." He yawned, shuddering with exhaustion.

"Any luck identifying the infectious agent yet?"

Khayatian tipped his head toward the oncologists. "We were just talking. We're pushing all kinds of antibiotics, but she's not responding. So we're looking at some other possibilities."

"Like . . . ?"

Richard Green answered for the resident. "Her CBC this morning shows pancytopenia and lymphoblasts, so we're scheduling a bone marrow biopsy."

"You think she has leukemia?" Phelan said with surprise.

Green shrugged. "We're throwing darts at this point. There's something radical going on inside this poor kid." Sanders sipped his coffee, judged it too hot, and asked, "How about your guy?"

"I'm going back in today to remove the eye. I'm treating the infection as if it's orbital cellulitis. I've got to get it before it infects the brain."

Phelan's pager went off, and he checked its readout. "That's the OR. Gotta run." He finished the dregs of his coffee and dropped the cup in the trash on his way out.

"Jimmy," Howie Sanders called after Phelan, "Do me a favor while you've got your guy under general."

"What's that?"

"Give him a double orchiectomy for me."

Phelan nodded, flashed a tired smile, and left.

Orchiectomy. From the Greek root word for *testicle*.

✸

While Abby was undergoing a bone marrow biopsy—a painful procedure that in the little girl's sad condition could be performed without lidocaine—Art was waiting for surgery.

Sheriff Bill Nottingham had paid another unwelcome visit only moments before, informing Art that he would be transported to the Gander Hill Adult Correctional Facility as soon as his doctors deemed him fit enough to travel—and assuming Art hadn't by that time managed to post the $250,000 bail set by Essex County Judge William "Big Mac" McLaughlin. (A former beat cop from Boston's Combat Zone, McLaughlin was notorious for expediting criminal cases in his courtroom, and handing down severe "McSentences" faster than a drive-thru window.)

"A quarter of a million dollars!" Art said, despite the preop sedative an RN had just injected into his IV. As the drug began to ripple over him, he watched himself as if from a great distance reach out to clutch the sheriff's coat sleeve. "Please, Bill, you've gotta stop this," he said. "I didn't touch her!" It occurred to Art, even through his druggy fog, that it was in the extremes of experience that melodrama lived, and that arriving there, unrehearsed and frightened, we had only cliches to grasp. (I'm innocent! You've got the wrong guy!)

The sheriff had forcibly removed Art's clutching hand from his sleeve and was about to cuff him to the bed rail when he was scolded by a passing RN.

"Do you honestly think this patient is in any shape to be a threat to someone?" The sheriff frowned, and returned the handcuffs to their place on his belt.

Now, twenty minutes later, Art was shifted onto a gurney and wheeled down the long corridors toward the waiting elevators that would transport him to the OR on the eighth floor. He felt a flutter of panic awaken deep beneath the sedation, like something small struggling for breath. *My eye*, he thought, giving into that panic; *They're going to take my eye!* (He'd signed the consent forms, but it hadn't seemed as real and final then as it did now.) And after they took his eye they were going to send him to prison, where the real sexual predators would cruise the shallows that, for Art, had been forever reduced to two dimensions.

By the time they reached the eighth floor, Art's panic had slipped the velvet restraints of sedation. The orderly left Art momentarily on his gurney in the corridor while he went in search of the nurse manager in charge of Prep and Holding. Art scanned the corridor, saw stainless steel refrigerators labeled PATHOLOGY SAMPLES, a waiting crash cart, a tall shelving rack stocked with surgical scrubs . . .

Small, Medium, Large, X-Large.

He rolled off the gurney, winced as he tugged the IV out of his arm. He didn't yet have a plan, but he was in motion. He snatched medium scrubs from the shelves. And began running . . .

In the stairwell he slipped out of his hospital gown and stood naked for several tense moments as he struggled to fit his clumsy limbs into the blue scrubs. Then he began descending quickly, the concrete fire stairs chilly beneath his paper booties. He'd just made it to the sixth-floor landing when he heard the overhead page echo through the stairwell.

"Security to the eighth floor, stat. Code Orange . . ."

Sheriff Nottingham was on his way out of the building through the ER when he heard security paged overhead and saw two guards run past him toward the elevators.

Eighth floor. Surgery . . .

He stopped at an admitting desk, asked the triage nurse, "What's a Code Orange?"

"Lost patient," the nurse said. "Means someone who shouldn't has just went ambulatory."

The sheriff began running in the direction of the west stairwell.

"What the fuck are you doing?" Art paused on the fourth-floor landing, saying aloud what the little voice of reason had been shouting at him since the moment he'd gotten off the gurney. He wasn't sure why he was running, or where he intended to go, but he knew he had to get out of this hospital and off of this runaway train headed toward prison and disfigurement.

Fourth floor . . .

They'd mobilized security pretty quickly, so he knew there would be guards covering the main exits from the building—he'd have to find an alternate route out.

Fourth floor . . .

He hesitated on the landing, staring at the number stenciled on the steel fire door. His pulse throbbed in his ruined eye behind the bandages.

Fourth floor . . .

And then a piece of memory fell on him: the Pediatric Intensive Care. Abby's floor...

Shit, no time. And yet he knew he had to take this detour to see her. Without knowing what exactly he intended to say when he found the little girl, he pulled open the fire door and dashed onto the PICU. He hoped his surgical scrubs would buy him a few moments unnoticed among the staff—

Whoa. The bandages. With his head still swaddled in gauze he might as well be wearing a sign that read BABY RAPIST. He ducked into a men's room and began tearing the bandages free, bracing himself for the horror he expected to see in the mirror. He was surprised to find most of the bruising had faded, and the minor lacerations on his cheeks, healed. If he kept his head down and moved quickly, he might slip by.

He exited the rest room and walked headlong into a security guard.

"Watch it!" the guard said, and pushed Art aside brusquely as he headed toward the stairwell.

Art hugged the wall, told himself to breathe again. He began walking briskly along the carpeted corridor, headed for the PICU. There was only one RN at the nurses' station, and she was too busy trying to clear a paper jam in the printer to notice Art.

Room 411... 412... 413—

Abby.

The sheriff burst through the fire door on Eight to find a half-dozen security guards surrounding an empty gurney. "Get downstairs—cover the exits!"

"Sir?" the nearest guard said. The sheriff didn't bother repeating the instructions, only snatched the man's walkie-talkie from his hip and barked into it: "I need someone watching every exit, Main, ER, Outpatient Clinic..."

He threw the walkie-talkie back to the guard, thrust a finger at two of the men. "You and you—with me. We'll sweep one floor at a time. The rest of you get downstairs and lock this place down."

He broke the huddle and led the search for the fugitive.

. . .

The little girl had been left on her side following the biopsy and lay now facing the windows. Art thought she might be sleeping, but when he came around the foot of her bed he saw her eyes open and staring out at the cloud-streaked sky. He said her name quietly and the eyes shifted, fixing him with an indifferent gaze.

She looked smaller than he remembered, there in the great mechanical hospital bed. One IV dripped a steady flow of antibiotics into her arm, while a second fed her a liquid breakfast directly through a G-tube in her stomach. From beneath her blankets, more tubes carried away her urine to a discrete receptacle. Worst of all was the steel halo that stabilized her head while her vertebrae healed. Art saw the fine surgical screws that fixed the hardware directly to her skull and felt his heart seize within his chest with sorrow.

He wondered how much she remembered of the accident, wondered if the gaps in her memory had been filled with the fiction of his supposed kidnapping. And yet she regarded him now with neither recognition nor fear, only that cool, horrible indifference of a sick child heavily medicated.

"Abby," he said, and crouched suddenly below the level of the bed as he saw two RNs stride by briskly outside the room. He was very close to the child now, his face close enough to hers that he could feel her breath against his cheeks, and smell the ghost of a child beneath the disinfectant.

"Sweetheart, you have to try to talk again," he whispered, as if sharing a secret. "You have to try to remember what happened, tell the police who has been hurting you."

She stared at him without blinking. He could see tiny versions of himself reflected in her eyes.

"Abby, do you understand?"

Nothing. He took her hand in his own, then wished that he hadn't: it was cool and clammy, a lifeless thing. He felt tears come then to his eyes, stinging, and he tipped his head against the chilly bars of the bed railing.

"I'm so sorry, Abby . . . ," he said miserably.

The little girl's mouth twitched—involuntarily, he thought. And then she spoke.

". . . name isn't . . . Abby . . . anymore."

Art froze, ice water beneath his skin. He felt her dead hand—impossibly—tighten around his own, seize him in an iron grip. He asked with great care, "What's your name?"

To which the little girl answered: "Sarah . . . Hutchins."

The elevator doors opened on Four and the sheriff emerged with the two security guards. The three men moved efficiently, fanning out as they swept through the PICU, checking each room.

The RN at the nurses' station looked up from her paper jam as they stormed past. Sheriff Nottingham trotted ahead of the other two as Abby's room came into sight—

Nothing. She was alone.

Art descended the fire stairs quickly, his paper slippers shushing across the concrete. Above, he heard loud male voices echoing in the stairwell.

Where now? Any advantage he'd had he'd lost by his detour through the PICU, and was certain now security would be covering all the main exits . . .

Except for one.

With the sounds of voices growing closer overhead, Art hurried down the stairs past the first-floor landing, heading for the basement . . .

Within moments, he was gone.

Later, Sheriff Bill Nottingham would replay the events of the morning and try to understand how exactly Art Leeson had managed to slip out of the hospital undetected. True, this wasn't a high-security facility, and the sheriff hadn't had either the time or the manpower to turn it into one. Yet they'd swept each floor methodically and posted men at every service entrance, fire exit, and back door.

In other words, at every exit a pedestrian might use to leave the hospital.

But Art hadn't left by a pedestrian exit. He'd left via the physicians' underground parking garage, where the only guard was a mechanical gate. Thus had he so effortlessly evaded the Windale police department and a team of trained security guards.

The sheriff vowed not to give Art a second chance at such evasion.

✦

Wendy arrived at Pearson Hall several minutes early for comp lit and immediately regretted it. Frankie spotted her before she could get through the doors to the classroom and hurried over. "I'm not speaking to you," Wendy said in a preemptive verbal strike.

"What are you talking about?" Frankie asked, genuinely baffled. Obviously Alex hadn't clued her in.

"I know," Wendy said. "Alex told me."

"Again, what are you talking about?"

"You told him," Wendy said, then whispered. "About the ceremony in the woods."

"Did he show up?"

"He followed me!"

"I thought he would," Frankie said. "Unless I underestimated him, he should have brought some wine and cheese and a selection of soft music."

"What are *you* talking about?"

"It's so obvious you guys are hot for each other," Frankie said. "Some people are so dense. I should have known better than to initiate a rapprochement between the sexes. So what happened? He scare you?"

"He spied on me!"

"Yuck! A peeper?" Frankie said.

"I'm pissed at you, Frankie," Wendy said. "I told you about the . . . about my ritual in private. And you told Alex to follow me. I thought you were my friend."

Frankie's eyes seemed to refocus. "You're serious, aren't you? You're really mad at me?"

"Furious. I really liked Alex."

"Past tense?"

"It's over now," Wendy said. "We can't go back the way we were."

"Look, Wendy, obviously I misjudged the situation. . . . I screwed up. Please don't be too quick to throw something away."

"Maybe you shouldn't have been so quick to violate a confidence," Wendy said, brushing by her and entering the lecture hall.

"Open mouth, insert Birkenstock," Frankie said sullenly.

Wendy rolled her eyes when she saw that Alex had saved a seat for her. *As if nothing had happened.* She climbed the stairs and walked by him without even acknowledging his offer. Alex caught her arm, and she noticed abrasions on his hands, like rope burns or . . . road rash. "Wendy, I need to talk to you," he said.

"I'm not feeling very talkative," she said.

He forced a grin. "Then I'll do all the talking."

"Save your breath," she said and walked back several rows to the next empty seat. She could feel his gaze on her back, but she ignored his attempts at eye contact then and all during the class.

Frankie took the seat Alex had saved for Wendy, and the two of them had a heated exchange before the start of class. Wendy couldn't help watching them, wondering at the dynamic that had managed to split both of them away from her. Frankie's meddling? Alex's unspoken curiosity? Whenever they happened to glance her way, she quickly averted her eyes. She was trying her best to pretend they no longer existed. It would be easier that way.

After class, Frankie and Alex made an attempt to approach her. Wendy turned her back on them and cut through one of the back rows, intending to go out the far door to avoid even having to tell them she *really* didn't want to talk about it, to leave her alone. That's what brought her to Jensen Hoyt's desk near the back of the class. The dark-haired girl had her head bowed over a sketchbook instead of her class notebook, her fingers methodically smudging the pencil illustration, getting the texture and the shadows just right. She seemed lost in the image she was rendering. Her long black hair, which hadn't been washed in a week, formed a curtain in front of her face.

Jen seemed to sense somebody standing over her. She looked up, revealing dark circles under her haunted eyes, and the curtain of hair parted from the drawing. Wendy gasped.

Jen had drawn the face ... the black, leathery face with the wisps of hair and the feral eyes that had stared back at Wendy from her bathroom mirror for the blink of an eye. The memory was an indelible image in Wendy's mind, and obviously, Jen shared the nightmare visage.

"What...?" Wendy's throat was suddenly dry. "What is that?"

"It's hideous, isn't it?" Jen said, as if that explained everything. Wendy nodded. Jen looked down at what she had drawn, then back at Wendy. "It's all I can see."

"What's it from?"

"It's the creature," Jen said. "The creature that took Jack."

Wendy's knees buckled, and she fell into the desk in front of Jen, sitting awkwardly and banging her elbow in the process. Alex and Frankie were watching her from the end of the row of seats, watching but maintaining their distance. They looked at each other, confused.

The rush of thoughts numbed Wendy's mind to everything else. Somehow, she really must be responsible for Jack's disappearance. Somehow she must have summoned this thing, this creature. It had come to do her bidding, to rid her of Jack, and now it was appearing to her, had come to collect its fee. Her free hand went to her mouth, her teeth biting down on her trembling lower lip. *What have I done...? My God, what have I done?*

"I have more of them," Jen said.

"More?" Wendy said, thinking, *How many of them are there?*
"In my dorm room," Jen said.
"Show me," Wendy said.

As Wendy followed Jen through the cinder block corridors of Bosch Residential Hall, she thought, *Maybe I'm not really missing anything by living at home.* The all-female dorm was a concrete bunker built twenty-five years ago in that great 1970s architectural tradition of post offices and public middle schools—all improbable angles and windows that wouldn't open. The carpet underfoot was an institutional shade of tangerine, the fluorescent lighting overhead flickered to some subliminal rhythm, and the air had a weird stale smell of dirty laundry. The closed doors they passed were hung with dry-erase message boards (J, YOU GO GIRL! T. AND BEWARE THE BAWL SAC!) and plastered with male models ripped from the pages of GQ. Through the occasional open door, Wendy glimpsed a dorm decor that was timeless: the Escher prints of stairs going nowhere, the liquor-store promotional banners for Bud Lite, the stuffed-animal menageries.

When they arrived at Jen's room at the end of the labyrinth, however, Wendy saw a bare door scarred with bits of Scotch tape. Jen fumbled with the keys, and gave Wendy a last dark look that seemed to say, *Abandon all hope, ye who enter here.* But behind that warning look there was another, wounded expression of frightened vulnerability. Wendy could see just how fragile the poor girl had become in these last few weeks, how she'd eroded under the pressure of a community's skepticism. As Jen hesitated with the key in the lock, Wendy understood the psychological risk she was taking bringing Wendy here—exposing herself to yet another devastating session of disbelief.

Wendy put a hand on Jen's arm and felt the girl flinch. "It's okay," Wendy said quietly. Jen took a breath, and her eyes brightened with tears. Then she pushed the door open . . .

"See . . . ," she said, raising a listless arm to welcome Wendy into her nightmare.

Wendy sucked in a sharp breath at what she saw, and stepped inside.

It seemed that she'd entered a hall of mirrors, where image upon image repeated itself endlessly on all sides...but instead of her reflection, the image she saw reflected back at her in a thousand charcoal variations was of the creature's feral face...

Taped to every open scrap of cinder block wall. Taped to bureau and closet doors. Taped to chairs and lamps. Papering out the daylit window; scattered across the floors...

The room was suffocating in paper, the studio of a schizophrenic. Wendy turned slowly in a circle, taking it all in. It would be easy to go crazy in this room, to join its frightened artist in her compulsion. She turned to find Jen, and saw the girl standing quietly in the corner, her expression changed now to one of passive acceptance of whatever judgment Wendy might bring. A strange little smile quirked the girl's lips, and she stole a furtive glance at Wendy.

"Do you like them?" she asked simply, and for a moment Wendy couldn't decide which was the more horrible sight—the gallery of leering monsters, or the lost expression of the artist who'd rendered them.

⊗

Karen was cramping so badly by noon that she canceled her lunch with Eva Hartman and asked her teaching assistant, Kristin, to lead her afternoon graduate seminar.

When she arrived home, she rushed inside and huddled on the toilet in the guest powder room and waited for the pain to subside. There were a few drifting blossoms of fresh blood in the bowl. To quell the nausea, she poured herself a tall ginger ale and applied an ice cube to the webbing between her thumb and forefinger—one of Art's little homeopathic tricks he'd picked up from his Chinese acupuncturist. She couldn't tell if the ice actually had some soothing effect on her stomach, or if the feel of it melting up her sleeve was simply enough of a distraction to take her mind off of the nausea.

In the living room, she found the answering machine filled with messages. All Paul.

Beep. "Hi. Just wanted to know if you're okay, if you need anything or—Okay."

Beep. "Hi, it's me. Are you screening your calls?" Long pause. "Guess not. I'd like to talk, but I'm willing to wait until you're ready."

Beep. "Please just give me a call and let me know you're okay. You don't have to stay on if you aren't ready to talk yet."

Beep. "Karen, please, we need to—"

She stabbed the erase button hard and stood listening to the whirring hiss of the tape. She held her finger down on the erase as if she were stubbing out an errant spark—an ember of longing for Paul she wasn't yet ready to acknowledge.

It had been three days since she'd last seen Paul, and in that time she'd withdrawn as well from colleagues and students and retreated to this nest of misery she was building. This was not depression, she told herself, but rather a kind of horrible patience. She was waiting for her baby to die. Waiting for the child inside her to finally succumb to its birthright infirmities. Paul *couldn't* understand what she was suffering; he was a man, with a man's self-protective instinct for blamelessness. Already she could hear it in his voice, this note of sad acceptance, already he was distancing himself from the raw immediacy of their loss. In his mind they were simple victims. If he'd been here he would grieve with her, yes, and comfort her, and hold her hand, but he would also mistake what she was feeling for simple depression, some female analogue to his own emotion. But she didn't feel depressed; she felt complicit. After all, who else was to blame if not her for bequeathing these crippled genes to her baby?

Her baby. *Oh God, my baby* . . .

In the basement below, something suddenly went thud. She felt the sound through the soles of her feet as much as heard it. She turned sharply. Had it just been the sound of some precariously stacked junk—the milk crates of old clothing, the ice cream maker she'd bought at a garage sale but never got around to using—shifting in the cluttered basement? Or something else . . .

Silence. She felt her heart's adagio flutter settle to a gentler rhythm: curiosity. She wasn't afraid; the house was flooded with late-afternoon daylight, was too bright for fear. She walked to the top of the cellar stairs and flicked on the light switch. The bulb brightened momentarily and then went nova, its filament exploding with a muffled pop. Shit. With a sigh she started down the rickety stairs.

At the bottom of the stairs, she peered out into the dark. Paul had strung a second simple light fixture midway around the basement's bend. She could just see it dangling from the open floor joists above. Around her, a lifetime's clutter crouched in shadow, moldering, making its own dust. She strode across the darkness to the light fixture and pulled the dangling chain. Nothing. Then she noticed the bulb had been smashed ...

Something shifted from among the shadows, and Karen spun, giving a small cry of surprise. Movement. A face—

"Don't be frightened," Art said. "It's just me."

He peered out from the dark place between the furnace and wall where he'd been huddled.

"Christ, Art! What the hell are you doing here?"

He emerged clumsily from his hiding place, kicking over a tinkling box of Christmas ornaments in the process. He was wearing blue surgical scrubs grimy with soot and grease.

"I didn't know where else to go. I had to break the padlock to get in. I'm sorry. But I couldn't go home ... and I couldn't go to Paul's. They'd find me there."

"Who?"

"The police," Art said. "Haven't you heard the helicopters all afternoon? I'm a fugitive from the law." He gave a rueful smile at the ridiculousness of the notion.

She was staring down at his feet, trying to decide what sort of footwear the sodden muddy masses had been once. "Hospital booties," he explained. "Not exactly all-weather gear."

"My god. Are you okay?" The maternal instincts were kicking in, and she led him closer to the dingy light cast by the basement's one high window.

"I didn't know where to go. I wasn't strong enough to get on a bus out of town. And I didn't know if I could trust Paul."

Karen gave Art a critical look. "That's not very fair to your brother. You know he'd never turn you in."

"No, but he'd try to talk me into turning myself in."

"And you think I won't?"

Doubt flickered briefly across his face. "I hope not."

"Art, this is crazy—" He hushed her with a raised hand, cocking his head at a sound only he heard. She listened, and then she heard it, too: the distant noise of a helicopter. "It's them," he said in a whisper. "The cops have infrared cameras and scopes, you know. Like night predators. They can see right through rooftops. I don't think they can penetrate to the basement, though." Karen felt the hairs on the back of her neck prickle. Art seemed unaware of how hard he was squeezing her arm, of the fact that he was hurting her.

He made her wait until the sound of the helicopter had faded to his satisfaction before speaking, and in that time of tense silence she studied his face: gaunt, muscles twitching involuntarily on the injured side. She wondered about the state of the mind behind that haggard mask, and when he let her speak again her first words were trembling, filled with pity for them both. "Oh, Art, what the fuck has happened to the two of us?"

"I have a theory about that," Art said suddenly. He sat on some nearby boxes and pulled her down into a conspiratorial huddle. "Okay, I've been working on this all day . . ." He took her hands in his own and announced with great certainty, "This town is cursed."

He squeezed her hands hard, as if to distract her from the disbelief and confusion that followed like a reflex. She winced.

"Cursed?"

"Or poisoned. Take your pick." He touched his cheek, then extended a hand to touch her belly gently. "I guess *poisoned* is the more accurate word in our case."

"Art, I don't understand what you're—"

"The birth defects. This mysterious 'infection' I've picked up. Think about it. You know, I came across an interesting statistic once, years ago, when I was researching my original dissertation.

At the turn of the century the infant mortality rates among residents of Windale exceeded the national average by forty percent. Especially among the textile workers."

She shook her head. "Art, you're not making any sense! What does this have to do with a curse?"

He grew excited. "That's the really cool part! See, it's like Jung's model of the collective unconscious, but with a Marxist spin. Flashback to the nineteenth century. No one in the community dares voice the suspicion that Windale's flagship industry is polluting the groundwater and poisoning their young. That'd be heresy. So—and here's where we add a dash of Freud to the mix—we *repressed as a community* our collective guilt! But, see, that kind of guilt can't stay bottled up forever, so it starts to bubble up to the surface again in interesting ways through local folklore. Particularly in a backwater little hamlet already predisposed to all things spooky. Presto—instant curse! Compound it with the usual centennial hysteria, and suddenly you have an explanation for everything and anything bad that happened in Windale circa 1899...and now in 1999. Livestock dying? It's the curse. Kids born with flippers? It's the curse. A mill fire kills thirty-eight workers? It's the curse."

"But I've never heard anything about a curse, and I grew up here."

"Ah, exactly! See, ever since the textile mills closed, we've forgotten the reason we invented the curse in the first place. But in fact the real curse is alive and well. You and me and that poor little girl are the latest living chapters in its story. Hell, the water table in this town must be saturated with whatever toxic shit those mills were pumping out in the pre-EPA days. I'd like to go back out to that witches' graveyard with a couple biochemists and a contamination suit..."

Karen grew frustrated at his paranoid logic. "What does this have to do with the witches' graves?"

"That's the poetic justice of it all! Think about it—what are Windale's witches but another example of our community's willingness to repress its guilt? We're so fucked up that we take our deepest sins and turn them into a parade! Hey, close down Main and invite the neighbors! That's why it's so beautifully ironic that both pasts intersect at that graveyard. It all comes together in a single perfect image of a little girl asleep on a toxin-soaked grave." His excitement turned with alarming speed to urgency. "Do you still have your laptop? Cause I'd like to capture some of this."

Karen looked at him sadly. "Art, I think you've got more immediate problems to worry about." Overhead, they could hear the choppers circling back again as the manhunt continued. In that light he suddenly resembled a disappointed child.

"You think I'm nuts, don't you?" he said quietly.

"I think you're tired," she said, reaching out to brush a wisp of hair that had escaped his ponytail. "And frightened. And sick," she said, feeling his brow for fever. He was cool. "I think we've got to talk about how you're going to turn yourself back in to the police, so you can get back to the hospital."

"Please," Art said, and the mad light was gone now from his eyes, replaced by desperation. "Just let me rest here a day or two until I sort this out. I really think I'm on to something."

"Why, Art? Why is this so important? What do you think you're going to prove?"

"That I'm not the town monster," he said. "That I had reasons for being in those woods other than hurting that little girl."

Karen was overwhelmed with a sudden stab of emotion and reached to touch Art's cheek tenderly. "Please," he said, and she knew she couldn't deny him this simple thing he was asking.

Christopher Perry never waited long for a ride. He'd learned years ago how to tug at the sympathetic heartstrings of the typical motorist. Came down to the three Ps: preparation, presentation, and poise. If you wanted to be a successful American hitchhiker, you had to follow a few simple rules.

How you looked was important; that's all you had at the outset. Jeans, the distressed denim variety, were fine, showed a practical side, a little needy. Top it off with a college sweatshirt—he wore Florida Gators colors at the moment because he was headed south for the winter. Higher education was respectable. Keep the hair trim on the sides for the grannies, long in the back for their grand-daughters. Try to shave at least every other day; with his blond hair, twice weekly was enough. Most important of all, you had to look harmless, whether you were or not. (He carried a decent-size switchblade inside his right boot.)

His *look* had been good enough to get him some manual work with that general contractor, Paul Leeson. Nice guy, but the town was basically dead. *Too depressing acting the townie here.* Wouldn't have stuck around as long as he had if not for the chance at some college coed action. But he'd grown tired of chasing and working to impress the pretentious bitches. The hell with them, the hell with the crummy under-the-table job, and the hell with Windale. Time to hit the road again. Time to get back in the groove of catching the perfect free ride.

Now he found himself standing with his back to a brutally cold New England wind, thumb freezing in a light rain, with nobody to blame but himself. In this shit-little burg called Windale (Windburn was more like it) nobody seemed to give a sweet damn if a poor-but-engagingly-handsome "college" student walked through the night till he froze his tight little ass off.

Half past eleven, he'd already given up on the carload-of-restless-coeds fantasy; he would have settled for a toothless granny on a protective undergarments midnight run.

Traffic too light. Like fishing in a mud puddle. He decided to rest his thumb, balled his fists in the pockets of his ratty jeans, back bowed to the fierce wind, teeth clenched to keep them from chattering, eyes toward oncoming headlights. Except there weren't any. *Was everyone in this town under a curfew?*

An empty soda can clanked behind him, startling him as it skipped across the asphalt. He cursed under his breath. Soon time to unfold the bedroll. *Sandy and Tina. Sexy Sandy and Kinky Tina; boy, that was some ride.* He smiled. *Well, two rides, technically. Where the hell had that been, Memphis? No ... West Virginia. Almost heaven.*

His smile evaporated as he smelled something foul. He'd tripped over some potent roadkill before, but even on the long desert strips out west, where the sun baked the hell out of it, it never smelled quite this bad. He looked down at his feet. Though he hadn't felt anything, he sure as hell must have stepped in it. Another step backward and he suddenly had the sensation of being watched. He whipped around.

It was sitting in the middle of the road, silent, a tall black boulder, like one of those statues on Easter Island, the wind tearing at tattered bits of it like moss. He stood still, paralyzed, too startled yet to be frightened, only confused. He heard a rustling, and then caught movement in what he'd at first taken to be a rock. It was unfolding, two long branches extending to either side, hypnotically. He watched, mesmerized, for the full twenty seconds it took for the branches to rise, and then suddenly it occurred to him that those weren't branches, they were arms, and as if in response to his realization, the creature began to unfold itself all at once. It stood in the silence, arms wide in a welcoming embrace, and then it came after him.

He tried to run, but with his first step his legs buckled beneath him. He scrambled forward, roadside grit biting into his palms. He fumbled for his switchblade, heard its tiny click, four-inch blade wavering in the darkness.

The monster towered over him, and Christopher fought hard to process the riot of details, the creak of black knotted muscle, the swell of belly as it took its breath, forest of rank hair between its legs.

The monster leaned down over him. One enormous hand came forward to gently touch his chest, dragging clawed fingertips down, down, then even more gently touching there in the crook of his jeans. The hand closed carefully, fingers halfway up his back again on the other side as it cupped him from beneath. The monster laughed, and Christopher Perry felt the bass rumble of the sound in his testicles. The monster's head moved in close, pressed hard lips against his brow. He smelled the blast of its breath over him.

He realized that this was a kiss. But then the kiss changed as the grip between his legs began to tighten like a clamp. Another hand closed on his shoulder, and he was suddenly hoisted in the air. A moment passed before he realized the monster was rising with him, the street falling away like a dark ribbon, details of the town blinking out with the dizzying height. The hard lips peeled back and he felt only teeth against his brow, teeth opening wide to accommodate him.

CHAPTER
SEVEN

On his final rounds of the evening of October 26, Dr. Khayatian, the chief pediatric resident at Windale General, noted the following on the chart of Abby MacNeil:

23:52, Temp: 99 p.o., Pt. A & O X 3 but still uncommunicative; persists w/o sensation distally

Which, in translation, meant that at eight minutes to midnight Abby's fever had abated to 99 degrees p.o. (*per os,* Latin for *by mouth*), that she was alert and oriented to time, place, and person, but still could not feel anything in her extremities when Khayatian pinched them . . . , which was, of course, consistent with a patient with a broken fourth cervical vertebra.

Khayatian freed the little girl's blond locks where they'd gotten tangled in her metal halo, wished her good night, and left for the evening.

By the morning of the 28th, when he was next on call, Abby was moving again.

"I want an LCS film stat!" Khayatian barked at the nearest RN, as the room began filling up with pilgrims to the site of Windale's resident miracle. At the center of the chaos, Abby lay watching with the placid eyes of a child lama. All eyes were riveted to every voluntary movement of her arms and legs as she shifted in her bed. Someone held out a Beanie Baby dolphin to her, the room fell to a hush, and then a collective gasp of amazement went out as her fingers closed around the toy.

Twenty minutes later, following a well-escorted trip to the X-ray suites, Khayatian stood examining Abby's LCS (lateral cervical spine) films on a light box. "Holy shit," he heard himself say; nearby, someone gave a low whistle . . .

The little girl's cervical fracture was healing like no broken neck Khayatian had ever seen before. A strange pattern of ossification was knitting the fracture together again. But it was more than simple healing . . . it almost seemed like *reinforcing*. Weird spiny growths were linking transverse and articular processes of the vertebrae, clustering like armored barnacles along the spine. The new bone showed in the murky films as hot spots; the little girl's spinal column, viewed in sections across the light box, lit up like a Christmas tree. And within that armored column, they could assume, an equally miraculous—and impossible—regeneration was under way . . .

"We'd better get a consult from Osteo and Neurology," Khayatian said, and then added for good measure. "Um, and maybe an orthopod and a couple PTs."

He'd recently turned thirty, had graduated first in his medical school class, and was generally considered something of a medical prodigy. But in his thirty years he'd also developed a keen sense of when he was in over his head. . . . And looking at the little girl's X rays now, he knew that time had arrived.

✦

Shortly after Wendy reported to work at The Crystal Path, her boss, Alissa told her she wanted to go in back to perform her morning *vinyasa*. The vigorous series of postures and breathing exercises known as a *vinyasa* had the unusual quality of being more strenuous and aerobic the more accomplished a yogi one became. "How's business this morning?" Wendy inquired before her boss retired to the back room and her yoga mat.

"Mostly tourists," Alissa said, "no true believers." She almost made it sound like a weather forecast, *Mostly tourists, with a slight chance of true believers.*

Tourists were often better for business than the true believers. True believers mostly came in to replenish perishables like candles or herbs or incense. Tourists, once they got beyond the gaping stage, were likely to purchase the more expensive trinkets on what Alissa called "travel whims." The feeling that they might never come this way again and didn't want to regret not shelling out a few extra dollars for that one-of-a-kind, handmade silver pendant. It was for that very reason that Alissa never put out duplicate items of jewelry. The local craftsman who turned out most of the work was indeed making handmade items, but they were so identical as to be all but indistinguishable from one another by anyone but the craftsman himself. Still, there was no deception in advertising when she placed the HANDMADE, ORIGINAL cards in front of the various pieces. The priciest items in the display cases even came with a certificate of authenticity, signed by the artist or craftsman. Every little bit of marketing and showmanship was needed to move them. But Alissa displayed these items under consignment, so she never had to employ high-pressure sales tactics to foist them on anyone.

Still, The Crystal Path could expect a slight boom in business in the week before Halloween, as that holiday was its retail substitute for a traditional store's Christmas season. Tourists would be more inclined to buy the various trappings of modern witchcraft now than during any other time of the year. The mood was just right for a little supernatural extravagance. And the Windale business community sure put on a show around Halloween, decorating windows and signs, stringing banners across power lines announcing the upcoming King Frost costume parade. Almost every business worth its marketing salt was giving out "Black Hat" coupons or "Broomstick Bargains" or "Fright Night Specials." The used car salesman on television was the worst, selling beat-up Buicks to a costumed "hag" witch who was trading in her broken broomstick. The lingerie shops used "sexy" witches in scantily clad outfits to move their "enchanted" and "bewitching" nightwear. "Your man will be spellbound!" Dating service "witch-counselors" turned frogs into princes. Even commercials for the state lottery featured crystal-gazing witches trying to forecast the lucky numbers.

In other words, Wendy's gag reflex was working overtime. Another hazard of growing up in Windale was the near constant bombardment of ridiculous witch caricatures. And no time of the year was worse than the week leading up to Halloween. Even though the holiday marked Samhain—a most important day on the witch's calendar—that's when Wendy felt the most misunderstood. In light of her recent squabbles with Frankie and Alex, she felt depressed *and* more alone than she ever had before. Frankie had left three telephone messages with Wendy's mom, to Alex's one. Wendy returned none of them, which drove her mother about as crazy as when she ignored a ringing telephone. People simply returned telephone calls, it was the polite thing to do. Wendy had just said, "If you aren't speaking to someone, isn't the telephone rather superfluous?"

The four oversize palmistry hands at the corners of the cash register island seemed disgustingly festive, and Wendy fought the urge to rip them off their suction-cupped springs and toss them under the next street cleaner to pass by. Hitting them was no good, since they just wobbled back and forth in their—Hi, *there! See ya!*—waves.

She had no boxes to uncrate, so she took the synthetic feather duster and walked to the shelf filled with crystal balls, where she began to touch up their stands. The last one rested on the coiled silver dragon. She held the crystal ball in one hand while she dusted the dragon with the other. The door chimes klinked together just as she was about to return the crystal sphere to the serpent's coils. Wendy turned and looked up as an elderly man wearing a rumpled black suit coat entered the store.

Her gaze met his as he said, "Witch—!"

The face belonged to Jonah Cooke, the lecherous magistrate she had dreamed about and had seen murdered by Rebecca Cole. Wendy gasped and her fingers went numb, losing their grip on . . . the crystal ball—which struck the floor with a sound like a faraway gong and shattered at her feet. She backed into the shelving and almost dislodged several more crystal balls from their ornamental pedestals.

"Sorry to startle you, young lady," the old man said, "I was just wondering, Which way is it to the Interstate? I'm from out of town and a little lost."

Wendy pointed to the east, the lump still too large in her throat to permit her to speak. Her heart hammered so strongly she felt the crystal pendant on her chest vibrating in a sympathetic rhythm.

"Do you need some help cleaning up that glass?" the man asked.

Alissa stepped beside Wendy, her slippered feet shuffling to avoid the jagged shards of crystal scattered across the floor. "That's okay, sir, we'll take care of it." The man nodded and backed out of the store with another mumbled apology. Wendy stared after him, deciding the resemblance to Cooke had mostly been a trick of the light and shadows cast by the spider ferns.

"Wendy?"

"I'm—okay, I think," Wendy said. "He just surprised me. . . . He looked like someone, somebody I've seen before."

"Where?"

"In one of my dreams," Wendy said. "A frightening man."

"So you are still having these strange dreams," Alissa said with a clear hint of accusation. Wendy had made the mistake of telling Alissa that she hadn't had the dreams anymore in the past several days. No sense complaining about it if Alissa couldn't help her *do* anything about it.

"Now and then," Wendy said. "I'm trying to not let them bother me."

"Obviously they are bothering you," Alissa said. "You need to relax. You need to remove the stress points from your life."

Wendy told Alissa that she'd had fights with both Frankie and Alex, without going into the specific circumstances of the ritual.

"Definitely stress points," Alissa said. "You need to resolve these issues to remove the stress from your life."

"I thought they were my friends," Wendy said, "but they think I'm a freak, just like everyone else. Who needs them?"

"I'm guessing you do, Gwendolyn," Alissa said. Wendy started to respond, but Alissa held up her hand. "Listen to me for a minute. People you let close to you, inside your social circle, if you will, are going to get curious about your lifestyle. They're bound to get curious! You have to make allowances for that."

"I know that, but—"

"If you are holding them up to normal, average standards of curiosity, they are going to let you down," Alissa said. "I bet they're not even sure how to phrase the first question about what you do."

"Frankie asks plenty of questions—"

"But I bet she's not even aware of how seriously you take this stuff. To her, it probably seems like an interesting lark, a different way to be mysterious. She doesn't see your attempts to connect to nature, to commune with nature and the elements. In a way, both of them probably can't see beyond the cartoons cluttering this town or the darker mysteries surrounding witchcraft."

"So what am I supposed to do about it?"

Alissa smiled wryly. "You have two choices. You can be alone for the rest of your life and mope. Or, you can talk to them, explain what it all means to you. How else will they ever understand?"

Grudgingly, Wendy began to see the wisdom of Alissa's assessment. Maybe it wasn't fair of her to judge them by the usual standards. Maybe it was up to her to cut them some slack. She thought it over while she swept the remains of the dragon crystal into a dustbin—she promised to reimburse Alissa in weekly installments out of her pay each week for the next month. By the time she had the floor completely clean, she had decided to give Frankie a call to apologize. As she reached for the telephone it rang beneath her hand. "Crystal Path," Wendy said into the receiver.

"Perhaps you can help me," said an old woman's voice. "I need the ingredients for a spell."

"A spell?" Wendy asked, skeptically. Crank calls were all too common this time of year. A fake voice?

"Yes," the old woman said, "a forgiveness spell. It seems I misjudged a situation involving two young lovers . . ."

"Frankie?" Wendy asked, smiling.

"The name is Frances, my dear," the old woman's voice said. "Frances Jane Lenard."

"Frankie!" Wendy exclaimed. "I'm glad you called."

"You are?" Normal, squeaky Frankie voice now. "Why?"

Wendy laughed. "Because I've been a stubborn jackass."

". . . But you're all better now?"

"I'm okay," Wendy said, feeling a weight lifting from her back, "better than fine."

"You got laid?"

Laughing. "No!"

"Well, you sound like you just had some good sex, woman. Speaking of sex, are you also fine with Mr. Dunkirk."

"Yes! No! I mean, I haven't called him yet."

"Well, you should . . . call him, I mean," Frankie said. "Guys who wear sunglasses and Hawaiian shirts really shouldn't mope."

"I have his dorm number," Wendy said. "I can try him there."

"Wanna split a pizza later? During your break? I have this intense mozzarella craving . . ."

"Okay—bring a pizza, in an hour," Wendy said, laughing.

"Make it a large," Alissa said, returning from the back room again. "No meat toppings."

"Hold the meat," Wendy said into the phone, then to Alissa, "What about cheese? I thought you were becoming a vegan?"

"I haven't made the total commitment yet," Alissa said. "But I'm leaning..."

Wendy spoke into the receiver, "Make that one large, leaning tower of pizza."

"Oh, you are shameless," Alissa chuckled. "I should dock your pay for that pun."

"Bye, Frankie. See you in sixty," Wendy said, hung up the telephone, then dialed Alex's dorm number. It rang nine times, and she was about to hang up, when the ringing stopped. After a moment, Alex's sleepy voice said "Hello" over the receiver. "Alex? It's Wendy."

Immediately he seemed more alert, but still tentative. "Wendy, hi! Good to hear your voice again. I was just dozing. Been a long day. Feel like I stepped in another cow."

"Stepped in what?"

"Never did get to tell you about the cow, did I?"

"Maybe later," Wendy said. Maybe he'd been drinking. "I just wanted to find out if you're still... curious."

"Curious? Yes, I am... Why?"

"I have some things I want to show you."

A white Jetta pulled off onto the shoulder of Route 33, and Sheriff Bill Nottingham looked up from his grim task of securing off a corner of a weedy utility ditch with POLICE DO NOT CROSS tape. Eric Beauregard, a local freelancer who pinch-hit as a crime scene photographer on those rare occasions Windale had a scene worth documenting, climbed out of the car with a cardboard carryall from the Witches' Brewhouse on Main.

"Got you a mochachino and an everything bagel," Beauregard said, setting the carryall on the hood of his car and walking over toward the ditch, at the bottom of which lay a greasy heap that not so very long ago had been a human being. Or, more accurately, part of one. There wasn't much left to identify the victim, which made looking at the mess—part of a torso, according to the medical examiner—that much easier for those who had to deal with it. Missing head, hands, limbs and any other distinguishing characteristics, it had been dehumanized to the point of roadkill.

Except that this roadkill had had a name at some point within the last six to twelve hours.

Determining that name was the sheriff's business, and there were beginning to be several candidates. This morning he'd arrived at his office to find a waiting room of concerned family members wanting to file missing persons reports.

First there was Lottie Brown reporting her husband, Larry, missing. An electrician by trade, Larry had last been seen working late into the night stringing lights along Main in anticipation of the King Frost parade. Then there was Jessie Burke, a pretty junior at Danfield, concerned that her roommate, Tina, hadn't come home after spending the evening cramming for a poly-sci exam at the library. And there was seventy-something-year-old Florence Reader, whose equally elderly "gentleman friend" George had never returned from one of his late-night insomniac strolls with their Boston terrier, J. Edgar. (Though Florence had found the dog sleeping peacefully on the front stoop that morning—still wearing its leash.)

By Windale's sleepy standards, it was a veritable pandemic of disappearances. Compound that with the earlier drowning-death of Jack Carter, his girlfriend's talk of monsters, and the rash of vandalism, and the sheriff was beginning to feel a sick little knot of dread just below his breastbone. *What the fuck was happening to his town?*

"Any idea who it is?" Eric Beauregard asked, beginning to snap photos from varying angles.

"No idea," the sheriff said. "Though I can tell you who I wish it was ..." Personally, he hoped it was Art Leeson, the fugitive he'd spent every waking hour of the last three days tracking. He had a hunch, though, that he wouldn't be so lucky to have that manhunt end here so easily, in a drainage ditch beside an old snow route.

The sheriff's instincts were serving him well: the human remains did not belong to Art Leeson ... or for that matter, Larry Brown, Tina Lewis, or George Gerdts. In fact they belonged to a drifter, but this piece of information would never be determined, and Christopher Perry would find himself interred eternally and eventually forgotten within a storage drawer at the Essex County medical examiner's office.

⬠

Wendy had fallen asleep sitting up in bed, a sure sign of her general fatigue. Her teeth were chattering and her skin was covered with goose flesh. *Why am I so cold?* she wondered. Her forehead was hot and damp.

It took a few moments for the fog of sleep to lift before she realized that her dark fingernails had clawed through her biology workbook, shredding lessons for the rest of the semester along with some of her blankets. Remnants of chapter summaries were scattered on her bed like confetti. Then she saw the blood and began clearing away the paper and shredded cloth to reveal the three slices she'd gouged in her thigh. That's when she realized her leg wasn't just stiff from sleeping in an awkward position, it ached from the wound.

She hobbled to the bathroom, poured a palmful of hydrogen peroxide over the cuts, then taped a gauze bandage the size of a coaster tight against her thigh. Splashed water in her face, grimaced at the few gray hairs that had popped up recently in her dark hair. Evidence of lack of sleep?

Yet she had fallen asleep—if only for a few minutes—and without preparing for dream magic: no valerian, no moonstone or amethyst. (Before she fell asleep that night, she'd have to remember to put on that old pair of leather driving gloves she had in the garage, to sheath her "claws.") This dream had been of the simple "being chased" variety, except the thing chasing her was some sort of dark, looming bogeyman, and it had the same hideous leathery face she had seen briefly in her mirror and all over Jensen Hoyt's dorm walls. She vaguely recalled trying to scrabble over a stone fence to escape, which was probably when her hands and her fingernails had lashed out. But this dream had affected her differently, completely draining her. Maybe because she was unprepared? Her sliced thigh alone was enough reason not to fall asleep again without the preparations.

A glance at her clock radio told her she was running late for her two afternoon classes, after which she'd have time to visit Professor Glazer during her posted office hours.

Her thigh wound had stopped throbbing in time to her heartbeat midway through her second and last class of the afternoon, so Wendy decided to skip the elevator ride and climb the stairs to the fourth floor of Pearson on principle alone. In addition to the new gray hairs she'd found before going to her afternoon classes, the circles under her eyes were well on their way to becoming bags. She had even borrowed some of her mother's makeup and expertise to make her eyes appear a little less frightful, enduring her mother's clucks of disapproval on how she was wasting her youth.

Despite a slight pause on the third-floor landing, Wendy finally made it to fourth-floor Pearson. A *little breathless*, she admitted to herself, *and a little wobbly in the pins, but here all the same.* Fourth floor was where most of the liberal arts profs had their offices. Wendy was looking for room 424.

She was ticking off the room numbers, only peripherally aware of the man mopping the floor until he called out to her, "Be careful!"

Startled, she turned and looked back at him. "What?"

"The floor," he said, pointing, "it's still wet down there."

"Oh, the floor," she said, feeling idiotic. "Thanks. I'll watch my step."

He probably thought she was being a wiseass, but lately concentrating on two things at once required more focus than she could muster. Checking door numbers and watching her step? She might as well attempt to walk and chew gum at the same time. *Absurd*, Wendy thought, then giggled to herself. *I am becoming frighteningly delirious all too easily these days.*

She found the door to 424 open but knocked lightly on the doorframe nonetheless. No answer. She poked her head in. Three small offices in the room, with name plates beside the doors: Theresa Renzetti and Anthony J. Zambino flanked Professor Glazer's middle office. Wendy stepped into the outer office/waiting area, which featured two chairs and a narrow table cluttered with all sorts of cautionary pamphlets and a couple academic journals. The doors to the Renzetti and Zambino offices were closed and, based on the dark vertical panels of frosted glass beside them, unoccupied as well. Professor Glazer's door was open, and she was sitting at her desk, elbow planted on an uneven pile of blue books, her chin resting in the curled palm of her hand. Wendy thought she might have dozed off and worried that her prof might fall into another seizure. "Professor Glazer?" Wendy called softly.

Karen startled slightly, making Wendy believe she really had fallen into a light sleep. She looked up, and her eyes seemed a little worn around the edges as well, from stress or lack of sleep. "Hi," Professor Glazer said. "Sorry—I must've dozed off. Come in. What can I do for you?"

"Nothing, actually," Wendy said, and saw the look of confusion on Professor Glazer's face. "I brought you something..."

She opened her purse and took out a small linen pouch, which rustled when she handled it and resembled a dollhouse pillow. It had a little cloth strap dangling from it. "I was going to give it to you after class the other day, but I chickened out." She found herself inexplicably nervous. "You may have heard some things about me. That I dabble in white magic."

"I've heard rumors," Professor Glazer said diplomatically.

"I bet. Anyway, this is a ... charm I made for your baby-to-be ... and for you. It's mostly parsley, sage, and rosemary with a turquoise stone for good luck. The seeds and leaves are supposed to bring beauty, health, vitality ..." As she began to run down the list of attributes she saw Professor Glazer's eyes drift off somewhere far away, and judging by the tears that began to well up, it wasn't a very nice place.

Wendy stopped abruptly, and reached to put a hand on Karen's shoulder. "Are you okay?"

Karen's eyes were filled with sadness. "No," she said quietly. "No, I'm not."

Wendy hesitated, unsure of whether or not she was being invited to intrude further into personal terrain. She decided to take a chance.

"Is it the baby?"

Karen nodded, and said with finality: "I'm losing her."

Wendy felt her professor's words like a sudden sharp blow to the chest. She felt something catch within her own throat in sympathy.

Karen looked embarrassed, began searching her desk for tissues. "I'm sorry, I'm sure you didn't come here to listen to me—"

"It's okay. Really."

Karen found a crumpled packet of Kleenex and blew her nose loudly. "Fifteen years I've been teaching, and I've never broken down in front of a student." She announced it more as a criticism than an explanation. "I've just been such a wreck lately. I can't eat without getting sick, can't sleep without having nightmares—"

Wendy fixed on Karen's last words. "Nightmares?"

And despite a long-held personal belief that teachers should maintain a professional distance from their students, Karen found herself confessing to Wendy about her dreams of Rebecca Cole . . .

Wendy listened without expression, nodding on occasion as Karen described the lucid tour of colonial Windale, the leering gaze of Jonah Cooke, the epileptic seizure. . . . And Wither. As she listened, she tried not to let her face reveal the sinking feeling blooming like a black flower in her stomach. But despite her best efforts at composure, when Karen finished, Wendy was reeling.

"Wendy, what's wrong? I'm sorry, I know it's not fair to vent my problems on you."

"No," Wendy said sharply. "I deserve this." *I deserve to know what I've set loose*, she thought, though she couldn't bring herself to admit this aloud to Karen. She stood suddenly, and took her professor's hand in her own.

"I'm going to stop this, Karen," she said. "I'm going to stop your nightmares." *Our nightmares . . .*

She gave Karen's hand a squeeze and hoped she took some little bit of strength from Wendy's grasp. She hoped, too, that she didn't sound as frightened as she felt inside as she made the promise.

It had to stop. Whatever plague of nightmares she'd set loose during that ceremony in the woods had to be put back into the Pandora's box from which they'd come. Before they wreaked any more havoc. Before they snatched any more innocents like Jack Carter. Before they invaded any more dreams...

Before they sapped Wendy's remaining strength and she was no longer able to fight them. *But how do you reseal Pandora's box? How do you trick the vicious genie back into his bottle?*

Still holding Karen's hand, Wendy looked out the window of the office at the gathering night. God only knew what was waiting out there for her, or what it wanted with this poor pregnant woman. But Wendy was going to find out.

She had an idea, but it would require Alex's complete understanding... and his help.

Karen wore the strange charm Wendy had given her close to her heart throughout the afternoon's blur of colorless events, slipped into an inner pocket of her cardigan like a secret valentine. Periodically she would take out the charm and study it, holding the fragrant little pouch to her nose. Like the tea-soaked madeleine that released the floodgates of nostalgia in Proust's masterwork, *Remembrance of Things Past* (a novel Karen team taught with Deb Schaeffer, from the Modern Languages Department), the witch charm's scent of sage and rosemary conjured up for Karen a series of warm memories: of the day she first told Paul she was pregnant; of an afternoon spent picking wallpaper for the nursery; of the evening she'd first felt the baby kick. The charm, and the memories it evoked, seemed to break something resistant within her, some tiny seal with which she'd been holding grief at bay. All throughout this horrible week she'd tried to safeguard her heart by avoiding

these memories of happier times, knowing that they would be cor-
rosive in their undiluted purity. But she was too tired now to resist
any longer; Wendy's charm—for better or worse—had convinced
her of that. When she pulled into her garage she closed her eyes
and listened to the ticking of her cooling engine, finally allowing
the grief to flood the inner recesses she'd fought to preserve.

And, unexpectedly, found herself relieved. She'd expected it to be
like the moment when a drowning victim can no longer hold their
breath and gives herself to the water. But it was not. As she gave herself to her grief, it ceased to be an infinite thing, ceased to be the vast
and life-smothering blackness she'd feared, and became instead
something finite, already lightening at its borders. Something that
could be endured. Something that could be survived.

Her eyes snapped open, and she saw with greater clarity now
the Volvo's speckled windshield in need of washing, the cluttered
garage in need of cleaning. Spring projects, after a long winter. She
felt a strange melodic calm, and far beneath it a counterpart melan-
choly, barely audible now, only a resonant hum. It was the aggre-
gate sound, she imagined, of microscopic healing. *Thank you,
Wendy*, she thought.

She got out of the car and headed inside with the take-out roast
chicken and stuffing she'd bought for herself and the fugitive she
was harboring. "Art?" she called, entering the house.

"Hey!" he said, coming across the kitchen toward her.

"Any luck on the 'Net?" she asked. She'd left him this morning
working at her laptop and modem, with an old paisley handkerchief tied across his eye, that made him look like a digital-age buc-
caneer. He relieved her of the burden of the take-out bag.

"No. I couldn't get access to any county records on-line. And
you can't exactly do a Yahoo! search for 'Town Curses.'"

He was just removing the Styrofoam containers from the bag
when the doorbell rang.

They both froze, turning in the direction of the sound.

"Who is it?" Art asked Karen in a frightened whisper.

"I don't know." Karen could see a man in profile through the
front door's leaded glass. She pushed Art back into the dark dining

room adjacent, out of the line of sight should the visitor at the front door choose to peer in through the windows.

Bracing herself for the sight of a half-dozen U.S. marshals on the porch, she walked to the door and opened it . . .

And found Paul. He stood shifting nervously under the porch light.

They stood in silence for several heartbeats, already becoming strangers to each other after only a few day's absence. He looked tired, she thought, and she felt a sudden unexpected tug of longing for him. He hesitated on the threshold of the house, round-shouldered and vulnerable, hands thrust deep within his pockets, as if he couldn't trust himself in the situation he was entering. As if he was afraid she'd turned to glass.

"You rang the doorbell?" she said, surprised he hadn't used his key.

"I didn't think I should just come in . . . ," he said miserably.

She opened her arms to him and he stepped forward into her embrace. She clung to him, kissed his sunburned ears, smelled the cigarette smoke in his shaggy hair. She clung to him hard, there on the front porch, within full sight of God and all the neighbors, and for the first time she didn't care.

He buried his face in her neck, and she thought he might be crying. She heard him say, "I haven't slept . . . I thought I'd lost everyone who meant anything to me. First you . . . then my brother . . ."

"You'd better come inside then," she said finally, breaking their embrace. "There's someone here."

Confusion crossed his face, but he nodded and allowed himself to be led inside by the hand.

✪

Art had been incorrect in assuming his brother would try to talk him into turning himself in to the police.

"We've got to get you the hell out of town!" Paul said. "Now! Tonight!"

"I can't," Art said. "They'll have notified all the bus and train stations within a hundred-mile radius. And there's no way I'd make it past airport security."

"You can take my truck, then," Paul said. "You can be in Canada by morning."

"I can't drive, not with one eye. My depth perception is shot." He didn't say that his night vision seemed to be improving in his bad eye. Reminded of his injuries, he adjusted his handkerchief eye patch. Even this tiny bit of movement ignited a roman candle behind the closed eyelid. At least the pain had subsided from the light shows, though.

"I'll drive you, then," Paul said.

"Are you kidding?" Karen said, leaning forward at the kitchen table. "I'm sure the police are watching you."

Paul frowned at this. "They *did* turn my place upside down looking for Art," he said.

"Of course they did," Karen said. "Bill Nottingham went to school with all of us, he knows how close you are with your brother. He'll expect you to try to hide him."

Paul sighed, knowing she was right. "He can't stay here, though. It's only a matter of time before they come looking for him here. We've got to take a chance to sneak him out of town."

Karen considered a moment, then said, "If you wait until Halloween, there'll be another twenty thousand tourists here for the parade, you won't be so conspicuous."

Art looked at his brother across the kitchen table, and Paul nodded once. It was a plan.

Art said, "I never thought I'd actually be grateful to the stupid fucking King Frost Parade—"

He stopped abruptly as the house lights flickered suddenly and died. The house was plunged in darkness. Paul went to the window, moved the curtain so he could look out at the street.

"Whole neighborhood's out. Must've blown a transformer."

"I have candles here somewhere," Karen said, and went to a junk drawer beside the sink where she kept every misfit item she didn't want cluttering tabletops: old batteries, picture hangers, a tack hammer, flashlight.

Candles. In a dozen loose varieties, birthday, practical joke (they sputtered back to life after you blew them out), plain white beeswax...

She took out two squat candles the diameter of soda cans, and borrowed Paul's Zippo to light them. She found herself strangely captivated by the lighter's blue flame as she held it first to one wick, and then the other. The second wick was stubborn, and as she struggled to get it to take the flame she smelled the mingling scents of butane and acrid wax—

And that's what triggered it.

"Christ, she'll swallow her tongue!" Paul said as he and Art crouched beside Karen on the kitchen floor. Her eyes were rolled back in their sockets so that only thin crescents of white showed beneath fluttering lids; her convulsing limbs drummed the kitchen's linoleum. It was a tonic-clonic seizure, and as the electrical storm cascaded through her nervous system she alternated between stiffened limbs and spasming.

Art began searching for something to wedge between Karen's clenched teeth. He snatched a hand towel from the refrigerator door and stretched it tight between his hands.

As he crouched down to try to wedge it like a horse's bit into her mouth, Karen suddenly froze, her face snapping toward Art.

"No!" she barked, and her voice was gravelly and deep, a guttural sound.

Art froze. In the flickering candlelight, Karen showed a horrible grin, and she fixed him with a hateful and pupil-less gaze.

"I did not!" she said again, filled with fury.

Paul recoiled from her, watching her head loll from side to side, as if a captive enemy of this spasming body. Finally he mustered the courage to try to approach her again.

"Karen, it's me, it's okay—"

"Stay back," Art said, motioning Paul to keep his distance. They watched as Karen dragged herself backward across the linoleum, like an animal with a broken back trying to crawl to the roadside.

When she reached the corner where counters came together she pulled herself upright into a seated position and lay there with legs splayed, a feral rag doll.

She glared at them, panting.

"Release me!" she roared, and Art felt his hackles rise as he realized there was a fourth person in the room with them.

"Who are you?" Art asked, trying to control the quaver in his voice.

"You know us!" she said, head thrashing side to side in agony. "You have accused us!"

Art shot a helpless glance to Paul. He began improvising, hoping if he stalled long enough the seizure would abate . . .

"I don't understand. Accused you of what?"

"Malefic doings . . . congress with the devil . . . murder!"

Art had a flash of inspiration. "State your name for the record!" he shouted imperiously.

"Rebecca Cole!" Karen shouted back at him. She'd hooked her fingers through drawer handles to either side of her, and thrashed now, as if manacled there. Art was glad for the delusion. "Would you? Would you?" She glared at him with lethal rage. She spat, catching Art on the cheek. Her saliva burned like molten wax.

"What's wrong with her?" Paul asked as Art wiped his cheek.

"She thinks she's one of the Windale witches. I don't know why—"

"WOULD YOU?" she barked at him from her corner, and when she'd gotten Art's attention again: "Would you send a child to your gallows?"

"What child? I don't understand—"

"Thou shalt not suffer a witch to live. But what of her unborn child?" She strained at her imagined manacles. "Would you cast your own babe into the Pit? Would you . . . , magistrate?" She pronounced the title of office with equal parts venom and derision.

Paul had inched his way toward the phone. "I'm calling an ambulance," he said in a harsh whisper. "We can't let this go on any longer!"

Art raised his hand. "I have an idea how to end it." Karen had begun screaming a torrent of obscenities at them both. He picked up one of the candles still burning on the table and held it out before him as he slid across the floor toward Karen. Her fury intensified, and dark blood began pouring from her nostrils. It stained her teeth a glistening crimson.

"Rebecca Cole!" Art said sharply, stilling her like a thunderclap. He held the candle up, and she fixed on it, following its slow hypnotic trajectory through the air. "Rebecca Cole, you stand accused of betraying your God and murdering the innocent—"

"Ah! WHORE-LOVER! YOU FUCKING—"

"If it is Satan's embrace you cherish, then it is into Satan's arms we shall send you—"

"I SHALL GIVE THEE BLOOD TO DRINK!" She screamed, and the kitchen drawers rattled as she convulsed, the first spilling free. Art didn't back away, even as she reached for him.

"...and so I sentence you to be hanged from the neck until dead!"

"NOOOOooooo!"

And Art blew out the candle. Instantly she slumped, going limp on the linoleum. Paul rushed to her, cradling her in his arms as she whimpered and drew herself into a fetal ball.

When her eyes fluttered opened moments later, she looked at them blankly. "What happened to me?" she asked, searching Paul's face. "Where am I?"

Paul threw his brother a helpless look, and so Art answered for him:

"The twentieth century."

When Wendy sat down to change the gauze bandage on her thigh that night, she was amazed that the parallel row of deep cuts had almost completely healed, leaving four five-inch-long red lines no more threatening than paper cuts. With a disbelieving shake of her head, she rolled up the bandage and tossed it in the trash can.

Just as she was buttoning her black jeans, her mother knocked on her bedroom door, leaned in, and told her that Alex had arrived.

"Don't sound so surprised, Mom," Wendy said.

"Stop being so sensitive," her mother said. "You are going to see him, aren't you?"

"Yes, Mother, we reached a détente," Wendy said. "Actually, I invited him over." And was she feeling a bit of "stage fright" now? She wanted to show him all of her magical items, try to make him understand, convince him to help her. But what if he thought all of it was ludicrous? Was she prepared for that? *No holding back,* she thought. *No turning back.*

"Send him up, Mom," she said.

"Wendy," her mother said, slipping into her cautionary mode. "Don't forget your father and I have that fund-raiser tonight. You have the house alone for the night...so please don't make me regret it."

"I won't, Carol. Believe me, I won't."

"Don't take that tone with me, young lady."

"Sorry," Wendy said. "I just wish you would learn to trust me."

"Trust has to be earned," her mother said, then nodded.

Wendy rolled her eyes and sighed.

A moment after her mother left, Wendy examined the scattered books and clothes, the soda cans and paper cups from a fresh perspective, and decided that some careful weeding might be in order. She picked up her trash can and quickly filled it with paper, plastic, and aluminum; a recycling sort could come later. She gathered clothing from her headboard, bookshelves, chair back, and exercise bicycle. She carried the bulky pile to her door, but heard athletically quick footfalls coming up the stairs. She'd never make it to the bathroom hamper unseen, so she turned 180 degrees and headed for her closet, wedging the wadded ball of clothes in among her shoes and trash bags full of sweaters. Knuckles rapped on her door. She kicked at the clothes avalanching out of the closet. "Just a minute," she said, forcing the door shut. "Coming." She ran to her bedroom door, took what she hoped was a calming deep breath, then swung the door open.

Alex stood there, smiling nervously. He was carrying a small paper bag.

"Come in," she said. "I work better sitting in the clutter." She closed the door. "Have a seat," she said, indicating the wicker chair by the window.

"Um, I brought you something," he said, looking down into the bag he was carrying. "I've been carrying it around most of the day." He took out a single red rose, stem cut short so it could be worn as a corsage. "Guess it doesn't look so hot anymore..." Discouraged, he dropped the rose back into the bag; Wendy took it from him, smiling, and carefully fastened it to her hair. She gave him a slightly awkward thank-you kiss. She didn't feel it so much as experience the brief pressure, the skip of her heartbeat. Her imagination raced ahead to a time when they might be comfortable at this.

Alex smiled and stumbled a bit as he sat in the chair, his eyes scanning the room, gaze resting briefly on the wooden pentagram.

"So, what do you think?"

She tried to examine her surroundings from his perspective. Scattered magazines. A large poster of a forest view pinned to the back of her bedroom door, a nature calendar on the wall by her closet. Aside from the unusually titled books and the wall pentagram, she saw nothing really bizarre. He asked about her exercise bicycle facing the wall map of the United States, and she explained her mental journey on the bike. "Can't wait to get to the French Quarter in New Orleans," she said.

"You'll probably make it to the Grand Canyon by the end of the semester," he said, chuckling.

"And not one sacrificial altar in the whole mess."

He took a deep breath and said, "I wasn't sure what to expect."

"All of my—" She was about to say magic, then realized how ridiculous that might sound to him. "Everything I do is related to nature, recognizing the power of nature, which feeds and nourishes us, and interacts with it."

"How so?"

"Long ago, some plants and herbs were identified as having certain medicinal qualities. Some could make you drowsy, or alert, or even heal you, like aloe heals burned skin. What I do is based on that foundation but extended to include other areas of life, such as emotions, luck, success, fulfillment. Extend that again to other areas of nature, bringing in the four elements: air, fire, water, and Mother Earth. So a diamond aids strength and builds everlasting ties, laurel promotes fame and victory, quartz is used to aid concentration." She smiled, touched her hair, and looked away briefly. "A rose facilitates love."

"And how do the elements figure into this?"

"The elements are the expression of the . . . magic," she said. "In magical grammar, the items—herbs or stones or whatever—are like words, and the elements are the sentence structure. Fire is used in banishings because it burns away whatever it touches." Alex frowned. "Say you had a bad habit you wanted to quit, you would write it on a piece of parchment, then burn it over a flame."

"Oh," he said, still slightly confused.

"Or water," she said, trying to clarify. "To receive the healing properties of parsley, you would measure the proper dose, grind it to powder, mix it with fresh water, and drink it."

"So you're absorbing the magical property because you're drinking it."

"Just like taking a pill," she said with a smile. "Except staying in touch with nature, instead of the machine that stamped out the pill."

She hopped off the bed, opened her cedar chest, and showed him some of her brass candleholders and burner. "I use these when I'm performing . . . incantations," she said, watching his expression intently for signs of disapproval.

"Why antiques?"

"They were made by hand more than machine, so they're closer to nature than assembly lines. The older, the better." She put everything away and closed the lid of the chest. "Let's go to the basement. Don't worry, no altars down there either."

Down in the basement, Wendy didn't comment on The Hunting Horror of her father's side of the basement except to ask, "You're not a hunter, are you?" Alex shook his head. "Good," Wendy said. She bypassed the old frame pyramid and continued on to her desk and wall shelves. She pulled the dividing curtain along its track to isolate her and Alex in her special place. "I keep all my herbs, seeds, flowers, and stones here."

"Where do you get all this stuff?"

"Most of it at the place where I work, a small store in a strip of shops on Theurgy Avenue. It's no Mall of America, I bet," she said. He smiled at her Minneapolis reference. "Some stuff I find on my own. Whatever I buy, I have to consecrate before I use." She looked through her collection of stones, hidden away in their pouches. She dumped one into her palm. "Here's a tektite stone, used for banishings. And here's a rutilated quartz," she said, showing him a clear stone with streaks like white thread running through it, "for creativity."

"Garnet," he said, pointing to a stenciled pouch. "What's that for?"

She dumped the deep red stone from its stenciled pouch. "To open yourself to life's pleasures and, um, sex."

"I'll just keep this," he said, pretending to pocket the garnet. Wendy laughed.

"Some of the herbs and flowers have properties that duplicate the stones," she said. "Just like rose quartz, parsley, and sage are used for health and healing." She picked up another lettered linen bag. "Thyme leaves in your bathwater give you courage and strength—good for an athlete. And here, witch hazel leaves make you charming and irresistible."

"You must have used those," Alex said, looking right at her.

To avoid the intensity of his stare, she looked again at her collection. "Let's see, a sprig of rosemary in an infant's room will make him or her safe and happy."

"And this?" he asked, pointing to another pouch, "foxglove?"

"Foxglove leaves," she said, trying to suppress a smile. "You have an uncanny knack for picking out certain varieties." She cleared her throat. "Keep powdered foxglove leaves in a box at your bedside to open your life to strong sexual love."

Alex raised his hands, palms up. "I may have a natural gift for picking them out," he said, "but you're the one who has them in her collection."

She slapped at his hand, laughing. They stared at each other for a moment, neither looking away. Finally, Wendy reached back on the bottom shelf. "This is my prize." She withdrew an object wrapped in layers of cloth and laid it in Alex's hands before unwrapping it. "Mandrake root," she said. "A strong, all-purpose charm. A complete one like this—with the entire man shape—is considered especially powerful." She carefully put it away again. "And that concludes our tour."

"I hope I'm not acting like a tourist," Alex said.

"Not at all," Wendy said. "I hope you understand me better now." *God, I hope that didn't sound condescending.* "I mean—"

"Wendy, I know what you mean," he said, "I was the one who acted like some perverted jackass..."

She touched her fingertips to his lips. "Forgotten," she said. "Except for one minor detail."

"A minor detail?" he asked, no doubt wondering at his penance.

"I need you to do something for me... to help me with something. If you really do understand all this now, it shouldn't be that big a deal." *Yeah, right!* she thought. *Maybe he thinks I should be locked up for my own protection. The moment he gets out of here he'll call the men with straightjackets.* "I've been having these really... intense dreams. They keep me up most of the night, almost every night. And, frankly, they scare the hell out of me." She saw no reason to mention that Professor Glazer was having similar dreams or that she felt somehow responsible for Jack's disappearance.

"And I can help you...?"

"You know the expression two heads are better than one?" she asked. "Sometimes in magic, two are stronger than one. I've been using magic and homeopathic remedies to help me, but I think I need to 'up the ante' against these dreams. To get control of my sleep, to get control of my life again."

"Are you trying to tell me this involves you *and* me in a... magic circle?"

"Yes."

"And we'd be, um, naked, of course."

"It works better that way," she said, smiling.

Wide grin. "So what's the downside?"

"This may sound kinky to you," she said, "but it's . . . serious to me." She almost said *deadly* serious, but that would definitely put him over the edge. "The downside for me is that it might not work. But I really need to try. I want you to be as serious about this as I am. If it's a dirty joke to you, it won't work. Magic rituals are all about a state of mind."

"So if I do this, and take it seriously, then you'll believe me about understanding it all?"

"It would sure help your case, young man," she said and grinned. She was using her leverage unfairly, but it was merely a hint of her desperation. He needed enough wiggle room to feel he could decline without hurting her feelings. "Do you think you can approach it with an open mind?"

He thought for a moment, sighed, and said, "I think so."

"Good," she said, kissing him again. But this was more than a thank-you kiss, it was a kiss filled with possibilities. With her hands light around his neck and his hands around her waist she could almost feel safe, she could almost hope.

"How long do I have to think about it?"

She dropped her hands, stepped back, breathed deeply. "Till nightfall. Come back when the moon is high. Let's say eight-thirtyish."

"Tonight?" he asked, stunned. "You're talking about tonight?"

"Unless you have other plans."

CHAPTER
EIGHT

At sundown, Saturday, October 30, residents throughout Windale began to take precautions against the night's anticipated mischief—turning on all available porch and deck lights, parking the nicer of the family cars in the garage, leaving the dog out in the backyard a little bit later. In years past, such precautions weren't really necessary; the worst anyone suffered were a couple of soaped windshields, a few clumsily thrown eggs splattered on the front walk. And, honestly, who didn't secretly chuckle at the sight of an old crabapple tree festooned with gently blowing streamers of toilet paper?

But this year was different. It was more than just the rash of vandalism that had claimed church steeples throughout the county; more than the mysterious vanishings; more than the strange animal cries heard in the woods at night. There was something palpably different in the air, a premature chill. True, the King Frost Parade was so named for a reason, and any day now local gardeners expected to wake and find that the first hard frost had crept in during the night and slaughtered the impatiens in their beds. But this early chill felt different, somehow, than other years. More wicked, in some indefinable way.

And so this Mischief Night as the first bats began flitting among the treetops, parents began breaking the bad news to their children that they wouldn't be allowed out this year to rove the neighborhoods in giggling packs. It wasn't a decision reached like so many others after supermarket consultations with neighboring couples, but rather a silent townwide consensus. *Something was out there*, the parents of Windale knew, fastening the front door's dead bolt at seven-thirty—though they couldn't exactly say *what* was out there, and were too many generations removed from superstition to call it by its given name . . .

The Curse.

On the Danfield College campus, however, it was another story entirely. The parents of these thirty-one hundred students were far, far away . . . while the need for a midterm bacchanalia was far more immediate. Like the collegiate rule that dictates weekends shall begin on Thursday evening, Halloween was declared by the students of Danfield a two-night holiday, and as the first long shadows began to overreach the campus the telltale sounds of early celebration could be heard: here a peal of surprised laughter as a girl was hoisted onto a shoulder; there the somber chords of some classic rock anthem blaring from a dorm window.

In town, Sheriff Bill Nottingham was deep into the paperwork that rose up on all sides of him, like water in a flooded basement. Twenty minutes earlier he'd grunted when his secretary, Agnes, had bid him good night, and now he looked up and saw with surprise that night had crept up on him. He was alone in the oasis of light cast by his single desk lamp. Outside the windows, which fronted the town square and the war memorial, darkness had gathered like an unexpected storm. He sipped his coffee and was surprised to find it cold.

In the next room, the police scanner chattered quietly, his deputies (Jeff Schaeffer and Reed Davis) reaching out to each other across the airwaves as they kept their lonely beat.

All quiet, the sheriff thought, and made a mental note to himself of the time—7:58. He hoped the town had seen the last excitement for the season. They'd earned it. Hell, with the last month's trouble they should've earned themselves good karma into the next century. But he'd be satisfied with one quiet night. Just one . . .

He would be disappointed.

✪

Wendy glanced out her window with a sense of apprehension, afraid her vicious genie was waiting out there in the night. Her parents had left for their fund-raiser. She grabbed her duffel bag and headed downstairs, where Alex waited.

"Are we going where I think we're going?" Alex asked.

"Same place," Wendy said. "It's usually secluded."

"Right," he said, chagrined. "Usually. So what's in the bag?"

"A few things I think I'll need," she said.

On the drive to Gable Road, Alex was unnaturally silent. He fussed with his sunglasses, turning them over and over in his lap. Earlier he had seemed ready to sit in his first magic circle, but she suspected that might have been pure bravado. When they passed the Windale Motel and Restaurant, he sat up a little straighter.

"Having second thoughts?" she asked. *What if he says yes? Can I afford to let him back out now?*

"No, I'm cool," he said, sounding nervous nonetheless. "You really think this ritual will help you?"

It has to! "I do," Wendy said, trying to sound calm. "Maybe it's just for my peace of mind," she said, offering him a rational bone to chew on. It was one thing to accept her "eccentricities" as part of her personality, but quite another for him to participate in them willingly. "Maybe my dreams and insomnia are psychosomatic and this is the placebo I need to get me back on track."

"Who knows?" Alex said, and she was grateful he hadn't jumped on the easy, rational conclusion she had offered. "If you feel you need to do this, then you probably do."

She braked suddenly and swerved onto the shoulder. Alex's hand clutched the dashboard. "We're here," she said.

"You asked me earlier about my self-control . . . What exactly . . . ?"

"I'll tell you what to do once we're in the clearing," Wendy said. "We have to get off the road before somebody sees us and decides to 'help.'" She stepped out of the car, taking the duffel bag with her. After she tied the soiled T-shirt to her door handle, she pushed in the lock knob and slammed the door shut. She started for the woods, then noticed Alex was still in the car. Returning to the car, she leaned toward his open window and said, "Alex? "

"Just trying to steel myself, get my head in the game," he said, then sighed and climbed out of the car. He tossed his sunglasses on the dashboard, then slammed his door after a reluctant shrug.

She kissed him lightly and said, "No altars. I promise."

"I know," he said, "I trust you." He followed her along the deer trail to her special clearing in the woods.

"Don't worry," she said, "we're all alone."

"Famous last words."

Well, she thought, *you should know.*

Alex watched patiently as she dug a circular groove in the dirt, filled it with flour through a paper funnel to form a white circle, then marked the four points of the compass with burning candles in antique brass holders. He sat down outside the circle as she placed a bowl of rice to the north, a cup of wine to the west, a brass burner ablaze with kindling to the south, and finally, the brass incense holder with three sandalwood sticks smoking to the east.

She removed the contents of the wooden chest, laid the mandrake root atop it, then unfolded her meditation mat. She stood in the center of the circle, her face set in an expression of grim concentration. Alex looked around the deep blackness of the woods, the red and orange and yellow of leaves that still clung tenaciously to gnarled branches, the tree trunks' stark silhouettes, strangely two dimensional in the cold light of the moon. His gaze always returned to the center of the glade. Glowingly alive within the four points of fire, sparks of flame glinting in her eyes, Wendy seemed the only thing of substance in this gray and black landscape.

She picked up her linen robe and stepped out of the circle, stepping carefully over the white line, to join Alex. "Everything's ready now," she said, draping the robe over her shoulders. "I used a smaller circle to concentrate the heat from the candles and the burner. That should keep us warm." She took a breath, then asked, "Are you ready to join me?"

"Maybe it would help if you explained again why this is necessary," he suggested.

"To stop the nightmares, to cure my insomnia," she said patiently. *And I feel like my life is coming apart at the seams.* "Something like this worked before, but I need your help to make it . . . stronger."

"Will I have nightmares about *this*?" he said with a nervous smile.

"Calm thoughts," she said. "Pleasant dreams. You'll be fine." Her smile was inviting, somehow comforting. "I'd like you to join me. I'm comfortable with you. I *trust you.* But if this makes you uncomfortable, it defeats the purpose of having you within the circle. It has to be your willing decision." Her confidence was a little false bravado for his sake: she was nearly ready to collapse from nerves. But the ritual was important. Though she wavered, she always returned to this certainty. She reached within her robe, began unbuttoning her V-neck sweater.

"And the nudity thing is important?"

"To be in tune with nature," she said. "Clothes dampen the natural power of your body."

"I thought that was a line only guys used," he said, smiling. He was blushing faintly, walking in tight circles with his hands on his hips, as if cooling down from a hard run. He kept steeling furtive glances in her direction. "Okay. All right."

She smiled, slipped her arms out of her sweater under the robe like a contortionist working free of a straightjacket, but her hands trembled nervously. She told herself, *It's okay. This is just like that time I went skinny-dipping with Scott Jones in Cooper Pond. I have nothing to be ashamed of. It's . . . natural. Completely natural. A French woman wouldn't even give this a second thought. And I really do trust Alex. It's okay.*

She breathed deeply, and that helped to steady her hands. She kicked off her cross-trainers, doffed her black jeans. She forced herself not to hesitate when she got down to her underwear. She hooked her thumbs in her panties and then skinned them down. *See how easy that was?* she thought. *Just don't think about it too much. God, is he looking?*

She had been able to remove the bandage from her thigh; the wounds she'd dug with her own nails had almost completely healed. Four faint pink lines were the only traces of the injury. She doubted she would even have scars. *Just another part of the strangeness that is my life.* She folded her clothes neatly atop the duffel bag, then finally looked at Alex. "I'm going to begin now," she said evenly. "You can join me up till the moment I close the circle by facing east—the incense burner—the second time. If you join me, I will guide you through the ritual. Leave your clothes here with mine and be careful not to break the circle when you enter it."

Without waiting for his answer, she turned her back to him to step into the circle again. She stood on her meditation mat, trying to calm herself and fight her own rising embarrassment. She was aware of his gaze fixed on her back. Maybe he thought she was out for revenge for his spying on her, to get him stripped down to his birthday suit. It was too late to ease that possible concern. He would just have to trust her.

With some degree of grace, she loosened the drawstring of the robe and let it slide down her body. It fell with an urgent whisper of cloth against skin.

She heard a sharp intake of breath as she turned to face Alex, who stood just within reach of the candlelight. He was looking fixedly in her eyes, and she was surprised to see a confidence there in his expression, too, a startling trust. The fallen robe formed a warm ring of cloth around her as she sat in the lotus position, facing east.

The night was colder than last time, but the flames were closer. She shivered in the cool breeze, welcomed each hint of warmth from the fire. She placed her herbs, flowers, mortar, pestle, and stones within reach, then closed her eyes and concentrated on centering herself. She must draw energy from the earth and the sky, from herself and her interaction with Alex—should he decide to participate—and hold all those energies within herself until it was time to channel them.

She fought to eliminate all outside awareness, trying to remove Alex from her consciousness. When she opened her eyes he might be gone. Or he might even stay, but not join her in the circle. The smallest possibility, the one she most desperately hoped for, remained. But as she had told him, that was his decision, beyond her control, outside her center.

When at last she felt completely focused, at peace, her eyes fluttered open, as if she awoke from a hypnotist's trance. Now she must commune with the elements.

"Welcome my mind to your essence, Air," she said, her voice trembling, her gaze climbing the fairy rope of incense smoke into the night sky. She shifted her position. "Welcome my heart to your essence, Fire." She was most conscious of Fire, as she ached for the warmth it provided. "Welcome my life to your essence, Water," she said, sipping wine as she faced west. Shifted again. "Welcome my body to your essence, Earth," she said, aware of the firm ground beneath her. Next, she must turn to the east again, to close the circle. Still no Alex . . .

As she lowered the cup, Alex stepped into the circle, naked, hurrying to sit down. "Sorry," he said quickly: either apologizing for waiting till the last minute, for his obvious physical arousal, or for his general embarrassment.

She took his hand, her nostrils flaring with the inhalation of fire and smoke, burning wax and cold, hard Earth. "That's okay. You don't have to stand at attention," she said, glancing down briefly with a grin. He blushed furiously, then said, "Just don't stare at my webbed feet." They both laughed together, the tension evaporating like gasoline, up and away, not quite gone but not quite as bad, either.

"Alex, I want you to close your eyes. Good. Now, think of something peaceful, a meadow in springtime, or a sheltered cove. Think of your own breathing, your heartbeat as the current in the stream, and flow with it, be soothed by it. Take your time." Minutes passed, she withdrew her light touch, leaving him alone in the circle.

"Okay" she said. "Open your eyes and look with me to the east, to the incense. I want you to picture yourself carried away with the smoke, floating upward into the sky, at peace. Take your time. Tell me when you feel it." She waited until he had nodded, then directed him to the south point and the incense burner. After he had looked to each of the four elements, turning again to east to close the circle, she nodded and said. "Now we're ready."

She ground chamomile flowers with the mortar and pestle, enough for both of them, then poured the powder into two ceramic cups and added fresh water. "Drink this," she said. "It prepares you for magic." After she drank her potion, he drank his, watching her over the lip of the cup. His lips pursed at the unfamiliar taste.

After placing their empty cups on the ground, she picked up two necklaces with tiny linen sachets of anise fruits. She slipped one over her head, then held one up until he bowed his head, then slipped it down his neck. Likewise, she had prepared two necklaces with moonstones in muslin pouches. In hers, she had added an amethyst to draw dreams. She would prepare the actual valerian infusion and drink it later before she pursued her dreams. Everything had started with the dreams, and in the dreams she believed there was a resolution. But first she would need the insight of divination.

She had powdered henbane in a small jar she reserved for poisonous substances. Turning to the south, the element of fire, she gathered a pinch of henbane between her thumb and index finger.

"Don't inhale this," she said.

"Why?"

"Poisonous."

"Good answer."

She held the pinch of henbane over the flames. "Henbane go where I cannot be; henbane look where I cannot see." When the breeze momentarily died, she tossed the henbane into the fire. The flames crackled and danced.

Wendy poured a small amount of fresh water over her hand, then dried it on her robe. "Now we begin for real," she said. All through the preliminary stages of the ceremony, she noticed that he was being careful not to look below the level of her chin. She almost loved him for how sincerely he was participating, how hard he was trying. But now she needed him to look at her. Now they had to get close. "Look at me," she said.

"I am looking at you."

"Not just my eyes," she said, smiling. "The rest of me. All of me. It's okay to take a look at the goods."

"As long as I don't have to stand anytime soon."

"It's a natural response," she said. "That's the reason I needed you here. Tantric magic. Psychosexual energy will boost the magical energies we've allowed into ourselves."

"You're the expert," he said. "What will you be doing while I look at you?"

"That's easy," she said, trying to sound as if she had actually done this part before. "I will look at you. And," she added, reaching out, "touch you."

Karen had fallen into a deep, exhausted sleep after returning from the ER following her seizure the previous night, slept throughout the long day and clear on through to the following nightfall. Paul kept a nervous vigil in a folding chair at her bedside, periodically refreshing the damp cloth on her brow. Briefly, at eight-thirty, Karen surfaced from the sleep, and smiled, and gave his hand a squeeze. He held her hand and looked into her eyes, neither of them speaking, and before a single minute had passed on the bed-side digital clock her grip loosened and she sank back under.

Eventually Paul's own exhaustion got the better of him, and lulled by the sound of Karen's breathing, he dozed off beside her, still holding her limp hand in his own. A breeze hissed through the window screen and stirred the lace curtains, while somewhere very far away a dog barked its unheeded warning...

This was the moment Art chose to slip away.

✪

He took Karen's bike, an old ten-speed with its ram's horn handlebars wrapped in fraying tape. It felt comfortable to be on a bike again (and it was true that you never forgot how to ride one), pedaling silently through the chilly dark. He felt invisible, invulnerable, and noted with satisfaction that he passed a night jogger and his tethered Lab without either seeming to notice.

He could smell winter on the horizon, crouching, impatient; the trees seemed to shiver in frightened anticipation of its arrival. The night was too dark, darker than it should be, given the full moon that hung fat and festering like a rotten gourd just above the rooftops.

But he was grateful for the dark, and the cover it would provide him once he reached his destination.

Ten minutes later he was there, hiding the ten-speed in the pool of shadow behind the town's municipal building. He removed a flashlight from the backpack he'd brought and ducked up the alley. He found the low window he remembered behind a reeking Dumpster. He wrapped his backpack around his wrist and punched out one glass pane, then reached inside and fumbled about until he felt the window latch.

For once, he was grateful the Leeson family's rugged build had bypassed his genetic makeup, as he wriggled his skinny hips through the narrow window frame and dropped down into the municipal building's basement.

He switched on the flashlight quickly to banish the claustrophobic darkness. He was in one of the airless rooms Town Council used for their interminable monthly meetings. *Spooky as shit down here*, he thought, moving quickly in the direction of the stairwell. He ascended to the first floor.

A corridor, with doorways to either side: the offices of the mayor and the sheriff. Weak light spilled out through the glass door from the sheriff's: someone was burning the midnight oil. Art slid along the wall, feet moving soundlessly over the buffed floor. Or at least, he hoped he was moving without sound; he'd lost all objectivity, given the tympani pounding of his own pulse in his ears.

Finally he reached the door of the historical society. Time now to separate the pros from the petty larcenists. He reached into his pocket and came up with a single key. His hand was shaking. *Would they have changed the locks in fifteen years?* The key slid inside halfway and stuck. Art's heart stopped. He jiggled the key. Nothing. He retracted the key, rubbed his fingers on his forehead to pick up oil on the tips, then applied them to the key.

This time it slid in with a quiet snick. And turned.

He slipped inside, and reminded himself to breathe. In the dark the only illumination came from Florence Reader's screen saver, a broomsticked witch bouncing merrily off the boundaries of the computer monitor.

And to think fifteen years ago he'd considered that internship with the historical society a waste of time.

⊗

Two hours later, Art was knee-deep in data, searching town records in the last century for deviations from the national average mortality rate. He was working on instinct, chasing some elusive intersection of hunch and hypothesis that hovered just beyond his reach. Could Windale's rise in infant mortality rates, birth defects, and unexplained illnesses be linked back to toxic waste from the textile mills?

This was the question that he'd come here tonight to investigate. But just when he thought he'd isolated a single thread of mystery, the image of Karen's terrifying seizure the night before kept intruding itself. Why had Karen hallucinated that she was Rebecca Cole, one of Windale's infamous three witches? (And why, for that matter, was an eight-year-old little girl hallucinating that she was Sarah Hutchins?) Try as he might to filter out these digressions from his pure line of inquiry, Art couldn't help feeling the two were somehow involved, that the same psychological mechanism that was causing a town to turn an ecological disaster into a "curse" was also causing two of its citizens to turn its witch-hanging legacy into a living nightmare.

Shit, but this was becoming complicated. He felt like a child who discovers too many pieces to a jigsaw puzzle. *Tough shit, professor,* Art thought, reminding himself that in the real world mysteries didn't come packaged as concise little thesis statements. *Figure it out. Go back to the data . . .*

He conducted another data sort, looking at death rates in various years over the latter part of the nineteenth century—good old Floss should get a civic commendation for transferring a mountain of old manual records into the township's computer system. Given the mill fire that had claimed thirty-eight lives, 1899, of course, was a banner year for Windale's morticians. As Art revisited that tragedy now, though, he saw something in the column of luminescent numbers that he'd glossed over before: the date the fire had occurred. October 28.

He frowned, began typing in commands. Told the database to sort the town's 1899 deaths by date. The cursor blinked at him as the PC worked, the hard drive humming quietly in concentration.

One hundred and forty-four deaths that year, seventy-eight of which clustered in the month of October. You didn't have to be an actuary to know that that was more than statistically significant. And you didn't have to be a physician to know that if these deaths were all attributable to toxic groundwater, they would've been more evenly distributed throughout the year . . .

Unless for some reason Windale's citizens preferred to die around Halloween.

He didn't trust the data and decided to repeat the sorted query; but when he typed in the command, he saw that his finger had slipped on the keys and he'd accidentally typed 1799. He was about to cancel the command when the data for that last year in the eighteenth century began scrolling down the screen.

And saw the same pattern the century before.

Art sat very still, staring at the screen as his hypothesis crumbled around him. The year 1799 was a full fifty years before the first textile mill opened in Windale. And while Windale had been a significantly smaller hamlet in 1799, a disproportionate number of its residents had died in the month of October.

October 1799.

October 1899 . . .

You didn't have to be an actuary to see that this was also statistically significant. And you didn't have to be superstitious to suddenly start believing in curses.

He logged out of the database, began gathering his notes and shoving them into his backpack. Time to get the hell out of here.

As he retreated through the dark, he collided with something hard and heard the crunch of glass. A display case.

Overhead, an alarm began ringing.

At the sound of the alarm, the sheriff opened his desk drawer and removed his service automatic. He bolted out of his office and scanned the dark corridor, looking for immediate and obvious signs of the break-in. The plate-glass front doors were intact. Must be one of the back doors. He started running in that direction, hoping he wasn't charging into a situation (without backup, no less) that he'd later regret.

He stopped abruptly as he passed the historical society's office. Something different about the place, though he couldn't specify exactly what. Something out of place . . .

The computer monitor.

It glowed faintly, the only light in the place after hours. Nothing unusual there; Florence always left her computer on, so she could access it from home. Then the sheriff suddenly realized what was bothering him...

Where was the screen saver?

The monitor glowed at the log-in screen. Someone had been using it recently.

The sheriff fumbled for his keys, unlocked the door, and slipped inside, his gun arm rigid at his right thigh. He scanned the historical society's single large room. No furniture besides Florence's desk, so there was no place to hide...

Except the Witch Museum. He could see the first two manikins—dressed as colonials—just inside the museum's entrance.

The sheriff chambered a round, and entered the dark museum.

Seen from above, the floor plan of the Witch Museum resembled, appropriately enough, the ideographic symbol for "female," so that visitors eventually were forced to exit via the same short hallway they'd first entered. Within the "loop" was a minitheater where an old PBS documentary on the Salem witch hysteria played continuously on a wall-mounted television, and it was in here that Art was hiding when he heard the sheriff call out, "This is the police. There's only one way out of here, and I'm standing in it with a gun. You understand?"

Art didn't answer. He slid along the round carpeted wall, hoping the sheriff wouldn't try to be heroic and come in after him.

Suddenly, the television in the minitheater winked to life. Art heard an electrical breaker being thrown and saw a row of theatrical lights just outside the minitheater brighten, throwing violet spotlights on a chamber-of-horrors-style black mass. On the TV, the documentary narrator said, "*While the Salem hysteria looms large in the American collective conscience, the episode merits barely a footnote in the greater European tragedy of seventeenth-century witch purges...*"

Art slipped out of the minitheater, clinging to the shadows. He scanned this part of the museum, looking for a fire exit, a window—anything. But the walls here were smooth, the windows plastered over and painted—

["In this so-called Age of Englightenment, one province of Alsace alone saw the public burning of more than five thousand ..."]

—like a stage backdrop to create an illusion of sky. Art found himself before the big showstopper of the tour: three manikins standing on a papier-mâché gallows, while a fourth—the Puritan hangman, perhaps a distant ancestor of the sheriff's—stood frozen in the act of lowering a noose around the neck of the youngest witch. The witches were portrayed here sympathetically, three young women sent to an ugly and untimely death by a paranoid mob. Art hesitated for a moment, face-to-face with the coven's supposed ringleader, Elizabeth Wither. She stared at Art with painted, lifeless eyes.

["... and though few today believe these women were responsible for the supernatural crimes for which they were hanged, many historians agree that at least some were in fact practicing witches, devotees of a domestic religious cult that predated Christendom."]

"Freeze!"—Art heard behind him, and when he began to turn. "Don't fucking move! Show me your hands!"

Art did as he was told. He felt the barrel of the sheriff's gun press against the back of his head.

"Put your hands there," the sheriff said, and Art placed both hands in front of him on the papier-mâché gallows. The rickety structure shifted beneath Art's weight, threatening to tip. The sheriff kicked Art's legs apart into a spread-eagled stance. Art heard the rattle of handcuffs being removed from the sheriff's belt.

Art gripped the gallows in both hands and gave a sharp sudden tug. The whole display toppled forward, crashing down on top of them. The crosspiece hit the sheriff in the face with a soft whump—knocking him backward. Art rolled free and came up in a crouch. He saw the sheriff's gun on the floor and kicked it away into the shadows.

Then he began running.

✪

Wendy was conscious that her breathing had quickened. She was nervous but hoped Alex was too distracted to notice. *This is just like heavy petting*, she told herself. *And you have tried that a time or two before, kiddo.* She nodded slightly to herself. *Okay, just like heavy petting. Very bizarre heavy petting. You can handle it, no pun intended. One step at a time. Center yourself. Hope he doesn't think you're a nutcase. Center. Here goes . . .*

Wendy reached out her hand and closed her fingers gingerly around Alex's scrotum.

He gulped convulsively. "Let me guess," he said. "This is where the self-control comes into play."

She nodded, smiling. "We have to . . . build each other's arousal level. As the psychosexual energy increases so, too, does the magical energy. Both energies travel along the same pathways in the body. You have to touch me, too—but don't break eye contact or we'll have to start all over again. Maintaining eye contact is . . . very important."

"What happens at the . . . peak?"

"I'll prepare an infusion of valerian to drink before I go to sleep."

"That's not what I meant," Alex said. "I mean between us. Do we ever . . . ?"

"Oh, no," she said. He couldn't hide his disappointment. "That would dissipate the magical energy too soon."

"Oh. I just thought," he began, "You know, seal it with a kiss."

"Not while we're in the circle," she said.

"We won't always be in the circle," Alex said.

"Good answer," she said with a smile.

"O-kay," Alex said. "Maintain eye contact. I think I can remember that. Self-control and eye contact. No problem."

"Good," she said, her hands moving lightly over him.

"So what happens if I . . . lose my self-control?"

"You can't!" she said quickly. "That would dissipate the magic."

"Not to mention other things," Alex said, then cleared his throat and shifted uncomfortably on the ground. "I'll try to keep that in mind."

"Let me know if you feel yourself losing control," she said. "I'll slow down until you're ready again."

"Thanks," Alex said.

"Just relax yourself," Wendy said. "And touch me."

"Touch you?"

"I need to build my tantric energy, too."

"I'm sure you do," he said, inhaling sharply as he felt Wendy's fingers stir where they held him.

The flecks of gold in his brown eyes seemed to grow larger as Wendy fought her own instincts and maintained eye contact. She was aware of his right hand moving, his fingers lighting on her breast, finding her nipple. A chill raced up her spine, arching her back, pushing her breasts slightly against his hands. Now she knew what he meant by a long night. "I'll let you know if I'm about to lose control," she said.

"That's only fair," he said.

At one point, as Wendy's ministrations became fevered with her own arousal, Alex said, "*Slow!*" and she stopped stroking him. Her hands drifted up his muscular abdomen, across the broad plane of his runner's chest, out to his shoulders and upper arms, then back in again. His hands slid down the inward curve of her waist then out with the swell of her hips, along the curve of her outer thighs, rounding her knees and in, along her inner thighs, meeting at the center, where the soft curls of hair hid a surprising warmth.

After a few moments, he said, "I think I'm okay now."

"Good," she said, and began to gently increase the motion of her hand on him. Her other hand fell to her side, where the small linen pouch of valerian root waited. In moments, she might begin to lose control.

She fumbled with the lip of the bottle she'd brought for the valerian infusion, poured the ground root down the long neck, spilling some on the ground. She was breathing hard, trying to set her hands to separate tasks, separate rhythms: she clumsily grabbed the bottle of fresh water she'd brought and sloshed it into the spell bottle. The mixture would be the most potent she had ever prepared. She stoppered the bottle, shook it briefly, then dropped it on its side as Alex's hand moved against her, fingers inside of her. She gripped his shoulder with her free hand now. She felt the brittle tensions that had been moving slowly up through her abdomen—balanced as carefully as a house of cards—begin to tremor; she heard rapid breathing, was confused for several instants whether it was hers or Alex's. And behind it all she was desperately alert to any change, a filament of the supernatural, woven deep down at the core, beneath all this sensation, some sign the tantric magic was working. Was that it? She lost it. There? A ripple, beginnings of the end . . .

"We're almost finished," she said.

"That's what I'm afraid of," Alex whispered harshly.

"One more spell," she said, fumbling out her tektite stone, and a piece of stiff sketch paper, twice folded. She worked it open with her free hand, momentarily dropping the stone to the ground. The sketch paper held the frightening image of her dark demon genie, the creature that had appeared to do her bidding, as misguided as it had been. Jen had given her one of the hundred sketches she had made, after Wendy had recovered from her shock at seeing so many faces, all the same, all hideous.

"What is that?" Alex asked, taking his eyes momentarily from her.

"One of my nightmares," she said. "A bogeyman."

The branches high above them began to sway and clack together. Down in the clearing, a brisk breeze picked up, scattering dust and fallen leaves. The flames in the candles at the compass points guttered wildly. The fire in the burner leaned into the breeze, away from Wendy.

With one hand occupied with Alex, Wendy hurriedly placed the stone in the center of the paper and refolded it. She held it over her burner as she repeated a banishing spell three times, "Leave us forever, that all the ill may recover." With each repetition of the spell, the wind gusted more strongly, but the flames remained lit. She let the folded paper fall into the burner flame, and as the edges caught, she said to Alex, "Stop!" She removed her hand from his erection but still felt his heat on her palm.

As his hands reluctantly fell away from her body, flames erupted from the burner with a whooshing sound, reaching out a fiery, arcing tendril that caught her wrist and swirled up her arm, contorting her body in an instant of agony.

Wendy screamed.

Alex grabbed her shoulders and pulled her away from the burner. He tugged on her fallen robe in an attempt to throw the cloth over her burning arm. But as quickly as it had engulfed her arm, the unearthly flame vanished. "What the hell was that?"

Wendy shook her head, weeping as he held her in his arms. Something magical had happened, she only hoped that the banishment had worked.

"Did you soak that paper in gasoline?" he asked, staring at the burner in disbelief. Up until the moment the paper had been completely consumed, the flames were wildly agitated, bursting high, sparks crackling and jumping, almost seeming to reach out for something else to burn. Human flesh? When the paper was nothing but black ash, the flame winked out with a hiss.

Wendy's arm appeared normal, but it ached, as if with a deep sunburn. She reached out with her other hand, gently touched Alex's face, which was coated with a fine sheen of sweat, and said, "We can break the circle now. Take me home."

After Wendy had dismissed the elements, Alex dressed quickly, then helped her get dressed and pack up her magical equipment. She leaned against him all the way back to the car. Alex offered to drive, and Wendy simply nodded acquiescence. Neither spoke of the fire until they were in the car and had turned around on Gable Road.

"I remember once when I was about ten," Alex said. "Playing with a Ouija board with my cousin Adrienne. I was skeptical about the whole thing, making jokes about it. Then that little plastic pointer thing started moving around the board, darting all by itself. Scared the hell out of me."

"Is that what this was like?" Wendy asked, smiling faintly as she tried to picture Alex as a ten-year-old.

"Worse," he said, taking his eyes off the road to look at her for a moment. "Much fucking worse."

She took his hand in hers and held it till they reached her house.

Wendy held on to Alex's upper arm as she pushed open her bedroom door. She was feeling better, but every now and then her legs went wobbly on her. "Thanks," she said, "I don't think I could have made it up our ever-so-grand staircase without your help."

"You're sure you'll be okay up here alone?" Alex asked, concerned. "When are your parents due back from their fund-raiser?"

"Not for an hour or two," Wendy said. "I'll be fine, but would you mind bringing up my magic stuff. I need that spell bottle. I'm afraid to sleep without taking that valerian potion I made."

"I'd be afraid to sleep with it," Alex said, then shrugged. "Back in a flash."

Wendy kicked off her cross-trainers, stripped off her sweater and slacks, then her underwear and socks. She put the pile of clothes in her seldom-used hamper and removed her flannel robe from its closet peg. She wrapped herself snuggly in the soft cloth and lay down on her bed with a shudder, then a sigh. *Good thing I had a witness or I might believe I am losing my mind.*

Alex tapped lightly on her door, waited till she called him in. He set the duffel bag on the floor beside her bike. All except for the spell bottle, which he put on her nightstand. "I guess that's everything," he said.

"Not everything," she said, motioning him over to the bed.

He sat beside her. "What did I forget?" he asked.

"This," she said and reached up to hold his face in her hands. She leaned up and kissed his mouth, his cheek, then whispered in his ear, "Make love to me."

He pulled back slightly. "God, don't think I didn't come prepared, you know, hope springs eternal and all that. But are you sure you're up to this?"

"Remember," she said. "Seal it with a kiss." She pulled him down into the circle of her arms, and if he was surprised at all by her strength, he didn't protest. His mouth fell to hers with a sudden passion as his hand slipped inside her robe to cup her breast. This is how she would always remember him, his sweet caresses, the way his arms trembled when he was inside her. Later, much later, she would attribute her invitation, her actions, to the henbane divination spell she had cast when they were alone in the circle together. She was sure she would have fallen into his arms eventually, but somehow, from some deep, instinctual corner of her mind came a whisper of mortality, the realization that time is so very precious after all. And never more so for Alex and her than at that moment.

After he left her—lying in a rapturous state of contentment, a feeling that maybe all the world's wrongs could be righted just for one day, one hour, one blissful moment of time when two people were so entwined with each other that *we* became a singular state of being and having—she drank the infusion of valerian. Almost as if she had consumed a fairy-tale sleeping potion, her head fell back on the pillow and the spell bottle slipped from her fingers and fell to the floor with a dull thunk. She slept...and she dreamed...

Elizabeth Wither is in jail with Sarah Hutchins and Rebecca Cole, her coven. The walls are brick with one small window set high and crossbarred. Rebecca stands on the tips of her toes and forces her forearm through a gap that is barely wide enough to accommodate it. "I hear children playing ...," she says wistfully.

The door is iron-bound oak with a single opening, a narrow slot for the passage of meals. Sunlight dapples the cell, which smells equally of old urine and fear, a stale mélange of odors.

Sarah Hutchins sits on the fresh bundle of straw that has been forked into the corner. Sarah hugs herself and rocks slightly. "So it has come to this," she says to no one in particular. "We are to be hanged tomorrow."

Rebecca looks to Wither, both hands now framing the child within her. "Elizabeth, you believe they will truly hang us?"

"All of us," Wither says. "Even you, Rebecca." But Wither's mind is awhirl with other plans. It is better that Windale put an end to this chapter in its history, better that the coven disappear and be forgotten. And that is Wither's secret, even from the two closest to her. Wither has gloried in the feast of fear and terror. But this need not be the end to them. Wither has one bit of cunning left to offer them here, now in their midnight hour. She has brought them to this place, where what she has to offer them will be their only escape. If she has chosen well, they will not resist an escape from the death and damnation that circumstances have brought them. They have been helpless victims empowered by her and would be empowered one last time, one final way. To escape death they must choose to surrender their humanity. "Would you die tomorrow for their amusement?"

"I spit on them," Rebecca says. "Even with my tongue swollen out of my mouth."

"And you, Sarah?" Wither asks. "Will that be your satisfaction?"

"You have a plan, Elizabeth?"

"I will let them hang me," Wither says mysteriously, walking over to an iron ring bolted to the wall and flipping it with her fingers. Rebecca looks in surprise at Wither, then Sarah, and back again. Wither meets her gaze. "But that will not be the end for me."

"Speak it, Elizabeth," Rebecca urges. Sarah nods slowly.

"We are sisters," Wither says. "But what I propose requires us to become true sisters of the blood ... of my blood." Wither pushes back her sleeves and shows her forearms to them, where the veins are closest to the skin, ... the black veins. When Wither clenches her fists the black veins throb. Her fingernails are as black as pitch now. "I am more than what I seem, sisters. Even now you see the transformation within me. It will make me stronger and live long beyond the day when even their memories are forgotten. But first I must sleep for long and long, safely tucked away. When I emerge all that you see around you will long be forgotten to all but the scholars and their dusty books, yet even they will not know the whole truth of it."

"You will rise from death?" Rebecca asks, awed.

"Not death," Wither says, excitedly. "But so it will appear to them, for my nature is as strange to them to be as unknown. I would need to sleep soon anyway, lest my different nature show too much upon me."

"Are you immortal, Elizabeth?" Rebecca asks.

"There are cycles even to this life, but there is something to the immortal in it, though I be not immune to death."

"You say you sleep but do not sleep, die but do not die, yet there is nothing of this for Rebecca and myself," Sarah said.

"There is if you choose it!" Wither says, taking Sarah's hands urgently in hers. "I do not bear children, that is not my way, yet each kind must spread itself as it must."

Rebecca says softly, "We may become as you."

"If you choose quickly, there is time for the change to begin in you," Wither says. "You will hang with me but will not die, though all who fear you think it so. Once the change is upon you, hanging will be as nothing to you. A gentle tug on your altered flesh and sinew, an unpleasant tightness, but no snapping of the neck."

"Then a spelled sleep placed upon us," Sarah says, ever the logical one, guessing the way of it. "We will sleep and seem to die. And they will bury our bodies. Alive and nothing but the cold earth for comfort. I would not live entombed in a much smaller prison than what these walls afford."

"Good, Sarah, you think ahead, but so, too, have I," Wither says, "I have made certain arrangements with a … gentleman in my employ. They will bury us quickly, that is their custom. Our sleep shall be short. As will be our entombment."

Rebecca steps forward. "I choose."

Sarah nods, a fateful gesture. "An easy choice when no other affords."

"Then we begin, so that my blood may acquaint itself with yours before our hour of reckoning." Wither pulls her sleeves back again and uses the hardened nail of her left index finger to slice open her skin in a line from the bend of her right elbow to her wrist. Then she repeats the procedure on her other arm.

Sarah gasps. Rebecca speaks with awe. "It is wonderful!"

Wither bleeds. But she bleeds unlike any human, her blood a swirling black that races with intent down her arms across her palms and out to her fingertips. Wither's eyes flutter up inside their sockets. Sarah realizes—even if Rebecca does not—that this is a natural process for Wither. She is not diminished by it. Rather she is aroused. Wither offers a hand, palm up, to each of them. "Drink it," she says breathlessly, "first drink, to prepare yourselves for mingling my blood with yours."

Rebecca grabs Wither's right hand and brings it to her mouth, the look of the lover in her eyes as she places her lips to the black-coated fingers. She takes them in her mouth and closes her eyes. The streams of black blood appear to hurry on their course to her mouth. Rebecca moans pleasurably, even as droplets of black blood stain her lips and run down her chin. Her legs swoon, and Wither allows it, falling on her knees beside the red-haired woman.

Sarah hesitates, staring at the fingers and seeing a final damnation . . . and a final salvation in equal balance.

Her eyes still closed, Wither says, "Quick, Sarah. It is the only way. My blood will prepare the way for your blood. Drink before the mingling of blood. Now!"

Sarah nods, takes the offered hand in each of hers, delicately at first, mesmerized by the black droplets of blood pooled there, waiting for her. As her mouth hovers close, Wither surprises her by shoving her fingers forward. A drop of the strange, black blood reaches her tongue and her inner struggle is over.

She falls to her knees, elated and trembling with exquisite exhaustion. Each of the fingers finds their way into her mouth, one after the other. The black blood races down her throat and fills her with an aching pleasure. She trembles on her knees, swaying back and forth and, though she doesn't realize it, in perfect rhythm with Wither and Rebecca.

Long moments pass, but Wither has not yet finished with them, though they lay besotted with her inhuman blood. She rouses them with gentle prodding until they kneel obediently before her *again. "Now we mingle your blood with mine," Wither says. "Bare one of your forearms to me." They do as instructed, unquestioning. "The pain will be less than you would have felt before tasting of my blood." Wither's coarse fingernails poise over their arms, one index finger over each, near the bend of their elbows. She cuts them quickly in a parallel motion.*

Both women gasp. "It stings," Rebecca says. Sarah grits her teeth. Wither bares her own forearms again. Whereas their red blood simply drips down to stain the straw, Wither's blood, which had already begun to settle and heal the self-inflicted wounds, becomes agitated again, as if sensing the presence of their blood so close. Black droplets chase around her arms, seeking . . .

Wither holds her forearms under theirs. "Clasp my arms as I clasp yours. We will become true sisters of the coven."

Rebecca and Sarah nod. Wither's black blood almost seems to leap upward, defying gravity, straining to meet theirs. Wither grabs their arms with a fearsome grip, even as they grip hers. When skin and blood contact each other, Wither hisses a single word, her eyes blazing. "Coven!"

As white-hot pain explodes within their bodies, scorching every nerve, Rebecca and Sarah scream! It is their last truly human act.

The pain was a burst of fire within Wendy, recalling the fiery tendril that had leapt out of her burner and threatened to consume her. She screamed and convulsed, writhing off the bed to escape the agony. Her head struck the end table, gashing her forehead just above her right eye. She roused slowly, propped against the unforgiving metal handles on the drawers of her end table. Naked and trembling with a new chill that seemed to seep down deep into her bones, Wendy was unaware that her pentagram had fallen to the floor.

She rolled into a fetal position, released from the dream, but still in a quasi-sleep state where reality and imagination overlapped and played tricks with her unconscious, fragmenting the details of the dream.

Memory. Flying over Windale, spiraling down among the trees. She sees him perched on the roof of the trestle bridge. She scoops him up, her clawed fingers digging into his screaming flesh. Below a pale girl-face watches in horror, mouth agape. And the memory ends.

The rush of flight again, not memory, but now. She is flying again, swooping down over the field of circles, where he is running, running in circles. Another boy. The one who interferes with her chosen. She swoops down to clutch this one, claws aching for the feel of flesh crushed beneath them. She wants to punish him, to tear him apart. He senses her, looks up, his face a pale blur of fright. He is . . .

"Alex!" Wendy's eyes snapped open, sleep instantly vanquished in a bright blossom of fear. She sat on the floor of her bedroom, shivering, arms wrapped around her bent knees, alone. It had been the worst dream yet. And she prayed it was only a dream.

She was lost without his heat beside her, maybe lost forever . . .

By the time he'd returned to his dorm room, Alex was wide awake. After the freaky fire incident in the woods, when he thought Wendy had severely burned her arm, he thought his heart would never return to its resting rate. Later, he had calmed down, but Wendy had completely surprised him by taking him into her bed. Despite a layer of physical exhaustion and the memory of sheer pleasures, his mind was bouncing around, out of control, trying to sort out everything that had happened in a few short hours. No chance sleep would come anytime soon, so he decided he might as well jog out all his kinks, give himself time to think in the familiar solitude of Marshall Field. In other words, a mental cool down.

He completed his stretching routine and curled his hands behind his neck, breathing deeply as he walked out onto the crumbling track. This was an old familiar place, he wasn't nervous here, even at night. He began his first lap at a light pace, breathing easily through his nose, not pushing himself. . . . Yet.

He also had to admit that while he found the ritual in the woods unusual in an extreme sense, it had also been incredibly sexy and . . . fun. "At least until it got really spooky."

Alex finished the first lap, reset the chronometer on his watch to zeroes, pressed the start button, and broke forward in a brisk run. Even though he could judge his pace accurately without it, the watch provided a backup when he was distracted. He quickened his pace after glancing at his watch, really wanting to work up a sweat tonight. His mind wandered to memories of intimacy with Wendy, leaving the immediacy of his physical exertion behind.

He came around the last turn of the track to complete his third lap. As he neared the home team bleachers, he felt a cold draft of air wash up from behind him, a rotten breeze. He gagged, glanced back, and nearly screamed at what he saw. A clot of night and shadow was nearly on top of him.

He stumbled, got quickly to his feet, and sprinted forward without looking back. *Never look back!* His coach's voice yelling at him in trial runs. He ran with every ounce of strength, crossing the lanes of the track toward the grass. He had just run his best ever hundred-meter dash time.

A mantra. *Don't look back. Don't look back.* But the scared, primal animal inside him was in command tonight, not the coach. He glanced back. Nothing behind him. *Where—?*

It hit him between the shoulder blades, slamming him to the ground. Rolling with the blow, he avoided its claws as they scored the ground where he had been a moment before. Back on his feet, moving quickly before it could adjust its attack.

Alex zigzagged across the grass, as if eluding a sniper's scope, then hurdled the Cyclone fence. Definitely not one of his sports. His pants ripped as he came down awkwardly. He fell to his palms just as the flying thing struck the fence with a rattling clang that bowed the Cyclone fence like one of those snag lines that catch landing jets aboard aircraft carriers. It shrieked at him, a strange, drawn-out, fear-inducing sound that made his skin crawl. Alex looked ahead at the home team bleachers. Twenty feet away. He could make it if—

—pain exploded on the side of his head as a clawed hand nearly ripped his right ear off.

Staggering, stumbling, he threw himself through the gap between the third- and fourth-row benches. The brittle concrete foundation scraped the skin off his arm from wrist to elbow. When he stood up abruptly, he struck his head on an iron support, a bright spike of yellow sparks lancing through his brain.

He listened for the flying thing, but heard only the ringing in his ears. Hunched over, he scampered deep under the bleachers until he had enough headroom to move about freely. He looked up at the horizontal slices of night sky visible between the wooden benches overhead.

Long moments passed in silence. Alex thought that it—whatever it was—might have flown away, that maybe he was safe. He rose from his hunchbacked position. The seat above his head exploded, spraying chunks of decayed wood like shrapnel at his face. In the middle of the ruptured seat, a black clawed hand shot down, grasping convulsively. And just beyond, a snarling visage filled with long yellow teeth. He dodged but felt the claws catch his nylon warm-up jacket. He pulled away, trying to wriggle out of the jacket. The cloth tore, and overbalanced, he fell to the ground.

The weight of the thing above him came down on the split bench with the force of a pile driver. Any moment the creature would come crashing through right on top of him.

Under the bleachers, Alex rolled across the concrete, avoiding the scrabbling arms. He was deathly cold, watching the flying thing's clawed arms and feet clang against the iron struts, raking furrows through the broken concrete, missing him by inches and less. The sheer bulk of the thing kept its whole body from dropping down through the rusted iron framework of the bleachers, but that barrier couldn't be trusted to remain sturdy beneath that incredible weight and ferocity.

His glimpse of the demonic face had brought with it a terrible recognition. A charcoal drawing, on sketch paper, before Wendy had folded it up and tossed it into the flames. Wendy had somehow known this thing existed, but how? She had been trying to banish this . . . "bogeyman." Obviously that spell had failed.

Suddenly the creature was gone, rising back into the starry sky, withdrawing long limbs from the ruptured bench. His scraped arm ached, and his torn ear throbbed with every rapid heartbeat. A sticky trail of blood ran down his neck. His only chance was to make a dash out from the bleachers, get into a building, somewhere, under a car, something, before the creature realized he had slipped free. But he needed a fair head start to make it anywhere close to a safe haven, if such a thing existed. Marshall Field, unfortunately, was isolated from the rest of the campus, so his only hope was some sort of diversion.

His gaze never left the slices of dark sky between the benches. That's why he noticed when a constellation of stars winked out to his left. He dropped to a crouch as the bench over him shattered. Scampering sideways, crab-fashion, he evaded the sweeping hand, flashing claws. Gone.

He looked frantically to the left and right. *Where the hell is it?*

The rusted iron framework above him had begun to creak under the stress. A fine grit of rust showered down on him, coating his sweats and stinging his eyes. Suddenly a large section of rotted timber struck his shoulder. He cried out in pain, falling even as the clawed hands burst through the debris once again.

One thick arm scooped him up like a doll, slammed his body against the broken bench seat and iron supports, trying to pull him through the splintered gap. He blanked out for a second, then regained awareness as he slipped free of the grasp.

He scrambled back, his breathing an agony. *Several broken ribs, definitely,* he thought, pressed in fear against an iron stanchion. His wrist was a mess, too, a bad sprain, already swelling. Was he still entertaining a mad dash across the Danfield campus with broken ribs?

The palm of his good hand pressed the loose concrete around the stanchion, a saucer-size piece shifted, scraped against the ground. He looked around, away from the ticket booth, and realized he had one chance to create a distraction. A large trash Dumpster sat fifteen yards beyond the bleachers.

Darkness streaked across the star-flecked sky.

He tossed the chunk of stone like a Frisbee toward the hulking Dumpster. The concrete wedge hit the side of the bin with a thundering racket, and in an instant, the thing pounced with a terrifying ferocity.

Alex scrambled to his feet, took a couple of steps, and knew it was useless. Behind him he heard the creature's ravenous destruction in the Dumpster. A momentary silence fell, which frightened him even more. When he couldn't hear it, he didn't know where it was, what it was doing. He trotted gamely toward the ticket booth. After that he would be out in the open and it was at least a quarter mile to the nearest campus building. He thought he might even be able to make it.... If he stopped gasping with every painful step. Why hadn't he borrowed Oz's car tonight of all nights?

Then the inhuman roar of the creature and the thunderous weight of it pounding across the bleachers seats, clawed feet splitting timber, the iron framework first creaking then groaning. All around Alex, reality distorted like a Dali-esque image, with the metal framework bending and twisting all around him. It felt like an earthquake and the sky was falling all at the same time. A creaking explosion as everything gave way and the ticket booth was still too far away.

He didn't even have time to look up as the tortured metal and rotted timbers came down to crush him like a giant's fist in one murderous instant, the last flash of pain so brilliant and quicksilver that it winked out in a merciful darkness.

He never heard the sirens.

✪

Paul dreamt he was a child again, cowering inside the doghouse he'd built for the family's beloved Lab. So lucid was the nightmare that close overhead he could see the plywood roof and rusted shingling nails he'd hammered in astray. Outside the doghouse, he knew (with a dream's dread certainty) something hungry was hunting him . . .

Thud!

Paul woke with a start, nearly tipping the folding chair in which he'd been dozing. He shook his head, still baffled with sleep. Karen lay sweat-sheened and feverish, the sheets kicked free and her nightgown raked up above her breasts. She gave a low moan and arched her back, as if the bed itself was burning, as if she was offering up the naked swell of her pregnant belly on some dark altar.

"Karen?" Paul asked, frightened, and heard her groan in reply. He saw a strange bruise at the base of her throat, a purpling of the skin, like a ligature mark—

Thud!

Something heavy landed on the pitched roof overhead, and in that single heartbeat's silence before the attack began, Paul knew deep in his heart that his nightmare had found him in the waking world.

"No!" Karen cried from her own fever-dream as the scrabbling overhead turned destructive. It sounded to Paul in those first furious moments like a wrecking crew attacking the roof with crowbars. He heard the stuttering pop-pop-pop-pop of roofing nails coming loose as whole sheets of shingles were torn free . . ., heard the explosive splintering of the first plywood being ripped from the frame . . .

The whole house shook beneath the attack, and a fine rain of powdered drywall sifted down like fairy dust over the bed where Karen lay writhing. In that instant Paul understood that the thing on the roof wanted Karen for itself, and would not be denied.

No time to think. No time to plan a defense . . . Paul ran to the bedroom window and threw open the screened sash. Ignoring the three-story drop, he swung his upper body outside and turned so he was sitting on the sill. He gripped the edge of the roof, the shingles gritty beneath his fingertips. He contorted himself until he managed to get his work boots on the windowsill, and then stood, hauling himself up onto the roof . . .

The full moon had brightened in its ascent until it became bone white and radiant, like a bleached skull. It cast a brilliant cold light over the rooftop landscape of chimneys and satellite dishes.

And illuminated the dark goblin at work on Karen's rooftop. It was enormous, a hunched black thing ... its spine a tortured ridge in the moonlight ... its crooked arms draped in tatters like Spanish moss.

The monster's back was to Paul as it focused entirely on its task of destruction. It tore another long sheet of shingles free and tossed it aside. Raised a claw like a cage of branches and punched through the plywood, shrieking as it worked—

Paul cast about for a weapon. Fixed on the crumbling chimney a few yards away. The mortar was rotten, the bricks leaning precariously. Project number four on his priority list of repairs before winter. He tugged two bricks free of the crumbling stack and had the fleeting thought *Don't be an idiot! You can't fight it up here. . . . This is its domain . . .*

He pushed the fear away and embraced the cold fury that shot through him like a current of mercury. He hurled the first brick—

It struck the goblin between its broad shoulders, and when the monster turned in outrage the second brick hit it full in the face. It shrieked in agony as the sun-rotten brick shattered, driving fragments of splintered brick into its eye.

Paul staggered back a step on the pitched roof as the goblin swelled in rage, its hunched back broadening around it like a cape. It fixed him with a look of pure hate, and though he'd never before seen a face so horrible he recognized it nonetheless as human . . .

Then it came at him.

✪

At 2 A.M., long after visiting hours had concluded for the night, Abby's father came staggering onto the Pediatric Intensive Care Unit. He'd been out drinking at the Tap Room all evening and reeked now of cigarettes and cheap beer. He was a self-pitying drunk, a barroom Job, and tonight as his drinking mates stood him one sympathy round after another he'd become increasingly maudlin, lamenting his shitty life . . . an even shittier ex-wife . . . and most of all the shitty twist of fate that had landed his little girl in the hospital . . .

His circuitous homeward journey behind the wheel of his Camaro took him through Windale's rolling hinterlands, and when he looked up suddenly and found himself outside Windale General he decided then and there that he had every right—as a parent, as a victim—to visit Abby.

He'd slipped easily past the groggy security guard in the lobby and rode the elevator up to the quiet PICU. For once, luck was on his side, and the night RNs on duty were occupied elsewhere as he passed their abandoned station.

He entered Abby's little alcove and sat by her bedside, listening to the quiet beep-beep-beep of her heart monitor. She was resting curled up on her side, sucking the two long fingers of her right hand while her left played absently with her blond hair. He didn't understand why she still wore the metal halo, didn't understand why they'd said at first she'd never walk again but had now changed their minds. Doctors. He knew only that he disliked them. Especially that smart-ass with the fucked-up foreign name who looked at him as if he had no fair claim to fatherhood.

Abby wasn't sleeping, but neither did she seem entirely awake, and lay staring past him at the wall. "Hey, baby," he said quietly. Nothing. She still wasn't talking; and he felt no urgency to encourage her. He felt nervous with her here, among strangers. Vulnerable. Both of them.

He reached out to touch one of her bare legs where she'd kicked free the blankets. He could feel his daughter's pulse at the knee, tiny and lost.

Her eyes flicked to him then, as if noticing for the first time he was there. "Hey, sugar," he said, giving her a smile that he hoped bound them, father and daughter, in secret covenant. He leaned across the space separating them to give her a kiss on the brow, and noticed the deep discoloration at her throat, as if she'd been caught in a garrote. At the same time he caught a whiff of something unpleasant exuding from her skin—

Her hand shot out and clamped around his Adam's apple. Her nostrils flared, and he thought he saw her smiling as he dropped to his knees at the bedside,.... trying to free himself from her crushing grip on his throat...

The little girl sat up, eyes rolled back in her head. With her free hand she wrenched the halo free, tugging until the cranial screws came loose. Thin rivulets of blood trickled down from her hairline. She swung her legs out of bed.

She released her father and he pitched forward, choking and retching on the floor. From his vantage he saw his daughter's bare feet on the tiles, and looking up he saw her move as if in a trance away from the bed. She didn't seem to notice the IVs she was trailing until the tubes grew taught; then she turned and with a single savage jerk yanked the needles free of her veins.

He lay curled up now, holding his bruised throat, looking up at his daughter. She froze suddenly where she stood, alert like a doe to some unseen danger. She cocked her head and listened, tracking the sound across the ceiling tiles. She made a weird warbling sound, a coo, and then she urinated, the stream soaking her hospital gown and pooling at her bare feet.

He cowered beneath the hospital bed and watched as the little girl who had been his daughter followed the sound she alone heard out of the room.

In the dream that wasn't a dream, Abby was walking again, the tiles chilly beneath her feet as she moved through the silent PICU corridors. She felt drawn forward by an invisible tether, like the irresistible sound of music playing in a distant room. Her eyes were closed now, she no longer needed them to follow the call that drew her through night-silent corridors. Her feet turned to a whisper as tiles became carpet. She trailed the long fingers of her right hand (her *becoming* fingers) along the wall like a blind girl, and with the confidence of the blind knew her touch would not betray her but would lead her safely through this unlit terrain . . .

Here. She opened her eyes and found herself in another short corridor, before a set of pine doors. The doors opened for her, and she seemed to glide forward weightlessly.

The chapel was empty, its darkness heavy with the smell of extinguished candles. The doors shushed closed behind her, sighing on their tired hinges. As she floated deeper into the waiting darkness she dropped her hands, fingertips gliding over the smooth ranks of pews to either side. Above the simple altar rose the chapel's sole adornment, a great abstract mosaic of stained glass through which the full moon shown.

Abby hung suspended before the altar, dappled in the kaleidoscope of filtered moonlight. She could hear the call of the moon beyond the glass, a single deeply resonant note, like the sound a mountain might make . . .

So intently was she focused on the moon's song that she didn't hear the chapel doors fly open behind her . . .

Didn't hear her father calling her name . . .

Or the sudden explosion of stained glass, as the angel came to take her.

✶

Flight. A dizzying somersault of light, stars, and streetlamps trading places as Paul was hauled aloft from the rooftop and carried screaming into the sky. His eyes and ears were filled with the icy rush of wind. His heart staggered midbeat on the exhilaration of flight, as for a fleeting instant he had a view of all of Windale spread out below him in its night colors, a horizon so vast he thought he could almost see the earth's curve.

Then they plummeted together, Paul and this nightmare that had seized him, rushing earthward . . .

He clamped his eyes shut against the stinging wind as they fell together, the creature's shriek keening like a hellbound missile. And then he was dropped—

He fell, tumbling, while the nightmare that had released him corkscrewed with a shrieking hiss up and up and up like a mad balloon—

Paul's death-descent lasted only a fraction of a second. He landed hard on metal, bounced once, again, rolled.

He was still alive. Bruised, not broken. He flipped over quickly, onto his stomach. Saw pale painted metal beneath him. A horizon of steel, glowing in the moonlight. His fingers found a welded seam. He pressed his cheek to the cool surface beneath him and waited for his heart to steady. *Where the hell am I?* The wind moaned in his ears. Wherever he was, he knew he was high above the world.

Calmer now. He raised a hand and brought the heel of his palm down on the surface below him. Heard the great echoing gong of hollowed metal. And then he understood where he'd been dropped . . .

On top of a water tower.

Time to think about climbing down from here. He slid forward across the painted dome on his belly, searching for a ladder. The wind came at him again, rising in pitch from a tremulous whistle to this keening shriek that wanted so badly to blow him off the tower. He shut his eyes against the stinging wind until it had subsided again. When he opened his eyes there were tiny beads of moisture clinging to them, and his vision had sharpened. He began crawling on all fours, the metal painful against his knees. He crawled carefully, fighting that primitive part of him that wanted only to hold on for dear life.

When he reached the curving edge of the dome he dropped back down again, flattening himself to offer the least amount of surface area to the wind, then inched forward on his belly. His mind was beginning to play tricks on him, convincing him of sudden unpredictable shifts in the metal surface so that he'd cry out and clutch the seams to keep from sliding. He braced himself against the vertigo, and peered over. He saw a strip of railing a few yards down, and a catwalk. If he could find the utility ladder that lead from the top of the dome to that catwalk, his chances of survival would suddenly leap into the double digits.

He shimmied around the perimeter of the dome on his belly until he found the utility ladder. It curved up one side of the dome and flattened out like train tracks near the top. He hoisted himself up onto the horizontal ladder, the metal rungs thin and sharp as dowels. He began climbing backward rung by rung; once the ladder had returned to the vertical it wasn't so difficult anymore. Except for the paralyzing numbness in his rubbery arms. And the ever-present shriek of the wind . . .

Don't look down . . . don't look down . . . Rooftops didn't bother him, but this was something else entirely. The dizzying vista hovered at the periphery of his vision, tempting him to look. He kept his eyes fixed forward at his hands upon the ladder, the spray-painted graffiti on the water tower's metal flank. JOE + STACEY it read in yard-tall letters.

His legs were shaking. The wind buffeted him, whipping and snapping his clothes like sails in a squall. His fingers were turning numb on the wind-chilled metal. He concentrated on his grip.

Steady now, you're almost there . . .

Something shifted in the corner of his vision. He turned in reflex and saw it, the goblin-thing, scrabbling around the side of the water tank with spidery grace. Coming back for him.

He let out a yell and lost his grip on the ladder. His foot slipped through the rung and wedged. The world inverted as he swung upside down, the back of his head slamming hard against the water tank. He saw the catwalk beneath him, scattered with trash—beer bottles, a discarded sneaker, cans of spray paint.

He heard the insane cackle of the goblin as it came at him. He crunched upward, contracting his hip and abdominal muscles to raise his torso high enough so that he could try to free his trapped ankle.

He pulled his leg up and out, and dropped suddenly, slamming down onto the catwalk with a huge metal clang. The short fall was violent enough to knock the wind out of him, and in the choking silence where his breath had been he felt the shuddering thunk of a great weight landing on the catwalk beside him. He turned, scrambling away from the thing that was approaching, its head cocked sideways in a horrible parody of human curiosity. As the nightmare advanced on him he realized—without understanding exactly how he knew—that it was female.

He scrambled backward, his hands knocking abandoned beer bottles across the catwalk. He smelled the sour dregs of stale beer, heard the bottles rolling clear of the catwalk and dropping through the darkness. He kept going until he bumped into an iron railing and could go no farther. His fumbling hands found spray paint cans the vandals had used to decorate the tower. He heard the hollow clank as the cans rolled across the catwalk, heard the distinctive rattle of the steel mixing marble inside—

Contents under pressure...

A chunk of memory fell on him from above, a childhood's reckless game with aerosol cans...

Paul fumbled in his shirt pocket and found his Zippo. The creature took another step. With numb fingers Paul flipped open the lighter.

The creature took a step forward and brought its face in close to Paul's. Its eye gleamed black as polished stone as it blasted him with a gust of rotten breath.

Paul lifted the paint can to its face and flicked the lighter.

The fire erupted in a startling cone of brilliant yellow, a scorching blast that engulfed the leering face.

The creature gave a furious shriek and reared back, blazing.

Burn, you son of a bitch! Paul held the funnel of fire out before him as he climbed to his feet. The burning creature howled in her agony...

And thrashed out, suddenly, one black claw striking Paul hard, tipping him back over the catwalk's railing...

I'm dead, Paul thought as he fell. No time to think of Karen, or the baby he would never know, his daughter... only the dizzy cartwheeling sensation of falling toward a darkness that was eternal.

✪

Art sped through the dark streets of Windale, pedaling furiously to outdistance the sirens that were just beginning to awake. He leapt the curb on Lore Avenue and dismounted smoothly, letting the ten-speed glide to a harmless collision with the forsythias. He dashed up the front steps to Karen's porch, fumbling out the spare house key she'd given him. Inside, he hid beside the front door, peeking out through the curtains, watching for the strobing lights of police cruisers. The sirens grew distant, and he knew for the moment he was safe.

Thump! His eyes shot to the stairwell at the heavy sound from above—as if someone had fallen out of bed. He hurried upstairs—

And found Karen, writhing in her sodden bedsheets, alone.

Where the ceiling once had been, there was now a ragged hole.

He rushed to her, tugging down her nightgown. She groaned and clutched at him, surfacing from her agony long enough to whisper, "Paul . . . it got Paul . . ."

The sheets were clammy and soaking, and when he looked he saw blood. At first he'd thought she was hurt, then realized that her water had broken, that the blood that soaked the bedsheets had been diluted by the rush of amniotic fluid.

It was beginning . . .

"C'mon, sweetheart," he said, sliding his hands beneath her. "Put your arms around my neck." He struggled to lift her, and staggered toward the bedroom door.

She was unconscious by the time he got her to the garage and lay her out across the backseat. He gunned the Volvo's engine and backed out of the garage with a squeal of tires.

Karen moaned from the backseat as they barreled down Lore and onto Main, headed toward Windale General. "Baby . . . the baby . . . ," she kept muttering, her eyelids fluttering. When Art turned to check on her he saw fresh blood on the seat beneath her, and a dark spreading stain across the lower half of her nightgown. She was losing the baby, and quite possibly hemorrhaging.

. . .

Ten minutes later he pulled to a screeching halt outside Windale General's Emergency Room. The automatic doors whispered open as he staggered inside with Karen in his arms. The triage nurse and two tired-looking MDs ran to meet him. He relinquished Karen to their care, backing away helplessly as the trauma staff went to work on her. When he looked down he saw blood on his shirt. At the sight of it he knew suddenly that he shouldn't linger here, that he would be recognized . . .

Simultaneously with that thought, a voice called, "Sir?" Art turned, saw a security guard approaching beside another triage nurse. Art began backing away. "Wait a second, sir—" the nurse said, closing the distance between them as the guard's hand went to his walkie-talkie.

Art turned, sprinting out through the automatic doors.

BOOK THREE

"WOMEN ALONE"
Halloween Night

Transcript of live-feed interview, WPVI, Channel 5 Action News

Reporter: This is Jade Welles reporting live from the steps of Windale's city hall, where final preparations began early this morning and will continue throughout the day for tonight's King Frost Parade. I'm joined right now by Windale's mayor, Alfonse Dell'Olio—Mayor, you expect quite a few spectators to your town this evening, don't you?

Mayor: That's right, Jade. Each year over twenty thousand folks from throughout the county come out for the parade. It's a tradition we've kept going for over sixty years—in fact, I remember marching in the parade when I was just this high!

Reporter: Well WPVI's weatherman is calling for clear skies through the weekend, so it looks like you'll have a beautiful night for it.

Mayor: Absolutely! Tonight we welcome in Old Man Winter. Or, as he's known locally, King Frost. So I invite everyone young and old to come out in costume tonight and enjoy the last outdoor blast for the season.

Reporter: Mayor, there are some who are criticizing your decision to hold the parade in light of recent alarming events in Windale—the disappearance of several Danfield College students and other residents, as well as one unsolved homicide. Do you care to comment?

Mayor: Those are isolated incidents of an unfortunate nature, and are still under investigation. But I will say that Windale always has been—and will continue to be—a safe place for children, parents, families, everyone—except witches, of course!

[He removes a tall black witch's cap from offscreen and puts it on the reporter's head.]

Reporter: Ah! So what d'you think my chances are of winning best costume?

Mayor: I don't know, Jade—there's gonna be tough competition in your age group! Maybe if we enter you under the category of Prettiest NewsWitch . . .

Reporter: Well! There you have it, folks. Down here spending a few hours with the ghouls and ghosts of Windale, this is Jade Welles, reporting live for Action News.

CHAPTER
NINE

The pregnant woman, Karen Glazer, thirty-eight-year-old white female just entering her third trimester, spent the predawn hours of Halloween morning in the Emergency Room, being poked and prodded and generally frowned over by the exhausted house staff. They replaced the blood she'd lost, noted that she was two centimeters dilated, monitored the baby's fetal heartbeat (still strong), and paged her OB/GYN. Throughout the ordeal the patient floated in and out of consciousness, mumbling with only occasional coherence about someone named "Paul" (her husband, it was presumed) who had disappeared, about monsters trying to steal her baby, and about a "hole in the roof."

The trauma staff pulled a blood sample for a toxicology screen, and while it was processed by the lab took bets among themselves on what cocktail of narcotics she'd ingested. They examined the deep ligature marks on the patient's neck and concocted their own cynical backstory of domestic violence and addiction.

When the tox screen came back clean, the chief resident on duty scowled. "Impossible," he said with authority and turned to the nearest RN. "Pull another two vials. Fucking lab techs must be smoking their Halloween crack." Then he promptly forgot about the pregnant head-case in Trauma Room A as he looked up at the sound of the automatic doors shushing open for his next customer: a townie cop, bleeding from a scalp lac that looked like it wanted stitches.

"What the hell happened to you, officer?" the resident asked.

The sheriff shot him a warning look and said simply, "Gallows."

Wendy sat huddled in the wicker chair by her bedroom window. She had slept fitfully through the night, for once more afraid of the dawn than of dreaming. She pulled her flannel robe tight, hugged herself, but could not banish the unnatural chill she felt. A *cup of hot chocolate might have done the trick,* she thought as she watched the sun climb over the trees. But she was imprisoned by the notion that if she left her room, even for a moment, the spell would be broken. Dream would become reality. And she could not bear that.

Soon enough, she heard a quick rapping on her door.

"Come in," she said, her voice quiet with resignation.

Her father opened the door and walked over to her, his expression grim. "Wendy," he said. "There's been an accident at Marshall Field."

She looked up at him, her lips pressed together to quell their trembling. Her voice would betray her if she spoke. Her father's concerned face blurred before her as tears welled in her eyes. She wiped them quickly, pretended it was only sleep there. Only divination or uncanny premonition could account for what she knew, had known since late the previous evening.

"Come downstairs," he said. "It's on the television."

She nodded, stood up, and suddenly wrapped her arms around him. "Love you, Dad," she said, her voice a strangled whisper. He patted her back, stroked her hair, his own voice lost. "It's about

Alex," she said, her voice firm now, but still only a contained whisper, enough to dam the flood of emotion that threatened to overwhelm her. "Isn't it?"

"I'm afraid so. It looks bad."

Elizabeth Wither stares defiantly at the hardened faces of the people gathered in the commons. She stands on a wobbly platform, Sarah and Rebecca on either side of her, too far away to touch even if her hands were not bound. A noose around their necks connects each of them to the rough-hewn timber above. The knot bites into Wither's flesh. The executioner moves down the line and kicks the platform out from under each of them. Wither feels the sharp pull of gravity until her body jerks at the end of the suddenly taut rope.

The crowd gasps. Wither can not breathe.

Her eyes roll back into her head and she lets the darkness consume her . . .

The sensation of falling caused Wendy to stagger into her father, who caught her elbows. She nodded at him that she was okay. But the long walk down to the family room was a blur forever lost to memory. Her legs were numb, her arms superfluous as she allowed her father to guide her all the way. She chewed her lower lip to hold back a wail that seemed to swirl inside her heart, battering her body like a ship on a storm-tossed sea, seeking escape. Her mother stood in the family room with her hands pressed to her mouth, her eyes wide, brimming with tears when she saw Wendy enter the room. Wendy choked back a sob, her mother's reaction releasing a force within her.

On the big-screen television, an on-the-scene reporter stood almost life-size near the fence at Marshall Field. In the background, Wendy saw the twisted, mangled wreck of the home team bleachers. ". . . as a freak accident. It is unknown at this time why the Danfield freshman was under the bleachers when they collapsed, although friends say he was in the habit of running on the abandoned track here. This is Michelle Lundquist, reporting live for WTKN, News Nine."

The station cut to the news anchor. "Thank you, Michelle," he said, turning away from his offscreen monitor to face the live camera. "Again, this was the scene last night after police received calls from a student in a nearby dorm who described what sounded like a series of explosions."

Video footage replaced the anchorman. Marshall Field again, cloaked in night, the two security lights at either end of the field barely enough to illuminate the field. In the foreground, a police cruiser with flashing red lights and an ambulance, also flashing lights as attendants hurried a collapsible stretcher into the back. Wendy caught a fleeting glimpse of a bloodied face a moment before the EMTs slammed the ambulance doors shut. The ambulance drove off, sirens screaming.

Cut back to the anchorman. "Police are attributing the collapse of the bleachers to extreme metal fatigue, but there was clear evidence of vandalism to many of the benches. If other students were involved, their identities are not known at this time. Police are looking into the possibility of a fraternity prank gone awry."

"Again, the Danfield freshman suffered broken bones, internal injuries, and some head trauma. Police have notified the family of the student, who has been identified as Alexander Dunkirk of Minneapolis. He was admitted to Windale General and remains in critical condition."

Wendy crumpled at the mention of his name, sobbing. *But he was still alive! She had been so sure he was dead.* Her father supported her with one arm around her waist and led her to the sofa. She covered her mouth, but made no effort to stop the silent tears streaming down her cheeks, and she choked.

Her mother took her other hand, pressed it within hers. "Wendy, dear, I know this is hard . . . but we need to ask you something."

Wendy nodded.

Her mother looked to her father for help. He cleared his throat, "The press called," he said. "They want an official statement from me."

Again, Wendy simply nodded.

"Honey," her mother said, "I left you with Alex last night . . ."

Do you know anything about what happened to him? That was the question Wendy prayed her mother would not ask. How could she ever answer that? "We went out for a while," Wendy said, finally wiping tears from her cheeks.

"To Marshall Field?" her father asked.

She shook her head vigorously. "No," she said. "We went for a drive . . . we came back here, but he left around eleven. Said he was going back to his dorm."

Her father sat down beside her, stroked her hair again. "We'll take you to see him later. I don't want you driving just yet."

Wendy buried her face in her mother's blouse and let herself cry. She hadn't realized just how much Alex meant to her. How could she tell them that she felt responsible for his "accident"? She was overcome with waves of guilt and relief in equal measure. *You'll be fine*, she had told him. And now this. *But thank God you're alive!*

She visited his bedside for only a few moments, which was all his doctor would allow and was almost more than she could bear. They had stopped the internal bleeding, bandaged his head, and put casts on both legs and his left arm. He was hooked up to an IV and had an oxygen tube up his nose. His face was a frightful study in contusions and abrasions. He was so pale from loss of blood, but his condition had been downgraded to serious.

He still had not regained consciousness.

Before she left his side, she squeezed his right hand, whispered fiercely, "I'm so sorry, Alex." She kissed him lightly on the cheek. Then she placed the cloth-wrapped mandrake root under his pillow. Maybe the nurses, seeing it could do no harm, would actually leave it there.

After Wendy returned home from the hospital with her parents, she was still so distraught her mother gave her one of her machine-manufactured sedatives—which Wendy swallowed without a single protest—and it took the harsh edges off of jagged reality. Exhausted and sedated, she fell asleep on the sofa. Before her father spoke with the press he carried her up to her bedroom, placed her gently on her bed, then stood back as her mother placed a comforter over her. As he stood looking at his daughter's tear-reddened face, Larry Ward couldn't help but notice all the strands of gray hair around her temples.

✮

"Karen?" a voice asked quietly, and she opened her eyes to see Maria Labajo looking down on her. It was late morning, and Karen was resting with eyes closed in the private room on the maternity ward to which she'd been relocated as she waited out the irregular Braxton-Hicks contractions of early labor.

The overworked ER trauma staff had been unable to reach Maria throughout the morning and had finally tracked her down to the Copley Square Mariott in Boston, where the obstetrician had been attending a medical conference on alternatives to hysterectomy.

Maria checked Karen's pulse now at the wrist, then held her patient's hand in her own.

"Honey, I'm so sorry about Paul," Maria said. The sight of tears spilling down Karen's cheeks brought tears to Maria's own eyes, and for the moment she put aside the clinical stoicism she typically held as a protective shield against her patients' sorrow. "They told me they'd informed you how he was found—"

"Yes," Karen said miserably. When she'd been told an hour earlier, the news had come as neither a surprise nor a shock, but only a confirmation of what she'd dreaded. She'd known he was dead the moment he went out the bedroom window; only the circumstances of his death were new. He'd died defending her, defending their baby, and for that she would love him always, and fiercely. Already, though, she felt the merciless erosion of memory, that self-protective healing instinct that begins to blur the face of our beloved the instant they slip from us. She couldn't bear it. And so she turned her attention willfully away from its own dissolution and asked Maria, "Is the baby coming...?"

Maria looked at her with concern. "Slowly. You're dilating at less than a quarter centimeter per hour, and the baby's hardly descended at all. At this rate you'll remain in prolonged latency for another twelve hours."

A male RN arrived with an IV bag of medication. "I'll take that," Maria told him, and connected the bag to an intravenous infusion pump. She connected it to the IV line already dripping hydrating fluids into Karen's arm.

"This is synthetic oxytocin—to speed up the labor," Maria said. "The contractions may be a little more painful, so let me know if you're hurting too much and we'll see about getting you some meperidine. The important thing now is to get you through this as quickly as possible, and without a C-section, if it can be avoided."

"What about the baby?" Karen asked. "Is her heartbeat still strong? Will she survive the birth?"

Maria heard the hope in her patient's voice, and knew in this rare case she should caution against it. "Maybe. But you need to prepare yourself that she probably won't survive the night. Frankly, I'm amazed the baby has survived this long. Whatever genetic defect is at work here has kicked her gestational rate into high gear. She's already the size of a healthy thirty-seven-week-old..."

"Healthy?" Karen said, clinging to hope. Maria took her hand and gave it a squeeze, looked at her patient sadly.

"I'm sorry, Karen."

Art learned about his brother's death on the noon news. He was holed up in the old vinyl archives of the WDAN campus radio station, where he'd come on foot last night after ditching Karen's Volvo.

He received the news in stunned silence on a little black-and-white portable TV he'd found among the junk of the back room. From its staticky screen he also learned that his own fugitive status had reached critical mass during the night, following his assault on Windale's sheriff, his suspected abduction of eight-year-old Abby MacNeil, and brutal murder of her father in the hospital chapel. Though not armed, the news anchor warned, Art Leeson should be considered "very dangerous."

Art didn't feel very dangerous. All he felt was miserable, squatting in a corner of a windowless back room that smelled of deteriorating cardboard and rotten carpet padding.

He wept loudly for his brother, confident he was buried deep enough in the cinder block bunker that he wouldn't be discovered by the daytime student DJs. Half of WDAN's back rooms were virtually inaccessible, the doors barricaded with collapsed metal shelves of archaic equipment and old record promos. Art cowered in the most remote one, wishing he could somehow stay here eternally and join the other obsolete junk—the eight-tracks and unspooling reel-to-reels—moldering quietly in darkness.

He tried to distract himself from his sorrow with questions: What had Paul been doing on a water tower? What had happened to the roof of Karen's house? Where was Abby? And what *was* this goddamned curse that had chosen Art and anyone with whom he came in contact for its victims?

He drew his knees up beneath his chin and huddled in darkness through the long afternoon, with only questions for company.

⊕

In anticipation of the parade, most downtown employers released their office workers at three-thirty that afternoon. Sidewalk cafés and lunch counters closed early (most would convert to food concessions later, serving everything from fried dough to lobster rolls), while the boutiques along Main Street and College Avenue moved their prettiest wares into storefront displays, tricked out in autumnal splendor. Though there would be no sales this evening (by official decree), most retailers took consolation in the fact that King Frost—by enticing twenty thousand out-of-towners to Windale's sidewalks—offered the year's biggest night of free advertising.

By four, deputies Jeff Schaeffer and Reed Davis began rerouting traffic around the central business district, while volunteers from Windale's lone engine and ladder company set up barricades and hand-painted signs in the four large municipal lots designated for festival parking. Parking alone was expected to generate in excess of fifty thousand dollars in revenue.

Meanwhile, at the pavilion outside the Danfield College gates (which also fronted the square), students from the school's Sound Technology department were laying cable and tweaking audio levels in preparation for a five-o'clock sound-check. After heated competition, seven local bands had been awarded the coveted thirty-minute sets scheduled throughout the evening. Showcasing a representative section of musical tastes, the evening lineup included such perennials of the Essex tavern circuit as George "Fatback" Johnson (Chicago blues), Tyrannosaurus Sex (ska), Margo Rita (Jimmy Buffett covers), D.K. (goth), Tackhammer (indie), Grym Reaper (metal), and the bizarre acoustic quartet Bob & Ted & Carol & Malice (folk).

Five on the dot. The bass-heavy power chords of sound-check carried on the clear night ... and could be heard as far away as the outlying residential neighborhoods of Windale, where the first trick-or-treaters were emerging. The bass gave the night an ominous pulse, an anticipatory heartbeat. In the neighborhoods, parents accompanying their little flame-retardant ghouls and drugstore goblins (not to mention Spice Girls) looked up at the sound of distant rumbling. Could that be thunder? But no—one look at the twilit sky dispelled that question.

It was that moment of an autumn sunset when lawns glow blue-green and the air turns the color of gasoline. The sky was untroubled except for the bellwether clouds that reached high smoky fingers from the west.

The air was hushed. King Frost was coming...

At that very instant downtown, strings of white festival lights and decorative orange paper lanterns twinkled on, as Mayor Alfonse Dell'Olio threw a ceremonial switch. Behind him, arranged on the steps of city hall, the Harrison High School Marching Band began playing.

The Sixty-Fifth Annual King Frost Halloween Parade had begun. Halloween was here.

✪

Matthias had more foul work to do even though the Eve had arrived, cleaning up after the witches, burying the scraps of flesh and bone they discarded, burning the clothes and any personal effects left over after their feeding. He'd have to go into the barn to remove the latest steaming carcass or two before the stench of rot became too powerful. One time he'd had to tie a rag dipped in kerosene around his face to combat the putrid odor of a long-gone corpse. He still remembered the time, years before that, when he'd gone in without any special preparation and heaved up his morning meal to the cackling amusement of the witches. This time, however, he wouldn't mind venturing into the barn, for the need was upon him again, as it came every month when the moon was heavy and bloated in the sky. It sickened him, his craving, but there was naught to do for it. By the time the moon was full, he'd walk through a sea of bloated corpses to have his need attended to by Wither or one of the others. As loathsome as the craving was, to deny it was a thousand times worse.

One time, sixty years ago and more, when the witches were lethargic and barely noticed him, he had tried to stay away, to wait through the cycle of the moon, to free himself from their hold. Wasn't long before he couldn't keep down solid food and not much longer after that when a mere glass of water triggered retching spells so violent he would black out from the coughing. He had crawled, squirmed almost, all the long way to the barn and had almost died with the effort of getting the doors open just wide enough for him to squeeze through. They made him come to them, that much he understood. If he died, they'd find another keeper. That cold winter day, his belly dragging in the dirt, he had discovered once and for all who was master and who was slave. Not that there had ever been any real doubt. When Matthias crawled within reach of her arms, Wither had offered him succor as always. But he had sensed her amusement to see him laid so low, weak as a runt-of-the-litter kitten, silent tears streaming down his leathery cheeks as he begged for the one thing only the witches could give him. That had been the last time he tried to break free of his servitude.

Freedom, he knew, would only come in death, and death for him, as it had been for his father, Warren, and for his grandfather, Ezekiel before him, would be a long time coming. Of course, he could always end his extended life prematurely, take his father's way out, with a bullet through the roof of his mouth. But Matthias had never had the conviction of spirit to put an end to his part in the witches' centuries-long legacy of evil. It was a small but essential part he played, and once a month he would be reminded of what they could give him for his service. Once a month made all the other days bearable.

He carried his old bloodstained shovel into the barn with him. Sometimes they would make him work first, other times he could sidle right up to them and have done with it. Usually they were contrary, so bringing the shovel, appearing ready for his gory chores, was his casual bit of insurance that they wouldn't taunt him first. It also wouldn't do to have the need so full upon him that he walked hunched over with the consuming ache of it. If they saw him on the edge of suffering, they'd take great pleasure in drawing it out, make him wait until the pain was truly exquisite and he was ready to drop to his knees and whimper for release.

This time he chose his time well. Near dusk was—he knew from long years of experience—the safest time to disturb them. With the approach of dusk, they began to stir from their daylight sleep so were less likely to lash out at sudden movements and sounds. And it would still be too early for them to be full of their cunning spitefulness and dangerous rages. He could expect to find them as docile and amenable as they ever were. Especially now that their Eve had arrived. They would be most powerful and destructive now, leading up to midnight. Tomorrow would involve a hellish cleanup if his long years of experience were worth a damn.

Sarah and Rebecca sat hunched in the deepest shadows, the farthest corners, deferring the vanguard position to Wither. They appeared as large, textured lumps to him, their occasional languid movements almost eel-like, serpentine as they unfolded their limbs in welcome to the night. Matthias stopped about six feet from the folded bulk of Wither, standing within reach of her long arms, as she demanded, but distant enough to be respectful. Even squatting she was almost as tall as he was. Her eyes were open, mere yellow slits but completely aware of him, he was sure, despite her apparent lethargy.

"The need is upon me," he said without preamble.

Wither stirred, her arms unfolding, reaching out toward him. So there would be no games this day. No taunting. He laid the shovel carefully at his feet and stepped forward, afraid to say anything that might change her relatively good mood.

She pricked the tips of her index and middle fingers with a curved thumbnail, releasing a trickle of dark blood. After nearly a century and a half, Matthias could smell it on the air, and the scent unhinged his arthritic knees. He fell before her, pulling the fingers into his mouth, sucking on the strange blood that coursed through the witch's veins. It satisfied a hundred needs within him, and hinted at a hundred more, secret pleasures forever out of reach but endlessly tantalizing.

Soon came the realization he was no longer with Wither. From where he lay, on a stale pile of straw clotted with fresh clumps of shit, he guessed she had tossed him bodily across the barn. He had been too lost in the rush of pleasure to notice the passage of time, the pain of his twisted arm, or the sickly sweet smell of her feces.

He rolled over, climbed to his hands and knees and retrieved his shovel. Wither had leapt up into the loft and completely ignored him now. Just as well, since he had work to do. He brought the wheelbarrow he kept by the door over to the remains of the first corpse and shoveled the one-eyed head in first. Generally they ate the internal organs and most of the thighs. The rest they left scattered around the barn for Matthias to find in what amounted to a grotesque parody of a scavenger hunt.

His wheelbarrow was soon overflowing with the remains of three different corpses, one of them female, wearing the tattered remains of a Danfield College T-shirt, which he would burn later.

⊛

Wendy dreams she is alone in the dark, on the verge of sleep or just arising from a deep sleep. Without moving, she can tell she is in a confined place. The air is stale and earthly. Her eyes are staring, wide, but there is nothing to see.

She reaches out with her hands, feels wood at her sides and wood above her, inches from her face. Her legs move and strike wood as well. She is confined within a wooden box ... not a box.

A coffin!

She has been buried alive. Wendy wants to scream but Wither will not allow it. Wither remembers. This is where she is supposed to be. Listen!

And she does. Her ears are hypersensitive, to her breathing, ... to her heartbeat, frighteningly sluggish ... to the steady chuff coming to her from above.

She has been waiting for just such a sound. The chuff chuff from above just as she expects. Wendy bites down on Wither's lip, fighting the urge to moan. Soon, Wither seems to promise her. Very soon now.

The chuff becomes a thud as the shovel strikes the lid of the coffin. In minutes the thuds become more urgent. The coffin lid vibrates and dust sifts down on her face. She blinks her eyes to free them from dust. Then she hears a squeak as the coffin lid lifts slightly, then it bangs shut again, slipping free of the numb fingers that pull against it. The momentary blast of fresh air revives Wither slightly. She breathes deeply of it.

The lid raises again, more carefully this time, and she sees a sliver of moon, a sprinkling of stars, then the sweaty face of Ezekiel Stone looking down at her, fear expanding the whites of his eyes. The shovel falls from his hand. It is one thing to be told to dig up a coffin. Quite another to actually find a live body waiting for you under the ground.

"You live!" Ezekiel Stone says.

"Of course, I live, Ezekiel," Wither says, "you would do well to remember that I do not die easily."

"I live only to serve."

"Then help me out of here and dig up the others quickly," she says. "They are bound to be more excitable than I at having been entombed."

Wither stands there as Ezekiel digs up the graves that have been placed on either side of hers. As she imagined, she can gradually hear each of the other women—first Sarah, then Rebecca—moaning softly under their cold blankets of wood and dirt.

As Wither waits for her blood sisters to be disinterred she makes plans for their future together. First they will need a place to sleep their long sleep, close to Ezekiel and his property. He and his descendents will keep them safe while the coven fall into their century-long stupor. And each time they arise to feed, she and her sisters will be further along the course away from human form. Sarah will be a perfect coven sister, strong enough, Wither hopes, to weather the changes in their life cycle. Others in the past have not always fared well, and Wither has had to put them down. No, Sarah will be fine. But what of Rebecca? Only time will tell. The child she conceived while human will remain inside her, maybe reclaimed into her flesh. Its life ended in the jail cell when they joined blood, became coven. Will Rebecca be able to forget the child she will never bear? Will her mind, precariously balanced as it is, stand the test of centuries? Only time will tell. Right now she just waits impatiently to greet her sisters, her coven. Their cycle has begun.

At seven-thirty, Art emerged from his hiding place in the vinyl archives, starving and stiff, and went foraging. He was alone in the radio station; WDAN was broadcasting prerecorded programming all evening, since it was always impossible to find student DJs willing to take a Halloween shift. As Art went in search of the stale granola bars he recalled he'd kept stashed in his office, he heard Frankie Lenard's prerecorded "Sisters in Song" playing.

No granola bars. He wandered down to Studio A, where he hit pay dirt: a half-eaten bag of nacho chips, and a fully loaded Pez dispenser. He said a silent prayer of thanks to the DJ who had ignored the station's "no food and drink" policy.

He plopped down heavily in the studio chair and wondered where Abby was hiding out in the darkness, and if she felt as alone right now as he did.

He lifted his sneakered feet and pushed off the console, to give himself some spin. The chair spun like an LP, at something less than $33^1/_3$ speed, and he had a dizzy view of the swirling studio: console, old sofa, venetian blinds, cork walls, console, old sofa—

There was a face at the window, upside down and looking in. A monster's face . . .

The window imploded as Art's chair tipped out from under him and he crashed backward, flailing at the consoles.

The face at the window was three times human size, and dark as scorched hide. It bellowed at him, thrashing in the window frame. The venetian blinds clacked and tangled as the thing fought to get at Art.

Art picked up his swivel chair hurled it at the creature in the window. The chair hit the furious black shape tangled in blinds, and seemed to only enrage it further. It struggled to wrestle its bulk in through the narrow window.

Art scurried backward beneath the console, cowering among the jungle of wires. From the studio speakers he heard Frankie

Lenard saying "Next we've got Elastica with 'Stutter.' Y'know, I'm still waiting for a follow-up to their 1995 album . . ."

If he could only get to the phone on the wall—

Wham! As if anticipating Art's thought, the creature in the window swung a massive arm through the air, sweeping two stacked CD players off the console and tearing the wall-mounted phones free.

Wham! The claw punched through the ceiling. Chips of acoustical tile came down in a feathery rain. If it managed to hit the console again, it would destroy the equipment broadcasting the prerecorded programs . . .

Was anyone listening? Would anyone notice the dead air and send help?

The console . . .

Suddenly Art realized he had the means to make the biggest fucking 911 call in history directly overhead.

The thing in the window bellowed. The cinder blocks of the outer wall began cracking under the enormous pressure.

Art took a breath. Slid out from beneath the console. Ducked to avoid the claw that thrust out to grasp at him. He punched a switch to kill the prerecording. Grabbed the studio mike.

The sign mounted over the door winked red: ON AIR

"JESUS CHRIST SOMEONE HELP ME! IT'S ALMOST—!"

He was screaming into the mike. The creature in the window glared, furious that he was just outside its lethal reach.

"IT'S ALMOST INSIDE . . . SOMEONE PLEASE HURRY—"

He saw the output needle on one meter bobbing in time with his crazed syllables. And wondered again if anyone was listening.

Frankie Lenard had brought a Walkman with her as she walked downtown to watch Windale's celebrated street festival, because she wanted periodically throughout the night to check out the "Sisters in Song" show she'd prerecorded yesterday. At a little past seven o'clock, as she waited for Tyrannosaurus Sex to pack up their trombones and switch out their drum kit for the next band, she slipped on her headphones in time to catch the weird disembodied sound of her own voice. *"... next we've got Elastica with 'Stutter.' Y'know, I'm still waiting for a follow-up to their 1995 album..."*

Jeez. Did she really sound that phony and annoying? She couldn't take it. She snatched the headphones off.

Onstage, Tackhammer's lead singer, Bryan, said into the mike, "Can I get more monitor?" He looked out across the crowd, forlorn, sleepy-eyed. "Someone? Anyone?" Frankie studied him critically from her position below the stage, his head of unwashed curls in stark silhouette against the increasingly cloudy night sky. Her opinion of Bryan, like her opinion of men in general, remained conflicted. Just look at this guy, he's a total indie cliché, with his Salvation Army bowling shirt and his bad posture and a bleary expression that said he'd only woken up twenty minutes ago on the sofa in the practice place in front of a rerun of *Barney Miller*. All of his songs were ironic little odes to television and convenience stores and how exhausting it was to work up the strength to kiss a girl, sung through a repressed yawn...

And yet, sweet Jesus he was hot. Okay, so it wasn't her fault— she was genetically programmed to respond to a guy with a guitar. You didn't have to be Desmond Morris to understand that a guitar was just an enormous throbbing electrified penis, wired for sound.

Bryan leaned into the microphone again and said, "Um, I really could use a little more monitor up here?"

It seemed like Tackhammer was having a few technical difficulties, so Frankie took the opportunity to check in on herself and "Sisters in Song" yet again, disapproving grimace at the ready. She slipped the headphones up to her ears—

"FUCK SHIT PISS COCKSUCKER—HELP ME!"

Behind the profane hysteria, it sort of sounded like Art Leeson, the fugitive station manager.

"—JESUS CHRIST SOMEBODY FUCKING HELP ME—!"

Then a loud crash, followed by static. Dead air...

What was that? Some kinda *War of the Worlds* Halloween prank? No, Frankie thought, feeling her chest tighten in fear: that was real terror in Art's voice.

She turned from the pavilion and waded into the crowd. She forced her way through the human tide, pushing aside kids with painted faces, sorority sisters dressed as prostitutes (how original), old couples with chemically glowing bangles and necklaces. Frankie spied a young deputy struggling hard to play the part of a "police presence." He didn't look very confident in his uniform; it might as well have been a costume. But he was wearing a real-enough sidearm, and she was sure he had a car nearby.

She ran to him.

⊛

The monster was inside the studio. The console exploded in a shower of sparks as she tore it free of the wall to get at her prey . . .

But Art was gone. He'd abandoned the flimsy shelter of the console only moments before, after a feeble attempt to remember all seven of the Seven Dirty Words the FCC forbade from broadcasting.

He was backing down the hallway now, into darkness. Listening to the destruction going on in the studio. The creature was creating a real light show of sparks and flame as she destroyed Studio A.

Art wasn't sure exactly when he'd begun thinking of the monster as *she*, but he was as certain of the monster's gender now as he was of his own. Despite the horrific proportions of her arms, the distorted nightmare of her face, there was something distinctly female about her.

CRASH! The wall of the studio collapsed, spilling mortar dust and cinder block rubble into the corridor. Art backed away a little faster, then turned, running deeper into the labyrinth.

He only paused long enough to seize a fire extinguisher—the nearest heavy object he could find. He heard the monster enter the corridor behind him, so big she nearly filled it. She swung her fisted claws from side to side, smashing craters in the corridor walls. As he ran, Art felt bits of cinder block shrapnel sting the back of his head.

In the confined space of the narrow corridors Art had the advantage of his smaller size. He cut a sharp right, tripping head-long over a box of CD jewel cases someone had left in the dark. He spilled forward, hit hard. Scrambled back—

She loomed over him, bellowing. He felt her pin him down with one claw as she brought her face in close to his. He shut his eyes—expecting a quick, violent death—then opened them again when it didn't come.

She cocked her enormous head at him, unmistakably a gesture of human curiosity. Her lips curled back from a vulpine snarl. She clamped a claw around his head, holding it like a melon, and sniffed him. Her eyes narrowed to slits as she turned his head left and right, her expression one of bafflement. She sniffed the ban-dana and the injured eye beneath . . .

A scream. The monster whipped her head around, instantly alert.

Frankie and Deputy Reed Davis stood several yards back in the corridor. The deputy had his firearm drawn and began wincing as he squeezed off shots. Six in rapid succession, deafening concus-sions in the confined space.

The monster roared as the bullets struck her. Art took advan-tage of her momentary distraction, and emptied the fire extin-guisher into her face, blinding her temporarily with chemical foam. She reared back, furious, and he scrambled out between her legs.

The monster turned and staggered after them in blind pursuit, thrashing. The deputy lingered a split second too long, emptying his gun into her. As she passed, she slammed him into the cinder block wall, crushing his rib cage. She lumbered past, bellowing at the fleeing Art and Frankie. Deputy Reed Davis slid down the wall slowly in a slick of his own gore, landing in a seated thump—splay-legged—like a broken marionette.

. . .

Frankie and Art ran hand in hand through WDAN's narrow hall-
ways, fleeing the nightmare. They burst through the station's front
doors and dashed across the short lawn to the deputy's patrol car,
its engine idling.

Inside the station, the witch roared as she struggled to wedge
through the tight doorframe, seeing her prey escape in a blaze of
headlights and a spray of gravel.

⬟

Wendy awoke, huddled in her bed, shivering with a phantom
fever. Her throat felt sore. From thirst, she thought initially, but
soon realized it was an external ache. Her hands went to her neck
and found abrasions there. She ran to the bathroom mirror and
discovered the abrasions were ligature marks circling her throat,
all the way around to the nape of her neck, as if someone had
tried to strangle her while she slept...Not *strangled*, she realized.
Hanged.

Wendy's recollection of the official events was sketchy at best,
but she recalled that the Windale witches had been hanged several years after the Salem hysteria had come and gone. That had
been the extent of Windale's brush with witchcraft. But her
dreams told a different story, a story where documented history
and the facts parted company at the gallows. Wither and her
coven had cheated the hangman's noose. They had even been
buried, in some sort of deathlike sleep or trance, waiting for the
gravedigger to come along. Could any of this really be true, or was
Wendy losing her mind? Witches with black blood and clawed
fingernails? Was that part of the "pact with the devil" aspect of
black magic and sorcery?

She rubbed some of her mother's skin lotion all over the red
marks circling her neck, soothing the dry burning sensation, and
returned to her bedroom.

What did the Windale witches, who had lived three hundred
years ago, have to do with what was happening to Karen and her

today? The dreams, the fatigue, the gray hair... *and now these strange ligature marks.* Were they being haunted? Had the witches placed a curse on Windale? Wendy looked down at her aching legs. *I'm losing all control of my mind and my body.* Then a chilling thought, *At night I dream her dreams and in the daylight she takes a walk in my skin.*

After checking that there had been no change in Alex's condition, Wendy went into the bathroom and prepared a purifying bath of lavender and thyme. She climbed into the steaming water, wearing her crystal necklace in the hope it would clear her mind. She lay back, her arms along the edge of the bathtub, head resting against the sloped back as the hot water eased her aching body. She imagined floating on a peaceful sea with no worries.

Floating...

Floating over colonial Windale... no, *flying.*

Fly agaric toadstools, body grease enabling witches to fly ... on broomsticks made from the wood of ash trees ... flying, *just like in my dreams.*

Wendy imagined the tales of flying were based on accounts of astral projection. Most of the Salem convictions had been based on spectral evidence, that is, the accusers said they saw the witches' specters—astral projections—leaving their bodies to do the accusers harm. Right in the courtroom where everyone could see ... but everyone *hadn't* seen. Only the accusers saw the specters of the witches on trial. When the spectral evidence was disallowed in Salem, the convictions ended. Never sufficient evidence of witchcraft to hang another accused witch in Salem. That hadn't been the case in Windale. The Windale witches were found guilty of the practice of witchcraft but had been convicted on damning evidence of murders.

Wendy sat up a little straighter in the tub with a simple but frightening thought. What if Wither and her coven had been more than murderesses? What if they *had* been real witches? Not secretive midwives or medicine women, mixing herbs and making foul-smelling poultices. But genuine, black-magic-practicing, card-carrying evil witches? *Like the ones all the fairy tales warned us about, the ones who made poisoned apples, cast malicious spells, and had an unsavory taste for the flesh of children?*

Her mother knocked on the bathroom door. "Wendy? Frankie is here to see you. She seems quite distraught."

Five minutes later, Wendy emerged from her house, dressed in black jeans and a cable-knit sweater, her hair still dripping wet. Frankie was pacing in tight little circles and muttering to herself.

"Jesus, Frankie, what's wrong?" At the sight of Wendy, Frankie flew into her friend's arms and began sobbing. Wendy held her tight and smoothed her blond hair, saying, "Are you hurt? Did something happen?"

"I saw it, Wendy," Frankie said, just this side of hysteria. "God, I really saw it!"

"What did you see?"

"The—thing—the thing that took Jack. The monster Jen Hoyt's been drawing in class, that—"

Wendy cut her off. "Where?"

"The radio station." As she said it, Frankie seemed to remember something. "C'mon, I brought someone else who saw it, too." She clutched at Wendy's sleeve and drew her down the driveway toward the street.

"Wait, Frankie, where are we going? What—?"

"Please! No questions! Just come with me."

Wendy followed Frankie off the mansion grounds and up the sidewalk. Two blocks away, parked in the deep shadows of an elm, was a police car. And there was someone inside. Wendy stopped short.

"You came here in that?"

Frankie nodded emphatically, jumpy, nerves fried. "I didn't want to freak out your folks, so we parked out here. The deputy was killed. It killed him—"

"Killed? Then who's that in the car?" Wendy felt her hackles rise as the passenger door opened and the haggard stranger came forward from the shadows. He looked like an escaped mental patient, a paisley bandana over one eye, face covered in fresh scratches.

Wendy thought at first his hair was entirely gray then realized it was covered in plaster dust. His shirt looked like it had been tie-dyed in blood.

"This is Art," Frankie said. "From the radio station." She turned to Art and said, "Wendy knows about these things. She's a witch."

"Why do you think it came after you?" Wendy asked Art.

"I don't know," he said. "I think it's the same thing that killed my brother last night. It might've been trying to get to his girl-friend, Karen—"

"Glazer?" Wendy said, a cold lump of dread in the pit of her stomach. "Professor Karen Glazer?"

Art nodded. "I took her to the hospital before it could come back for her. I think maybe that's why it's pissed off at me." He looked Wendy up and down, obviously reconceiving his notion of what a witch looked like. "Do you know what it is?"

Wendy looked down at her hands, realized she was rubbing her thumb raw against her fingernails. The nails were dark, coarsened. *Inhuman.* What was she becoming? The witches in the jail cell. The dream was finally coming into focus, the mingling of blood. "Better than that," Wendy said. "I know *who* she is." Art and Frankie looked at her in surprise as she told them: "Rebecca Cole."

"The Windale witch?" Art shook his head, trying to process what Wendy had just said. "As in the infamous Windale Three? But she was hanged, it's in all the town records of the period."

"Hanged, buried, and then dug up again. She survived her reported death. Trust me, I've seen it. . . . Or, actually, dreamt it."

Frankie said, "But the thing we saw wasn't human!"

"She's three hundred years old," Wendy said. "She's getting a lit-tle long in the tooth."

Frankie shook her head, struggling to understand. "Wendy, if this monster—this Rebecca Cole—has been around for three hun-dred years, how come no one's ever seen it before?"

Good question. Wendy was about to admit she didn't know when Art provided the answer.

"Someone has." All eyes turned to him. He seemed to be a little surprised himself, as if he'd just realized the explanation. "Every hundred years, during the last October before a century's end. It's the Windale Curse. Just look back at the historical records.

Wendy nodded. "They must undergo some sort of dormancy period..."

"They?" Art repeated, the blood draining from his face.

"It only makes sense," Wendy said. "There has to be more than one of them."

"How do you know?" Art asked.

"Because a different one is after me. Just like Rebecca Cole has targeted Karen," Wendy said, feeling a sick lurch in her stomach as she said it aloud for the first time, "Elizabeth Wither is after me."

She began speaking aloud again, as much to herself as to Frankie and Art. "Wither is the leader of their coven. She recruited the other two." Wendy's eyes unfocused and her voice fell to a whisper. She spoke as if from a great distance. "She made them drink her blood, then infected their blood with hers ... so they would become—different—just like her."

Art recalled something he'd seen on a plaque once in Windale's Witch Museum, a detail he'd never granted any significance. "The other two were young, Rebecca Cole and Sarah Hutchins. Born here in the colonies. But Wither arrived later to the community. Whatever she was, or is, she brought it from the Old World, like a plague."

His words brought Wendy back into focus. She met Art's eyes, the two strangers united suddenly in a moment of mutual understanding. It was Frankie who finally interrupted, with the simplest of questions.

"If Rebecca Cole is after Professor Glazer, and Wither is after Wendy, then what about the third witch?"

"Sarah Hutchins," Art whispered and felt his throat tighten as he flashed back in that instant to a hospital room in the Pediatric Intensive Care Unit.

"Abby MacNeil."

"Who?" Frankie asked.

"An eight-year-old. I found her sleeping on Sarah Hutchins's grave in the woods. The witch must have kidnapped her from the hospital last night." He flashed Wendy a desperate look. "The police think I snatched her."

Wendy said, "So you're the 'fugitive' they've been looking for."

Art caught Wendy's arm. "Do you think the little girl is still alive somewhere? What does Sarah want from her?"

Wendy held up a lock of her prematurely graying hair. "The same thing Wither wants from me."

Frankie looked at Wendy's drawn face, eyes ringed with dark circles. "*She's* doing this to you, isn't she?"

Wendy's hand went to her cheek, found a new line there. "Draining me."

"Why?" Frankie asked, horrified.

Wendy shrugged. "Sapping our—life force, energy, whatever you want to call it. Draining us like batteries."

"How much longer . . .?" Frankie began to say, and let the thought trail away. She touched two fingers to Wendy's face.

"It ends tonight," Wendy said. "One way or another. It's the biggest magical night on the calendar." Wendy felt her knees go soft and gave in to it, sitting on the curb, turned to Art. "You saw it yourself, the 'Curse' is an October phenomenon. That means by midnight all three of us will be drained dry. Karen. Abby. Me."

She looked up at Frankie and Art, standing to either side of her. Her expression hardened, eyes narrowing. "At least, that's what Wither would like to think . . ."

"You think you can stop this?" Art asked.

I tried once before, but I didn't know all the facts and I failed. Now I know just what I'm up against. Wendy stood suddenly, determined. "I think it's time to write a new ending to this fairy tale."

Twenty minutes later they separated, Art cruising off in the deputy's patrol car with the headlights off, Wendy returning inside with Frankie in tow to make preparations for battle.

Throughout Windale, jack-o'-lanterns grinned from porch steps while paper skeletons waved from parlor windows. Downtown, the King Frost Parade had spilled outside the boundaries of the square and into side streets. As the hour grew later the costumed crowd grew rowdier with alcohol and adrenaline, seething now with something slightly feral as the clock crawled toward the witching hour. There were no police now to control them; the sheriff had departed moments earlier in response to a panicked radio call from deputy Jeff Schaeffer, something about the WDAN radio station, and an officer down . . .

At 11 P.M., Mayor Dell'Olio felt something hard ping him on the top of his head. He pulled off his rubber Ted Kennedy mask and searched for the offending projectile . . . and saw it bounce off through the crowd.

A golf ball—?

Then the turbulent skies opened, and the hail began.

CHAPTER
TEN

The bruised sky above Windale roiled like something alive, the heavy clouds pregnant with ice. When they finally burst, the hailstones spilled forth in a single biblical tumult that scattered the twenty thousand downtown and sent them screaming for shelter. Several paraders were knocked unconscious by the larger hailstones, and two were blinded when they looked up in fear at the angry sky. Hailstones pelted sidewalks and shattered streetlamps, ricocheting through storefront windows. The crepe paper floats were battered to wet pulp; scraps of costume were left in sodden heaps by the fleeing paraders.

In the outlying neighborhoods, those few residents of Windale not in attendance at the King Frost Parade downtown emerged in confusion on doorsteps and lawns beneath a brilliantly clear night sky and listened to the faraway screams, commingled with the otherworldly chorus of a thousand blaring car alarms.

Racing across campus with headlights extinguished, Art found himself in a sudden skid as the hailstorm started. "What the—!" He fought to regain control over the patrol car as it fishtailed, back wheels spinning on the hail-riddled asphalt. Hailstones big as chestnuts drummed off the roof and dimpled the hood. A dozen starbursts freckled the windshield.

The patrol car went into a spin and did a complete 360 in the intersection of Montgomery and Old Winthrop. In one of those magically cooperative moments between fate and physics, the patrol car came out of its spin and to a final stop pointing westbound on Old Winthrop—precisely where Art had been headed in the first place. He gave a nervous hiccup of laughter and stamped on the accelerator . . .

One hour until this was over—which meant only one more hour until the witch finished draining Abby dry. One hour left for Art to try to find the little girl and wake her from the nightmare she'd been living. As he drove, he remembered the day he'd first stumbled across Abby in the woods, sleeping sweetly on the grave like some spellbound fairy-tale princess. It was back to these woods that he was now driving, recklessly and with only a vague sense of a plan; back to the place where this had all begun for him.

He had no idea if he would find Abby held captive there. But he knew the grave site in the woods had been her special place, and perhaps it held some sentimentality as well for the witches—their intended graves. Their first victim had been snatched nearby. . . . Wouldn't it be reasonable to assume that the newly woken witches, still sluggish from their long dormancy, wouldn't venture far for their first feedings?

But how did you kill a witch? She wasn't like any of the other monsters out of folklore, defeatable with silver bullets or crucifixes. In fairy tales—"Hansel and Gretel," say—she was vanquished by guile. Lured into her own oven by the ingenious siblings . . .

Art doubted if guile would work against one of the creatures he'd met earlier that evening. So he was hanging his hopes on the deputy's pump-action shotgun he'd found in the trunk and carried now on the passenger seat.

He wouldn't get to use it.

Suddenly, another patrol car roared out from a cross street and broadsided Art. He had a split-second's glimpse of the sheriff behind the wheel, and then he was slammed sideways and sent spinning.

The patrol car slammed into a utility pole. Art's consciousness blinked out with the collision. Some uncertain amount of time later he awoke to the sound of a car horn blaring a single unmodulated wail. He couldn't see anything; the world outside the car was obscured by spiderwebs of shattered safety glass. He raised the back of his hand to his lip and it came away bloody.

The driver's side door was suddenly wrenched open and Art was hauled out unceremoniously. He heard the menacing *shunk-chunk* of a pump-action shotgun chambering rounds. He winced, rolled over onto his back in the sandy grit of the roadside.

The sheriff stood over him, and said with deadly calm, "On your belly. Hands behind your head." Art was stunned, hurting. "Do it!" the sheriff said, and jabbed the shotgun at him.

Art obeyed. The sheriff straddled him, twisting first one and then the other hand around painfully behind his back. Once handcuffed, Art was jerked roughly to his feet and thrown against the sheriff's car, which had survived the collision with only a crumpled grill and one shattered headlight.

"I didn't ... kill him ...," Art said, having trouble breathing. His ribs hurt. "The deputy ... I didn't ..."

"Shut up," the sheriff said. He returned to the open driver's side door of his patrol car and talked quietly into the radio. Art could just make out Nottingham's words to his lone remaining deputy: "Ran into him. Literally. I spotted him fleeing in Reed's patrol car ..."

Art leaned back against the car and looked up at the menacing sky. The clouds that writhed like a canopy over downtown Windale were spreading now, passing overhead in a kind of meteorological race for all horizons. They devoured the stars and screened out the moonlight.

Art heard the sheriff say, "I'm bringing him in." Then the crunch of the sheriff's boots on the roadside gravel.

"C'mon," he said, and gripped Art's arm hard. He maneuvered him in through the back door of his car, careful to keep Art from banging his head on the frame. The back of the patrol car was fitted with hard plastic bucket seats with a deep well to accommodate handcuffed fists.

"Bill, listen to me—" Art began once the sheriff had climbed behind the steering wheel. "We don't have much time. The little girl, Abby—there's still a chance we can save her—"

The sheriff ignored Art. He slipped the car into gear, executed a U-turn in the middle of Old Winthrop Road. "Bill, please!"

Nothing. A brick wall. Art slumped in the backseat. No time for this ...

Then, an idea. He leaned forward, speaking through the perforated Plexiglas separating them.

"I'll take you to her right now," Art said, then steeled himself for the lie. "I'll take you where I'm hiding her."

The sheriff didn't turn, but his foot eased on the accelerator. Debating. Art upped the ante.

"She's still alive. You can still save her."

The sheriff stood on the brake, and Art was thrown facefirst into the Plexiglas. He bounced back against the bucket seat, his nose streaming blood. The sheriff turned around to glare at Art. Calling his bluff.

"Show me."

Ten minutes later they were tramping through the woods, Art in the lead with the flashlight, the sheriff following with the shotgun. The trees had shed their leaves during the previous week, and now dead leaves crunched underfoot as the two men walked in single file. Art played the flashlight's tight beam over the deer path they were following. His heart was hammering high in his chest and his mouth was dry. His mind raced through scenarios of what he'd say once they arrived at the grave site and found it empty.

"How much farther?" the sheriff said.

"It's just up ahead," Art lied. Nothing looked familiar, and he wondered if he'd gotten them lost. It had been weeks since he'd last navigated these woods successfully, and back then he'd had the advantage of daylight.

They tramped on, their footsteps hypnotic. Art saw a clearing ahead, but when they arrived at it there were no gravestones, and no little girl. Art slowed, and felt the shotgun barrel butt him between the shoulder blades.

"Where is she?" Nottingham asked.

"Not yet," Art said, trying to invest his response with a confidence he didn't feel. He took up his forced march again, resuming with it his old appeal to reason. "Please, Bill. You've known me for twenty-five years. Do you really think I could've done that to your deputy? Or the little girl's father? Do I really look like that kind of monster to you?"

The sheriff said, "If you don't show me where the little girl is in the next five minutes, you won't leave these woods alive."

Art turned suddenly to face him. The shotgun resting lightly against his sternum. "If we find her, neither of us will." He saw the sheriff frown in confusion. He said, "I'm telling you, Bill. Turn around. Go back to your patrol car. And go home to your family. Because if we find Abby, the thing that killed her father, and killed your deputy, and has killed god knows how many other people in this fucking town over the last three centuries is going to be there guarding her."

The sheriff looked at Art strangely then, though it might've been a trick of the shadows thrown by the flashlight. For a moment it seemed like he might be considering Art's words. Then he poked Art with the gun barrel, uttering his one-word refrain: "Where?"

Art sighed, turned, and resumed his march. Ahead, something resolved out of the darkness, a great ramshackle outline behind the screen of trees. Art felt his scrotum tighten, a primal reaction to something sensed just below the level of conscious perception: a smell, a subliminal sound.

A barn, standing alone in a clearing in the middle of dense woods. A barn that seemed to hold contained within its rotting boards a darkness deeper than the night's.

He lifted a hand and pointed at the barn, and gave the sheriff his answer: "There."

✪

As the ER house staff welcomed the hailstorm's first walking wounded, Karen was being transported from her private room to the hospital's new Childbirth Wellness Center.

Annexed to the west wing of Windale General, the Wellness Center had been built the preceding year according to a more enlightened paradigm of childbirth, eschewing the chilly tile delivery rooms of yore for the kinder pastel schemes of "birthing environments." The facility was state-of-the-art and even boasted a large heated tub into whose gently circulating waters Essex County's more adventurous mothers could expel their progeny. (The idea being that the transition from womb to water exposed the newborn to a lesser shock.) And yet, despite the center's soothing murals and discrete natural lighting—provided by skylights in each suite—technology was never far from sight, and at a moment's notice any room in the center could be converted into a fully equipped surgical unit.

Karen was wheeled into Birthing Suite D. The room was decorated in a simple abstract print wallpaper, was scented lightly with something artificially floral, and lighted at a more muted wattage than elsewhere in the hospital. There was nary a stainless steel instrument to be seen. From somewhere unseen overhead they were piping in Lite Jazz—a sax solo so chastely inoffensive it would never grace a love scene. Maybe that was the idea, to subliminally snuff out any conflicting stimuli below the waist.

And yet, despite the center's best efforts at concealment, Karen noticed in one corner of the suite a "crash cart," complete with shock paddles and defibrillator; and over there, behind a scrim of surgical drape, wasn't that an anesthesiologist's ventilator?

Suddenly another contraction seized her, and Karen was wrenched away from any interest in her surroundings.

"Breathe through the pain," she heard one of the RNs say. "No pushing yet."

Fuck you, no pushing, she wanted to say, but she kept quiet, focusing her energy on the task of clamping down on this pain. Her breath hissed through clenched teeth. Around her, the RN was busying herself like a scrub-clad chambermaid, humming along with the Lite Jazz.

The contraction subsided, and Karen tipped her head back into the damp pillow. Maria appeared at the bedside, wearing surgical scrubs.

"Not much longer now," the obstetrician said, glancing at the wall clock. "The pain will be over before midnight."

She fed Karen ice chips from her hand. Karen tasted latex from Maria's gloves. Another contraction coming. Less than a minute apart now. She tipped her head back and saw the ceiling overhead, painted to look like a sunny afternoon sky, complete with airbrushed clouds. It would've been a more complete illusion if not for the skylight amid the clouds, like a dark hole punched through the midday sky.

It was the biggest magic circle Wendy had ever drawn. Big enough to accommodate her Gremlin within its circumference. She had parked on the shoulder of the back road, more than a hundred feet from the covered trestle bridge that had serviced the Windale Textile Mill once upon a time. The place where Wither had attacked and captured Jack Carter. *The place where she first appeared,* Wendy thought, *I suppose it's only appropriate that it end here.* Silently, she began laying out her magical implements.

Frankie watched as Wendy poured flour through a paper funnel, fiddling with the disposable camera she had insisted they stop for at a convenience store on the way to the mill road. "I want proof," she had said adamantly. "No one's going to believe this shit without some hard evidence." Now she was a bundle of nerves. When the flash went off in her face she nearly dropped the camera. Satisfied with the camera's operation, she slipped it into the pocket of her jean jacket. She rubbed her arms to ward off a chill that had less to do with cold than fear. Wendy had watched her confidence dwindle the closer they came to the covered trestle bridge.

As Wendy laid out the bowl of rice, the cup of wine, the burner, and the incense, Frankie asked, "What if it doesn't work?"

Since Frankie had placed her life at risk by staying at her side, Wendy had felt an obligation to tell her about the strange things that had happened at each ceremony she had performed. "You mean, what if I can't summon Wither? What if I can't banish her?" Frankie nodded. "Some of my spells worked, since the nightmares began. Wither opened some sort of mental *circuit* between us. She's been siphoning energy from my soul"—*Jesus*, Wendy shuddered, *this is creeping me out!*—"but she's also opened a flow of magic from her to me. That must be why the spells worked. Maybe she found me amusing, her little witch in training, while she sucked me dry. Maybe I can overload that circuit, create a feedback loop powerful enough to finish her off, once and for all."

"If she's been . . . draining you from afar," Frankie said, still coming to grips with the idea that the witch—rather the monster, which had apparently been a flesh-and-blood witch three hundred years ago—was sucking the life energy right out of her friend's body. "What's to stop her from finishing the job without getting her hands dirty?"

"You have to understand, when she touches my mind, I touch hers. I'd be lying if I said I understood how she thinks. But I've had a taste, and that qualifies me more than anyone. I don't think she can resist the challenge. She's the leader of the coven, she has a chip on her shoulder, she has something to prove."

"Next problem," Frankie said, with the quirk of a nervous smile. "What if it *does* work?"

"What do you mean?"

"Well, if I'm down with these magic rules and regulations, this circle is supposed to protect us, right?" Wendy nodded. "Well . . . what if she shows up—hell what if the whole coven shows up—and it turns out they don't give a fuck about the rules of magic circles and pentagrams and whatnot." Frankie stopped herself abruptly, realizing how shrill she sounded. "I mean, hypothetically speaking."

"Then I'll use this," Wendy said, and withdrew one of her father's hunting rifles from her bulky duffel bag. "I hope we don't need it, but if you see me go for the rifle, you'll know we're screwed."

"That's comforting," Frankie said with caustic irony.

Wendy tossed the rifle through the open car window, to the passenger seat, where it would be easy to retrieve.

"Running away isn't an option anymore." Wendy looked at her. "I have to do this, not just for myself, but for Karen and her baby, and for that little girl, Abby." Wendy looked meaningfully at Frankie. "You could still go. Maybe you're not on the hit list. Take the car. Come back for me after midnight. Maybe all of this will have been a bad dream."

Frankie seemed to stand straighter, shook her head decisively. "I could never live with myself if I left you alone here, no matter what happens."

"I understand," Wendy said softly, secretly grateful she wouldn't be alone for the witching hour. She wrote swiftly on a piece of parchment paper.

"What's that?" Frankie asked, obviously trying to distract herself in the details.

"If you're in a foreign country, it helps to speak the language," she said, narrating the process. Wendy raised her arms demonstratively within the circle. "This is the language they speak." Frankie nodded. She fiddled with her camera again as she sat on the hood of the Gremlin, glancing up as Wendy donned the white linen robe and sat facing the incense holder at the east compass point of the circle.

"Do you usually perform magic with your car in the circle?" Frankie asked. Wendy's closed eyes snapped open as the question broke her concentration. "Oh, sorry. Didn't mean to interrupt."

"I'm breaking some rules," Wendy said. "I obviously can't compete on her level. If I want to win . . ."

"You have to cheat?"

"If she played by the rules, she would have been dead three hundred years ago," Wendy said, then returned to her meditation. Frankie was silent.

Wendy's hand trembled as she drank her chamomile mixture. But she was having trouble centering herself, focusing her thoughts. Many lives were at stake. The tektite banishing stone was in a pouch around her neck, beside her crystal and anise sachet. Tonight, she'd brought a ceremonial dagger with her. She had purchased the dagger in the early days of her fascination with witchcraft, though she'd never had the courage to cut herself with it. That, too, had changed.

She stood over the parchment paper, dagger held in her right hand. With a quick jab, she pricked her thumb and let drops of blood fall to the paper. The pain came a moment later, but when it arrived it was surprisingly fierce, a stinging that throbbed in time with her heartbeat. The drops of blood blotted out part of the charcoal writing, but she could still read the spell. She read it to herself three times. *Wither, Cole, and Hutchins, I banish thee; these lives are not yours, so set them free. Abandon forever what you intend; the damage you've caused may begin to mend.*

She picked up the paper and set it afire with a woodstove match, watched the smoke drift heavenward. She held the parchment over the burner with one trembling hand, recalling the way the fire had leapt up her arm last night—*God, has it only been one night!* In her other hand, she clutched the tektite stone. She repeated the spell three times aloud, feeling more foolish with each repetition. The words were instantly consumed by the night, drifting up and away like the thin candle smoke, devoured by the hungry moon. From the center of town, dark storm clouds rolled across the sky, blotting out the stars one by one. Wendy was left feeling small, ridiculously young: a little girl with useless nursery rhymes. *Like whistling in the dark to scare away the evil spirits,* she thought.

Amazingly, the cut on her thumb had already closed, the wound healing as quickly as the deep wounds in her leg had. She might be getting older, but she was healing much faster. She slipped the dagger into the side pocket of her robe. The pocket hung down slightly where the thread had unraveled, but that was the least of her worries. She joined Frankie and waited. Then waited some more.

Nothing.

"What now?" Frankie asked after a long silence.

"We could take off our clothes and dance naked counterclockwise."

"You're not serious?"

"I'm not making this stuff up," Wendy said with a nervous laugh. She jumped off the hood of the Gremlin and moved the duffel bag in front of the grill. She glanced at her watch: 11:27. "Shit," she said. "I've had enough of this waiting."

"We're leaving?" Frankie said, relief in her voice.

"Not yet," Wendy said and stepped outside the circle. "If I'm right, my clock runs out in about thirty minutes. Doesn't matter where I go."

"Um, Wendy, I thought you said it was a real *bad* idea to leave the circle."

"I did. Stay put."

"But you're—"

"Breaking my own rules again," Wendy said and nodded. If the circle really afforded her protection, maybe it was keeping Wither away. Maybe the only way to lure Wither to this place was by exposing herself outside the circle.

She walked toward the dark bridge. It was a link to a dead past, a hulking anachronism, as much out of place in the late twentieth century as witches and ghosts and things that go bump in the night. Perhaps she should have made her circle on top of the bridge, where Jack had stood the first time Wither had appeared. She shuddered. Much too vulnerable up there.

"Wendy, don't even think about climbing up there!" Frankie said, almost reading her mind.

"Don't worry. I won't make it that easy for her," Wendy replied. Wither might not be able to resist an encore performance of her infamous bridge snatching. Wendy walked closer to the gaping mouth of the bridge. She looked down the embankment, at an old oak's exposed roots. The tree seemed as if it wanted to escape, was prying itself out of the ground one tortured root at a time. Wendy stepped into the dark passage of the bridge and tried to feel some connection to the witch. Her appearance here had coincided with Wendy's first ceremony. She should feel some lingering—

The hair on the nape of her neck rose. Wendy felt a slow vibration building under her feet. "Oh my God!" she said.

"What?"

"I feel something . . ."

"Wendy, get out of there!"

"Right," Wendy said, realizing her tactical error. She promptly stepped out from the maw of the bridge. And the sensation was gone. *Damn!* She thought her challenge to Wither had begun to work, but it was probably just her overactive imagination playing tricks on her.

Wendy clenched her teeth in anger, making her jaw ache. Her fists curled into tight little balls that caused her mutated fingernails to bite painfully into her palms. Suddenly, her rage was so bright and crimson it scared her. She was near the breaking point and felt utterly helpless. She wanted to scream her frustration. It wasn't fair that Wither should be able to wring the life out of her without showing her face here in the last few minutes of Wendy's life. More than anything, Wendy wanted to tell the bitch to go to hell.

"Wither!" she called, yelling so loud that her voice cracked. "Elizabeth Wither, I know who you are. I know what you are. I know you've been playing with me. Using me!" She wheeled around, directed her voice to another part of the sky. "You were a gutless killer three hundred years ago and that's all you are now. Show your ugly, fucking face and let's get this over with!"

"Wendy, you're scaring me," Frankie called from within the circle.

"Don't be afraid," Wendy said to her, shouting theatrically as she stared into the starry, silent sky. "She's not worth it. Wither and her coven are cowards! Preying on the innocent. Hiding themselves. They're afraid! Come down and face me, you sorry-ass, sickening bitch!"

She waited, waited, closed her eyes and listened, imagined the sight of this huge circle seen from above, fires burning at the compass points, a hypnotically bright image in her mind's eye. Nothing. Waiting. Finally, Wendy threw down her hands, her voice in shreds. Walking toward Frankie, she croaked, "Sorry I wasted your time."

"Look on the bright side," Frankie offered. "Maybe your spell worked and you really have banished her. Maybe they're all gone."

Wendy stepped into the circle, reached for her duffel bag. "We can only hope," she said. "What's that godawful smell?"

"*Oh. God! Oh, Jesus!*" Frankie cried, scrambling down off the hood of the Gremlin. Wendy turned in time to see Elizabeth Wither come screaming down from the night like a dark meteor. She struck the roof of the bridge and it exploded into a million flying splinters and boards.

Wendy gagged, thinking of this thing crawling around in her mind for months, using her, feeding off of her. "Don't leave the circle," she whispered to Frankie. "Take the keys."

"I'm not leaving without you!"

"Just be ready to get us out of here," Wendy yelled. "Get in the car. Just in case . . ."

Wendy walked to the edge of the circle. Her legs were so weak she worried they might buckle at any moment. "Elizabeth Wither!" she called as the cloud of dust from the ruined bridge began to settle. As she feared, she had only succeeded in getting Wither's attention, not the two other witches. But Wither was the leader of the coven, so maybe that was good enough to end this.

The witch appeared from the ruin, clambering over the leaning mass of timber. She leapt to the ground with a gravity-defying grace and covered the distance from the bridge to Wendy in a few strides, stopping abruptly just outside of the circle. The ancient witch cocked her head to the side as she studied the line drawn with flour, the way a dog will as it considers something curious. The blast from the bridge had disturbed the continuous line, blotting it out in several places . . . , breaking it. The witch chuckled hoarsely, a rumbling bass sound that made Wendy's stomach buoyant. It was a sound full of death.

With the circle broken, all Wendy had left was pure bravado. "Get the fuck out of my life!" she shouted from her side of the circle. "I performed the spell. I banish you and your coven!"

The chuckling stopped.

"You'd better start the car," Wendy called back to Frankie.

The witch took a long, slow step over the circle's perimeter, growling. Wendy heard the Gremlin's engine cranking behind her. Suddenly it turned over, and Wendy spun around. The witch lunged, shrieking.

Frankie leaned out the driver's side window and snapped a picture. The flashbulb bleached the night bright white for one instant, and the witch paused, shrieking again, this time painfully, her eyes squeezed shut. Wendy knew instinctively the witch hated bright daylight and what was the camera flash, but a modern day spell of localized daylight!

Wendy swung the car door open, grabbed the rifle off the seat, and turned to face Wither. The witch whipped her large head around, as if trying to pick up a scent or shake off the afterimage of the flash. She seemed to stare at the Gremlin for a moment, then lumbered forward. The Gremlin's engine sputtered and stalled. Frankie began slamming her hands against the steering wheel. "Your spells aren't working!" she yelled, cranking the ignition again.

"This might," Wendy said, leveling her father's hunting rifle at the witch. "Elizabeth Wither, I banish you!" she said as she squeezed the trigger. The rifle leapt in her arms; the bullet ripped into Wither's stomach, exposing tender red skin underneath the black hide. Still the witch stepped forward. Wendy worked the rifle's action, fired again. A black splash, and a bright raw blossom opened on the witch's throat. Then came the blood, spraying Wendy's arm, so hot it burnt her. She hastily wiped it on her jeans. The witch punched the claws of one hand right through the Gremlin's roof. Wendy smelled the witch's blood, the sharp tang of her own fear, and the witch's rancid hide.

She also smelled gasoline. The Gremlin's engine was flooded.

The sheriff shoved Art out from the stand of trees into the clearing, saying, "Take me to her."

Art glared at him. "Quietly," he warned, and then pantomimed that they should approach with stealth, keeping low. Then he dashed across the open weedy space between the woods and the rotting wooden structure. The sheriff followed a few paces behind. Together they crouched against the side of the barn.

"Jesus, what's that smell?" the sheriff whispered. He'd grown up in farm country, had visited morgues and crime scenes, so he'd known the worse kind of stenches rendered by the living and the dead. This was neither, a ripe, fetid reek that seemed to coat the back of his throat. He shook out a handkerchief and pressed it to his nose. "It stinks to high—"

Art raised a hand to silence him. He gestured, and the sheriff turned to see movement, a figure emerging from the trees at the opposite side of the clearing from which they'd come. As the figure neared they saw it was an old man carrying a kerosene lantern in one hand and a double-barreled shotgun in the other. His features in the play of yellow lamplight were flat, dead, as if whittled out of wood.

Without hesitating the old man hauled open a door of the barn and entered.

Art said quietly, "Must be their caretaker ..."

"Whose caretaker?" the sheriff asked. Art fixed him with a pitying look. He was about to find out.

✪

Through the skylight, Karen saw an apron of cloud envelop the moon.

"Okay, honey, we'll give this a try the old-fashioned way, " Maria Labajo said, peeking up from beneath the sterile drapes that tented Karen's legs in the stirrups. "The baby's presenting feet first, I'm going to try to reposition her." The obstetrician turned to the RN assisting her and said, "Page anesthesia. If we can't manage a vaginal birth in the next fifteen minutes I'm doing a C-section." The RN ducked out of the room.

Karen looked at the big cheerful clock on the wall and made a mental note of Maria's deadline. It was now eleven-forty-five.

Maria turned back to Karen, said, "Now you can push."

Karen gasped in relief, gathering what little reserves of strength were left in her after the nearly twenty-four-hour labor, and pushed—

The room shuddered as something heavy landed overhead. The lights flickered. Doctor and patient looked up simultaneously.

The sky exploded.

Glass showered down on them in jagged splinters from the shattered skylight. Maria screamed, trying to shield her patient with her own body. Karen looked up and saw a monstrous face leering down at her. Maria saw the look of shock and horror on her patient's face, and followed her gaze up to the skylight.

Despite her Western training, the Filipino obstetrician had been raised in a culture with a healthy respect for the supernatural, and when she saw the feral thing leering down at them through the hole in the painted sky, she recognized it as a creature out of a nightmare. The witch reached down with one long arm and swept Maria aside like a rag doll. Maria hit the wall and collapsed in a heap.

Karen rolled off the bed just as the witch's claw came thudding down, shredding surgical drapes and mattress. Karen cowered beneath the bed as the witch's grasping claw knocked over the IV stand and scattering sterile instruments. Suddenly Karen doubled in pain as her insides clenched around another contraction. Simultaneously, the witch's furious attack ceased. Karen peeked out from her hiding place below the bed and saw the witch bent double as well, making a strange warbling moan, as if in sympathetic agony.

Karen took advantage of the monster's momentary distraction to crawl across to where Maria lay. She pressed her fingers to her friend's throat until she found the pulse.

The contraction was subsiding. Overhead, Karen heard the warbling turn to a shuddering growl.

She looked up, and the thing that had once been Rebecca Cole let out a roar.

✪

Art said, "The little girl is inside the barn. I know it." The sheriff listened gravely, checked his shotgun, glanced up at the menacing clouds as a farmer might before making a decision about his crops.

"We'll wait till the old man comes out. I don't want any shots fired in the dark if that little girl's inside."

"Okay, but—"

Blam! The plank wall between them splintered outward as buckshot ripped through the rotten wood. Art fell back, his ear ringing from the blast, and saw the sheriff roll across the weeds and come up in a crouch.

Blam! A second shotgun blast widened the exit wound created by the first. The sheriff didn't return fire, unwilling to risk a random shot into the dark where a child was hidden. He crouched, waiting with the shotgun held high,... waited until the old man materialized from the shadows and peered out through the hole he'd blasted in the barn wall ...

Then the sheriff swung around in a single lethal arc, smashing the butt of the shotgun into the ancient face.

The old man's leer split in a ragged cleft the fissure of nose and lips. He dropped his shotgun and raised his hands to his ruined teeth. With a gravelly curse he lunged at the sheriff through the hole in the barn wall.

But the sheriff was ready. He stepped clear and swung the shotgun in an uppercut that snapped the old man's head back and sent him staggering across the weeds.

Only now did the sheriff level the business end of the shotgun at the old man.

"Stop right there! Don't move!"

In the cloud-smothered moonlight, the old man's bloodied grin looked black, like a hole punched in a rotten tree. He shambled forward.

"I said don't. Fucking. Move!"

The old man kept coming. The sheriff fired into his chest. At this close range the sound was deafening. The old man was staggered but remained standing. His shirt was shredded by the blast; the blood that came from the dozen fresh entrance wounds flowed sluggishly.

The old man kept coming. Some trick of the moonlight transformed his bloody mouth to a leer.

"Stop!" the sheriff said, and when he didn't, fired another blast. This one stopped the old man less than a yard away from the sheriff. But still he didn't fall, only lowered his head as if in prayer and let out a long sigh. He took another shambling step, this time shorter in stride.

Blam! A final blast, fired from point blank range. The old man's hand closed gently around the barrel of the sheriff's gun, not to wrench it away from the younger man but rather simply to steady himself... the way any old widower might pause in midnight relief after the long journey from bathroom back to bed with his hand upon the doorknob.

The two men, old and young, stood connected by the shotgun for several long heartbeats, the old man's eyes downcast, the young man's disbelieving. The old man was dead long before the sheriff gave him the nudge that toppled him.

Wendy shoved the rifle into Wither's jaws and pulled the trigger. Black mess exploded out the back of the witch's long head, and Wendy felt a distant pain echo in the back of her own head. Far from fatal, the wound seemed only an annoyance to the witch. And the stomach wound was already beginning to heal. Wither whipped her head from side to side, tearing the rifle from Wendy's grasp, crushing the stock and flinging it aside.

Wendy jumped in the car, slammed her door shut. "Now would be a good time to get out of here!"

From where she sat hunched over the steering wheel, Frankie gave Wendy a brief panicked look, and she desperately twisted the ignition key. She pounded the dashboard. When the engine finally spurted to hesitant life, she was so startled she almost forgot to put it in gear. She stomped the accelerator repeatedly, as if she were keeping time to some weird song of destruction, coaxing the sputtering engine into a roar. The Gremlin leapt forward.

Wendy looked back out the hatchback window, saw nothing. "Where the hell is she?" Then she remembered the witch could fly.

"*Jesus!*" Frankie said.

Wendy looked out the windshield just as Frankie swerved the car, narrowly avoiding the witch's descent. She almost drove past Elizabeth Wither—but glass shattered as the back of the Gremlin dipped like an overbalanced seesaw. Both rear tires blew out with twin, deafening concussions. Wendy looked back at the black, leathery arm that had driven through the wide hatchback window like a railroad spike through a china plate.

Frankie floored the accelerator, but the Gremlin only swerved side to side, metal squealing in protest.

"It's pinned," Wendy said, amazed at the brute strength of the witch.

"If she lets go, even for a second, I'll drive on the fucking rims!"

But Wendy knew they wouldn't be able to outrun the witch, even if the Gremlin still had rear tires. "Maybe noise," Wendy said. "Try the horn!"

The sound of metal and cloth tearing was almost completely muffled by the shrill horn. But Wendy felt the car tremble, smelled a blast of foul air, and looked up as clawed hands peeled back the roof of the Gremlin in a single jagged strip. Wendy's own fingernails throbbed in sympathy. When the dark hand reached for another ragged section of metal, Wendy pushed off the seat and raked her nails into the witch's exposed skin, gouging deep furrows. The witch howled, either startled or in pain, and snapped back her oversize hand.

"We'll have to run for it," Wendy said. "Head for the trees, anywhere she can't fly."

"Here goes," Frankie said and pushed her door. She pushed again with a grunt of effort. "Shit! It's stuck." The battered roof had crimped the metal doorframe.

Wendy tried her door, managed to shove it open with a protesting squeal of metal. "This side," she called. "Give me your hand."

Wendy edged around the door, pulling Frankie by her arm. "Hurry!" But Frankie's feet got tangled up, and her disposable camera fell out of her jacket. She scooped it up, pushed off against the edge of the door, and started to run, but was spun around forcefully. She looked back, saw the witch's ruptured face, dripping black blood and gore as it leered down at her, an unnatural hunger in her eyes. The clawed fingers of her long reaching arm had snagged Frankie's jacket.

The witch tried to haul Frankie into the air, but her claws ripped through the fabric of the jacket, and Frankie fell hard, bruising her ribs. Wendy pulled her to her feet as the witch tugged her other arm free of the debris in the back of the hatchback. Black blood speckled the length of that arm as well as the one Wendy had clawed. *Maybe if she loses enough blood, she'll pass out.*

"Come on," Wendy shouted. With a quick nod, Frankie scooped up the camera and raced down the hill with her. They veered toward the tree line, but Frankie's chest burned with the effort of the run, as her lungs strained her sore ribs. Her stomach became dangerously queasy. Wendy slowed to help her.

She looked back in time to see the witch lift the Gremlin onto its side and roll it down the embankment. The crumpling sound of metal was punctuated by the loud cracks of trees snapping until the car slammed into the trunk of a red maple.

Wendy noticed the camera in Frankie's hands. "Is the flash still good?"

"Think so," Frankie said.

"It's the only spell that's worked tonight," Wendy said. "Keep it ready. Quick, into the trees."

Wendy glanced back, but the witch was already floating down from among the trees right in front of them. "Hurry!" she screamed, almost losing her balance as she pulled up short. "The flash!"

"Smile!" Frankie yelled insanely and took another picture as the witch swooped low, ragged cloth fluttering behind her. The flash-bulb made a short popping sound as it lit the night.

Wither shrieked, lost her bearings, and toppled from the sky, crashing into the trees on the rising embankment. As the witch struggled to her feet, eyes staring without focusing, Wendy and Frankie veered around her.

Wendy staggered, strangely blind as well. As the phosphorous green supernova faded from her retina, she saw two young girls running downwind of her, running from her; a moment's disorientation and she realized she was one of those girls . . . Her mind had overlapped the witch's when the flash disoriented her. The line between them seemed to blur. It had to be very close to midnight. Time was running out.

"Are you okay?" Frankie asked, her arm on Wendy's as she stumbled around, confused.

"Run!" Wendy yelled, too late. With Frankie hobbled and Wendy blinded, they had barely made it across the road to the tree line.

The witch was loping toward them, reaching out with long clawed hands. She struck down a sapling with a sound like a rifle shot. Wendy ducked under the swiping arm, but Frankie's reflexes were slower, diminished even more by her bruised ribs. The camera fell and Wither was quick to stomp on the cardboard and plastic contraption, pulverizing it. Frankie screamed as the witch hoisted her into the air and shook her like a rag doll.

"Frankie!"

The blond girl flailed at the witch, but Wither hardly noticed the blows. "Run," Frankie shouted to Wendy through gritted teeth, her eyes wide with fear, brimming with tears. "Get the hell out of here!"

The witch shook the girl again, viciously—and Wendy suddenly felt her friend's weight in her own arms, tiny and insubstantial. Wendy felt a sickening hunger for her friend's flesh, and a deeper hunger, a hunger ripe with ecstasy and power . . .

Instead of trying to screen out the witch's sensation, Wendy drew on it, opened herself to the connection, and in that moment felt herself gain enough control of Wither's limbs to force the witch to drop Frankie.

Wither looked over at Wendy and roared in indignation at being so easily manipulated. Wendy fought to screen out the connection between them but couldn't react in time to prevent the tidal rush of pure demonic rage. The witch glanced down at Frankie's helpless form, the power to snuff out her life in a heartbeat all too clear in the disparity of their sizes.

Wendy had to distract the witch, get her away from Frankie once and for all. "Here, Wither! I'm here," Wendy called. "You want me? I'm right *here!*" The towering witch took a step in her direction. Wendy backed away, luring the witch away from her friend. Glancing back a moment later, she saw she wasn't being pursued. The witch stood over Frankie, was reaching down, her mouth opening wide to expose long yellow teeth, thick strands of bloody saliva.

"No! Right here! Here *damnit!*"

The witch towered over Frankie, who was too petrified to even crawl away from her.

"You want me! Remember!" Wendy screamed. "*I'm your fucking battery!*" And, with those words, she opened the circuit wide.

Wither turned to Wendy.

Dizzying flood of sensation, her vision split in two, this hideous, bullet-scarred body superimposed within the outlines of an eighteen-year-old girl, like the shape beneath the shadow, the woman this monster had once been, this young girl about to become a monster. She felt a great petrified strength within her young limbs and a swooning freedom from the pull of gravity. She imagined Wither's inky poison within her own veins pulling her down to a warm place where she could breath water or soil as she slept in silent darkness, where she could listen only to stones and the heartbeat of the earth itself . . . She let herself go, and it was as effortless—this consumption—as rest, easy as two opened palms, simple as sleep.

Wither had begun to feed.

✪

Karen had just managed to drag herself to the exit of Birthing Suite D when she suddenly doubled over again, wracked by another fierce contraction. From the skylight overhead she heard the witch bellow in sympathetic agony. The pain was so intense this time she almost blacked out. She clutched her abdomen.

The witch, trapped in the narrow frame of the skylight, reached out to Karen in a gesture that seemed almost imploring. As the black claw opened like some spiky desert bloom before her Karen felt the baby lurch violently. She heard the witch's curious warbling, saw the raven eyes fixed on her abdomen . . . and understood finally that it was her baby the witch wanted.

"No!" Karen said, and crossed one arm protectively across her middle. The witch hissed, lips curling back from a hundred glistening teeth.

Karen pulled herself up into a crouch, steadying herself against the dizzying rush of blood to her head. She staggered, supporting herself against the wall. Overhead, bits of ceiling plaster were falling. The walls shuddered as the witch thrashed.

She scanned in desperation for a weapon. Nothing. Only hospital equipment, heart monitor, ventilating machine, oxygen tanks, defibrillator . . .

She grabbed the crash cart, wheeled it around. Began tugging open its drawers looking for anything sharp. As she scattered the useless contents of each drawer, her eye fell on the canary yellow defibrillator unit. Printed along with the instructions on top was a warning: DANGER! EXPLOSION HAZARD IF USED NEAR FLAMMABLE ANESTHESIA OR CONCENTRATED OXYGEN.

The shock paddles had fallen off the top of the unit and dangled at the end of their long cords.

Karen turned, scanning the room, finally spotting what she was searching for: the oxygen tanks attached to the ventilator. She hurried—doubled over, cradling her stomach with one hand—to the nearest tank and cranked open the valve. She could feel the tight little funnel of pure oxygen on her face. She tipped the tank onto its side and rolled it, hissing, to the crash cart.

Overhead, the witch slipped a shoulder through the widening hole in the sky.

Karen focused on her work, entwining the shock paddles around the hissing oxygen valve. Another contraction, so fierce it dropped her to her knees. She crawled toward the door, sat down against it, and used her body weight to tip it open backward. Maria was crawling toward her now, and Karen helped push her out of the birthing suite and into the hallway.

Karen grabbed the rolling crash cart and pushed it out through the door, trailing its shock-paddle leads. The leads weren't very long, only a few feet, and they stretched taut now where they wrapped around the doorframe.

Karen felt her strength fading. The room seemed darker now. The bright blue flame of fury she'd felt only moments before was dwindling ... But she had to finish this thing that had taken Paul from her, and was trying now to take her baby.

She crawled out through the open door, and heard the door to Birthing Suite D close behind her.

With a sudden crash, the witch came plummeting down in a shower of debris. Karen cranked the voltage knob on the defibrillator all the way to the right, 360 joules.

She looked in through the window. Rebecca Cole was standing in the middle of the room, looking back at her. The witch hissed, took a lunging step forward—

Karen pressed the two red buttons on the defibrillator simultaneously, discharging the electric shot ...

A flash. A rush of igniting oxygen ...

Karen was blown backward against the corridor wall by the white-hot flash. The last thing she remembered before the blackness closed over her was the shrieking wail of the witch in flames.

⊛

Art and the sheriff entered the barn. They saw the old man's shotgun lying in the straw beside the kerosene lantern. Art carried the flashlight, though its beam seemed outmatched by the seething darkness. Far overhead was just visible a ragged hole in the roof, through which they could see the silent drift of moonlit cloud.

"Abby?" Art called into the shadows, his voice high and trembling. "Abby, can you hear me?" He panned the flashlight beam across the hayloft, the support beams hewn from rough wood. The sheriff walked farther into the dark, craning his head back to peer up into the rafters. He thought he could make out something up there, a knot of deeper blackness.

"Over here," the sheriff called. Art joined him. The sheriff pointed, and Art shone the flashlight toward the high ceiling.

There. The flashlight's beam found the little girl suspended from the rafters, trussed like a spider's prey. Her eyes were open, staring down at them, bright in the flashlight beam. She wasn't moving, and for a moment Art thought they were too late. But then she squirmed, and turned her eyes from the painful light.

"She's alive!" Art said. The sheriff pushed him aside and called up to the little girl: "We'll get you down, honey."

The sheriff began climbing the ladder to the hayloft, still holding his shotgun. Art waited on the ground.

Once in the hayloft, the sheriff stepped out onto one of the rafters and began edging out carefully across the open. When he reached the little girl she cried out and tried to squirm away from him, but he talked to her soothingly, humming a favorite Raffi song of his own six-year-old daughter. The little girl quieted. The sheriff laid aside his shotgun on the rafter and took out a clasp knife. He sawed at the tarry scraps of cloth that bound her.

Art watched from below. Behind the bandana, his eye throbbed with his racing pulse. "Hurry," he called up to them. *Where was the witch?* He scanned the dark corners of the barn, alert to any movement. *Why had she abandoned her prize?*

Up on the rafter, the sheriff swore to himself as the sticky goo gummed his knife's edge. He scraped the black mess off on the rafter and resumed sawing at the tarry cloth. Finally the little girl dropped into his arms. She hugged him around the neck instinctively. "Hold on real tight, sweetheart," he told her, and kissed the blond crown of her head. With the little girl cradled in one arm and the shotgun in the other, he began edging back along the rafter toward the hayloft. When he reached it he lifted the little girl off of him and dropped her gently into the waiting hay. Art stood at the base of the ladder and beckoned her down to him. "Just a little farther now, Abby."

The child hesitated at the top of the ladder, giving Art a dark look.

"She's afraid of you," the sheriff said.

"It's okay, Abby," Art called to her, trying not to allow his own panic to frighten her. "I won't hurt you."

She looked back at the sheriff a few feet above her, as if for permission. He nodded toward Art and said to the little girl, "It's okay, sweetheart. Just climb down to him."

She extended a dainty bare foot to the top rung and began her slow descent. By the fourth rung she was within Art's reach, and he lifted her clear of the ladder and hugged her, saying over and over again, "I've got you now, it's okay, I've got you . . ."

She clung to him, and he felt tears well up in his eyes, sharp and stinging. He called to the sheriff, "You'd better hurry and climb down from there—"

He stopped, alert. He heard the little girl draw a sharp breath beside his ear, and felt her pulse quicken.

Abby said, "She's back." She was staring up into the rafters at the far side of the barn.

Movement overhead, sudden and violent, the shadows coming alive. Art spun, trying to fix it with the flashlight beam, but the witch was moving too fast. The flashlight bulb imploded with a quiet pop. Art dropped it to the hay underfoot.

"Bill, get down from there!"

Too late. They heard a startled cry as the sheriff was snatched from the hayloft and carried aloft high into the rafters.

BLAM! BLAM BLAM! Three deafening shotgun blasts exploded in quick succession, each strobing nightmarish shadows. The witch shrieked and dropped the sheriff. He fell across the twenty-foot open barn and landed hard on the hard-packed dirt floor. Art ran to him and saw a splinter of bloody bone jutting from his thigh.

The barn shuddered around them as the witch leapt from one rafter to the next overhead. Art tried to track her movement through the dark, but without the flashlight it was impossible. He set Abby down and began dragging the groaning sheriff toward the barn door. Abby held on to Art's pant leg, whimpering.

Art tripped over something in the hay underfoot and looked down—the old man's old double-barrel shotgun. He broke it open, saw two fresh shells inside . . .

The witch had already survived three blasts at close range. He'd have to make these last two count.

Where is she? He could see nothing. The only remaining light was cast by the old kerosene lamp resting on the floor a few yards away. The wick had burned down to a dim blue flame, as if the darkness itself was smothering it. *Where are you, Sarah Hutchins?* Art thought, hefting the shotgun.

He shouted up into the rafters, "I know you're up there, Sarah."

At the sound of her name the witch hissed from a high corner. Art immediately trained the twin gun barrels in the direction of the sound. "You've overstayed your welcome," Art shouted up to the witch. "There's a grave waiting for you, Sarah."

And now came a new sound, echoing from a dozen directions at once, impossible to pinpoint: laughter. A deep, liquid rattle. Art felt his stomach clench at the distinctly human sound and was reminded that his enemy was not some brute animal who could be easily provoked, but a malevolent intelligence . . . with an equally malevolent patience. She was waiting . . .

Then suddenly she was in motion. He heard the shuddering thud of her moving from one rafter to the next, tried to track her across the dark. The movement stopped, and as the echoes rippled away the silence returned like a still and impenetrable surface.

The witch could be anywhere now. She was playing with them, enjoying her advantage over them in the dark. Beside him, Abby whimpered. Art picked her up and she buried her face in his shoulder, crying. She wrapped her arms around his neck, accidentally brushing his bandana awry . . .

And the darkness became suddenly visible.

His injured right eye saw through the shadows. The darkness deepened into a textured landscape of surface and shadow.

Suddenly what had been a blanket of darkness became a terrain of varied night shades, blues and grays and violets. He saw the barn's complex framework of rafters and supports, saw the ancient hayloft in exquisite detail, saw the old rusted baling hooks dangling by chains high above them ...

She was on the ground with them, only a few yards away, crouched beneath the hayloft. Watching them, motionless as a cat. Thinking she remained unseen in the dark, that she alone had the advantage of night-sight.

But the witch was wrong. She herself was indirectly responsible for the gift of this night-adapted eye.

Art let her think he couldn't see her crouching there, yards away. He fought the impulse to turn and fire at her. He could wait as well. He watched her rise slowly, silently from her crouch and stride toward them.

Closer. Come closer, Sarah.

She stood within three yards of them. "Sarah!" he called up into the empty rafters, as if he thought she was still hiding there. He saw her lips curl back in a snarling smile. Pleased with herself, playing with them.

He spun and emptied the first barrel into her.

The blast knocked her back a step, roaring in surprise. Furious, she lunged at them.

One shell left. Art didn't aim at her this time, though, but at a different target.

The kerosene lamp. The blast sprayed flaming kerosene against the witch, setting her tattered rags aflame. The fire spread to the hay beneath her. She bellowed in agony.

Art threw aside the shotgun. One arm cradling Abby, he grabbed the sheriff by the scruff of his jacket and dragged him toward the barn door. Behind them, the witch screamed from within the liquid flame that engulfed her. She staggered, thrashing, trying to beat out the flames, and collided with one of the barn's support beams. The old barn shifted and groaned, collapsing in on itself ...

Even as the flames rushed across dried straw to the four crumbling walls of the dilapidated barn, Art dragged the sheriff clear, then collapsed beside him outside in the witchgrass. Abby sat in Art's lap and stared up at the fire with solemn eyes. Together, the three refugees of the blaze watched the biggest bonfire any of them had ever seen send hissing embers spiraling up to the midnight sky.

✸

Now that it was too late, Wendy finally understood. Wither's presence mingled in the confines of Wendy's body and mind, acquainting her with Wendy in the most intimate way possible. Wither hadn't been draining away Wendy's life. Seasoning her maybe, weakening her soul possibly, preparing her body for a demonic transfer of life's energy—a soul—definitely. But she'd had it completely backward. The witch needed to replace Wendy's life and soul with her own. There were cycles within cycles. Waking every hundred years to feed, to grow, to change, but every three hundred years the hardened, monstrous body had to be replaced, sloughed off to start a new cycle, when the ancient life fitted itself in the confines of a fresh young body. To start another three-hundred-year cycle of growth in Wendy's body!

Wendy wondered helplessly if her mind, her memories, her soul would be cast in the discarded, weakened carcass of the witch, a useless husk that would quickly shrivel and die.... Or would the witch consume that which was Wendy, her essence, in the process of taking residence in her flesh. And would anyone, even her family, know that a being of pure evil now wore her skin like a suit of clothes?

The process had weakened Wendy's will. She felt herself winking out, her consciousness like a flickering fluorescent lightbulb. Each flicker was longer than the last. Wither's mind raged within her, testing the body, the reflexes, rooting in the corners of her mind, stirring up lost memories and blotting them up, filling them with her own, and revealing herself to Wendy. Wither no longer saw Wendy as a threat or an obstacle. She was making herself at home in a young woman's mind, a mind that Wendy was surrendering to an ancient evil force. Wendy felt diminished, losing herself, but seeing Wither for what she was at long last ...

Another time, over three hundred years ago. A carriage ride ... Elizabeth Wither, the woman who was Elizabeth Wither, returning to London. It is night, and the coach careens wildly as the horses scream. The coachman's scream follows, but it is all too brief. Charles Wither pats her hand in comfort, but his eyes widen in terror. A black arm, impossibly long, bursts through the carriage door, plunges into his chest and pulls him into the night. He is dead before he can scream. The arm comes again, but this time slowly, lifting Elizabeth gently through the shattered side of the carriage into the night for an embrace that Wendy has finally come to understand ...

Other times, other faces, other women in endless three-hundred-year cycles ... Wendy looks back in time through the inverted telescope of Wither's predatory mind. In Wither's mind, Wendy sees the fall and rise of Rome, she sees the first trilithon of Stonehenge raised on Salisbury Plain, a monument that will require more than fifteen hundred years to construct, she sees the moon god's ziggurat of Ur in Sumeria. She sees the collapse of science into superstition, technology into barbarism, cities into huts, the countless faces of a line of women stretching back to the belief in pagan gods and demons, and if the gods have proved false, the demons are all too real. And Wither, or that which has become known as Wither, has been there all along, hiding in the shadows, just beyond the light and warmth of the first campfires, preying on humankind. She can not be understood by any one religion because she has outlasted them all, she has always been there ... feeding.

Frankie watched horrified as Elizabeth Wither held Wendy in a bizarre lover's embrace, her nearly hairless, black head poised inches from Wendy's face, their mouths parted, as if in anticipation of some unholy kiss between woman and demon. From the witch's mouth came a long, guttural, clotted sigh, and the air between them rippled like heat waves, but Frankie knew it was something else moving between them, some vital energy. Wendy had said Wither was draining her life force like a battery, but it looked to Frankie as if the transfer was moving in the opposite direction. Wendy seemed to vibrate with energy, while the nine-foot-tall monster that held her in its grip appeared to be diminished with each passing moment. Wendy's eyes had rolled back in their sockets, her head lolling from side to side in a weakened struggle, even as her limbs trembled with nervous energy. Slowly, Frankie was coming to a horrible realization, but the progression of her thought was interrupted as the ceremonial dagger fell from the frayed pocket of Wendy's robe.

Frankie saw the flash of metal. The blade struck haft first, fell with the point facing her. No magic in the dagger, Frankie now realized. She had reserved a small corner of faith for Wendy's magic circles and banishments, had believed Wendy might somehow be able to protect them from a real witch—hell, a coven of them. But Frankie's belief had crumbled as each gesture and incantation had proved empty and useless against the witch's evil.

But a knife was a knife, magic or not.

Frankie crawled forward, reached for the dagger, then winced at the sharp pain in her side. She clutched the dagger within her intertwined fingers, both hands trembling violently. She raised it above the knotty span of the witch's clawed foot, then slammed the point of the dagger down.

In a last fading moment of coherent thought, Wendy understands she is just the latest victim, one more sacrificial host to Wither, in a line stretching back over five thousand years. Wither is a plague on mankind and an abomination to nature, which she has always had the ability to pervert in the service of her evil. She is a malevolent force that has never been denied. All thoughts of resistance slip through Wendy's ability to concentrate. She is almost gone . . .

A shaft of pain lanced through the darkness. As Wendy's eyes fluttered open, the witch drew her head back. Wendy felt an echo pain in her own foot, and the more immediate agony of the witch's crushing grip on her arms. A smothering veil of despair had been lifted from Wendy's mind, providing an instant of clarity. She had snapped back from the brink of oblivion. The witch had been suppressing Wendy's ability to resist, her ability to even consider the possibility of resisting, by making her believe, truly believe, her situation was hopeless. The reprieve might be short-lived. Wendy didn't hesitate. She reached for Elizabeth Wither's gnarled face and plunged her thumbs, with their mutated nails, deep into the witch's bulging yellow eyes.

The witch screamed, dropping Wendy as both clawed hands reached for her own damaged face. Wendy fell to the ground, momentarily blind as well, rolling quickly out from under the witch's stomping feet. She heard the witch bellowing in pain, the heavy thudding blows of her feet as her long arms lashed about in their blind search for her prey.

Wendy focused on her own identity, to seek her sense of self, independent of Wither. Her *self*. Her family, her friends, her profs, her classes, her stupid Gremlin, but more deeply, her hopes and dreams, her happiness at what she and Alex had shared, followed by her grief and guilt over what had happened to Alex. She climbed to her feet. "Quiet!" she shouted to Frankie. Her vision began to clear. She searched for a piece of deadwood, found a branch Wither herself had broken from a maple tree, and began to swing it back and forth, thwacking it against the trees, the dead leaves at her feet, until finally, Wither followed the sound.

Wendy ran through the trees at full speed and burst onto the cracked blacktop of the condemned Windale Textile Mill's parking lot. Raging and blind, Wither swatted trees from her path and followed Wendy's noisy retreat, the witch's loping strides quickly closing the distance.

Wendy's immediate goal was to lure Wither as far from Frankie as possible. Beyond that she only wanted to stay out of that fateful embrace. She felt as if she'd been given a death row pardon, and she would rather kill herself than let the evil of Wither creep into her mind again, to devour or discard her soul as she took up residence in Wendy's body.

Nowhere to hide ... but inside the long, sprawling building. The nearest door was hanging from one rusty hinge. Wendy slipped through the opening with a squeal of protest from the door, then into the shadowy darkness of the condemned mill. Most of the windows, high and low, had been shattered over the years by bored teenagers throwing rocks. The machinery of the mill had been removed long ago, along with copper tubing and anything else of even marginal value.

By the time Wendy had surveyed her enclosed surroundings, the door screeched as Wither slammed into it, ripping it off its one remaining hinge. The walls of the building seemed to quake with the impact. Dust rained down on Wendy's head, along with several chips of plaster. The witch hurled the metal door into the building and smashed her way through the door frame after it.

Wendy could hear a low, keening moan in the building, decayed metal straining to hold its form as the witch battered against the walls. Wendy worried the place would come down on her head any second.

Suddenly it dawned on her. She'd read that a pile of stones had crushed an accused Salem witch or a wizard in an attempt to extract a confession. And right this moment, Wendy was fresh out of bullets, stakes, or fire.

She looked around quickly. How to bring down the house, collapse a building, even a condemned one? She had seen the implosions of demolished buildings on the news all the time, but that involved the strategic placement of explosives. *Think*, she told herself. *How—?*

Now that Wither was inside the building and not pounding against the door frame anymore, the vibrations had begun to subside. The imminent danger of collapse had passed, unless she could help the process along by knocking out a load-bearing wall. She remembered their old house, before they'd moved to the president's mansion at Danfield, how her mother had wanted to knock down a wall between two small rooms to make one medium-size room.

The contractor told her the wall had to stay, because it was a load-bearing wall, supporting the weight of the upper floor.

Wendy realized that the second-floor row of offices was held up by the line of four plaster columns, probably with a girder of steel at their core. She walked carefully behind the first one and rapped on it with her branch. Bits of lath fell from the crumbling column. Wendy just hoped the process of entropy—nature's most unrelenting force—had had sufficient time to work its decaying magic. Wither came charging at the rapping sound, like a bull spotting the toreador's cape. The witch seemed to loom incredibly larger with every loping stride.

At the last moment Wendy dodged toward the second column. Wither hit the first with the force of a locomotive. Lath exploded in a cloud of debris, and the steel underneath was dislodged from its mooring. Incredibly, Wither wrenched the girder even farther out of position. The creak and moan of steel above Wendy's head became a discordant song, punctuated by the crack of splitting plaster and crumbling cinder blocks. She would die, but she would take Wither with her.

The second column had already begun to buckle. Wendy swatted it with her branch. "Over here!" she shouted. Black blood oozed from Wither's gaping eye sockets. She bared her teeth and charged, lowering her shoulder as she reached for the sound of Wendy's voice. But Wendy had sidestepped, and the second column crumpled under the witch's onslaught. The witch grinned through broken teeth, pleased with this intimidating demonstration of her power, that ramming herself into human constructions wasn't hurting her at all, probably thinking to demoralize Wendy.

The groaning above became more pronounced, and the far end of the row of offices seemed to lean downward. Popping, crunching sounds rang out above. Wendy didn't think she'd need to have Wither charge the remaining two columns. *Just keep her under here!* Chips of stone and dust began to rain down on them. "Over here," Wendy whispered. Wither slowed, as if warned by Wendy's cautious tone, perhaps thinking there might be a hole in the floor before her. The witch's feet lifted off the ground and she moved forward, floating. Her head just inches beneath the crumbling ceiling. The third column was bending, twisting, lath popping and spraying as the tortured metal underneath slowly gave way under the pressure from above. Wendy backed away, the sounds of her cross-trainers crunching bits of debris now drowned out by the sudden, escalating roar above her. Wither was still unaware the ceiling was about to come down on both of them. And Wendy was looking for a corner to hide in when she realized the window behind her was broken, a V-shaped hunk of glass missing. A last chance, maybe, but she would have to wait to the last second or risk Wither following her out into the safety of the night. Wendy slipped out of her robe and wrapped it several times around her forearm, creating a thick padding.

It came as a deafening roar. Wither finally raised her face, lifted her hands above her, reaching for the ceiling, but it was too late. Wendy ran full speed toward the window, choking on the clouds of dust rising around her. She raised her padded arm and dove through the window. She felt it burst out before her, prayed a sliver of glass wouldn't slice through her throat, and heard the tremendous din behind her, then a sound like a sudden explosion before the concussion whumped through the window, blowing the remaining shards of glass out into the night. Wendy rolled down the hill on the far side of the ruined building, carried by her momentum into overgrown bushes. She looked back at the mill and saw that the entire outer wall had followed the collapse of the offices inward, piling tons of brick and mortar on top of the witch.

Minutes later, Frankie found her standing outside the shattered window, staring into the dark interior of the mill as the dust settled. They could make out one long, gnarled black arm protruding from a mountain of rubble. The arm had been severed, crushed paper thin at the shoulder. Black blood spread like crude oil, seeping out from under the stones, collecting motes of dust.

Later they poured gasoline collected from the Gremlin's ruptured fuel tank through the window, over the pile of stones. When they lit it, another loud whump filled the night. The remaining windows flared golden.

As Frankie put an arm on her friend's shoulder, Wendy crossed her arms and hugged herself.

She looked down and realized her fingernails had begun to return to normal.

EPILOGUE

The fires raged all night.

Overwhelmed by the magnitude of the hailstorm's fury, Engine and Ladder Company Number 14 called in fire companies from neighboring townships to fight the multiple blazes burning throughout Windale. Ipswich's volunteer firefighters converged on the fire that had engulfed Windale General's Childbirth Wellness Center; while faraway Salem contributed two pumper trucks to douse the strange woodland bonfire off Old Winthrop Road. (Due to the absence of hydrants so far out of town, the Salem company was forced to draw water from a nearby creek to fight the raging fire.) Meanwhile, Windale's Company Number 14 concentrated on controlling the blaze threatening city hall and several other municipal buildings. That fire, believed to have been started by power lines felled by the apocalyptic hail, was finally brought under control by 2 A.M., but not before it had claimed one municipal casualty: the historical society's Witch Museum.

To those refugees of the storm huddling in storefronts and church foyers, the hail had seemed to cease with the stroke of midnight. As the survivors of the Halloween of '99 emerged from their temporary shelters and looked up in wonder at the dissipating clouds, they saw restored to the autumnal sky a scattering of twinkling stars. Dawn was still many hours away on this first day of a new month, but already they tasted a difference in the air, like the acrid smoke of an extinguished wick, foretelling of an early winter.

At two-thirty in the morning, Windale General welcomed its second miracle of the season. Though several months premature, Hannah Nicole Glazer weighed nearly nine pounds at birth and scored a perfect Apgar. Despite her own injuries, physician Maria Labajo assisted at the delivery.

The miracle infant—who at one time hadn't been expected to live through her first night—was kept for the first three days of her young life in Windale General's neonatal unit, where she quickly established herself as the unit's heartiest resident. By her fourth day she was relocated to a crib adjacent to her mother's room.

On Hannah Glazer's fifth day, she welcomed her first visitors.

"She's beautiful," Art said from Karen's bedside. He'd come with Abby and the sheriff, who looked uncomfortable on crutches. The little girl clung shyly to the sheriff's air cast.

Art slipped an arm around Karen's shoulders. She was surprised to find it felt comfortable there. "She has your eyes," Art said. Karen looked down at the little bundle squirming sweetly in her arms and said, "No. She has her father's eyes."

It was true. Hannah's eyes were deep and piercingly blue; Karen could see herself reflected in them as the baby studied her, processing Karen's every expression in puzzled wonderment. She'd been born with a shock of black hair shot through with gray, though the nurses thought this would eventually grow lighter, like her mother's.

"Do you want to see the baby?" Karen offered Abby. The little girl approached the side of the bed gravely. "It's okay," Karen said, "You can touch her."

Abby took the baby's hand in her own, and showed a rare smile as Hannah's fingers curled instinctively around her own. The thick, discolored nails of Abby's right hand had fallen off two days ago, revealing new growth underneath, the cuticles pink and healthy. The sheriff's wife, Christina, had painted Abby's other fingernails with bright red polish, but this had already begun chipping as Abby played outside with the sheriff's two young sons and his six-year-old daughter, who was already looking at Abby as if she were an older sister.

"It's getting crowded in here," Maria Labajo said from the doorway to the private room, her arm in a sling.

"Room for one more," Wendy said, entering the room with an autumn-themed bouquet of flowers, which she set down on the bedside table.

"Thank you, Wendy," Karen said, squeezing her hand briefly.

Maria Labajo checked to see that the infection in Karen's arm was responding to the antibiotics she'd prescribed, then that Hannah's umbilical stump was healing. She tickled the bottom of one of Hannah's bare feet with her fingertip. The baby kicked vigorously at the air.

Wendy smiled broadly at how healthy the baby seemed.

"You know," Maria said, "in the Philippines, breech babies are believed to have healing powers." She leaned over the baby and laughed as Hannah rested one splay-fingered hand on her injured arm in the sling. "Oh yes, this one's definitely got the Touch!" she said approvingly.

The baby startled at the unfamiliar sound of laughter around her, just one of the million human responses that lay ahead of her to learn. She was still months away from her first voluntary smile, and so she lay there now among these strange beings and gave them the only expression she'd perfected: rapt fascination.

A half hour later, Wendy stood near the nurses' station, waiting there until Alex's parents and his sister, Suzanne, took a break from their vigil to get something to eat in the hospital cafeteria. She had felt far too guilty to introduce herself to them.

She entered his room, wearing a green jogging suit, with a diagonal black stripe across the chest. Four days ago, she had lugged her exercise bicycle down to the basement, torn down the wall map of the United States, and traded in her cross-trainers for specialized jogging sneakers, which she wore now.

Alex looked peaceful. His color had returned, but his face was still mottled with bruises. She took his right hand in hers and said, "Hi, Alex. It's me, again. Wendy. You're—" She felt his hand squeeze back and she gasped.

When she looked up at his face, his eyes were open and focused on her. "Oh God! Oh God, am I happy to see you!" she said, tears of disbelief streaming down her face. "I—I'll get a nurse. A doctor!"

"It's okay," he said, smiling. "They know. I regained consciousness this morning. I was dozing."

"I'm sorry," she said. "I'll come back later."

He held her tight. "No, not yet. I want to look at you for a moment." He glanced at her outfit. "You've taken up jogging?" She nodded. "Doc says I'll need physical therapy, might even have a slight limp."

She smiled, wiped away a tear. "So I'll be able to keep up with you then."

He chuckled. "That won't be a problem."

"Oh," he said and reached into the bedside table's drawer. "I have something of yours." He handed her the bundle of cloth.

She opened the cloth, revealing the man-shaped mandrake root. But when she touched its coarse surface, it crumbled into ash, as if the protective charm had been burnt . . . or completely used up.

She refolded the cloth carefully, covering the ashes.

Alex took her hand again. "You're okay?"

"I'm fine," she said, then smiled again. "Everything's fine . . . now."